BLACKEST
OF
FRIDAYS

Other books by Joe Smiga

Fiction

Behind the Lies

Gateway to Terror

A Cowboy's Vengeance

One Came Back

Silver Lake's Transformation

Non-fiction

Tova

What Keeps You Going?

BLACKEST OF FRIDAYS

JOE SMIGA

Library of Congress Control Number:		2016906678
ISBN:	Hardcover	978-1-5144-8782-2
	Softcover	978-1-5144-8781-5
	eBook	978-1-5144-8780-8

Print information available on the last page.

Rev. date: 04/25/2016

To order additional copies of this book, contact:
Xlibris
1-888-795-4274
www.Xlibris.com
Orders@Xlibris.com
731147

Contents

Dedication

I felt I wanted to write a police thriller. My wife told me I was into terrorism, not police thrillers. I thought about this for a while and arrived at the idea of combining a police thriller with terrorist bombings similar to what happened in Boston at the marathon race.

I dedicate this book to those whose lives were lost in that senseless attack, and to those who were injured in any way—whether it is physical or emotional. Let us learn to combat these terrible acts of death and destruction in order for people to be safe and unafraid.

Prologue

2017

At 3:00 a.m. on Black Friday, the day after Thanksgiving, twelve men are dropped off near the strip mall where they've rehearsed their plans over the last two months. Each one carries a backpack and all of them are heading to stand in line alongside shoppers waiting to get into the stores when the doors open at 5:00 a.m. It is the official opening day of the Christmas holiday shopping season.

Shoppers are standing in the cold night air, drinking hot beverages to keep up their body temperatures. Many of them wonder why they do this every year, and most of them will return next year. It seems to be a ritual for those who continue to come back.

Each of the men looks like any other member of the local population. Each group of three has one member wearing a jean jacket and a Boston Red Sox baseball cap. A second person in the group is wearing a leather jacket and has Western-style boots. The third is the conservative one wearing a tweed sports coat with leather patches protecting the elbows. One thing they all have in common is the color and size of their backpacks. They divide up the way they trained, heading toward the four stores they have in mind.

When they reach the lines standing outside their particular store, they mingle with the crowds but split up so as not to draw attention to themselves. No one pays any particular attention to the men.

At 5:00 a.m. the doors of each store open and the mad rush to get inside to get the best gifts at the best prices for the holidays begins. It begins for the shoppers, but the twelve have something else on their minds.

Chapter One

They're Off

Across the nation, nearly every retailer is opening its doors before dawn even breaks on Black Friday. Huge crowds are stampeding their facilities in search of bargains and new ideas for Christmas gift giving. When the crowds enter the stores, it seems as if they have a plan as where to head first, and how many of their competitive shoppers they can outdo.

They look like horses released at the starting gates of a major track event. When the gates (or doors, in this case) are opened, they race into the aisles the same way race horses do on a track.

Each member of the terrorist team, shouldering their backpacks, proceeds to the locations they are assigned.

Team One is entering a store that handles multiple lines of clothing and household goods. Their main target is to set their backpacks where the explosions will create shrapnel from metal goods and glass products.

Team two is entering a children's toy store. Their objective is to place their backpacks where metal toys are displayed and in the area that dolls are located. These should be areas where many shoppers should be congregating.

Team three is entering a second store with multiple lines of clothing. Their assignment is to place their packs where the greatest number of consumers seems to be at the time. One of them will deposit his pack in an area where you try on clothes.

Team four is focused on an appliance store where there is everything to furnish a home, from televisions to sound systems, plus washers and dryers. When their explosions occur, there will be a great deal of twisted metal to add to the body count.

*   *   *

By the time the teams enter their locations, it is around 5:20 a.m. Each one selects a shopping cart and places their backpack underneath the carriage. They are moving toward their goals while they add items to the carts to make themselves look legitimate.

Trying to maneuver around the many shoppers clogging the aisles takes time, and it is vital they don't force issues to raise attention to themselves and possibly be identified by the authorities later.

It is close to 6:00 a.m. when all four teams have placed their backpacks into areas where they will do maximum damage. The timers on the C4 explosives are set to explode at 6:30 a.m.

They leave their shopping carts in the aisles and head out of the stores to the designated pick-up area.

Around 6:20 a.m., all twelve have been retrieved by their leader. Ahmad pulls their vehicle out of the parking lot and parks the van just outside of the parking perimeter. Ahmad wants to witness the effect of their work. He needs to report to his superiors the results of their efforts.

*   *   *

Inside of the store where the third team laid one backpack nearby the women's changing area, the lady clerk manning the dressing rooms notices that someone left a backpack under a clothes rack. She reaches down to pick it up to see if there is any identification on it, and the bag explodes in her hands.

There is no one left alive within a ten-foot radius of the explosion.

Within moments, there are eleven other explosions inside the four stores.

*   *   *

Ahmad smiles and pulls away from the curb before emergency vehicles and police arrive.

Ahmad says, "No one said Allahu Akbar, did they?"

The twelve reply they refrained from saying anything as they were instructed.

"Good, they will not be so sure that this act of terrorism was from Islamists or from some homegrown group. That will confuse them for a while," replies Ahmad. "We have more to accomplish today. Remember, you will not speak Farsi even when we are alone. It is important that you condition yourselves to speak in English."

*   *   *

Inside of the stores the carnage is unbelievable. There are dead bodies scattered in many directions. People are in shock that need to be treated or wounded and are either down on the floor or trying to regain their footing. Along with the merchandise, shelves, and racks, it looks like a war zone. Managers and employees in all of the four stores are doing their best to clear shoppers who weren't injured by the bombings. The stores need to be cleared as best as possible to allow the emergency personnel to administer aid to the injured. Each person lying down would have to be checked for pulses to ensure they weren't killed in the blast.

One manager states, "Who is so rotten to be able to do this? Most of these people are women." Tears run down his cheeks as he checks the bodies to see if anyone is either unconscious, injured, or dead.

*   *   *

When the EMTs arrive, they radio headquarters to explain the dilemma they are facing. Emergency vehicles are being called in from adjacent communities.

At the same time the EMTs arrive, the local Natick, Massachusetts, police cruisers arrive and the sergeant in charge just says, "Jesus H. Christ." He calls it into main headquarters, and they too call for local community assistance.

*   *   *

Lieutenant John McNamara, a ten-year veteran on the Natick Detective Force, is called upstairs to the captain's office. He is placed in charge of the detail to handle the four stores.

"Jack, I don't know what we're dealing with yet. There are 911 reports of bombings at four stores that opened early this morning. Pick your teams and get me a report."

John, who likes to be called Jack, requests a four-man team to handle each store and is given the manpower to solve this quickly before the community panics. All off-duty detectives and police officers are being called into active duty effective immediately.

Chapter Two

Gathering Information

As soon as the sufficient numbers of detectives arrive at the station, Lt. Jack McNamara holds a meeting with the sixteen members assigned to the investigation. A half hour of time has lapsed.

"Right now all of you have a great number of questions, and I do as well. At this moment, all I can say is, for some reason some fanatics have bombed four stores located off Route Nine. It happened at 6:30 this morning and there are hundreds of deaths.

"I want us to get there quickly to do the best investigative work we can. From the list of names the captain gave me, this is who I want as team leaders of four teams: Steve Donovan, Henry Kostovich, Peter Chang, and Mark Rosen.

"I want you four to pick whoever you want on your teams so each of you needs to choose three other detectives. I feel we will accomplish more if you are comfortable working with people you've had experience with before. I'm giving you ten minutes to make these decisions and I will meet all of you out in the parking lot. See you downstairs."

Mark Rosen says, "Jack, are these terrorists jihadists?"

"Right at the moment, Mark, I can't say that for sure." Jack closes his notes and walks out of the room.

*   *   *

Outside in the parking lot, Lt. McNamara assigns each team a store to investigate. They head out to Route Nine in five cars. The lieutenant rides alone in order for him to move freely between teams.

*   *   *

Arriving at the location of the stores, Lt. McNamara exits his car and has the four team leaders meet with him. He gives them further instructions on how to begin and work with the patrol officers who have arrived on the scene before them. He knows they understand procedure; however, this is an extremely unusual situation and he doesn't want anything overlooked.

Each of the men nods their approval and returns to their vehicles.

McNamara reenters his car and drives to where he knows the senior patrol command center is located to learn whatever he can.

*   *   *

Arriving at the trailer where the command center members were located, Lt. McNamara exits his car and heads for the door of the trailer. Before he tries to enter, he flashes his badge to the patrol officer standing guard outside.

Entering Lt. McNamara sees his friend Ryan, a sergeant on the force, is in charge of the center.

"What do you have so far, Ryan?"

Turning to see who is calling his name, Sergeant Ryan looks over his shoulder and spots Jack. He smiles but the smile is short lived.

"I got word that you are heading up the investigation. Right now we are bare bones. There were three explosions in each of four different retail stores. We don't have a death count yet, but we are guessing in the hundreds. There will also be hundreds maimed by the blasts. Do you have teams out here yet?"

"Yes, I have four teams of four. I wanted to speak with you before I go into the stores and speak with each of them."

"Jack, I've got twenty years on the force, and I have never seen this kind of destruction here in our community before."

"I know it's hard to believe. I guess we live in hard times," says the lieutenant.

"If you can't give me any more than what you already have, I'll go now," remarks the lieutenant.

"May God be with you, Jack, and please catch these bastards."

"We will, Ryan, we will."

*   *   *

The local media is surrounding the area and reporters are doing their best to get information as to what happened, who might be responsible, and how high the death toll is.

Media helicopters are flying over the stores and their broadcast vehicles are staged around various portions of the parking lots.

*   *   *

Fire personnel, emergency medical vehicles, county medical examiners, forensic specialists, and various other medical personnel are deploying to the area. The job is overwhelming. The injured are being sent to hospitals as far away as thirty miles because of the lack of beds.

The dead are being identified, if possible, and placed in body bags.

*   *   *

Lt. McNamara enters the first store after leaving the command post. Jack crosses under the crime scene's yellow tape encompassing one of the bombed areas. Looking around for his team, he realizes what Sergeant Ryan meant when he said he has never seen anything so horrific in the community before.

Jack spots one of the rookie detectives heaving his guts out. He avoids him so as not to embarrass the man. He hopes the detective isn't destroying some evidence they need. Although Jack had been there many years ago, he wonders if his stomach will handle the vast devastation he is looking at. For a quick moment, Jack wonders how another human being can live with themselves after causing so much devastation.

Chapter Three

Kostovich's Responsibility

Moving around EMTs, fire personnel, medical examiners, and bodies lying all over the floors, Lt. McNamara works his way over to his team leader. Henry Kostovich is leaning over a figure of a woman who is definitely dead, from what Jack can surmise. However, the lieutenant is intrigued by the examination Henry is doing at the moment.

As Henry rises from his position, the lieutenant asks, "What did you find, Henry?"

"She didn't just die from the explosion; she has about a dozen holes in her body, probably made from BBs.

"Sir, this bombing is not the job of locals who try to hit and run. We need the FBI and/or Homeland Security involved. I'm sure we are going to find that the traces of explosives used are not the types used by amateurs."

"So, are you saying you want the feds in on this?"

"Yes, sir, I don't feel we are going to solve this by ourselves."

"Henry, from what I have observed, I believe you are right. I'll head out to the command center and make the call."

"Lieutenant, you know you're going to get static."

"Believe me, you're right. If they want the truth, they are going to have to accept our limitations. I saw one of your detectives throwing up. How is the rest of your team?"

"The one throwing up is new with the squad. We've all done it. He's a good man. He'll be okay. He's probably more embarrassed than anything else. The other two are seasoned guys. They'll be okay."

"When you've completed your investigation, plan on meeting back at the station. Make sure the techs collect every piece of evidence that can help us identify what caused the bombings, leading us to who did it."

"You'll have it, Lieutenant."

"Also make sure the patrol officers collect names, addresses, and phone numbers of those who survived. We need to talk with them as well as the store employees."

"Yes, sir."

* * *

Before Jack McNamara walks over to the command center, he visits with his other three teams. Each team leader has suggested the same course of action even though he has not shared Henry's opinions with them.

Jack McNamara knows what must be done in his first report of this crime scene, even though he knows deep down the top brass is not going to like what he will say. He dreads this next phone call.

Lt. McNamara gives each team leader the same instructions he gave Henry about having the patrol officers collect data from the survivors.

Chapter Four

The Mall

At ten o'clock the same morning, the twelve terrorists are let off at the mall located five miles west of their early-morning strike. They proceed to the areas they rehearsed for the last two months. Within the mall are some large stores with popular names, and numerous stores owned by individuals and smaller companies. Six of the men will penetrate the larger stores and six will lay their explosives in smaller locations.

As the men disperse around the mall, one of them decides he will locate his backpack near one of the water fountains across from a busy music store. He removes his pack and places it under the cooler in the hallway. He bends down to drink and casually begins to walk off.

Roger Demers, a security guard, notices the man drinking. While this is not unusual, he saw the man place his backpack under the cooler. In this morning's briefing, the security forces were warned to be on the lookout for anything unusual because of the earlier bombings. No one suspects there would be additional attacks on the same day, but they were warned never let their guard down.

Roger notices the man is leaving without his backpack and he hollers out to him that he left his pack behind. Instead of returning for the pack, the man begins to run.

Shit, what the hell is going on, thinks Roger. His first instinct is to clear the building. He reaches for the fire alarm and as he does, he hears the sound of an explosion in another wing of the mall. Roger pulls the alarm.

He begins to yell for everyone to clear the corridors and the stores. Repeating himself, Roger begins yelling, "There is a bomb threat here."

No matter what state of mind you are in, a fire alarm tells you to clear the building, and that is what saves many people's lives.

Emergency rear exit doors in the stores, as well as the main entry doors, automatically swing open and the crowds rush to leave the building.

*   *   *

The fire alarm at the mall signals three fire stations to respond. Firemen get suited quickly and the trucks begin to roll.

Mall security places a 911 call to the police station telling them of explosions going off. The dispatcher taking the call wonders, *What the hell is going on?*

The police chief is thinking how he is going to have the manpower to deal with all of this. At that same moment, his captain knocks on his open door and requests a moment saying, "We have a report from Lt. McNamara, and you're not going to like it."

Chapter Five

First Report

"What am I not going to like?" the chief says to the captain. "I don't see how this day is going to get much worse. We already have a second series of bombings at the mall and we barely have the manpower to cover both bombings properly."

The chief sits behind his desk and motions for the captain to take a seat.

"What do you have from McNamara?"

"They are not through with their investigation, but the body count is already over three hundred. Indications are there are at least five hundred wounded and some of those may not make it. The wounded are spread over a number of hospitals to obtain treatment. John says he and his teams feel we need to call in the feds on this."

"Shit, I felt this was going to happen. Do you have any word from the teams at the mall yet?" remarks the chief.

"No. sir, my gut feeling is these attacks are a well-coordinated move by the same group, either domestic or foreign. Whoever they are, we could use the assistance based on what we're looking at."

"I realize that the damn feds don't give assistance. They take control over everything."

"Chief, if you don't mind my saying it, we need to get the public some answers quick or we're going to have major problems on our hands in more ways than one."

"I'll call the Boston office of the FBI and ask for assistance. They'll have plenty of people here in a couple of hours."

*   *   *

At the command center where Sergeant Ryan is located, he is arranging a media interview to satisfy the reporters. Ryan is also trying to figure out how to rearrange the patrol officers to have some transferred to the mall. He knows the emergency medical teams are having the same problems he is.

*   *   *

Alice Broadwell, FBI special agent in charge in Boston, assures the chief of Natick's police department there will be agents on the scene within two hours. Alice knows the chief from past experience, and realizes this call must have been a tough choice for him.

Chapter Six

Press Release

Sergeant Ryan has officers set up a podium near the entrance of Parking Lot A for his announcements. His method is to keep the media as far away from the crime scenes as possible. There is too much going on to have reporters walking on the interior of the perimeter.

At 11:00 a.m. he begins stating his findings. There are over two dozen reporters from newspapers and television stations clamoring for information. Stations from all areas of New England and New York are present.

"I would like to thank the media for respecting the crime scene areas. We have too much happening, and if you had not remained outside of the perimeter, our job would be more difficult."

The reporters look at each other in amazement. This approach was something new for them to hear. They are wondering what comes next.

"We have found evidence there were twelve explosions within four shopping centers early this morning. I am sad to say right now the death total is slightly over three hundred and we are not finished. Over five hundred wounded have been taken to hospitals within a thirty-mile radius. We wish them a speedy recovery. At this time that is all I can give you."

One reporter shouts out, "Who the hell did this, sergeant?"

"At the moment, I cannot tell you, but we will find them. We have four investigative teams working inside the stores and I have just received word that the FBI is sending agents to lend assistance."

A second reporter asks, "Sergeant, is it true while we were here, there were bombings at the main mall up the road."

Ryan hesitates for a moment, wondering how much he wants to divulge. "You are correct. Approximately ten o'clock this morning, there were a number of explosions at the mall. How many, I cannot accurately tell you at this point. However, the building's fire alarm sounded and thank God many people escaped injury."

A third reporter asks, "Is this the work of foreigners, Sergeant?"

"I ask that you do not imply that in your reporting. Right now we don't know who caused this. We will find out, and you will be given the factual information as the department reaches a conclusion. I assure you, we will find them."

Sergeant Ryan turns and leaves the podium.

*   *   *

Each one of the reporters begins communicating with their offices. Some do so by stepping inside of vans, some by calling directly on cell phones, and some by sharing the information on to the helicopters that are circling overhead who will then pass this on via satellite communications.

Every reporter notes Sergeant Ryan was tearful and angry at the same time. Most of them know the sergeant, having lived here most of their lives. By their standards, he is a first-class police officer and they trust him.

Chapter Seven

FBI Arrives

Two hours after the special agent in charge of the Boston FBI office spoke with the chief of the Natick Police Department. Alice Broadwell and a combination of twelve agents arrive at the Natick Police Department.

Alice told the agents they are to wait in the vehicles while she goes inside to decide how and where the team will work the scenes.

Special Agent Broadwell walks into the police station and flashes her FBI identification in front of the duty sergeant.

"Oh, give me a moment and I will contact the chief. We didn't expect you so soon."

"Why not, Sergeant? This is very serious business we will both be dealing with. I venture to say you will be seeing a lot of me for a while."

The sergeant doesn't reply, but the grimace on his face reflects his feelings.

The duty sergeant places a call to the chief's secretary. He also places a call to Captain Green.

Alice wanders away from the duty desk to look at their bulletin board.

* * *

Three minutes later a policewoman arrives at the duty sergeant's desk to escort the FBI agent upstairs.

As they climb the stairs, Agent Broadwell says, "How are things progressing, officer?"

"Right now the detectives and the patrol cars are at the scenes. That's all I know."

At the top of the stairs, they meet Captain Green. After introductions, the captain walks with them down the hall to chief's office.

Chief Winters stands and moves from behind his desk and shakes Alice's hand. "Thank you for coming so quickly. Our detectives on the scene suggested we call you."

"I have twelve agents waiting in vehicles outside. Fill me in on the details so we can head out. I remember you saying there were multiple scenes."

"Let's everyone sit down," says the chief.

Alice and the captain take seats and the police woman returns to her desk.

The chief begins telling Alice the details from the first 911 call to the last 911 call that came in from the mall. Then he tells her about Lt. McNamara's report.

Alice thinks for a moment before she responds to his statement. "What I want to do is put eight of my agents at the four locations in the strip mall. I will place four agents and myself at the mall. Who are the officers in charge at these locations?"

"Lt. McNamara is at the strip mall and we have a command center there. Lt. Richards is at the mall. Sergeant Ryan is in charge of the command center."

Standing up, Alice says, "I'll head downstairs and get started."

Captain Green escorts Alice downstairs and wishes her success in solving this tragedy.

Chapter Eight

Precautions

Driving away from the mall bombings, Ahmad reflects on how this operation first began with an idea in Iran. As a religious leader in one of Tehran's largest mosques, Ahmad was called into the office of the senior mullah. Seated at the end of a table, he was facing three very stern-looking mullahs, Ahmad had no idea why he was being called into this meeting.

The mullah seated at the opposite end begins. "Ahmad, we have a project that we need a leader to excel in. One who is a born leader and has military strategic capabilities. Your previous background experience indicates you might be the proper choice to do this assignment. If all goes well, you would be given the honor of being known as an imam. You would no longer be merely a religious leader."

Ahmad is getting anxious. Being offered to be raised to the position of imam is what he has been dreaming of. He wonders what this project is. Of course he will accept the assignment; he would be a fool not to. Ahmad doesn't stop and think of how they played him with the words *"merely a religious leader."* His ego is in high gear.

* * *

Pre-occupied with his thoughts, Ahmad has to slam on the brakes of the van. He nearly rear-ended a car stopped waiting in line at a red light.

That was close, Ahmad thinks to himself. *I must focus on what needs to be done and leave my dreams to when I can afford to address them. Having an accident near the mall in a van packed with twelve men would be a terrible mistake.*

I will drop the men at the residence and then return the van to the rental agency. We cannot afford someone spotting this vehicle and giving away the description and possibly the plate number to the police.

*   *   *

A half hour later, the twelve bombers and their leader return to the property they leased. Lunch will be sandwiches and cold drinks. The noontime news is sketchy about both bombing locations. The men have high expectations for what the evening news will announce.

After they eat, they spread their prayer rugs around on the floors and face east to do their midday prayers.

Ahmad leaves when his prayers are done. After returning the vehicle, Ahmad will rent another vehicle from a different agency. He doesn't want his face being too familiar with any one group of people.

Arriving at the rental company, he tells them he is returning the vehicle early because it is larger than what he needs.

They ask if he would like to rent a different vehicle; he tells them he has a friend loaning him one for the remainder of the time period he needs a car.

*   *   *

Three blocks away from the first rental company, he enters the office of a second firm. "Do you have a van that will accommodate a group of people?"

The blonde-haired gentleman, no older than in his twenties and with an earring in his right earlobe, walks around the counter to shake his hand. "Yes, we have three sitting on our lot right now. They seem to be a hot item, so you should make your decision fairly quickly."

Ahmad realizes he is being handed a sales pitch that is really a pitch without any merit. "Let me take a look at what you have."

The clerk moves back around the counter and removes three different sets of keys from the cabinet behind the desk.

"Follow me!"

Outside in their yard, they walk over to the three vehicles. One is a white van similar to the one he recently turned in. That leaves it out.

Next, he sees a red one, which would stick out and become easy to spot. The third one is a dark green Ford E series, which is a wagon van. There is plenty of room to move his members and the green should be less likely to be noticed.

After going over the details of fees, mileage, leasing agreements, and insurance, Ahmad agrees to lease the vehicle until the end of December.

The clerk tells him there is a holiday special going on this month, which will also continue into December.

After writing up the paperwork the clerk asks for his credit card and driver's license. The credit card processes without any difficulty. Ahmad receives the keys and he pulls the van out of the lot. This van was slightly larger than the one he turned in.

* * *

When Ahmad arrives back at the house, some of the men are napping and the others are playing cards. Their conversations speculate how much damage they caused.

* * *

Close to five o'clock, Ahmad places pizza orders. He calls four different locations and orders four different large pizzas for pick up. Fifteen minutes later, he directs four of the men to take the van and on how to pick up the pizzas. A different man is to go into each store so that the amount of pizzas purchased and who is picking them up isn't too noticeable. Ahmad gives them enough money to make the purchases.

Tomorrow he will begin planning their next assignment and he wants their full and undivided attention when he explains what they will do next.

*   *   *

As the terrorists begin devouring their slices of pizza and have cold drinks, the six o'clock news hits the television waves. All of the men's eyes are glued to one of the three screens located in various rooms.

Each station's reporters begin with what is called, "Breaking News on Today's Bombings."

The Natick police were very smart to allow a small number of reporters and cameramen onto the sites at midafternoon.

The carnage being shown looks as if the areas are war zones instead of shopping centers. There are shelves, racks, inventory scattered in all directions. People are still lying around the area waiting to be treated. There is blood splatterings everywhere you look at each bombing site.

The more serious have been sent off to every available hospital within a thirty-mile radius; the dead placed in body bags and moved off to an empty warehouse for later identification.

The number of dead at the early-morning bombings is listed at 561. The number of injured is 828. The number of dead at the mall is 136, with the total number of injured at 75. It is reported that the fire alarm at the mall saved many lives.

*   *   *

Meanwhile the terrorist leader Ahmad wonders in silence while the others are celebrating. Let them celebrate, he thinks. He has more concerns than with casualty counts. His first concern is that he only heard eleven explosions at the mall. Someone's bomb didn't explode.

His concern is one of the men made an error in assembling their bomb. His next set of plans is to split the group up into two sets. He is going to be making a decision without knowing all of the facts. He will pray to Allah for him to select a good leader for the second group. He needs to be nearby to get the next operation set and activated. Then he will meet the second party near the third location.

*   *   *

Back at the Natick police station, Lieutenants McNamara and Richards are feeding their men. It appears that tonight pizza is a popular item. While the men try to eat some food and wash it down with cold drinks, they are given instructions by each of the lieutenants as to how they are going to fill out their reports and begin their investigations. When the men are finished eating, they are told to go home with instructions to be in at eight the next morning.

Chapter Nine

FBI's Investigation Begins

Special Agent Alice Broadwell exits the door of the police station and walks over to the three cars in which the twelve agents are waiting for her. She asks them to exit their vehicles. "Before I go into details, you ladies and gentlemen are welcome to use the facilities before we leave here. I strongly recommend it, because from what I've been told we are going into what looks like a war zone."

The agents are relieved for the break and walk to the station door and go inside.

When all of them return, Alice has them standing in a circle in the parking lot.

She selects the eight agents who will head out to the strip mall to the command center. They are to check in with Sergeant Ryan for the whereabouts of Lt McNamara. They have their orders to work alongside McNamara's people but to begin their own findings.

The other four will head over to the mall with her and make contact with Lt. Mike Richards.

*   *   *

Arriving at the command post, one of the agents enters the trailer and makes their presence known to Sergeant Ryan.

Ryan gives him the information on which stores were bombed so the agents can proceed with their investigation.

"Let me call Lt. McNamara and find out where he is. One of you should connect with him before you begin."

The sergeant picks up his cell phone and dials McNamara's cell number. He tells Jack the FBI has arrived.

"Ryan, have them stay at the trailer. I want to meet them there. How many arrived?"

"The agent said there are eight of them for this location and five of them for the mall."

"What's going on at the mall, Ryan?"

"I'll fill you in when you get here."

"Okay!"

Before Jack heads over to the command post, he phones each of his team leaders and advises them to take a quick lunch break by twos. This way two of them will always be on site until they decide to wrap it up.

As he rides over to where the command trailer is, he wonders what Ryan is going to tell him about the mall.

Chapter Ten

At the Command Post

Lt. McNamara pulls up near the command trailer. As he steps outside, he sees a ring of agents trying to stay warm. He assumes they are tired of being cooped up in their vehicles and would rather deal with some of the cold air.

"I'm going inside for a few minutes, gentlemen, then I'll be out."

Heads nod in agreement, wondering as if they have a choice.

Inside Ryan sees Jack entering. He asks, "How is the investigation going?"

"Slow and very painstaking. What are you going to tell me about the mall?"

"Around ten thirty this morning, there were explosions at the mall. Right now that is all I can tell you. I know Lt. Richards is in charge there and the captain said four agents and the special agent in charge from the Boston office are headed there."

"Good Christ, what the hell did we do to deserve this shit," yells Jack.

* * *

Outside of the command trailer Lt. McNamara introduces himself and says thank you for the support of the FBI. "We have a hell of a mess on our hands right now. I realize you will be doing your own investigation here and that's fine with me. When we can get back to the station and put our notes together, maybe we can figure out who did this. Sergeant Ryan told me you already know which buildings had the bombings. I call them sites one through four. Why don't you decide as a group which sites you'll take and meet the team leaders when you get there? I'll be floating around to each of the sites, making sure we cover everything. Do you have any questions?"

Not getting asked any questions, Jack says, "I'll meet you at the sites; you might want to leave your vehicles here. The walk isn't too far and you'll avoid the mess of vehicles already near the buildings."

Jack leaves them and heads back to be with his people.

*   *   *

Special Agent Alice Broadwell and the four agents she chose to be at the mall with her arrive at the main entrance. The captain had given her Lt. Richards' cell phone number. She enters his number into her contacts and then places the call.

Lt. Richards' phone rings and he notices it is a Boston area code. Immediately he realizes the FBI has arrived. "Hello, Mike Richards here!"

Alice introduces herself and asks Mike where they could meet to put a plan together and be of assistance.

"Right now I'm close to the main entrance. Why don't I come out there and we can get started."

"Sounds like a plan to me. Give me some clues on what you look like."

"Before or after this damn thing started." That gives Alice an idea of what he's like.

Alice realizes that he hasn't totally lost his sense of humor in the midst of this tragedy. That's a good sign.

*   *   *

Alice sees a man coming out of the main entrance looking similar to the image Lt. Richards gave her. He is tall, about six feet, blond hair. That he is not wearing a tie is really the first thing she notices and realizes he wouldn't be an FBI agent dressed like that. She enjoys the dress code of FBI agents in the field.

At the same time, Alice notices Mike; he sees her and four other agents so that is a dead giveaway for him to head over to them.

Reaching the small group, Lt. Richards sticks out his hand to shake with Alice. "We are glad you're here. I have three teams of two inside and this is becoming overwhelming."

"Lieutenant, I suggest you take these men inside and divide them up as you see fit with your people. I have something else on my mind that I want to check with mall security, if you don't mind."

"No problem, madam. Let's go, fellows, we have lots of work to do."

Alice heads into the mall and looks for the mall office so that she can speak with mall security.

* * *

Meanwhile local media is putting the word out over television, radio, and in the newspapers about the bombings, plus deaths and wounded totals. Somehow they have also learned that the FBI has been called in on these matters.

* * *

Finding the mall security office in disarray, SA Alice tries to get someone to make a decision if one of their personnel set off the fire alarm, and what could have caused them to do so before all of the bombs detonated. This action very definitely saved many lives.

Finally, one of the staff offers to contact each security officer by radio and ask the question, if they were the one to set off the fire alarm.

On the tenth call, Roger Demers replies that he set the alarm off.

"Please have Roger tell you where he is right now and tell him to expect me to be there in a few minutes," says Alice.

The message is passed onto Roger and he tells the staff member where he is located.

Alice receives the location and is given directions on how to get there by the shortest route.

"Thank you!" replies Alice.

*   *   *

With a general physical description of Roger, Alice sees a security officer looking left and right as if he is expecting someone.

Sure enough, as she identifies herself, Roger returns his identification.

"Roger, your action saved many lives. I am wondering what caused you to set off the fire alarm."

"At our morning briefing today, we were made aware of the earlier bombings. No one really expected there would be additional attempts, but we were warned to be on our guard."

"So what happened to make you take action?"

"I was near the record store in the next wing at the time. I watched a fellow place his backpack under a water cooler and lean down to take a drink. In itself that is quite a normal occurrence, except when he finished drinking, he left the bag there."

"So what did you do then?"

"He started moving through the crowded hallway and I hollered out to him that he left his bag behind."

"Then what happened?"

"Instead of returning for the bag, he started running away from the cooler. His running triggered my instincts, and I started reaching for the fire alarm switch. As I was doing that, I heard what I thought was an explosion in another wing of the mall. I didn't hesitate, so I pulled the switch."

"Would you mind walking me to where the music store is to see if there was an explosion there?"

Roger turned a little pale at that point, hesitated, and then agreed to take Alice there.

* * *

Coming up on the music store, Roger points out the bag that is still under the water cooler. He offers to go and pick it up.

"Don't touch that!" Alice says. "I want you to call your office on your radio and inform them that we need the bomb squad here right now."

Roger looks at her, "Should we remain standing here?"

"Only until we finish roping this area off so no one enters it within at least fifty feet."

Roger calls his office and the call is put out as a 911 call to the police station.

The Natick police receive the call and the chief says, "Christ, I have the bomb squad working as patrol because we don't have the enough manpower here."

"Captain, get on the horn with the state police and tell them we need their bomb squad at the mall immediately on the direction of the FBI."

The call is made and the state police direct their bomb squad to the mall.

The mall office relays the information to Roger by radio.

"Now, what do we do?" asks Roger.

"First, I call Lt. Richards and tell him what we found and ask him to bring us plenty of crime scene tape. Then we wait for bomb squad to do their job."

Chapter Eleven

Bomb Squad

Within twenty-five minutes the state police bomb squad arrives at the mall. SA Alice Broadwell and mall security officer Roger Demers meet them as they arrive at the mall entrance closest to where the backpack is located.

Roger explains to the senior officer what transpired just before he pulled the fire alarm. He goes on to say the same bag is still under the water cooler across from the music store.

Alice says, "If it's safely possible, it would be vital to the investigation if they could remove the bomb and make it inert. The bomb's components could lead us to the perpetrators of this carnage."

"We'll do our best, ma'am."

The officer walks into the mall and looks over the situation at the cooler. Reaching for his radio, he calls his team and tells them to send in the lead lined box they use to recover small to medium devices. He also wants one of the team to bring in the ten-foot pole with the mechanical arm to lift objects.

The box is placed near the cooler and the top is removed and placed on the floor alongside. The two men who brought in the box retreat outside.

The squad member, wearing protective clothing, announces on his radio that he is ready to begin moving the pack. Very carefully so as not to jar the pack, he takes his time attaching the mechanical arm to the loop at the top and begins to move the pack about six inches off the floor.

Very slowly he inches the pack toward the position of the box. When he has it close, he lifts the pack higher so that it will clear the top. Then he moves the pack to the center of the top portion and uses the cable on the arm to make the pack descend into the box, moving it slowly inch by inch.

When he knows it is resting on the bottom of the box, he detaches the arm and proceeds to secure the cover on top with the use of the pole.

Once the box is secure, he radios to the team that two men can safely come inside and remove the box.

SA Broadwell and Roger Demers are anxiously waiting for the box to be removed to the special bomb vehicle.

"What happens next?" she asks the senior officer.

"We take it to our safety area and see if we can accomplish what you requested. Give me your cell number as this will take some time. I promise to call you with whatever we find."

Alice continues, "If you can decommission the bomb so it can be used as evidence, I will have an FBI lab team pick it up from your facility."

"That works for us. We would like to be able to nab whoever is doing this."

"Thank you for coming so quickly!" Alice remarks.

Chapter Twelve

End of a Long Day

As Jack McNamara is driving up to his two-story condo at nine that night, he notices a light on in his living room. He didn't think he had left it on. After parking in his assigned slot, Jack walks up the stairs to the front door; he reaches into his right front pocket to get his keys. Jack is surprised the door opens and Jennifer Stone, his fiancée, is standing there.

"I can only imagine what your day has been like. I didn't want you to be alone when you came home."

Exhausted, Jack steps through the doorway and gives her a quick kiss. "I'm glad you're here. Right now I don't even want to talk about it. Please pour me a drink and make it hefty."

"Give me your coat and I'll pour the drink. I've been watching the news since I got here around seven. God, this is terrible."

Jack snaps, "It's more than terrible. It's devastating!" He removes his 9mm semi-automatic from his shoulder holster and places it on top of the refrigerator. The holster gets tossed onto the counter.

Jennifer realizes how much anger Jack is holding inside. She hands him a tumbler half full of SKYY vodka with two ice cubes in it.

"Have you had anything to eat?"

"A couple of slices of pizza at the station. I sent everyone home to get some rest. The guys have been working on adrenaline all day."

"I know you're beat but you need to keep up your strength. I picked up some Chinese food on the way over. There's plenty left, if you would like me to warm some for you."

"Maybe later, right now I would like to finish this drink and maybe have another one. Please sit down next to me. I need you close to me."

Jennifer sits down on the couch on Jack's left side and he places his arm around her. She feels his body tremble slightly, probably some from the trauma and some from rage.

* * *

Lt. Mike Richards goes home to an empty house. His wife divorced him a couple of years ago. She moved back to New Hampshire, taking their two sons to her family's farm in the North Country.

Mike enters the house and its darkness makes him uneasy tonight. His mind is tired of looking at bodies and destruction. In the eight years he has been with the force, he has never experienced this kind of devastation before.

After turning on some lights, Mike pours himself a large glass of Johnny Walker. He moves into the kitchen and decides he needs a sandwich to top off the two slices of pizza he ate at the station.

Two hours later, Mike wakes up on the living room couch, soaking wet from perspiration. He had a terrible dream. It felt as if he was somehow responsible for the carnage. It reminded him of being in the middle of dead comrades over in Iraq.

Chapter Thirteen

Next Day

Lt. Jack McNamara is at the conference room one at 7:45 a.m. His team of sixteen are due to be on time for 8:00 a.m.

Lt. Mike Richards walks into conference room two at 7:50 a.m. His team is also supposed to begin at 8:00 a.m.

By 8:00 both conference rooms are filled with the detectives from the areas of the bombings.

Jack McNamara is standing in front of the white board on the wall. He is clearing the board of the previous investigation posted as the investigation is finalized.

"I hope you gentlemen got some much-needed rest," Jack says.

There are all kinds of responses from his group. Some detectives are trying to put a little humor into the conversation, knowing how serious the talk will turn to in a few moments.

"All right, let's begin. We're going to post the four sites as numbers one through four across the top of the board. On the left hand side of the board, we are going to post categories. Between us we will fill in the blanks on the board. You've all been through this before so you understand what I am talking about.

"Henry, let's start with you and go around the room. Take your time and be as thorough as possible. Many times we will be repeating information. We need to see what kind of picture we have to make some intelligent decisions." Jack will be adding columns to the whiteboard as needed.

Henry begins: his report goes on for twenty minutes. As the detectives take their turns from making their observations at the crime scenes, some take fifteen minutes and some take as much as thirty minutes.

Jack breaks them for lunch when only nine have spoken. He knows how hard they worked yesterday and what they've suffered because of this. He wants them to feel he appreciates them.

"Not pizza again," he hears someone comment.

"No, today you buy your own lunch. Save the department some money."

A number of laughs come out of the group.

* * *

On his way out of the conference room Lt. McNamara sees Lt. Richards. "How's it going, Mike?"

"Slow and tedious!"

"Do you think both attacks are the same group?" asks Jack.

"I would bet on it."

"Mike, you look awful tired. Are you okay?"

"I didn't sleep well last night."

"I'm not surprised; Jennifer came over and spent the night. She said I tossed and turned and even whimpered a couple of times. If she wasn't there, I probably wouldn't have gotten the sleep I did. Mike, let's go have lunch."

"Let me drop off some paperwork and I'll meet you outside."

* * *

At 1:00 p.m. the detectives are back in their designated conference rooms.

"Let's continue," Jack says.

The remaining seven give their reports and afterward Jack explains what his report to the captain and the chief will be like.

As they looked at the whiteboard. it appears to the detectives in Conference Room 1 that there is no clear-cut avenue to try and identify who the bombers are yet.

Jack advises everyone that he has been told by the FBI they are picking up the remains of an unexploded bomb from the mall, and should be able to identify where the components came from. This should give them something more to work with.

Meanwhile everyone has to hit the pavement to do some good old investigative work.

Jack has already planned ahead for this and he begins to hand out assignments to the men.

*   *   *

As some members of the FBI task force are eating lunch, Special Agent Alice's cell phone rings. "Special Agent Broadwell."

"I am the duty sergeant at the state police barracks. I have information for you from the bomb squad."

"Can you read it to me?"

"Sure!"

"The bomb has been dismantled and it is safe for your people to pick it up."

"Thank you. Where should I direct the technicians to go?"

"Send them to the barracks on Route Nine and we'll have it ready for your people."

"Thank you, Sergeant. Tell the bomb squad I said thank you as well."

"Will do, we are happy to oblige."

Alice shuts off her phone and smiles for the first time today since she woke up. "Well, ladies and gentlemen, we may have just gotten our first break."

Alice feels good enough to continue eating her lunch.

Chapter Fourteen

Bomb Report

Two days later, Special Agent Alice Broadwell enters the Natick, MA police station. The chief is expecting her.

The desk sergeant contacts the chief's secretary as soon as he sees Alice walk through the door. Alice realizes she is developing a name and recognition for herself when she hears the sergeant make the call.

Captain Green arrives at the entry and escorts Alice up to the chief's office on the second floor.

"You have the report from your lab?" he asks as they climb the stairs.

"Yes, a high priority was put on this situation by the president."

They enter the office and Chief Winters stands to be polite as he greets her.

"Please sit down. Captain, would you join us."

Captain Green is kind enough to take her coat and hang it on the coat rack.

Alice is wearing a dark blue suit with a pink blouse, which makes her very attractive.

The chief is wondering how such a lovely-looking lady decided to join the FBI.

Alice breaks his train of thought by stating, "Chief, the bomb components we found in the backpack were manufactured in the Middle East. It is difficult to say what their nation of origin is. However, we are positive they did not come from American manufacturers."

"Are you saying we are dealing with international terrorists?" asks the captain.

"It is the belief of the FBI that these bombers are not homegrown terrorists. We are dealing with trained infiltrators and for some reason, they've picked your community to cause this destruction."

Chief Winters replies, "There are no reports of anyone yelling 'Allahu Akbar' at any of the sites."

"It's my personal opinion this was done deliberately, possibly to delay an investigation from looking for foreign terrorists. In other words, for some reason they are trying to buy some time. However, it is entirely speculation as to why.

"The president has ordered the FBI to increase the number of agents working on this event. In two days there will be at least fifty agents in the area."

The chief asks, "How will it be possible for us not to get in each other's way?"

"The assistant director from Washington is flying into Boston this afternoon. He is going to take personal charge of this operation. I need to talk with him on how he wants to run everything."

"I would suggest that after the two of you meet, both of you come to this office and we can develop a mutual plan," says the chief.

"That sounds reasonable to me. I'll bring him. I will call to see when you have time for us. Hopefully his flight isn't delayed or cancelled. It's snowing in Washington right now."

Alice rises and shakes both the men's hands. The captain gets her coat for her and assists her in getting her coat on.

Alice thinks, *It is nice to have a gentleman around.*

*　　*　　*

While police officials are meeting with the FBI, the detectives are meeting with employees of the stores bombed and customers who were in those stores at the time. It is a long and tedious process. The detectives and the patrol officers are working twelve-hour shifts.

Captain Green set up staff members to call relatives of those who died in the bombings, giving the department's condolences. There are hundreds of calls to make. It is a difficult assignment to explain to people about the loss of a family member.

Meanwhile the media has camped out at each bombing site and is giving up-to-the- minute coverage on any new evidence found—or rumors—whichever may come first.

*   *   *

On the six o'clock news, the local stations begin broadcasting that there was an unexploded backpack and the materials used to create the bomb inside of it came from foreign sources.

"Shit," Chief Winters says. "Who the hell let that information out of the bag?"

*   *   *

At 7:00 p.m. Captain Green takes a call from SA Alice Broadwell. Alice advises him the assistant director landed and if they would like to meet him this evening, she would head out to Natick.

The captain places her on hold and inquires from the chief what he would like to do. "Have them come here at 8:00 in the morning. We need to wrap up some issues tonight."

Captain Green passes the chief's message and Alice says, "We'll be there for eight."

Alice turns around and gives the assistant director the message.

"Good, I've been running all day trying to put things together for this trip. Join me for dinner so we can chat some more."

"Yes, sir."

Chapter Fifteen

Meeting with Assistant Director

At 7:55 a.m. Assistant FBI Director Douglas Risner and SA Alice Broadwell enter the Natick Police Station.

Captain Green is notified they are here and he comes down to the lobby to greet them and escort them to the chief's office.

As they enter the chief's office, Chief Winters is on the phone. He motions with his hands for them to take a seat.

As soon as the chief is off of the phone Captain Green stands and begins making introductions between the chief and the assistant director.

AD Risner begins by saying, "Today there will be fifty FBI agents covering the bombing sites. We will do a complete analysis of what happened and what types of hardware caused it."

The chief is biting his tongue. "What do you expect my detectives to accomplish?"

Before he says another word, Doug thinks about what he wants to say and then goes on to say it.

"Chief, you know we have the expertise to handle this. What can your department offer in this type of investigation?"

The chief's face turns beet red. "What do we have to offer? We haven't even discussed what we have found. I've been in another location where I've seen the FBI waltz in and take over everything to get the credit."

Likewise Doug's face begins to redden. "Chief, let me ask you one question."

"Go ahead."

"Are you a cop or a politician?"

That statement hit the chief's hot button. He says, "Captain, I am going to ask you and Alice to leave us for a few minutes. I'll have Maggie let you know when you can rejoin us."

The captain and the SA rise, wondering where this is all going. However, neither one has a choice but to leave.

When they stand outside of the office, neither wants to say anything that would seem disloyal to their bosses.

*   *   *

As soon as the door is closed, the chief turns to the AD and says, "Mister, don't you ever call me a politician. I am a police officer and politics doesn't enter into my decisions."

Hearing that, Doug responds, "Sorry to put it to you that way, Chief, but I need to know which way you lean. For me, I will never be the director of the FBI, because like you I am not a politician. Now let's put something together so we can nail these suckers"

The chief waits a couple of minutes for both men to regain their composure and places a call to Maggie to have the captain and the SA return to his office. He also tells Maggie to have coffee and water sent in.

*   *   *

When the captain and Alice are seated inside of the chief's office, neither one of them knows what to say at the moment after what just happened.

Chief Winters begins, "The assistant director and I have cleared the air while the two of you were out of the office. I didn't feel the need to drag both of you into our personal situation. Captain Green, I would like you to begin telling the AD what we've learned so far and with that we can formulate a plan. Proceed, Captain."

Captain Green looks at Alice, and then he decides to proceed.

"I would like to suggest we go downstairs to the larger conference room. Lt. McNamara's handiwork of the bombing investigation he is responsible for is still on the white board, and I believe you will get more out of my conversation by looking at his chart."

Chief Winters says, "Captain, take the AD and his special agent and work out the details. Let me know when the three of you have reached a consensus. I would like to meet with all of you before you leave the building."

* * *

Captain Green leads the way to the lower level and the conference room. "Why don't the two of you take off your jackets? It might take us some time to do this properly and with keeping the doors closed, it can get pretty warm and stuffy in here."

Doug and Alice remove their suit jackets and place them on the backs of the seats they are using.

Alice unzips her binder and Doug takes out a recorder from his briefcase.

"You don't mind my recording this, do you, Captain?"

"Absolutely not, if at any time I am not making myself clear, please let me know."

Captain Green begins with the lieutenant's report and for the next two hours they talk back and forth to make sure the picture of what has happened at the four shopping centers and the mall is fully explained.

When they are finished, they have a good working plan on how the bombing portions of the events will be handled by the FBI and the police investigative work will be handled by the Natick Police Department.

Each force will be focusing on their expertise to find these criminals and bring them to justice.

Both Lt. McNamara and Lt. Mike Richards will be liaisons from the police department to the FBI and in the reverse order for communication purposes.

Captain Green remembers the chief wanted to be called and he lifts the receiver of the phone hanging on the wall then dials directly into the chief's office.

When he hangs up, he tells Alice and Doug the chief will be down in ten minutes.

* * *

When the chief arrives, Alice and the captain control the review of their efforts. The chief is satisfied and Alice and Doug leave the station.

In the car Alice says, "I thought when you called him a politician you were going to give him a heart attack."

"It needed to be said, and I thought it was the best way to do it."

Chapter Sixteen

Investigative Work

Natick's police chief announces he will assign twenty detectives, including the two lieutenants, to interviewing employees of the bombed-out stores and customers who were survivors, and check leads that are being called into the department. He holds back six detectives to do the regular crime requirements in Natick.

The twenty begin an enormous task; they will be working twelve-hour shifts to be able to acquire information that could help them find who set off the bombs.

Reports must be made out for each person interviewed and the paperwork generated will be huge.

*   *   *

While the local police are interviewing, the FBI task force is collecting more evidence from the crime scenes and adding their deposits to those already collected by the Natick Police.

The assistant director of the FBI rented a large facility for them to lay out what evidence they collect, in somewhat the same manner one would do for an airplane crash. Four days later, the technicians arrive and begin field testing all of the evidence. There are six teams of technicians.

*   *   *

The detectives gather together each day after filling out their reports. At the end of the first week after interviews began, one detective states he spoke to a woman who was outside at the parking lot entrance in a line of traffic when the explosions began.

The woman told him she saw a number of men enter a white van just before the explosions started. The van exited the lot and parked on the opposite side of the road. After the explosions ceased, the van took off. She thought that was kind of strange.

"Did she think to get a plate number or manufacturer of the van?" asks Lt. McNamara.

"All she got is a partial as the van drove by her. After the explosions, she was more interested in getting the hell out of there."

"Alan, call the DMV Monday with the partial, and see if they can tie that partial to a white van for us," says Lt. Richards.

The rest of the conversations are repeats of the reports from the first six days, providing no new information or anything else significant.

The detectives begin to bitch and moan not only because they are tired, but they have little to show for all of their efforts.

Lt. McNamara says, "I hear you, but I'll be out there with you so until we get some good leads, we need to continue hitting the pavement."

Chapter Seventeen

Department of Motor Vehicles

On Monday morning, Detective Alan Singer is on the phone as soon as the Department of Motor Vehicles opens for business.

On the third ring, someone answers the phone saying, "Motor Vehicle Department, Becky speaking."

"Becky, this is Detective Alan Singer of the Natick Police Department. I am looking to check out a large white van, no make, with only three plate numbers. Can you do that for me?"

"Is this relative to the bombings, Detective?"

"It might be, that is all we know right now."

"I'll do my best, but it will take time. What are the three numbers and were they the first numbers or the last numbers?"

"Numbers are 285 and they were the first numbers."

"Do you have a direct line, Detective?"

"Just call the department and ask for the detective's office. I'll be here."

"I'll call you back as soon as I can with whatever I find."

"Thank you. That is all I can ask."

* * *

It has been ten days since the bombings occurred. Ahmad has made a decision on how he will approach the next two bombings. He has given this considerable thought because they are miles apart, and to do them effectively, he must have good surveillance and planning to be successful.

Today, he will tell the men his plans. It will be good because they are full of excitement after their successes and need something to focus on. He decides to speak with them in the afternoon.

*   *   *

Assistant FBI Director Douglas Risner and Special Agent Alice Broadwell are comparing reports from the FBI lab in Washington regarding the samples that were sent in the week before from the wreckage of the bombings.

"Alice, are there any concrete leads coming from the Natick Police?"

"Right now, Doug, they are sorting through all of the information they are developing, along with the facts we have given them so far. Albeit that hasn't been a whole hell of a lot either."

"Nobody believes this is going to be easy, Alice. Thank God we have one unexploded bag to work with. Bomb residue really doesn't tell you a whole hell of a lot."

Chapter Eighteen

Ahmad's Next Plans

After noontime prayers, Ahmad has the twelve men assemble in the largest room in the residence. When they are settled in and comfortable, he begins:

"When you were recruited from your cells, you were advised that this mission will have multiple targets. It was deliberate that the information was vague in case any of you were arrested.

"The bombings we did ten days ago were just one part of our plan. Those attacks were not only to terrorize civilians but also to affect the holiday economy. The reports that are coming over the television seem to indicate we have been successful in those avenues. Retail businesses don't know who will be attacked next and shoppers are somewhat reluctant to venture out in public. At least this is what is happening in Massachusetts, but I'm sure shoppers in other states are wondering as well.

"This afternoon I want to split this group into two factions. One will stay here with me in Massachusetts to do one more assignment near here. The others will leave us to travel elsewhere to begin surveillance of another project. Both of our groups will join together after we finish here. Are there any questions?"

No one replies.

"I want the following men to remain in this room and the rest of you can wander around the property until I am finished with them.

"Renza, Omid, Sohrah, Turan, Vahid, Younis, and Zurvan. The rest of you can leave now."

* * *

"Renza will be your leader. In two days, I will take you by van into Boston where you will catch the Amtrak into New York City. Six of you will travel in pairs and not be seated near each other. Renza will have the information for you where to depart the train and where you will be staying. He will also give you an idea of what your new assignment is about. I suggest you take the time to do laundry and repack your belongings. I do not want any of you to discuss where you are going with the members remaining behind. Likewise they will be instructed not to discuss their assignment with you. This is for security's sake. You can leave and tell the men outside it is time for them to come in."

* * *

The five remaining men are seated but are wondering where this is all leading. Their eyes begin to wander to each other's faces and they seem to be in a state of confusion.

Ahmad enters the room and smiles. He loves to see the anxiety he has put into their thoughts. Each one of the twelve comes from a different cell and they feel totally vulnerable right now. They felt more secure as a larger group.

Ahmad begins: "The five of you and I will handle the one remaining project I have in mind. We will not discuss the project or how it will work out until the others have left. You are instructed not to ask any of them where they are going. Is this understood?"

Each of the men nods their head in an affirmative manner.

"Now you are free to go back outside and have Renza come back inside."

* * *

It is close to three o'clock when Becky from the Department of Motor Vehicles returns Detective Alan Singer's morning call.

"Detective, it took me longer than I expected, but I do have one match for you."

"Thank you, Becky. I'm sure it was a trying experience to be able to match the vague information I gave you with only three numbers," says Alan.

"Actually, it wasn't as bad as I first thought it would be. I don't know if this is any help to you. The vehicle, if it is the one you are looking for, is registered to a rental company in Worcester. It is the Rent and Drive company located just off Route 9."

"Becky, thanks for your help. We'll see where this leads."

Alan hangs up his phone and calls over to Lt. McNamara's office to give Jack the information he received from the DMV.

"What do you think, Alan?"

"I'm going to take a ride over there and see where this winds up."

"Call me as soon as you are finished talking to them. I don't want to leave any stone unturned in this matter."

"I'll call you before five, Jack."

* * *

Detective Alan Singer arrives at the rental agency. Entering the front door of the office, he notices there is only one person inside.

"Is the manager in?"

"No, sir, he's been out sick with the bug for five days now. Can I help you?"

The young blonde named Maria gives Alan a once-over and likes what she sees. Maybe this customer could be more than a customer for the rental agency.

"I'm sorry to hear that." Alan hands over his identification and the blonde turns whiter than her hairdo.

"I'm aware you have a white van in your company with a plate having 285 as the first three numbers, according to the DMV."

"Let me check the records," she says, as she walks over to her desk.

She looks up vans in the agency records and finds the vehicle. Turning she says, "It's here on the lot. Would you like to look at it? Did it have an accident? It was returned about a week and a half ago."

"I would like to take a look at it, if you don't mind," remarks Alan. He doesn't respond to her question.

"No, I don't mind, I'll lock up the office and walk you through the yard."

Chapter Nineteen

The Van

Alan Singer looks the van over. He turns down the offer of keys as he didn't want any of his fingerprints on the van. He takes out his cell phone after Maria walks back to the office.

Alan rings Jack's office number. He tells Jack everything he sees, which, of course, isn't much help. The remaining numbers 1441 Alan received from the DMV are the numbers on the plate of this van. The lady in the office told him she couldn't give him any customer information about who previously rented the van without authorization.

"Alan, go back into the office and tell the lady that the van is not to leave the yard. The FBI will retrieve it tomorrow for inspection. By then we expect she will have authorization."

He goes into the office and follows Jack's orders.

After hearing Alan's instructions, Maria says, "Oh my God, oh my God, are we in trouble?"

"Right now, all we know is you have a van with the same three numbers. I will be back tomorrow with the FBI and a warrant for the information about who the last customer was who rented it. Can you handle that?"

"Yes, sir, I'll be here at eight."

"Fine, so will we."

*　　*　　*

Lt. McNamara places a call to SA Broadwell. When she answers her cell phone, he tells her what is happening.

"Jack, have your detective meet us there tomorrow morning. We will work out the warrant because this is now being considered a federal crime against homeland security. This could be a big break for us. Nice work, Jack."

*　　*　　*

At eight o'clock the next morning, Detective Alan Singer, SA Broadwell, along with two other agents are waiting for the rental office to open. They have the warrant necessary to remove the van and for the information as to who the last customer was that used it. The FBI also arrive with a tow truck and a long flatbed to place the vehicle on.

Maria shows up at 8:05 and is astonished to see the number of people and equipment waiting for her to open the door.

SA Broadwell shows the lady her identification and the FBI immediately went about loading and removing the vehicle. Showing her credentials also enabled her to obtain the information they wanted without even showing the warrant.

When Alice walks toward the office door to exit, the blonde asks, "Who is going to pay for the time the van is out of the yard. I mean we might be able to rent it."

Alice takes a look at her and says, "If we find nothing on that van, the company will be compensated for its time out of your yard. If we do, we expect full cooperation of your company to find those who used it." Alice turns and walks out of the door.

Chapter Twenty

Inspecting the Van

The FBI took the van to the building they are renting. The building looks like an old Quonset hut. It appears to be almost as long as a football field. There is evidence laid out in an organized manner with each group designated as having come from a particular store location.

The tow truck pulls into the front set of overhead doors, and after being directed he drives about halfway down the right hand side of the interior. Parking the truck, the driver proceeded to remove the van from the flatbed, with the help of the two agents who were along at the rental agency.

When the van is on solid ground, the tow truck driver drives out of the rear exit doors. They didn't tell him anything, but he figures he has a good guess as to what is going on.

* * *

Special Agent Broadwell moves over to the assistant director and hands him the paperwork for the warrant.

"Alice, didn't you give the rental office a copy of this?"

"The lady working there was so shook up, she never even asked for a warrant."

"We will have a team on the van within the hour."

Alice leaves Doug standing by the van and departs to head over to the mall with the two agents who accompanied her this morning. They have other work to do.

* * *

While the FBI is preparing to inspect the van, Ahmad is advising Renza, who is the second team leader, about all of the details his group will need to set up their operation in New York. Ahmad goes over each and every point a number of times, because Renza must record this to memory. There cannot be any written notes regarding their projects.

Three hours later, Ahmad says, "Now repeat what I just told you."

Renzo looks a little bewildered, hesitates a moment, and begins. He needs some reinforcement three times; however, Ahmad is pleased.

Ahmad says, "I have watched you over the last three months and I see you are a leader. You also have good memory skills. That is very important. Tomorrow morning we will meet again and you will repeat everything back to me one more time. The following day, I will drive you and your team into Boston for the Amtrak."

* * *

Lt. McNamara is preparing to meet with the investigative team covering both bombing sites at 4:30 p.m.

Lt. Richards walks through the door of Jack's office and drops down in one of the chairs in front of Jack.

"Any luck out there today, Mike?"

"It's the same story over and over again. No one has seen anything out of the ordinary. People seem to be afraid to talk about it."

"I think I can understand that to some degree. Their minds are refusing to adjust to the horror of it."

"What do you plan to discuss with the troops when they come off the streets?"

"Something I hope is positive, but won't know for a couple of days. We may have found the van that the bombers used to get around.

"I'm waiting for Alan Singer to tell us what went down with the FBI this morning."

"The men need to hear something positive happening. This is their home and they are feeling inadequate dealing with nothing much to work with," says Mike.

"I know, that is why I think Alan's report might cheer them up a little."

"I hope so. I'm going to check my desk and meet you down in the conference room."

*   *   *

Nearly four that afternoon Assistant FBI Director Doug Risner gets a call from Washington on his secure satellite phone.

The call is from the director himself. "Doug, the credit card the renter used is legit; however, it has some peculiarities about it. The mailing address is a post office box in Massachusetts, which doesn't exist. The bills are paid electronically and are paid in full each month. We need to find the ISP address so we can see who handles this card. Right now that is all I can tell you."

"Well, that makes me more anxious to find something on this vehicle."

"I hope it works!"

"Me too," says Doug. "Thanks, I'll pass this on to Alice."

"How is she handling this?"

"She is doing a first-class job if you ask me."

"Good, someday I have other plans for her."

Douglas Risner calls Alice on her phone. He tells her everything he just heard from Washington.

Alice thanks him and when she signs off, she immediately calls Jack McNamara.

She gives him all of the details, wanting to live up to her promise they would work together.

Jack appreciates the call especially since her call came just before his meeting. Now the wheels of ideas are starting to spin in his head.

*　　*　　*

Lt. Namara begins his meeting in the same manner he always does. He begins asking if anyone developed new information other than what they already have.

Alan Singer knew this was exactly the kind of situation Jack wanted. Alan advises his fellow detectives what he has been working on.

When Alan is through, Jack asks if anyone else has something to offer.

When no one does, Jack says, "Alan, I want you to pick one other detective from the group because I have some ideas."

Alan says, "Henry, you up to working together?"

"No problem, guy!" remarks Henry.

"All right, the two of you stay for an extra five or ten minutes and the rest of you can go home and hit the pavement again tomorrow."

There are a number of frustrated exasperations as the men leave.

Jack explains to Alan and Henry what he wants them to do tomorrow.

Chapter Twenty-One

Personal Time

Following the meeting with Alan and Henry, Jack checks in with the captain and advises him he will be in by 7:30, if that is convenient. He has items to discuss with him.

"I know you have a dinner date with Jennifer tonight. Get out of here. I'll make time for you in the morning."

Jack smiles as he appreciates the captain not demanding they speak right now.

*   *   *

Jack makes it to his condo in fifteen minutes and quickly rushes inside so he can shower and shave before Jennifer arrives.

As he is tucking his shirt into his pants, Jennifer rings the doorbell.

Shit, I was hoping to be ready by the time she got here.

Jack answers the door and says, "I'll be ready in a couple of minutes."

"Don't worry, I'm early."

Ten minutes later, Jack and Jennifer leave his condo and are driving into Boston. They have reservations at the Chart House on the pier, one of their favorite restaurants in the area. Traffic isn't too bad, and they arrive fifteen minutes before their reservation time.

Jack wants to be out of Natick, because he knows being on the police force, he would get many questions from other diners about the bombings. This way he feels safer that he and Jennifer could have some quiet time together.

They are seated almost as soon as they arrive and have a grand view of Boston Harbor.

The waiter arrives at the table and pours water. When the waiter finishes, he asks if they would like cocktails. Jennifer orders a glass of shiraz and Jack orders a double wild turkey on the rocks.

The waiter asks Jennifer if there is a particular shiraz she would like. She says, "No, the house brand will do." Then he turns to Jack and asks, "Regular 80 proof or 101?"

"101 will be ideal." The waiter smirks, hands them menus, and figures this is going to be one hell of a night.

Jennifer says, "Sounds like this was a rough day. You don't usually drink bourbon."

"Let's say, I'm celebrating a couple of things. First, being with my wonderful fiancée. Second, I think we have a break in the case. It's too early to tell, but my gut instinct says yes."

Right then the waiter arrives with their drinks and takes their entrée orders. When he leaves, Jack continues to tell some small portions of what they found.

Before they are finished eating their salads, their entrees arrives: Jack ordered the filet, while Jennifer ordered the broiled salmon.

Jennifer says, "We are going to have to take some of this home."

"I agree!" says Jack.

As they continue to eat, Jack says, "Jenn, you know as much as I can tell you, so tell me what has been going on the last two weeks for you."

"Well, for starters, the public defender's office has offered me a position as one of their defense attorneys."

"First, let me say congratulations, and then let me ask if that is what you want?"

"I have two weeks to decide. I'm not sure. If I accept the position and I have to accept a case which you are involved with, I would feel very torn."

"Is there a way you could ask to be dismissed from that particular case?"

"Again, I don't know. I will have to check. There's also the side of me that wants to go into private practice. The state's public defender's office made me an offer as soon as I graduated law school even before I passed the bar."

"So you feel obligated."

"Somewhat!"

"I will accept whatever decision you make. Does that make you feel better?"

"Yes and no! I know I must make this decision myself. I will by the end of two weeks."

"What are you planning to do next weekend? I mean Sunday, I will probably work Saturday," asks Jack.

"I hear there might be some snow coming over the weekend. Why don't we drive up to the Berkshires and do some skiing, and if there's not enough snow, we can hike. I know of the perfect place in Lenox," responds Jennifer.

"I like that. Will you make the reservations?" asks Jack.

"Sure, I can do that, I know you get busy as soon as you hit the station house."

"I'm afraid so!"

When they eat what they can, they ask for carry-out containers to take home.

Jack pays the waiter.

"Do you feel okay to drive? You had a powerful drink."

"The food I ate soaked up what my stomach hadn't. Yes, I'm okay."

* * *

The plan was that Jennifer would stay overnight with Jack. When they arrived, Jack placed the leftovers into his refrigerator.

"Let me go and change into something comfortable."

"While you do that, I will make us some drinks."

Jack pours Jennifer a half glass of Bailey's Irish Cream. Then he pours himself a double of his favorite SKYY vodka. Both are on the rocks.

Jennifer walks into the living room with a new sheer cream0colored silk negligee, which is waist high and has matching panties.

Jack takes one look and says, "Guess I might as well get comfortable too."

"I thought you would like it. I bought it two days ago—special for tonight."

"Well, it looks special and what it barely covers looks even better."

* * *

The two lovebirds sit on the couch and cuddle as they have their drinks. Jack's hands begin to wander and Jennifer says, "I think it's time we changed positions."

Jack knows this is her favorite saying for "Let's go to bed."

Chapter Twenty-Two

Station House

Jack gives Jennifer a quick kiss goodbye before he walks out of his condo at 7:00 the next morning. Jennifer doesn't need to leave for another half hour.

He arrives at the station house at 7:20. He walks over to the captain's office and lets him know he is in so they can talk.

"I'll call you in a couple of minutes as soon as I am through here."

Jack walks into his office and sees the night cleaning shift forgot to empty his wastebasket again. This is one of his little pet peeves, but not a big deal.

*　*　*

Looking up from his desk, Jack sees Captain Green standing in the doorway.

"Do you mind if we talk in your office?"

"No, not at all!" Jack thought this is a bit unusual.

Entering Jack's office, the captain closes the door behind him.

"What's with the secrecy?"

"We have a leak to the press in the department and I want an update on what is happening. You being the senior lieutenant, I figure you have the best handle on it. I hope you have something for me to pass on to the chief.

"Detective Alan Singer checked with the DMV. We have a possible ID on a van at a Worcester rental company. Alan went there yesterday morning along with the FBI, and they've taken the van to their storage area to see if they can come up with anything that can help the investigation.

"At our regular afternoon brainstorm session yesterday, I told the men what SA Alice told me over the phone about the credit card for the renter. Alan and Henry are going over there this morning to see what else they can dig up.

"I also asked them to canvas other rentals in the area because I have a gut feeling whoever used the van was smart enough to dump it just in case. Now, we wait to see what the two of them come up with."

"Okay, I'll fill the chief in; let me know when you hear from Alan and Henry."

"I'll call you as soon as I hear from them."

"Jack, is the FBI making any other progress?"

"They are trying to identify where the bomb components were purchased from, even down to the backpacks. That's all I can tell you."

"The press and city hall are beginning to drive us nuts looking for answers." Rising, the captain says, "I'll be in my office all day if you have anything for me."

"Yes, sir!"

* * *

At the Worcester rental agency, the manager is back to work after being out sick. Alan and Henry enter the agency. The blonde secretary remembers Alan and she turns away from facing the counter. The manager notices her move so he walks up to the two men.

"Gentlemen, can I help you?"

Both detectives show their IDs and Alan proceeds to ask questions about the renter of the van. He also asks questions about the credit card transactions made for the rental.

"The van was returned. Let me check." He goes to his computer and looks for the information. Walking back to the counter, he says, "The van was returned six days ago. The gentleman said he didn't need such a large van and he had a friend loaning him a vehicle. We never had a problem with getting paid from that credit card so we had no reason to suspect anything."

Henry said, "We understand, you haven't done anything wrong. Would you mind if we send an artist down to have you recall what he looks like so we can get a composite of him?"

"Not at all, I'll be happy to help in any way I can."

"Thanks for your help; we'll let you know when we can get an artist here."

*   *   *

Outside in their unmarked car, Alan says, "Jack wants us to check around other agencies to see if the guy rented elsewhere."

Henry replies, "We don't have a photo or a composite of him, but we do have the credit card number."

"Let's give it a shot!"

An hour and a half later, they are walking into the fourth agency to inquire.

The man with the earring at the counter says, "How can I help you, gentlemen?"

They show their IDs and he hesitates for a moment.

Henry continues, "We are looking for someone who might have rented a van of some type. We don't have a photo to describe the person; we do have the credit card number he possibly used to make the transaction."

"Did you rent a van say, within the last week or so?" asks Henry.

"Our customer's information is confidential. I'm sorry I can't help."

Alan says, "Look, we are going to give you the credit card number and all we want to know is if it is the same as the person who rented a van from you."

The manager looks at both detectives a couple of times and says, "Okay, write it down for me. It will be easy as we only rented one van recently, and it is still out. So the credit card number will be active in the system."

Going to his computer, he brings up the transaction and begins to compare the credit card numbers. He looks stunned because they are identical.

Walking back to the counter, he says, "It's the same card number. What do you want me to do? It's rented until the end of December."

Alan asks, "Will you give us an address the renter used?"

"Sure, no problem. If you pick this guy up are we going to lose this vehicle?"

"We will also need all of the vehicle identification, plate numbers, color, size, etc.," remarks Henry. Neither detective answered about losing the vehicle.

The manager supplies them with everything they asked for. He is also advised not to repeat what just happened to anyone without their authorization.

"One more thing, we would like to send an artist here so you can recall what he looks like," says Henry.

"Sure, sure, anything I can do to help."

When they leave, the manager plops down in a chair at his desk. He's never experienced anything like this before. Oh shit!

*   *   *

Back in their vehicle, Alan says, "Who makes the call."

"Hey, guy, you started this thing, I'm only along for the ride."

Alan pulls out his cell and dials Lt. McNamara's number.

In his office, Jack sees a call coming in from Alan Singer.

"I hope you've got good news!"

"We've got more than good news. There is too much to explain on the phone. Jack, we're going to need a sketch artist to do two composites. Work on that while we're driving."

"How long before you get here?"

"Thirty minutes unless we hit a lot of traffic. Make sure the coffee pot is full!"

Jack laughs, "Okay, I'll do that."

Hanging up his phone, Jack calls the captain. When the captain answers, "Captain, it's Jack. Singer and Kostovich will be here in a half hour unless they hit traffic. They have some good news; I would like you to hear it from them when they report in. They also want a sketch artist to do two composites."

"Two composites?"

"They'll explain when they come in. Do we have someone who can do composites?"

"We haven't done one in years. Why don't you call the FBI for one?"

"Good idea, but not until we hear what happened in Worcester?"

"Jack, I want to do this downstairs in the small conference room."

"Yes, sir."

*   *   *

Alan and Henry walk in the detective's portion of the police station holding two McDonald's bags. The receptionist starts laughing when she sees them.

"What's so funny, we've been pounding the beat all morning and we figure we can have lunch here after we make our report."

"Who is expecting you?'

"Lt. McNamara"

"Thank you, I'll call him." When Jack gets the message, he tells the receptionist to send them into the small conference room."

Jack calls Captain Green saying he would meet him downstairs.

*   *   *

Singer and Kostovich are sitting in the conference room with the aroma of their lunch lingering in the air. Kostovich's stomach is starting to growl.

Lt. McNamara walks in and much to their surprise, so does Captain Green.

Lt. McNamara begins, "Okay, guys, start from the beginning."

Alan begins telling them everything that happened. Henry interjected a couple of items he thought Alan overlooked.

The captain looks very pleased. "The two of you did an excellent job. I know it is already two o'clock and by the sound of your growling stomach, I'm sure both of you are starved. Have your lunch here unless someone else needs the room. Lt. McNamara will handle it from here."

Alan asks, "What do you want us to do after lunch, Lieutenant?"

"I think both of you deserve the afternoon off. Get out of here."

Alan and Henry look at each other, amazed at what just happened. However, after lunch they haul ass out of there.

* * *

Going back to his office, Jack puts in a call to SA Alice Broadwell. He gets her voicemail.

Ten minutes later, she calls Jack back.

"Alice, I need a sketch artist to do two composites. Can you provide one?"

"What's going on, Jack?"

"Too much to tell over the phone. Let me know if you can get an artist and if you want to meet later this afternoon here at our station."

"This sounds good, Jack."

"It is Alice, it is."

* * *

Alice Broadwell calls the assistant director. "Doug, things are happening with the Natick police. They are requesting a sketch artist and want to meet later this afternoon. I'm still at the mall. Do you want me to pick you up or are you willing to meet me there?"

"I'll meet you at the station. No sense in you going that far out of your way. What time should I be there?"

"I sense that if we get them the artist, we can pick a time."

"Good, I'll get one from DC." Looking at his watch he says, "Tell them we'll be there for three-thirty."

Alice calls Jack back and informs him there will be a sketch artist available in two days from Washington. The assistant director and she can meet him at three-thirty this afternoon.

"Thanks, see you then. By the way, Captain Green will be meeting with us."

Jack calls the captain and advises him of what he set up.

* * *

Just before 3:30 in the afternoon, Assistant Director Doug Risner and Special Agent Alice Broadwell walk into the station house.

Lt. McNamara greets them at the sergeant's desk and leads them into the small conference room. "Captain Green will be with us in a moment."

As Jack is making this statement, Captain Green walks into the conference room. Handshakes are done, and Lt. McNamara begins to explain what two of his detectives found.

Alice's emotions show as she is excited for this break. Doug tells Jack and Captain Green that the artist will be arriving in two days.

Jack says, "If you don't mind, I would prefer to have Detective Alan Singer meet your man at the plane and take him around. We already have enough faces on this job."

Doug thinks about it a moment and answers, "Yes, that is a good idea. Tomorrow I will call you and give you the name of the artist and his flight times."

Jack responds, "Unless you want him for something else, we can return him to Logan."

"Actually that will work out quite well," says Doug.

With everything finalized, the two FBI people leave the station house.

Inside of Alice's car, Doug says, "You might want to keep your eyes on that lieutenant; he's someone I would like on our team."

"Will do," she told her boss, and not just for reasons of the FBI.

* * *

Right after the FBI people walked out of the conference room, Captain Green places one of his hands on Jack's left forearm. "Take a minute. I want to talk."

Jack looks puzzled.

"Jack, I know you didn't see what I saw, you are a little young in this business just yet. The assistant director was impressed that you took leadership in handling the investigation and handling the artist. Not because he doesn't have the manpower, but you want control.

"He admires your dedication. At some point throughout this investigation, you will be asked to join the FBI."

"You're kidding, Captain, that is the farthest thing from my mind."

"I know, I am just giving you a heads-up so when it comes about, you make the best decision for you."

Jack looks a little stymied, but says, "Thank you, Captain, I just want to do a good job."

"Keep that thought in mind, Jack, so your ego never gets bigger than your goal."

Both officers leave the conference room.

Jack feels very pleased with himself and Captain Green couldn't be happier.

Chapter Twenty-Three

Next Day

At the morning detectives' meeting, Lt. McNamara shares what happened yesterday and what could come of it. He wants the men to realize even though progress is slower than what they wish for, it is happening.

"Okay, hit the pavement, watch for the slightest thing that can give us more breaks. Alan, check with me at the end of the day. I am assigning you to go to Logan tomorrow to pick up the FBI artist and bring him to Worcester for the two composites."

"Got it, Lieutenant!"

* * *

Around 9:30, Ahmad loads Renza and six members of his team into the van. They pull out of the driveway and head for the Massachusetts Turnpike. They enter Boston and drive to South Station to pick up the Amtrak heading to Penn Station in New York. They will take the 11:15 train getting them into Penn Station at 3:15.

Ahmad drives off after the seven exit the van. They walk into South Station and by twos walk over to the ticket counter for Amtrak. Each one has been given cash to purchase their ticket and some meals. Now they just wait for the train.

* * *

Doug Risner and Alice Broadwell are discussing the report of the sweep of the van. The report states that the van had been thoroughly wiped clean of fingerprints before being returned. It did state there were two overlooked areas for prints, which people tend to forget. They have partial prints from the bar below the driver's seat, which positions the seat back and forth. The second place was inside of the glove box. There are three prints from what appears to be from a right hand.

Fibers that were very identical appeared at various locations throughout the van. It is assumed these came from some carry-on bags.

There is no evidence of explosives in the van.

Dirt and clay from shoes or boots show up throughout the vehicle even though someone vacuumed the van.

Doug turns to Alice, "What do you think?"

"I'm not surprised the vehicle is wiped clean. That alone tells us something. I don't think we'll find much from the prints because we undoubtedly won't have a match in our system. We need to match the fibers found with the bag the bomb was in. That could tell us a whole lot. The dirt and clay could possibly tell us where they are hiding out. That could be like looking for a needle in a haystack, but this is all we have to work with so far."

"I agree," says Doug. "I'll have the lab working on matching the fibers with the bag. We'll have to have Washington tell us where the dirt and clay could be located around the state. Let's keep our fingers crossed that the composite finds us a suspect."

* * *

Ahmad arrives back at the house they were renting. Its lease is paid for six months and is good to the end of the year. They are leaving today and going to the second place he leased, which is closer to where they will hit next.

Going inside, he instructs everyone to begin packing as they are leaving right after lunch.

The remaining five men look puzzled. First he splits the team and now they are moving somewhere else.

*   *   *

Close to 2:00 in the afternoon Assistant Director Doug Risner calls Lt. McNamara.

"Lieutenant, the FBI artist's name is Alex Walker. He is arriving tomorrow. His flight is due in at 10:05 on a United flight number 375 from Dulles. He knows your man will be picking him up. He has a return flight back at 7:40 p.m. Once he works over his composite, he will send you and I pictures. Hopefully they will give us a break."

"Thank you, Director. Alan will be there in plenty of time and stay with him all day."

Jack's next two calls are to the rental agencies who agreed to do the composites. He set them up with two appointments: one for 1:00 p.m. and the second for 3:00 p.m.

*   *   *

Renza and his teammates exit the Amtrak at Penn Station. They sat separately or in twos on the train. Now they walk together. Their instructions are to connect with a local bus to take them to Queens. Renza has the address and the directions.

As they head out of Penn Station, they are amazed at what they see around them. Each one has always come from small communities even when they arrived here in the States.

Renza asks for directions and he takes his merry group toward where they have to catch a bus.

*   *   *

Late in the afternoon, Detective Alan Singer calls in to Lt. McNamara and learns where and when he will need to be in Logan to pick up the FBI artist. In one way he is pleased he doesn't need to go into the station the first thing in the morning. Yet he knows tomorrow will be a long day.

*   *   *

The New England evening news channels announce that one-third of those who died in the bombings have been buried at this time. The FBI announces that it will take another couple of weeks to completely finish the burials due to the difficulty in identifying each body.

Chapter Twenty-Four

Multiple Happenings

Detective Alan Singer kisses his wife and his two small children goodbye. It is 8:00 a.m. and he wants to make sure he has ample time to get to Logan airport. You never know how Boston traffic will be. Alan worked it out with Lt. McNamara; the lieutenant would advise SA Broadwell, Alan would be holding up a sign reading NPD at his gate. Alex Walker shouldn't miss him.

Alan woke up a couple of times the night before hoping that the composites were similar so they can post it to the media.

They need some breaks on this case.

*   *   *

Assistant Director Doug Risner is looking at the report from the lab regarding the multiple fibers that were found in the van. They are identical in color to the bag containing the unexploded bomb.

The manufacturer's label inside the remaining bag indicated the bag was manufactured in China.

Doug dials Alice Broadwell. "Alice, I received the lab report on the fibers from the van. They all come from the same material similarly used in backpacks. They were all the same color, black. Since we are looking at low-cost bags, I want you to put out a dozen agents to stores like Walmart and anywhere else these bags could have been sold. We know there were supposed to be two sets of twelve bombings. Have your agents find out who and when someone or a group purchased two dozen bags."

"Yes, sir, I'll get right on it."

* * *

Ahmad and the five remaining members of the terrorist gang are now situated in Oxford, MA. The house they have leased sits on the west side of town and situated so that very little traffic moves by. It is good cover for them.

Ahmad says, "We will begin surveillance tomorrow for our next project. We will be attacking a Catholic church when they least expect it and we have information the building should be full of parishioners when we hit. The infidels will see what the wrath of Allah is."

Amir asks, "What will we use? I thought we used all of our explosives in Natick?

"True, we did use all of them; however, I have made arrangements for additional explosives to come in two weeks, plus six weapons. I am under the impression all of you have fired weapons before."

Each one nods his head or states "Yes."

Marduh says, "What are we going to do with the weapons?"

"I will explain everything tomorrow after you see the place."

* * *

Meanwhile in the Queens borough in New York, Renza is explaining the targets they will attack in the city. He assigns three two-man teams to locate the entry and exit places of the subways between Queens and Time Square.

The men are familiar with surveillance and know how to go about it. He hands them money for lunch and says, "We will meet here at five this evening to have some dinner."

As the three teams leave the flat, they are wondering how all of this is going to fit together. Each one is also wondering what the other half of the members left behind are doing. They realize how security conscious Ahmad is. Not one of them has ever had anyone they worked with previously act so cautiously.

*   *   *

Alan Singer meets the artist at the United gate. He wasn't expecting what he saw. Alan thought he would see a guy about five feet five and very nerdy looking. Alex was six foot and very athletic looking. He noticed the surprise on Alan's face but didn't comment. They made it to Worcester in plenty of time to have a decent meal for lunch before their 1:00 appointment.

Alan knows of a Moroccan restaurant up on one of Worcester's hills that is outstanding. He and his wife hadn't been there in a long time so he won't tell her where they had lunch.

Alex is amazed at the number of people eating lunch in this magnificent restaurant. "Do you bring your wife here often? This is beautiful. If the food is as good as the place looks, I will be very satisfied. I really appreciate you taking me to a place to have a decent meal. I didn't have much for breakfast and certainly won't have much for dinner. This will make up for it."

"My lieutenant told me to take good care of you. We appreciate what you are putting yourself through to get these two drawings."

Just at that moment, the waiter brings their salads out.

"Oh, this could be a meal in itself," remarks Alex.

As they eat the salads, their lamb plates arrive and Alan can see Alex's face light up.

Alan says, "Enjoy, compliments of the Natick Police Department."

Both men eat as much as they can and wish they could bring the leftovers home. Neither one of them will be anywhere near home until late tonight. The food would spoil.

* * *

The 1:00 p.m. appointment is at the first rental place. Alex goes to work with the manager because he spent most of the time with the client. Alan is amazed at the questions Alex asks to draw out what the suspect could really look like. Alan also notices the blonde secretary paying attention.

When Alex is finished, he too noticed the secretary paying a lot of attention. "Miss, could you take a look at what I've drawn and see if you can add anything to it."

The lady is sharp. She doesn't deserve any blonde jokes. She points out three things she thought the manager overlooked. Of course, women look at men one way, and men look at other men differently.

* * *

They arrive at the second appointment exact at 3:00.

Alex begins his magic and asks the same questions. He must have a tablet for questions in his memory.

By 4:30, Alex feels satisfied he drew a composite that spoke the features given by the manager.

The manager with the ring in his ear feels like a celebrity this afternoon.

Alex and Alan walk outside to the car.

Alan asks, "Are these two composites of the same man?"

"Yes, the human eye and mind focuses on different points. I feel I have been able to put the better of the two composites together. I will send your lieutenant and the assistant director, who I know is running this operation, a final comparison tomorrow. After you receive it, I recommend you put it out to the press."

"Alex, it has been a pleasure working with you. If you are ever up here on vacation, let me know in advance so I can arrange time to spend time together."

"Thank you for the compliment, Alan. Likewise for you and your wife, if you are in the DC area, let me know in advance."

There isn't enough time to have a sit-down dinner so the two men discussed which drive-through they would both enjoy.

McDonald's won and Alan knew of one close to the airport.

* * *

Lt. McNamara was still in his office at 6:30. His phone rings and his caller id said it was Alan Singer.

"How did it go, Alan?"

"It went well. Like the credit cards, this is the same person. You will have a perfect sketch tomorrow via fax. Alex will also copy the FBI director in charge so they have it. He suggests we push the hell out of it with the media."

Sitting back with a smile on his face, Jack says, "We will. You can be assured of that."

"Alan, good detective work, I'm proud of you."

"Thanks, Lieutenant, however, the idea was all yours."

"That's what teamwork is all about, Alan. Go home and have a great evening with your wife and kids."

Jack calls Jennifer on her cell, "Do you have time to spend together tonight?

"Today, we got a big break; I'll tell you all about it. I'll even pay for dinner."

"Wow, that's two in a row, big spender. Yes, I do have the time, I figure I'll work off calories another way instead of going to the gym."

"Are you bringing your cream-colored outfit again?"

"Of course, it worked wonders last time."

Chapter Twenty-Five

Composite Arrives

At 8:30 the next morning, Lt. McNamara's computer signals he has a priority message. Jack opens the message and sees it has a jpeg attachment of the composite. He opens it and says, "Wow, this guy is good. The clarity is amazing and it's in color." Jack forwards the email to the captain and the chief.

The chief takes one look at the attachment and advises his secretary to have the captain and Lt. McNamara come into his office.

As both men enter, the chief asks the captain, "Did you see the composite?"

"I was looking at it when Jane called."

"Captain, get this out to the media and set up a press conference with the media at eleven this morning. Tell them we are forwarding the composite to them and we want them to make it public right after our press conference."

"Yes, sir!"

"Jack, I want you to contact Special Agent Broadwell and have her here for the press conference."

"You only want Broadwell, not the director?"

"Top brass always have their faces on television. She is doing a lot of work on this incident. Let's give the Boston office of the FBI some publicity."

Jack smiles because he also realizes having a pretty face on television adds a lot to what the media does with it. Plus the chief wants points with the Boston FBI office.

Both men leave the chief's office.

*   *   *

Special Agent Alice Broadwell arrives at 10:40; she hurries off to the ladies room to make sure her hair and makeup are all right for the live broadcast.

At 10:58 the chief is standing at the podium in the large conference room. He has Captain Green to his left and Special Agent Broadwell on his right. There are numerous reporters standing in front of him waiting to hear about the breaking news.

At 11:00, the chief begins, "Ladies and gentlemen of Natick and all of Massachusetts, through the joint efforts of the Natick Detective Squad and the Boston office of the FBI, we are announcing there is a composite drawing of the man who leads the death squad. The man who is responsible for the bombings at the four stores off Route 9 and at the mall. He is to be considered armed and dangerous. Do not try to apprehend him. If you see him, you are to call the Natick police or the Boston office of the FBI. He rented a second van, which is green in color and the license number is Massachusetts plate 979-0003.

"Both the Natick police and the FBI are working on other evidence to bring the killers to justice." Chief Winters turns to his right, looking and smiling at Alice. She returns the smile.

"Thank you for coming. There will be no questions." The chief steps away from the microphone.

The reporters scramble to get outside and begin calling their headquarters.

Special Agent Broadwell says, "Jack, can I speak to you in your office?"

"Sure, Alice, follow me."

Alice and Jack enter his office and Jack closes the door behind him.

"What's on your mind, anything I can help with?"

"We found a quantity of patches of black threads at different locations in the van. We assume they are from the backpacks used by the bombers. We have men scouring the sporting goods people looking to see who might have purchased them."

"This sounds promising."

"It is. However, we need to find where the bombing materials come from."

"Right now, Alice, we have no clue. We were hoping that you would come up with that information."

"Understandable, right now we don't know either. I also want to compliment you on finding the van the way your people did."

"It's a start and hopefully it will lead to more things to bag these guys. Look, it's almost noon. Would you like to go out and have something to eat? I'm starving."

"I'd enjoy that. We can hash over some more ideas over lunch."

* * *

As Ahmad and his men are driving toward Worcester, they hear the breaking news flash over the radio. Ahmad pulls over to the side of the road. He cannot believe what he is hearing. He has been so careful with all of the details. Ahmad reverses direction and heads back to Oxford.

Javad asks, "Does this mean we have to abandon your plans?"

"No, we will have to make some adjustments to how we operate. First thing I want to do is change the plates on this vehicle. When we get to that shopping center we passed, I want one of you to remove the front plates from two vehicles. Remove the plates off this vehicle and we will drop them off in the dumpster at the end of the parking lot. Place the seized plates onto this vehicle. Not many people look at their plates often so that should work for us. We only need to be concerned for a couple of weeks, and then we will head south. By leaving the rear plates on the other vehicles, it is less likely that a police officer will stop them."

When they pull into the shopping center, Ahmad drives to the far side where there are a number of vehicles and the exchange should not be noticed. The other men either work on exchanging plates or act as lookouts. They finish quickly and take off.

In the center of Oxford, Ahmad pulls in front of a store where they can obtain hair coloring and over-the-counter eyeglasses. Ahmad gives Dariush instructions and money then sends him into the store. He doesn't want to make himself too noticeable until he has been able to alter his appearance somewhat. *Damn, why did this have to happen.*

They head back to the house and put on the television to watch the noontime news. Waiting for the news to begin, the men make lunch for themselves from the supplies that Ahmad placed into the refrigerator.

Ahmad and his men hear the same message once more, but this time they see the composite on the television. It is pretty clear it is Ahmad.

Ahmad rises and selects the hair dye off the kitchen counter and heads for the bathroom.

The men are beginning to get antsy. They felt safe and secure until now. Thoughts of their being captured are running through their heads.

*   *   *

A half hour later, Ahmad is satisfied with the depth of color change he has created. His black hair looks a decent shade of auburn. When he puts the glasses on, he feels a little more comfortable than he did after seeing his composite.

Ahmad gathers the five men together and begins, "I will not do any daytime surveillance. I will only go out after dark to be safe.

"I am going to give you the address of the church we will attack on their Christmas Eve. I want each of you to spend time inside of the church and when you return, we will make our plans."

Amir asks, "What do you want us to look for inside of a church?"

"If we plant semtex bombs to go off during their service, I want to know where we should position them to get the maximum effect of having parishioners run out into the street."

Kazem says, "Why do you want them to escape?"

"They will not be escaping, they will be running into us, and we will be holding AK-47s."

* * *

"Do you like Mexican, Alice?"

"Yes, I love it."

"Good, there is a great place five minutes from the station."

There is plenty of parking available so Jack has his choices of spots. He gets as close to the front door as possible because it looks like rain.

Inside the waitress guides them to a quiet table and places chips and salsa dip on the top. She returns with menus and asks if anyone would like something to drink. Both Alice and Jack order unsweetened iced tea even though it is fall outside.

"What do you recommend here?"

"Whatever you choose will be good, I guarantee it."

When the waitress returns with the tea she asks, "Are you ready to place your order?"

Alice replies, "I would like the Nachos Santa Fe."

Jack says, "I'll have the Veracruz plate."

The waitress collects the menus and says, "Those are good choices."

When she leaves, Jack remarks, "They always say that no matter what you order."

"Do you eat here often?"

"I would say at least once a month."

"How long have you been with the Natick Police?"

"Ten years last month, and you with the bureau?"

"Eight years in three months."

Each one is eyeing the other, wondering where and how this conversation is going.

"Why didn't the chief invite the director to the press conference? I thought it was a little odd he asked me."

"If you want my gut feeling, it's because the director doesn't look like you, and second because I think he's still a little pissed at how the director treated him when they first met. The captain told me what happened."

"A grudge, huh?"

"I would say it's a small one. He'll get over it. I think my first feeling was the main issue. You know as well as I do that a pretty face drives the media."

Alice blushes.

Their food arrives and they begin eating.

"This is very good. I won't have to cook tonight when I get home."

"Neither will I."

"So you are single. Did you ever think of changing jobs and maybe joining the bureau?"

"Not really, I was in the military police before the department. I know how the government agencies work. The chief and the captain give me a lot of leeway in doing my job."

Alice changed the subject and they brainstormed some thoughts they each had about the bombings and who might have caused them and why.

When they are finished and the check arrives, Alice says, "This is on the bureau. I heard what your detective did for our artist."

They head back to the station house. Each one goes their own way after getting out of Jack's vehicle.

Chapter Twenty-Six

Making Progress

The five terrorists, who left to do some surveillance of the church, find it is locked after dark. They need to come back in the daytime. This requires some planning as they don't want to be seen exiting from the same vehicle. They will create a grid this evening for them to use tomorrow.

*   *   *

Meanwhile in New York, Renza and his crew are sharing pizzas and cold drinks for dinner. The evening news begins and on the national portion of the news, the press conference for the Natick police is displayed along with the composite drawing.

Renza nearly chokes on the piece of pizza in his mouth.

"That drawing looks like Ahmad," shouts Younis.

"Quiet," shouts Renza.

"What should we do?" asks Turan.

"Nothing has changed for us. Ahmad is not arrested. He will advise us."

The men quibble back and forth, feeling uncertain with this new development.

*   *   *

Ahmad's group is looking over the layout of the church. While they are gone, he calls his supplier.

"Things have changed. We still need the supplies. However, I would like you to drop them off where we are now located."

"I understand from what I saw on the television, you don't really care to be out in public."

"You are correct. I will call you in two days with a list. This will provide us with everything we need for the next project and finally a third. Did you locate the AKs?"

"Yes, I have six AK 47s just like you asked for, and three thirty round spare magazines for each one."

"Good, I need to calculate how much semtex we will need and call you back."

"How far away are you right now?"

"It will take you about an hour to get here. We should plan to meet mid-morning sometime. We can set a date when I call you."

*   *   *

Ahmad's next call is to Renza.

Renza recognizes the number and answers, "Are you safe?"

"I'm fine. We should only speak for a couple of minutes. I want you to find a dozen large fanny packs. Do not purchase all of them in one location. We are still on schedule. Tell the men I am fine and not to be anxious."

"Good, I will have the packs here for when you arrive."

"See you soon." Ahmad looks at his watch; the call was only two and a half minutes.

*   *   *

FBI Agent Rodney Wilcox walks into a small sporting goods store in Shrewsbury, MA. He identifies himself to the man at the counter and asks to speak with the owner or the manager.

"I'll get her for you. I know she is in her office."

Diane is a slender brunette who looks to be in her thirties. As she approaches the counter, she enjoys watching the agent give her a once-over. It is all in good taste and she feels complimented.

"My name is Diane. I own the store. Can I help you."

Rodney quickly explains the reason for the visit. "Has anyone purchased one or two dozen backpacks from you recently?"

"Recently, no, but back about four months ago, we had a request from a scout leader saying he needed two dozen packs all in black. He told me larger chains couldn't place such a small order as they only order their inventory once a year."

"Would you mind looking at this composite?"

Diane takes her time and she tells Agent Wilcox she is positive this is the same man.

"Did he have you ship them to an address? Did he use a credit card?"

"Yes, he gave me an address; I will have to look it up for you. Also, I can give you the card number as I should still have it on file."

"Can I wait while you do this?"

"Right now I am in the middle of inventory. Can I get back to you tomorrow? Leave me your phone number."

Rodney gives her his card with his cell number on it.

"Thank you. What time can I expect to hear from you?"

"If you don't hear from me by noon, call me." She hands him a card.

*   *   *

Rodney contacts SAC Broadwell and tells her the details. Alice is thrilled to hear the news. If they can find the manufacturer of the bags and check out where they were delivered to, they might have a better trail to follow.

Alice places a call for Doug. He could use a boost right now as well.

*   *   *

Jennifer Stone has made her decision and is meeting with a law firm in the Boston area tomorrow. She knows she will be starting at the bottom of the barrel but she feels this will make her happy. She wants to surprise Jack with her decision.

Chapter Twenty-Seven

Happenings in Motion

At ten the next morning, Diane calls Agent Wilcox and tells him the name and phone number of the manufacturer she ordered the two dozen bags from. She also gives him the credit card number used for the purchase.

"Do you have the ship-to address handy?" asks Rodney.

"Oh, yes I almost forgot." She gives him the address in Shrewsbury, MA, east of Worcester.

"Thank you for all of your help!" remarks Rodney.

"My pleasure, Agent. Go get those bastards."

*   *   *

Agent Wilcox immediately calls Special Agent in Charge, Alice Broadwell.

"Alice, I have the name and phone number of the backpack manufacturer, confirmation of the same credit card, and best of all the ship-to address."

"Where is it?"

"In Shrewsbury," and he proceeds to give her the information.

"Rodney, call me back in half an hour. I will be going and bringing ten additional agents to that address, who will be heavily armed. Do you have your gear in your vehicle?"

"Yes, ma'am."

"Good, when you call me back I will give you a location where to meet us so we can proceed together."

*   *   *

Thirty minutes later, Rodney calls SAC Broadwell. He writes down the location, places it into his Garmin GPS, and heads over to meet with the team she put together.

They meet four blocks away from the house. Alice is outside of one of the cars and she is using its hood as a desk. She had a blown-up Google search map of the location. From the details she can tell the house is secluded. The closest neighbor is at least a quarter of a mile away.

Seeing what she is dealing with, she assigns the crews for each car to have three occupants. They are armed and wearing protective vests. The cars will proceed to the location in three-minute intervals. Each car is designated a location to arrive at and on command, they will proceed to surround the property.

Alice says, "I will be in the first car in the front passenger seat. Should there be any shots fired before we all arrive, come in shooting. Understood!" The men nod their heads. "Let's roll."

The driver of the first car is doing thirty miles an hour. A speed slow enough to handle most circumstances, yet not too slow to arouse suspicion.

As they near the property, Alice says, "What the hell?"

There is a woman hanging up a sign for a real estate company stating, "For Lease."

Alice tells her driver to pull over in front of the lady and exits the vehicle. "Call the remaining cars and tell them to stay put, John."

Upon seeing a woman dressed with an armored vest and a shotgun slung over her shoulder, the woman begins to tremble.

Alice is the first to speak. She identifies herself, then she says, "Where are the occupants who were living here?"

The realtor replies, "We had a six-month lease on this building and were supposed to get a renewal in December. I have tried to contact the gentleman. However, he never returns my phone calls. I came out here to look for myself and found the place empty and it is a shithouse inside."

Alice continues, "This is a national security issue. Right now you need to take down that sign and we are going to consider this part of a crime scene. When we are through with it, you can put it back on the market."

"My boss isn't going to be happy about this!"

"Sorry, but we're not too pleased with it either."

*   *   *

Minutes later, Alice is on the phone with the assistant director, requesting teams of technicians to scour the inside of the house. Doug promises to make the calls that are necessary.

Next, Alice calls Lt. McNamara.

Jack picks up the phone and says, "I hope this is good news."

"Well, Jack, some of it is good and right now most of it is bad." She apologizes for not informing him sooner. She didn't want to lose time. Alice told Jack that her director is calling the Shrewsbury police to inform them the FBI has invaded.

Jack smiles at the remark. He feels he would have probably handled the situation exactly as Alice did. He doesn't feel slighted.

Alice's final statement before she hangs up, "Are we still good, Jack?"

Jack knows what she means. She doesn't want him upset with her.

Knowing how the FBI usually dominates, Jack wonders about her last statement.

"Yeah, we're still good."

Jack hangs up his phone and now has to tell the captain everything that went down.

*   *   *

At the end of Jack's report to the Captain Green, the captain remarks, "We'll just have to continue on as we have been. Something should crack for us soon."

"Captain, do you figure they left and have high-tailed it, or are headed for another job somewhere else."

"They may have gone underground somewhere because of the composite. I don't believe they are through their reign of terror yet."

"Why not, Captain?"

"My gut tells me this holiday horror show is not over yet, Jack."

Chapter Twenty-Eight

Planning for December 24

The next day, Ahmad and his men are reviewing their plans for placing blocks of Semtex explosive under the seats of the church. Each one of the men who did surveillance inside made suggestions. The final decision is to place a block under the third row of seats in each of the aisles. This will cause many casualties in the front pews and send others running in panic outside. Ahmad and his men will be waiting outside for them.

Ahmad explains that each of the blocks will have a cell phone attached to it with a detonator, which will be inserted into the block. When the cell phone receives a call, the charge will be sufficient to ignite the Semtex. The blocks need to be attached underneath the seats in the designated rows. "Four of you will work in pairs. One will secure the block and the other will sit nearby and be a lookout. This shouldn't take more than fifteen minutes. Based on your surveillances, the ideal time will be midafternoon for you to do this."

Amir asks, "What are we going to use to attach the blocks?"

"We are going to cut the blocks in quarters to reduce the weight because of the cell phone weights. Duct tape will work very well when you use a sufficient amount of it. You will be placing eight blocks. The remainder of the blocks will be used on our third bombing."

Javad asks, "Are the materials here?"

"They will be here tomorrow," replies Ahmad. "Any more questions?"

There are no more questions so the men move about keeping themselves busy.

*　*　*

Ahmad calls his supplier, "I need you to be here tomorrow morning. We need four blocks of Semtex, sixteen detonators, fuse wire, two rolls of duct tape, sixteen prepaid cell phones, plus the weapons."

"I will arrive around ten. I need your address."

Ahmad gives him the address and shuts off his phone so he cannot be tracked.

*　*　*

Special Agent Broadwell is trying to obtain a warrant to get the cell provider to give the FBI the in-and-out call history for the phone number the realtor used to contact the party renting the property. She hopes that this will give them more information to stop these fanatics.

*　*　*

Scores of FBI technicians are scouring the rental property in Shrewsbury for any evidence they can come up with to identify and track these killers.

Chapter Twenty-Nine

December 23

Around 9:45, Jerry Walsh, Ahmad's supplier shows up. They chat briefly outside and Ahmad signals for two of the men to help carry the supplies inside. Once all of the supplies are unloaded, Ahmad and his friend hug each other and wish each other well.

Inside, Ahmad begins to instruct the men on cutting the blocks of Semtex into quarters and attaching cell phones on the four blocks they will use in the church. The phones must be positioned correctly for the cell phones to work properly when the phone rings. The detonators will not be attached until tomorrow just before they leave.

Ahmad's supplier is wondering what will happen next. He knows better than to ask. He will wire his contact in Iran with a bill for the supplies and his services. Within twenty-four hours his offshore account will have a deposit. Iran is only one of a dozen clients Jerry has.

*   *   *

At 10:30, Jennifer takes a call from the law firm she interviewed with a couple of days ago. The call is to arrange a luncheon with the two partners and her. She is thrilled and cannot wait to share this with Jack.

It's not a job offer yet, but a step in the right direction. The luncheon is set for December 27.

* * *

Two o'clock in the afternoon, Jack receives a call from Captain Green. "Jack, can I interrupt you for about a half hour?"

"Sure, Captain, I'll be right over."

As he entered the captain's office, the captain waves his hand, indicating he wants the door closed.

Jack is wondering what the hell is going on.

He closes the door.

Settling down in front of the captain's desk in a comfortable chair, Jack says, "What's up?"

"You know how the rumor mill runs with something."

"Sure do, I've seen it in action a number of times and most times it's wrong."

"That's how I feel. However, this could be serious in a number of ways."

"How so?"

"How close are you to Lt. Richards?"

"Friendly, but not really close. In our small department, he doesn't answer to me; he goes directly to you."

"Since the bombings on Black Friday, I've noticed a change in him."

"What kind of change?"

"He does his work, only he seems to be daydreaming a lot."

"You know, Captain, his wife left him and took the kids. She couldn't deal with the job. It is the start of the holiday season and he may be getting sentimental."

"Maybe you're right, although I've been hearing some remarks from some detectives who don't want to come forward, but say things in a way they know I will hear their remarks."

"Serious things?"

"Nothing serious, only I'm concerned about him."

"So you want me to pay some attention to what he is doing?"

"That would be helpful."

"I'll do it only because I know how important it is for us to be conscious of what is going on around us. I don't want anyone getting hurt unnecessarily. I'll have to work out my not feeling like a snitch in my own head."

"Welcome to management, Jack. You know I plan to retire in two years, I want you to follow in this chair."

"Does the chief feel the same as you do?"

"I believe so. Thanks for coming in. Just keep me posted if you feel I should know something."

"Will do!" Jack rises and makes his exit. He is uncertain how to handle this new set of events, yet he is also pleased that he may replace Captain Green when he retires.

* * *

Back in his own office, Jack wonders what he should be looking for once he settles into his chair. Then his little voice of intuition tells him he will know. It has always served him well. He listens to it.

* * *

At 3:15 Jack receives a call from Jennifer.

"Are you all right?" he asks.

"Yes, as a matter of fact, right now I am on cloud nine. Can we have dinner this evening, my treat?"

"Well, since you put it that way, of course."

"Why don't you meet me at Legal Seafood on the pier around six-thirty, is that okay?"

"That's fine. I can make that. How about we stay at your place tonight instead of mine?"

"Really, you like my dumpy studio apartment?"

"Only because it has you in it!"

"Oh, you're a good butter-upper."

"See you tonight, love you!"

"Love you too!"

Chapter Thirty

December 24

Children are anxious about what presents they will receive the next day, and parents are frustrated about getting everything all set up for Christmas. Meanwhile six men are planning death and destruction on holiday worshipers tonight. They review their plans time and again to ensure everyone knows where and what to do correctly. The Semtex bombs are in place under the pews.

*   *   *

Captain Green walks into Lt. McNamara's office. "I thought I told you to take the day off. You've been working a horrendous amount of hours since Black Friday. Take Jennifer and do something together."

"Jennifer is working today; we had dinner last night and a lovely evening together. I cannot get an uneasy feeling out of my head that I am having today. It's like I'm missing something."

"Do you have any more feedback from the FBI?"

"No, they are trying to decipher everything they are picking up at the Shrewsbury house and make sense out of it. I don't expect them to have anything until after Christmas. They did determine the van they picked up was used in the bombings. They based that on the materials from the backpacks that they confirmed with the manufacturer of the bags.

"Do you know where Mike is?"

"Yeah, he's out doing some last-minute shopping for his kids. He plans to go to midnight mass tonight and get up early to drive up to northern New Hampshire to spend time with his children tomorrow."

"Good, maybe that will calm him down."

"What are your plans, Captain?"

"The chief and I are both leaving after lunch today. I'd appreciate it if you would leave too. You are making me feel guilty, Jack."

Jack laughs, "Now that is one for the books, sir. Okay, okay, if it makes you feel better, I promise I'll get out of here after lunch."

*   *   *

Special Agent Broadwell is trying to get some shopping done before the stores close. She needs to get gifts for her parents and her brother and sister. Alice is not married, nor is she attached to anyone. She feels it would be very difficult to have a serious relationship and do her job well, although on holidays she wonders if that is a wise decision.

*   *   *

Jennifer Stone is wrapping presents and looking forward to having Christmas Eve dinner with her family. This is the first time that Jack is included in this event. Her brother and his wife, along with her sister and her brother-in-law, will be there. She wants to show Jack off to her family.

*   *   *

Last-minute shoppers are still in the stores at eight o'clock. However, the crowds are beginning to diminish. Staffs in the stores are anxious to get out of work and home to their families. It seems that some people can never get their gifts early enough so the stores can close earlier.

* * *

At eleven o'clock it starts to snow; not heavily, more of a light dusting. The forecast for tomorrow is two to three inches of accumulation. Everyone tends to want a white Christmas, or at least most people do.

* * *

Catholic churches around the city are preparing for midnight mass. This mass and the mass on Easter Sunday are the two with the largest attendance all year long. The priests love to see the pews filled with congregants.

* * *

Ahmad has one of his men put some mud on part of the rear license plate of the vehicle. He doesn't want any possible chance of the plan falling apart.

At 11:30 they head for Worcester. The next incident will happen after midnight.

* * *

Ahmad pulls the van into a parking spot a block from the church. It is parked in a way that nothing will block their departure, which will be hastily done.

Turning to speak with the men, "Everyone knows what their assignment is. I will make the first phone call and the three of you holding cell phones will make your calls following mine. This will set off all four of the charges. It is now 12:15 a.m. When we leave the van, head to your positions on the sidewalks outside of the doors you have been assigned. Make sure your weapons are concealed under your coats until you use them. When the crowds begin to run outside, wait for them to get halfway down the steps before you open fire. Make sure you shoot women and children as well as men. This is to be done in the name of Allah. Once you are out of ammunition, head back to the van. Don't waste time."

* * *

A local police cruiser is parked two blocks away from the church. The officers are drinking coffee and having a donut to celebrate Christmas.

The driver says, "Hell, this is my fourth Christmas Eve duty in a row. It gets so quiet around this time of year; it almost seems to be a waste of manpower and money."

"It's my second," says his partner.

An explosion rocks the quiet.

"What the hell?" says the driver. Then three more explosions follow the first one.

"Call it in," says the driver.

His partner picks up the mike and contacts the dispatcher. "Car 114 is two blocks from the Saint Joseph's Catholic Church in our sector. We just heard a series of explosions over that way. Wait, now we hear gunfire. We are en route. Send backup."

* * *

"Dispatcher to all cars in the vicinity of Saint Joseph's Catholic Church, Car 114 is reporting explosions and shots fired; you are directed to be backup units."

* * *

Screams and panic are what is happening inside of the church. Parishioners within the first five pews in each aisle are either dead or seriously wounded. Those unhurt are running for the exit doors. Priests, some of whom are bloody, are shouting for calm.

As directed, Ahmad and his men begin to open fire as people exit the church. When the first victims begin to fall, those running out of the church try and reverse themselves, but there are too many behind them to get back inside.

Car 114 pulls up close to the church and one of the shooters immediately sprays the driver's side, killing the officer behind the wheel.

His partner grabs the riot gun from its rack and rolls out of the passenger door. Looking for the shooter of his partner, he sees him and puts a round of twelve gauge double oo buckshot into the terrorist.

The terrorist's partner sees what is happening and begins to line up his sights on the police officer. Both men fire at the same second and kill each other.

In the middle of parishioners coming out of a side door, Lt. Mike Richards sees a shooter firing at people in front of him.

He pulls his Sig Sauer and shoots the terrorist in the head. Another terrorist sees Mike and fires at him. Two shots hit Mike in the left upper portion of his chest. He collapses on the stairs with people running around and over him.

All of a sudden, there is calm as the shooting stops and additional police units arrive.

Ahmad and two of his men survive and high-tail it to the van.

*   *   *

Inside the van, the terrorists are working from adrenaline. Their nerves are frayed and they are also in shock since they suffered three losses.

Ahmad starts the van and pulls out before a police blockade can be organized.

*   *   *

Four cruisers and a command car come from different directions closing in on St. Joseph's Church.

The command car stops near Cruiser 114 and checks out the bodies of the two downed officers. The captain shakes his head and proceeds to walk toward the fallen terrorists. His men have already checked them out and assured him they weren't living.

"It's a good thing because if they were, I might have shot them myself," says the command officer.

Someone notices Lt. Richards on the steps and moves over to see if he is alive. "The lieutenant is a lucky man. A little bit farther to the left and he would be pushing up daisies."

Ambulances and medical technicians are arriving. The captain has his men set up crime scene tape around the front and the sides of the church.

"Somebody call Lt. McNamara of the Natick PD. I don't have his number, but Natick dispatch will give it to you. Tell him we have Mike here and he's wounded. Witnesses say he took out one of the bad guys. Let the lieutenant know which hospital Lieutenant Richards is being sent to," says the command officer. "Look, the damn media will be here any minute. Let's get our shit together, people. We have to keep the media far enough away so medical emergency people can get in and out.

"Damn, tell dispatch to wake up some detectives. We have to work Christmas Eve. They don't get a free ride," he says as he looks horrified at what just happened.

*   *   *

Lt. McNamara and Jennifer are asleep at his condo. His phone rings. Looking at the clock, he wonders who could be calling this late.

"Jack McNamara, who's calling?"

"Lt. McNamara, this is Worcester police dispatch. Our command officer on the scene asked that you be called. We had a bombing at St. Joseph's Church. Lt. Richards was wounded and is on his way to Saint Vincent's Hospital. We thought you would want to know."

Hesitating at first then replying, Jack says, "Thank you, I'll be at the hospital shortly."

"Jack, what is it?" asks Jennifer.

"I need to get to Saint Vincent's Hospital in Worcester. Mike Richards was wounded in a bombing at Saint Joseph's Church tonight."

"Oh my god, you don't think it is the same people from Black Friday."

"I would lay money on it. Now where will they hit next?"

Jennifer gets up and puts on the television in the bedroom. Jack begins to get dressed.

Jennifer starts to shriek and cry, "Jack, look at what the bastards have done."

Jack comes over to the television and sits on the end of the bed. "Oh shit, it's them again. I cannot believe how sick these people are."

Jack puts his arm around Jennifer, "If I leave, are you going to be all right?

"I think so," she says sobbing. "How can people be so cruel? Look, they've even killed women and children."

"I really cannot give you an honest answer to their methods. My job is to stop them and I will do that."

"Promise me you will."

"I promise," Jack reaches over and gives her a kiss.

"I don't know when I will be back. Stay in touch okay."

"Yes, I will. Take care of Mike. He's a nice guy."

Chapter Thirty-One

December 25

Once in his car, Jack thinks a minute about calling the captain and the chief. He decides he will wait to find out about Mike's condition. This way he can give them a clearer picture.

He starts his car and pulls out of the condo parking lot. Normally it would take him a half hour to get to Saint Vincent's Hospital. Jack puts his flashers on and makes the trip in twenty minutes.

*   *   *

Media vans are now surrounding Saint Joseph's Church in Worcester. All the majors are there: Channels 4, 5, 7, and Fox. The police have directed the media to one area and the media are not pleased with the police force or their command captain.

*   *   *

Emergency medical units are moving around the bodies to see which ones are alive and in need of care. They begin with those lying on the stairs before going inside.

Those that are dead are lifted as courteously as possible to clear a way to the church entryways. The injured are being lifted and treated by the ten different ambulances that arrived at the scene.

"Christ, we don't have enough medical personnel to deal with anything this big," says the command captain.

* * *

Inside of Saint Vincent's Hospital, Lt. McNamara inquires about Lt. Richards. He identifies himself and a nurse takes him aside and tells him Mike has two gunshot wounds in the upper chest. Right now he is in surgery.

Jack thanks her and moves off to wait and see how the surgery goes.

He realizes now is the time to call the captain and the chief.

After making both calls, he makes a third call.

"Hello, Alice Broadwell, who is calling?"

"Alice, it's Jack McNamara. Put on your television. You might want to make a trip to Worcester tonight."

"Oh God, no? Do you think it is the same group?"

"I'd bet a week's pay on it."

"I'll be there. Where are you?"

"I'm at Saint Vincent's Hospital. Mike Richards took two bullets in the chest. He is in surgery."

"I'll go to the scene. Do you know anyone there?"

"Not that I am aware of, but evidently the command captain knew my name and had their dispatch call me about Mike."

Chapter Thirty-Two

On the Scene

The mayor of Worcester and the chief of police arrive on the scene at the same time.

"What's going on, Captain?" says the chief.

The captain briefs the chief and the mayor about what his men have learned from interviewing some of the parishioners.

"Do we have a death total yet?" asks the mayor.

"No, sir, we're trying to tend to the injured so they get the care they need. We do have three bodies of terrorists."

"Any identification on them?" asks the chief.

"None that we found."

"Fuck," says the chief.

Special Agent in Charge Alice Broadwell walks over to the captain. "Captain, Lt. McNamara from the Natick Police Department called me. I am the head of the Boston FBI office. Do you want our help?"

The chief looks over to Alice and says, "That's up to my office and the mayor to decide."

The mayor looks over to Alice and says, "Yes, get your people here as soon as you can."

"I'll have people here in about six hours. With it being Christmas, it will take some time to put together. I will call the assistant director now that I have your decision for us to get involved."

Alice walks away and takes out her cell phone. She calls AD Doug Risner.

* * *

"Captain, has anyone made contact with the priests?" asks the chief.

"One of my officers said there were three priests inside and they were trying to give comfort and aid to the wounded. I thought it best not to disturb them."

The mayor says, "I'm going over to speak with the media. Chief, do you want to come with me?"

"Sure, I'll be right there."

The command captain turns around and shakes his head. *Fucking politicians,* he thinks to himself.

* * *

Meanwhile, Ahmad is driving the van along Route 20 westbound. He doesn't want to use the turnpike in case the police stop him and he cannot exit easily.

Driving through the town of Charlton, he is doing ten miles more than the speed limit. Suddenly he sees blue lights appear behind him.

Marduh says, "Police. What are we going to do?"

"Stay calm!"

The cruiser pulls behind Ahmad when he is stopped alongside of the road.

Before he exits the cruiser, the state trooper radios in that he is stopping a vehicle on Route 20 inside the town of Charlton. Then he exits the vehicle.

Slowly walking over to the van, he notices the rear plate is not clearly visible due to some mud or something stuck to it.

Ahmad lowers the driver's side window. It is dark in the van so it is difficult for the trooper to see Ahmad's features.

"Do you realize you were speeding?"

"No, Officer, I didn't realize it."

"You been partying and drinking tonight."

"No, just heading home."

"Where's home?"

"Sturbridge."

"Why don't you get out of the van. You have something stuck on your rear plate. You clean it off now. I'll forget about giving you a ticket. Consider it a Christmas present."

Ahmad smiles.

The officer turns around to head back to the cruiser as he hears Ahmad opening the driver's side door.

As Ahmad steps out of the van, he raises his automatic pistol and shoots the trooper three times.

"There's your Christmas present."

Ahmad steps back in the van and pulls onto the road.

The trooper is still alive. He calls in on his shoulder mike. "Officer down, officer down in Charlton." Then he dies.

*   *   *

Close to three in the morning the doctor who operated on Lt. Richards comes out of surgery and gives good news to Jack. Mike survived the surgery, but he wants Jack to be aware that the trauma seems to have affected him severely.

"What do you mean, Doc?"

"Before the surgery he was delusional, shouting as if he was in combat. You might want to have him see the department's therapist after he recovers."

"Thank you, I'll pass that on to our superiors. Can I see him?"

"He'll be out for hours. I'm sorry, I cannot stay and chat. Bombing victims are arriving and I'm needed."

Jack calls Jennifer and brings her up to date. "Look, I want to go and visit the crime scene to see what I can learn. I will call you when I get near the condo so you don't think someone is trying to break in."

"Hurry back!"

"I will."

Chapter Thirty-Three

Back at Saint Joseph's

Jack McNamara arrives at the scene of Saint Joseph's Church. It looks very similar to the scenes he saw in the strip mall stores. Only a church tends to have more respect and this incident doesn't offer any. As a matter of fact, it shows a total lack of respect. Jack promises himself he is going to get these bastards no matter what it takes.

Jack quickly finds the command center and thanks the captain for calling him about Mike. Mike is doing well, he tells the captain. No need to go into the other crap.

The captain is appreciative of Jack having called the FBI. He tells Jack that the agent in charge was here exactly when the chief and the mayor were here. They would have looked like fools not to ask for help.

Jack smiled. He understands the politics of situations.

Jack hands the captain his card and says, "If I can be of any help, let me know."

"Thank you, I will pass your card on to the higher-ups. Don't know if their egos are too big to be able to ask for help, but I'll do it."

"See you around, Captain, and thanks again for the call. Mike will recover."

"Great, I learned he drilled one of them through his forehead."

"Knowing Mike, he wasn't taking any chances of body armor."

"I would say you got that right."

* * *

Walking away from the command post, Jack calls Jennifer. "I'll be back in half an hour."

"I haven't slept since you called me before. I'll have drinks ready for the two of us."

"Great lady, one of the things I love about you. You're always one step ahead of me."

"I can't wait for you to come home, Jack."

* * *

Ahmad realizes since the trooper he killed was state police, there was probably a camcorder on his dashboard recording a video of everything that happened. *This is not good. They have the vehicle and me on screen. Besides, I shot him in the back. There will be hell to pay if I am captured.*

"We need to change vehicles. With only three of us on board, we can acquire a smaller one." They start to look for one.

Before they arrive at Route 84, there is a restaurant that is open 24 hours. Ahmad has an idea.

They pull into the parking lot and wait.

Kazem and Marduh say they are hungry. He gives them some money and tells them to get something for him, and make it quick.

They enter the restaurant and place an order to go. They order three burgers and three large fries. They also order three large Dr. Pepper drinks.

They are back in the van in ten minutes. With the aroma of the food, Ahmad realizes how hungry he is.

It doesn't take long for them to finish their food.

Ahmad says, "Look, a four-door sedan is pulling into the parking lot. There doesn't seem to be anyone in it beside the man that is going into the place. I want that one."

The other two had no choice but to agree.

They wait for ten minutes. Nothing happens; evidently the man is eating inside.

He'll live a little longer more than he realizes, thinks Ahmad.

Ten more minutes and the man returns to the parking lot. As he approaches his car, Ahmad steps behind him, grabs him quickly, twisting his head and snapping his neck. No noise. A quiet killing.

Kazem and Marduh help place the body about a hundred feet into the wooded section behind the restaurant.

Ahmad has the keys, and he also took the man's wallet so that he has the registration in case they get stopped. The real reason is so no one knows the vehicle and the plate numbers of the vehicle they stole.

They head for Route 84 south and look forward to a more comfortable ride.

Ahmad uses the cruise control so he doesn't exceed the speed limits and gets stopped again.

*   *   *

State police barracks covering the Charlton area receives the officer down call. It's Christmas and the patrols are skeleton crews.

The lieutenant in charge says, "How many cruisers are nearby?"

The dispatcher replies, "We have three, each of them anywhere from 30 to 50 miles away."

"Contact each one and get a time estimate to Charlton. Call a local ambulance service near Charlton and have them look for our cruiser, hoping to keep our man alive."

After contacting the three, she says, "The car in the Webster area says he can be there in less than thirty minutes. I told him to proceed with lights and sirens."

"Good call; now let's hope we find our man alive.

"This is Christmas, how the hell is this happening?"

The dispatcher turns around to the lieutenant, "Don't go blaming yourself, Don! We are doing everything humanly possible."

"Right, like that makes everything easier."

"Let's hope and pray is all we can do."

*   *   *

Thirty minutes later, the trooper from Webster reports that Trooper Andrews is dead. He was shot in the back three times with armor-piercing bullets. There was nothing either he or the ambulance could have done for Trooper Andrews.

He pulls his comrade off the road so no one runs over him.

A team of investigators leave for Charlton. The ambulance leaves without anything left for them to do. The medical examiner from Springfield is called to the scene. He is not too happy for the call.

Chapter Thirty-Four

Later on the 25

Lt. McNamara arrives back at his condo. Jennifer is waiting for him with open arms. "Thank God, you are safe. Your job is beginning to worry me."

"Don't let my job worry you. Mike is okay, and this is Worcester's problem, not Natick's. We still have to solve our problem. The thing is, I feel our problem just left our area and we'll come up with nothing."

"You mean they're escaping and nobody knows who they are, and why this is happening?"

"Before we continue this conversation, I would like that drink you promised me."

"I have it on the counter for you. I find this feeling of dread is terrible."

Jack picks up his glass of vodka and takes a good mouthful.

"Jennifer, since neither one of us is going to sleep soon, let's turn on Channel 4 and see if we can learn anything new."

Jennifer picks up the remote and turns the television on.

*   *   *

Scenes from the church bombing and the havoc that was wrought onto the congregates are being flashed on screen. The residents of Worcester have no idea why this is happening. They were expecting to be celebrating a joyous Christmas.

*   *   *

From Channel Four's news room: "Breaking News: It was reported by the Massachusetts State Police that one of their patrolman was gunned down during a routine stop on Route 20 in Charlton. More details when they become available."

"Son of a bitch, those bastards are heading for Route 84 and probably going west. Let me get my notes."

Jack walks into the room he uses as an office. The file he is looking for is on the top of his desk. He grabs it and calls the state police and gives them the information of the second van the terrorists rented.

The state police put out a statewide alert for the van. Hopefully, they will catch them before they cross over into Connecticut.

*   *   *

The graveyard shift manager at Joe's 24/7 Eatery is taking a smoke break outside. He sees one vehicle in their parking lot. It is a van. However, there is no one inside eating. He checks the men's room. No one is inside. He knocks on the door of the ladies room. Getting no response, he announces he is opening the door because he is concerned for an individual who might have hurt themselves. No one is in the ladies room. He walks outside and circles the van a couple of times. There doesn't appear to be anyone inside.

He goes back inside and calls the Sturbridge police.

*   *   *

Within five minutes two Sturbridge cruisers arrive at the restaurant. One parks on the right side of the van, the second one parks behind the van so it cannot back up.

An officer from the one in back gets out and asks, "Is there anyone inside of the van?"

"Not that I can see," says the night manager.

The other officer looks at the back plate. "Part of the plate is covered as if someone did this deliberately. Do you have something I could scrape off whatever is on there?"

"Let me get one of maintenance's tools. I'll be right back."

The manager shows up with a putty knife.

The officer starts to scrap. "Jim, I think we have the van the state police are looking for. Call it in!"

Dispatch orders the cruisers to stay in place until the state police arrives.

The officer named Jim says, "They must have carjacked someone who was coming in to eat. They either took that person with them or their body will dropped off near here or down the road somewhere."

*　　*　　*

At 4:00 a.m. the headline news is: "One hundred killed at Saint Joseph's Church bombing and shooting. Numerous victims are hospitalized with various injuries. One quarter of those attending midnight mass are now dead."

The FBI has been called in to work with the local police.

*　　*　　*

The camcorder video was downloaded from the cruiser and sent to the state police labs. Molds of the tire tracks in front of the cruiser are made. The head of the state police has cancelled all leaves while the search for the terrorist goes on.

The bodies of the three terrorist who died at the church are in the county morgue and are being looked over with a fine-toothed comb.

*   *   *

Meanwhile Ahmad along with Kazem and Marduh cross over into Connecticut on Route 84. To the best of their knowledge, no one knows anything about this vehicle, including its license plate information.

They stop at the first rest area they find to clean up and slow down their anxiety.

*   *   *

Once the state police investigative team is through in Charlton, they move on to the Sturbridge location.

Chapter Thirty-Five

Camcorder Video

Trooper Andrew's camcorder provides a visual of exactly what happened just before he is shot. The voice communication is only clear one side until the end when he is killed. Trooper Andrews advised the driver he was speeding and since it was Christmas he would forgo giving him a ticket if he properly cleaned the rear license plate before moving on. Up to this point, the audio from the driver does not exist or is unclear. Andrews turns to return to his cruiser when he hears the driver opening his door. At that point the audio and visual of the driver is very clear. The driver says, "Here is your Christmas present" and fires three shots into the back of Andrews. The driver quickly gets inside of the van and it departs.

The supervisors watching the recorder are thoroughly shocked by the vicious murder that happened.

The senior officer says, "Get a blow-up of that man's face and I want it out in every media and our network now. Make sure it goes throughout New England."

* * *

The state police investigative van arrives at the Joe's 24/7 Eatery. The Sturbridge police are waiting for their arrival.

The investigative team has two officers. The senior one gets out of the passenger side and says, "Have you tried to get in the van?"

Jim replies, "No we haven't. We didn't want to disturb any prints."

The officer continues, "Good, we know this is the van that was involved with a shooting in Charlton. We are taking possession of it. If the party or parties involved stole someone's car, you may find a body nearby. That will be Sturbridge's responsibility."

"If we do find someone and we'll call in our detectives, hopefully they might be alive."

"These creeps just killed one of ours for no good reason. We have the whole thing on his camcorder."

Both officers respond saying they are sorry.

*   *   *

The restaurant's manager gives the Sturbridge officers free coffee and asks if they would like anything else. "Can you tell me what is going on?" he asks.

"Right now the state police have taken possession of the van. It appears whoever was driving killed one of their patrolman in Charlton."

"Oh my god, that is terrible."

"We have tried searching for a body, but it is too dark. We are waiting for it to get a little lighter. We suspect there may be a body lying on or near your grounds."

"No!"

"Oh yes, these things do happen. Merry Christmas," the officer says sarcastically.

Chapter Thirty-Six

The Search

Sturbridge officer Jim says to his partner, "We drank plenty of free coffee and it's getting light enough outside to do a search. Let's go!

"You take the far side of the van and I'll take the other side near the van." Jim notices the state police are still working here.

The two officers walk slowly around the property. For the first twenty minutes, nothing is found. Then Jim sees a body. This is exactly why he chose to search near the van. His partner is young and just learning police work. He doesn't know if he could handle this yet.

"Jeff, call dispatch. We have a body."

"Really!"

"Yes, really, now make the call." Jim's eyes roll up in his head like he can't believe what was just said.

There is not much else the patrol officers can do except tape off the area as a crime scene.

The eatery's employees are dealing with this in various ways. Some are surprised; some seem to feel sorry and others want to know if they can close so they can have the day off.

Customers are still trying to enter the restaurant's parking lot to get something to eat. People appear curious but not rude and inconvenienced.

Customers are asking about what is going on in the parking lot. The employees say they cannot reply.

* * *

While things are happening in Sturbridge, the FBI has arrived in Worcester. SAC Alice Broadwell sets up the crime scene by FBI standards. Alice has twenty agents with her, and probably that many unhappy families somewhere because today is Christmas.

* * *

The Sturbridge police department has two detectives on its force. Both men arrive at the restaurant within minutes of each other.

"What the hell do we have here, Jim?" asks Dennis. "Damn, this is Christmas Day."

Dennis continues, "Worcester is up to their ass in alligators with bombings and shootings. They cannot send a medical examiner. I'll try and get one from Springfield. They're closer than going to Boston."

Al, Dennis's partner, says, "There's not much more to do until the ME gets here. Let's have breakfast."

Patrolman Jim offers, "Here are the details as we know them. Do you need us hanging around? Shit, we have other things to do and reports to make."

"We'll take it from here. How are the state boys? Are they communicating with us?"

"So far they have been busy and haven't said much. They're really upset over the shooting in Charlton."

"We would be too if it was one of ours," says Al.

The two patrol cruisers check in with dispatch and head off to other issues.

Chapter Thirty-Seven

Worcester

The Sturbridge police are waiting for the medical examiner from Springfield, a man who is not happy being called out on Christmas. Ahmad, Kazem, and Marduh have crossed into New York state and are headed for the address in Queens.

* * *

The FBI team at Saint Joseph's Church is attempting to identify every fragment of the bombed pews and marking the positions where each victim lay when the bombs went off. It is a horrendous job. There are ten agents working inside of the church and ten working the stairs outside to do the same thing they are doing inside.

Fortunately, the snow that began last night ended. The temperature is bitterly cold and some of the agents aren't prepared to be working outside. Alice makes changes to get those without sufficient warm weather clothing inside, plus she rotates the agents periodically. This is very difficult work.

The three parish priests are trying to clear the altar area of debris and are having difficulty with what happened. Their meek and mild manners are not prepared to deal with these kinds of tragedies. One of them seems to be in a state of shock so Alice suggests that he seek medical care.

Just as they did in Natick, the FBI arranges for a location to move the dead and the debris for identification.

What surprises the FBI was there were six AK 47s left once the weapons were empty of ammunition. Three had partial magazines because the shooters were killed before the weapons were emptied. Evidently the terrorists have no fear of anyone having their fingerprints.

*   *   *

The local and state media are camped outside of the church while the investigation is ongoing. All kinds of rumors are beginning to float around comparing the Natick bombings with this bombing. What they don't realize is they are partially correct.

Residents of the city are stunned. Christmas is supposed to be a day of celebration.

The Worcester Police Department gave the FBI full autonomy over the situation.

*   *   *

At 10:00 a.m. visiting hours begin at Saint Vincent's Hospital. Lt. McNamara and Jennifer arrive to visit Mike Richards.

Entering Mike's room, Jack and Jennifer see that he is barely awake. Neither one has the heart to wake him.

Jack turns and goes down to the nurse's station. "If I leave a message for Mike Richards, would someone read it to him when he is awake?"

"Of course we will. He's been sleeping a great deal. The doctor on call said to let him sleep."

One of the nurses hands Jack a piece of paper and a pen.

Jack writes: "Mike, Jennifer and I were in to see you. We didn't have the heart to wake you. I took the liberty to call your ex-wife so the kids know why you haven't come up for Christmas. I am sure they will miss you today, and be glad that you are safe. I'll come by tomorrow. Everyone at the station sends their regards."

Jack thanks the nurses and walks back down to Mike's room to pick up Jennifer.

When they are outside, Jennifer says, "I'm glad that's not you in there."

"I understand, just remember though he wasn't on duty. He had gone to midnight mass."

Jennifer doesn't say anymore. She gets the message as much as she doesn't like it, and knows he is right.

They get into Jack's car and begin the drive to visit with Jack's family today. Last night was spent with her family. She was pleased everyone accepted Jack.

*   *   *

The coroner completes his work on the John Doe; the body will be moved to the morgue for an autopsy. The autopsy will be done over the next couple of days. Physically it is apparent he died from a broken neck. Someone with powerful arms did him in.

Detective Dennis begins taking photographs of everything he believes will be pertinent to the crime scene, including the body. He takes duplicate shots hoping someone can identify him. Without his wallet right now, he is unknown. Besides some bastards have his vehicle.

*   *   *

As the coroner's vehicle is departing with their John Doe, the state police flatbed truck pulls into the eatery's parking lot to remove the van.

The investigative unit has finished with what they can do in the field. The van will be stripped down further, hoping to find more evidence tomorrow after Christmas.

*   *   *

Two hours later, Ahmad arrives close to the apartment. He knew there was a parking garage ten blocks away. He drives to the garage as he plans on disposing of the car there. He will have no further need of it.

Ahmad, Marduh, and Kazem walk back from the garage to the apartment. Neither of the other men knows anything about this place or for what their reason is for being here. Ahmad has not said he was abandoning the car.

The morning air is cold and the wind cuts through them as if it had knife blades in it.

After five blocks, Marduh says, "How much farther?"

"Not much, would you like me to leave you here?" says Ahmad.

Marduh sulks and doesn't reply. This man is a bastard to work for.

Chapter Thirty-Eight

Late Morning December 25

Five blocks later, Ahmad walks up the stairs to the front door. He rings the bell. Renza is surprised to see Ahmad. He opens the door and lets the three inside. Questions run through his mind, but there will be time for that later.

"Get us some food. We are starving. I'll talk to you as I eat," says Ahmad.

"Yes, yes, come with me. I will prepare some warm soup and sandwiches."

The two men who were traveling with Ahmad sit in chairs in the kitchen area. They drink some tea that was warmed up in the microwave.

As Renza is opening cans of soup, he asks, "Where are the other three?"

"Let me get some food in me before I begin to tell you what happened."

*　　*　　*

In the morgue in central Massachusetts, the three dead terrorists are having autopsies and all identifying markings on their bodies are being recorded since they have no identification. Their fingerprints are taken by an FBI technician.

*   *   *

In Springfield, Massachusetts, the John Doe who arrived is going through a similar process. There are two big needs to be dealt with. One: to identify the man; and two: find out what kind of vehicle he drove in order to continue tracking the surviving terrorists.

*   *   *

After Ahmad has his first sandwich, he begins telling Renza what happened at the church.

"Everything went as planned until that lousy police car pulled up. Amir killed the driver. His partner rolled out of the vehicle and killed Amir. Then Dariush and the second policeman killed each other. As we were shooting people coming out of the church, Javad was shooting and a man shot him in the head. By that time there were multiple sirens heading toward the church and the three of us dropped our AKs and ran for the van."

"Where is the van now?"

"That's a long story too!" Ahmad tells Renza about killing the police officer in Massachusetts and carjacking a car at the restaurant."

"Won't the car owner report what happened as soon as you left?"

"Not in the state I left him in!"

"I see," Renza says.

"Where is the car now?"

"I parked it in an overnight parking garage down the street. It is ten blocks away. I am not planning to use it again. The three of us need to get some sleep. Wake us up for dinner. I will explain what happened to the men you have here."

"It would be better if they hear it from you."

Chapter Thirty-Nine

December 26th

Lt. McNamara is in his office at 7:30. He is generating a report on what happened at the Worcester Catholic Church bombing and how Lt. Mike Richards became involved. Why Lt. Richards drew his service revolver and fired. Also, how Lt. Richards came to be in the hospital with gunshot wounds.

Standing in the lieutenant's doorway, Captain Green says, "I knew you would be here early this morning. Did you get to enjoy the holiday?"

"Some of it. Jennifer and I spent time at her parents Christmas Eve and time with my parents on Christmas Day."

"I assume you are writing a report of why you were called in by Worcester."

"You are correct, there is something else you need to know, but I don't want to put it in print."

"What might that be?"

"Captain, take a seat so we can discuss this for the good of the department."

Captain Green seats himself in front of Jack after closing the door to Jack's office.

"What do we have to discuss? I thought everything was pretty cut and dry?"

Jack goes on to remind Captain Green about his observances of Lt. Richards, and then what the doctor at the Saint Vincent's told him how Mike was reacting before the surgery.

"You think he is suffering from PTSD?"

"It sounds reasonable that it started in the military. No one picked up on it and maybe he never said anything. The Natick bombings and the Worcester shootings and bombings have brought it to a head."

"I'm glad you told me. What I will do is require him to see our therapist due to his receiving gunshot wounds. I hope that will make it appear we are unaware of your findings. Mike is a good man. Let's hope he can get through this."

Captain Green says, "I plan to visit him in the hospital today. I'll fill the chief in on what we suspect so he knows. Thanks, Jack!"

The captain leaves and heads for his office.

* * *

Meanwhile in Queens, New York, Ahmad and Renza are eating breakfast away from the rest of the men.

"I can see the men are shocked by the fact we lost three of the group, when I explained what happened last night. The reality of what we are doing is beginning to take hold. Do you think we will have a problem with one or more of them?"

"Their fantasy project has now gone full circle, and they are faced with the real world. I doubt if any of them has had former combat experience of any type. So this is not surprising as to how they are reacting. I suggest we pair them up and give them some money to blow off some steam. When are you planning to do the third project?"

"I had planned to do it New Year's Eve. Now with my face on nationwide television, I can imagine they will suspect that we could be planning something for New Year's. I think we should play it cool and make them wonder. Maybe they will think we went away."

"This new plan sounds like a good move. It will also give the men time to recover from the shock of what happened."

"Agreed, you give them some leeway on what they can do, but don't let them get away with too much," says Ahmad.

"I'll handle it!"

* * *

The phone on Lt. McNamara's desk rings. He answers, "Jack McNamara." The receptionist downstairs tells him that SAC Alice Broadwell is on the phone for him.

"Hello, Alice, what can I do for you?"

"Jack, we need to talk and I would like to do it face to face."

"This sounds very ominous. What's going on?"

"Can we meet late this afternoon or for dinner?"

"The FBI has money in its budget to take me out to dinner. Wow, this must be important."

Alice has never had a man talk to her like this before. One side of her wants to say fuck off and the other side of her wants to give in. Alice gives in.

"I am told by our composite specialist your detective took him to a Moroccan restaurant in Worcester. Meet me there for six."

"I know the place. It has great food. I'll be there. You will need reservations. I'll handle it."

* * *

The autopsy of John Doe from Sturbridge is beginning. It will certify how the adult male died. Approximately what time he died and that it was a homicide. In the old days, someone with experience would have looked at the body and made most of those decisions.

* * *

The autopsy reports of the three Worcester terrorists are being sent electronically to the FBI headquarters in Washington. There are hopes that something can be learned from their fingerprints.

*   *   *

The commander of the Massachusetts State Trooper is doing his best to see how the murderer of his man can be found and prosecuted. Right now the best he can do is to arrange for Trooper Andrew's funeral and make sure his wife and children are being cared for.

*   *   *

Knowing what Route Nine and Worcester traffics are like, Lt. McNamara leaves his office at 5:00. He keeps running it through his mind what he believes Alice will tell him.

Jack arrives at the restaurant at 5:50. It is still a little early for most people who eat out so there are sufficient parking spaces available. He goes inside and sees Alice has already arrived.

"You made it," Alice remarks.

"I left at 5:00 anticipating heavy traffic; however, it wasn't too bad."

Alice tells the hostess her guest is here and they are seated in a quiet corner, which she had requested.

When they are seated, water is poured for them and the waiter asks if they would like cocktails.

"What kinds of wine do you have?"

"Let me get you the wine list along with the menus. I'll be right back."

"Have you had a break since the Worcester bombings happened?" ask Jack,

"What's a break? My life has been a roller-coaster since the Natick bombings happened."

The waiter arrives with the wine list and the menus. "I'll give you a few minutes to review everything," he says.

"Do you enjoy wine, Jack?"

"Sometimes"

"If I order a classic merlot, would that be fine?" Jack nods affirmative.

Both of them decide they will have the house special lamb dinner.

When the waiter returns, Alice orders a bottle of wine and their dinners.

Jack speaks, "What is going on, Alice, why the face-to-face?"

Alice hesitates then says, "Assistant Director Risner feels we will not learn any more than we have by continuing in Natick. He plans to move us to Worcester."

"That doesn't surprise me, only I don't feel you're going to get much out of Worcester either. I suspect these people are no longer even in Massachusetts. You know they left Shrewsbury. Where they holed up is like looking for a needle in a haystack. I will lay you odds it was somewhere around Worcester. I doubt they returned there.

"Why are you telling me this instead of the chief and the captain?"

The waiter returns with the wine and pours some in each of their glasses.

"You have been our communication link is why I am speaking with you."

Just as Jack is ready to speak, their meals arrive. He holds off on the conversation.

Alice says, "This looks and smells so good, I am starved. I haven't had a decent meal in two days."

"Then why don't you start eating before we continue our conversation," says Jack.

After a couple of mouthfuls, Alice is ready to continue. "The AD wants me to offer you something."

"What could he be offering?

"He is inviting you to be a member of the FBI. He has observed how you handle yourself and feels you would be an asset to the organization."

Jack stops chewing what he has in his mouth and needs to take some water before he answers.

He offers to refill Alice's wine glass then he will continue. "I appreciate the offer. I feel honored. Natick would be in a bind if I left, with Mike being laid up with gunshot wounds."

"You don't have to leave immediately. The offer remains open. When you complete your training, I can arrange for you to work out of the Boston office so you are close to home."

At that moment, Jack realizes it's not just the FBI who wants him.

Jack doesn't speak much about his personal life with other agencies. Alice is probably not aware he is engaged to be married next year.

"I will give the offer some thought, and I will pass the information over to the chief and the captain about your move out of Natick." Jack doesn't want to tell Alice about Jennifer. Now things are making sense to him about how she always needed to know that she was okay with him in previous conversations. *She wants me to work near her in the Boston office because she is looking for someone in her personal life. For whatever reason, she has her sights on me.*

This time Alice pours more wine in Jack's glass. Then she refills her glass a little more.

"I received word from Washington today that the phone number the Shrewsbury realtor had was a disposable phone. Likewise the other numbers that were called by the number were also disposable phones. It is very difficult for us to get good information with those types of phones."

"So, we won't know anything about the calls from Barre, Massachusetts, or Queens, New York."

"Not at the moment. We have NSA paying special attention to those numbers if they were to be used to make calls. It's a long shot but something to work with."

They are finishing their meals and Alice asks, "Would you like some dessert?"

"Just coffee will be fine!"

"I'm going to have some."

"Enjoy, you've earned it many times over, I'm sure."

Alice smiles at him with a gleam in her eye.

Two hours later they leave the restaurant and head out to their vehicles.

Alice says, "Please give our offer serious consideration, Jack."

"I will and tell the AD I said thank you for the offer." *How the hell did I get in the middle of this mess?*

Chapter Forty

December 27th

Jennifer wakes up and is very excited. Today is her scheduled luncheon interview with the two owners of the law firm who contacted her. After showering, she takes her time selecting the best suit and blouse in her wardrobe. Navy blue with a pink blouse makes her look very exquisite. She puts on just enough makeup to look attractive, but not overly done. She remembers the outfit she selected is the same one she wore when Jack paid attention to her at the party where they were both invited.

Jennifer takes time for a quick breakfast and heads out to her office to arrive early to make sure her desk is clear before lunch. She had penciled into her desk pad an hour and a half for lunch.

* * *

Worcester media as well as the Boston media are now going full bore with their blitz of stories, theories, spins, and anything else they can print or place on television about the "Midnight Mass Massacre."

Reporters continue to camp outside near the church. The crime scene tapes don't allow them to get too close. Some of this is necessity and some to control the media.

*   *   *

SAC Alice Broadwell and Assistant Director Doug Risner locate a warehouse where they can deposit evidence from the church crime scene.

Alice begins to wonder how many more years can she deal with the scenes of death and dying. The only thing that keeps her going is she lives with the hope of getting the criminals. Alice wants to get convictions and put these people away where they will never harm society again. At least that is supposed to be the way it works, only too many times that never happens.

*   *   *

Lt. Jack McNamara is sitting with Chief Winters and Captain Green.

"I met with SAC Alice Broadwell last night. She wants me to pass on where the status of the FBI investigation in Natick is." Jack hesitates. "The FBI has decided to give up working in Natick and is moving to Worcester."

"Just like that, they walk and leave us with a mess," says the chief.

"I'm afraid so. They feel if they are going to get any more out of what happened here, it will be from their labs and not their fieldwork."

"Do you agree with their move, Jack?" asks the captain.

"We are now five weeks into what happened in Natick. I think they are correct in that sense, only I don't feel they are going to get much more out of Worcester."

"Why?" asks the chief.

"Number one, I think these guys are now out of state. The reports from Worcester indicate there were six terrorists. We know there were at least a dozen to begin with. Where are the remaining terrorists?"

"Where do you suppose they are, Jack?" asks the chief.

"If I had to put money on it, they are down in New York somewhere."

"What makes you say that?" asks Captain Green.

"Just my gut feeling, Captain, that's all I can give you."

"Did you tell Alice how you felt?"

"No, because I have nothing to base it on."

The chief continues, "We will maintain what we have been doing for another month to see if we can uncover more evidence to nab these guys. After that, we will need to rethink where we will focus."

The captain says, "I agree."

"I agree too," says Jack.

"Oh, there's one more thing of which the two of you should be aware."

"What's that?" says the chief.

"Alice made me an offer to join the FBI. I don't want either of you hearing it from someone else."

"And your response is?" asks the chief.

"I told her if I was to leave the department with Mike in the hospital, the department would suffer. I felt it was a good distraction."

"Did she accept that?" asks the captain.

"She said the offer was open ended. She said she wanted me in the Boston office."

"And your reply was?" asks the chief.

"I thanked her and said I would think about it. I don't plan on leaving, so don't either of you go getting nervous. I just thought I should tell you."

The chief shakes his head. "I guess this shouldn't surprise me. They see a good candidate and want to grab him."

"Sir, I couldn't work for the government and be a robot. I like the freedom I have here in the department."

Finally, smiles appear on both faces of the chief and the captain. The chief says, "You had me worried for a moment there."

* * *

After Jack leaves the chief's office, the chief turns around to the captain. "Can we trust what he just said?"

"Yes, sir, you notice he told us—number one, Number two, he said he cannot be a robot. Number three, for some reason he knows Alice wants a piece of him."

"How do you know that, Captain?"

"I've watched her feminine ways and she is trying to latch onto Jack. I think Jack is smart enough not to get her jealous so our operation wouldn't be jeopardized because of a lady scorned."

"It's that bad?"

"I think so, Chief. Jack has been oblivious to what she has been doing up until now. Now he has smartened up. He is a great police officer who doesn't want his ego in the way of the case. Alice is the problem, not Jack, but her track record with the FBI will make heads roll somewhere. Jack doesn't want them rolling onto us. The man is a pro!"

*　*　*

At 4:30 Jack's phone rings, "Jack McNamara," the receptionist says, "Jennifer is on the phone."

Smiling, Jack loves the way the department treats Jennifer with respect.

"Hello, hon, how did it go?"

"I got the job. I told them I needed to give notice and they had no problem with that. I want to take you out to dinner tonight."

"I know you are thrilled you got the job and I'm happy for you. You paid last time so I should pay this time. Something happened recently that I want to share it with you so it's my treat. Let's meet at the Chart House"—Jack looks at his watch—"at six. Is that okay with you?"

"I'll be there before you, and sucking on a martini."

"Remember, you have to be sober to drive to my place."

"I know, I know I just feel so good I want to celebrate."

"Tell you what, put us up at the Hilton at the airport. The cars aren't charged parking if you stay there. We can both call in sick tomorrow."

"You wouldn't dare, Jack!"

"Try me!"

"Oh my God, this is going to be one hell of a night! I love you, Jack McNamara!"

"I love you too!"

When Jack hangs up the phone, he realizes how much Jennifer really means to him. He remembers how she changed legal positions so their careers would not conflict. He has a first-class lady on his hands.

Chapter Forty-One

Celebration Time

Jennifer had made reservations at the Chart House. Fortunately they were able to get a table for two in a small corner of the dining room. The Chart House has such great food, which is the main reason their dining room is full most times. The number of diners increases the noise level exponentially.

Jennifer orders a bottle of their best Merlot wine when the waiter arrives at the table to give them menus.

When the wine is delivered to the table, Jack indicates that Jennifer will taste-test the wine. The waiter looks a little puzzled. Usually that is left up to the man.

Jennifer lifts the glass with the sample of Merlot and rolls it on her tongue and swirls it around her mouth before swallowing it. She approves the bottle.

The waiter is also impressed. He's never seen a woman do that before.

The waiter takes their entrée orders and leaves.

While they each hold a glass of wine as a celebration salute, Jennifer says, "I've got the job and I start in two weeks."

Jack says, "In two weeks."

"Yes, I want to give the district attorney's office fair notice. They gave me time to decide what I want to do and I know they can find someone within that time to replace me."

"That's very ethical. I assume Walkman and Associates were impressed by that too."

"I think so. The two partners' names are Harry and Ben—two nice Jewish guys. They want a third person because Harry wants to retire in five years. At that time, if I measure up, I could be made a full partner. We would then begin a search for another junior lawyer because Ben wants to retire."

"Retire, yes, but they want their share of the business you will build."

"Jack, of course, they've built it and should expect a long-term return on investment. I am starting at a salary that is fifty percent more than I make. I will be eligible for yearly bonuses as well."

"Okay, moneybags!"

"You sound jealous!"

"No, I am teasing you. I was offered a new job yesterday."

"What, in the department?"

"No, the FBI wants me."

"Oh?"

"Relax, I am not accepting it. I cannot work like a robot as their agents work. I don't want to be shipped all over the country at someone's whim and our futures are more important than any job."

Jennifer looks at him and smiles.

"Besides, the FBI doesn't know our captain is retiring in two years, and he and the chief are in agreement that I will replace him."

"Oh, that is wonderful!"

"I think so too, and we might want to hold our conversation while our meals are being served."

Both of them ordered baked stuffed lobster. Their side dishes are coleslaw and mashed potatoes.

Jennifer says, "It's been so long since I had lobster, I don't remember where to start."

"I always start with the claws and work down from there. I enjoy sucking out the legs and then finishing up with the body. I eat the stuffing as I go along."

"My mind is getting sexual and I can visualize you sucking something else."

"Keep that thought in mind while you eat and don't lose it," says Jack.

"If you were older, I would call you a dirty old man."

"You love it and you know it."

They finish their dinners and Jennifer pays the bill. Again the waiter is a little taken back. However, he appreciates the tip Jennifer gave him.

*   *   *

After checking into the Hilton at the airport, Jack and Jennifer decide to take showers. Jennifer said, "I was nervous during my interview and I could feel my armpits perspiring. Thank God my deodorant works well."

"Go ahead, shower. You ordered a bottle of SKYY vodka and I assume it will be up shortly."

Jack no sooner said those words than a knock came on the door. He checked the peep hole and sure enough, there was a waiter with a cart standing there.

Jack opens the door and the man tells him there is a bucket of ice and four glasses for them. Jack signs the slip and posts a tip for the waiter. The man says, "Thank you."

He positions the cart near the bed and pours two glasses half full and adds ice.

Jennifer comes out of the shower with a hotel terry cloth robe on. Her hair is wet, wrapped in a towel, and she looks lovely.

"Do you feel better now?"

"Yes, I needed that. Why don't you shower now and we can let our dinners digest and totally relax. I'm glad you took the day off tomorrow. We need some time together without all of the hassles of everyday life and jobs."

"I'll be right out!" Jack heads into the bathroom.

*   *   *

When Jack is finished with his shower, he puts on the same type of terry cloth robe that Jennifer is wearing. Similar to Jennifer, his head is wet, but minus the towel.

Jack walks over to the cart and picks up the drink he poured. "Ah, this is nice and cold—the only way to drink vodka.

"Jack, with all of the emotions of the day, I am tired. Do you mind if we don't make love tonight?"

"Of course not, we'll do it twice tomorrow."

"You clown," she says as she throws a pillow at him.

Chapter Forty-Two

The Day Off

As they sit up in bed with pillows supporting their backs, they are enjoying their second drink.

"When are you going to tell the chief and the captain about the offer from the FBI?"

"I told them yesterday."

"Wow, I thought you might want to think it over for a couple of days."

"What's there to think over, it's not something I want."

Jennifer places her right hand in his left hand and says, "I'm glad. I wouldn't want you traveling all over the country."

"It's not something I want either. It's funny, the captain told me two weeks ago about his retirement. It made the whole decision process much easier. I do want to get promoted somewhere, but not at the FBI. Do you realize how many thousands of agents would be ahead of me for promotion?"

Jennifer seems astonished, "Promotion is important to you, isn't it?"

"Not so much the title. I have ideas of leading, which are not even happening in Natick. I'm not about to ruffle any feathers right now. One day I will get my chance."

"Yes, you will, Captain McNamara."

Jennifer drains her glass and says, "Honey, I need to sleep."

"Go ahead, I'll finish my glass and join you shortly. Do you mind if I turn on the news?"

"Go ahead, I'm so worn out today. I'll never hear it."

* * *

Jennifer lay cuddled up to Jack all night long. Near daybreak, she begins kissing him and waking him up.

It wasn't difficult to wake him and they begin making love.

Their love and respect for each other brings a whole new dimension to their sex life. It also gives them the freedom to try different things with each other and make each other happy.

* * *

An hour later, Jack says, "You're wearing me out, woman."

Jennifer smiles and says, "I'm glad you enjoy sex as much as I do!"

"Well, it's good for the both of us!" says Jack. "It will keep our weights down."

Jennifer smacks him in the shoulder. "I'm going to take a shower."

"I'm going to call the station desk and tell them I won't be in today."

"Remind me to call the DA's office to tell them the same thing."

Jennifer heads into the bathroom.

* * *

After they are both showered, they head down to the restaurant to have breakfast.

* * *

Following breakfast, they need to decide what both of them would be happy doing. For them, this is a special day. A day they have never taken before, because they are so work-oriented. Today is just for the two of them. They begin to realize it is not so easy to decide what each wants, wondering if the other would want that too!

"Jennifer, let's create a list of five things each of us would like to do today, and then compare so we can decide what we would mutually like to do."

"Is our marriage going to be like this?" she asks.

"No, by the time we get married, we will have a better feel of what each one of us likes. However, if we have difficulty deciding, then we can resort to this exercise."

"You know, Jack, this is an excellent idea. It lets us put everything, or almost everything, on the table."

"It's called an exercise in strategic planning. Our lives are the most important thing we have. Everything else is irrelevant."

"Jack, what a beautiful statement."

"I mean it, Jennifer. You are the most important person in my life. After you, I am a police detective because that too is an important part of me."

"I know and that's what makes you such a wonderful man, Jack."

"Let's stop with the mushy stuff and pick some places to spend our day," says Jack.

Jennifer realizes he can only take so many compliments.

*   *   *

Jennifer and Jack agree on three possible sites to visit. They chose the aquarium, the museum of fine arts, and the science center.

Those three will keep them busy until dinnertime.

*   *   *

SAC Alice Broadwell receives a call from her Boston office. "The NSA director would like you to call him," says her caller. "His name is Scott Warner and I emailed you his number."

Alice looks at AD Doug Risner and shrugs. "I have to call the NSA."

"This sounds interesting!" says Doug. "Better than what we are finding here."

Alice checks her email and places the call.

When Director Warner picks up his phone, Alice identifies herself. "I'm glad you called so quickly. This information is fresh off our system. One of the disposable phone numbers you gave me went active a half hour ago. It contacted a cell number in Brattleboro, VT. That number is not disposable and it is located on the campus of one of the area's colleges. We now know the disposable is located in the Barre, MA area."

"Thank you, Director. Please continue to monitor the three numbers." She asked for the Vermont number and thanked him again.

Chapter Forty-Three

A Day of Discoveries

The commander of the state police calls his captain into his office. "John, what are we finding on those three 9mm casings we found alongside Trooper Andrews body?"

"All three had partial prints from the same individual. Whoever loaded the gun, they never wiped anything clean. Our lab is running more tests to see where they will lead."

"John, I want you to get one of those casings and meet with the head of the FBI. They are working on the Worcester bombings and evidently AKs were left behind from the shooters. I can understand the three that were killed, but there are three more. Something doesn't fit. Have them check out the partial on the casing and see if it matches one of the weapons. I have a feeling that one of the escapees is our man."

The captain realizes how the commander is boiling mad about what happened to his man. It looks like he is going to turn heaven and hell over finding those responsible.

John exits the command center and pulls his car onto the highway, heading for Worcester.

* * *

The FBI is unable to find any usable prints from the home in Shrewsbury, MA. Whoever used it may have left it in a mess for the realtor to clean, but every conceivable area you might find fingerprints resulted in nothing.

The feds know the terrorist stayed somewhere else close by in order to do the Christmas Eve bombings, but where? It's like looking for a needle in a haystack. They need some breaks in this case.

*　*　*

The prints from the John Doe picked up in Sturbridge confirm he is Peter Bent from the Boston area. They place his identity, vehicle information, and the phone number of the Massachusetts state police on every media outlet available.

*　*　*

One hour after Peter Bent's information goes public, the state police receive a call from one of Peter's relatives in Vernon, CT. They explain he didn't show for Christmas as he normally did. They tried to reach his home, only to receive his voicemail each time. No one ever thought the body found in Sturbridge would be Peter. "Oh God," the woman cries into the phone, "how did this happen?"

The officer taking the call allows the woman to express her grief and rage. He knows this is not the end of it. However, right now she needs to vent.

Trooper O'Brien thanks her for the call and asks if someone can meet one of the state police detectives at her home this afternoon. She agrees to meet with whoever arrives at four.

The state police commander has his secretary get the phone number for the nearest Connecticut State Police barrack to Vernon, Connecticut.

With the number, the commander settles down a moment before he makes the call. He feels he is on to something, but doesn't want his emotions to blow it.

The commander places the call and it is received with the warmest sympathy. Connecticut's investigator will meet the detective from Massachusetts in Vernon.

* * *

The state police captain arrives at the building where evidence is being laid out for the investigation of the church bombings and shootings.

"I am looking for the agent in charge," he asks an agent at the doorway.

The agent looks over his uniform and says, "I'll be right back."

Inside the agent finds the AD and the SAC reviewing evidence.

"We have a state police captain outside who wants to speak with the agent in charge."

Alice looks at Doug and says, "I'll take it."

Alice exits the building and sees the captain standing with his hands in his pockets because of the cold.

Noticing his rank she says, "Captain, what do we owe this pleasure to?"

"I don't mean to seem rash, but this trip is not a pleasure."

"Come inside where it is warmer and we can talk," says Alice.

Inside the building, the captain begins to tell Alice why he is here and what happened to their trooper in Charlton.

"Oh God, I've had so much on my mind I haven't put that shooting together with the terrorist attacks in Natick and Worcester, I'm sorry."

"I understand, ma'am. We heard on the news that there were six AKs found outside of the church, but you only have three dead terrorists."

"That is correct. We have identified each terrorist with one weapon. We have separated the other three for further investigation."

"Our commander feels that one of the weapons will have prints similar to the partial on this 9mm casing. We have a recording on the trooper's camcorder, which gives us a good facial. We feel the two incidents are connected."

"Here is my email address," says Alice. "Please forward me the picture from the cruiser. We have composite drawings from someone involved with the Natick bombings. There is a chance your man is also part of this group."

"I'll do that as soon as I go out to my cruiser. Here is my card. Please call me if you find anything at all."

"I promise, Captain. I know how painful this whole affair is."

Inside his cruiser, the captain gives Alice's email address to the commander's secretary. She promises to handle it immediately. John thanks her.

*   *   *

In the parking lot where Peter Bent's sedan was left, the attendant is finally notifying the company that manages the lot. He's not about to make a decision about what to do with the vehicle.

*   *   *

Fifteen minutes after the captain left, Alice's computer rings indicating she has an email. She opens it, finding it came from state police headquarters.

Opening the attachment, she is astounded. The picture on the camcorder is the same as the man in the composites. "Doug!" she yells.

Chapter Forty-Four

It Gets Worse

AD Doug Risner hears Alice shout. She is almost embarrassed she did. "What is going on, Alice?"

"Look at my computer!"

Doug takes a look, "Where did you get this?"

"Ahmad, or whatever his name really is, murdered a Massachusetts state trooper after he and his partners left Worcester. I lay you ten to one they are no longer even in Massachusetts."

"You're probably right, based on the direction they were headed, they are either holed up in Connecticut or New York. Is there an APB for them and their vehicle?"

"The pieces are starting to fall together. A trooper gets killed; a motorist is killed in Sturbridge, so now they have a new vehicle until we can identify the owner and the vehicle."

"Alice, take it easy, you sound like you are beginning to blame yourself."

"Doug, this is a special holiday time and all these creeps are doing is causing death and destruction."

"Email the state troopers that this photo matches our composite. We are looking for the same person. Alice, go take a break for at least a half hour."

Tears begin to stream down her cheeks. "You're right, I am beginning to take it personally."

The other agents in close proximity see what happened to Alice. Part of what she is suffering from they can understand; the other side of the coin, they want to know if things continue to get tough, will she fall apart as their leader.

* * *

Outside in the cold Alice realizes what happened to her. The stress along with the death and destruction on a beautiful holiday can be an awesome burden. Maybe she should start looking for a new career.

While she is in thinking mode she remembers to call her Boston office. She advises her second-in-command that he is to contact the cell phone company for the name of the party with the number she just sent him from her phone. He is to request the phone records and, if need be, get a warrant. When he has accomplished that, he is to call her back.

* * *

The owners of the parking garage could give a shit about an abandoned car. They tell the attendant to call the towing company on file and have them haul it away. They are not about to ruin their holiday.

* * *

Alice calls the captain back to confirm Ahmad is the same man they are looking for.

Chapter Forty-Five

Where Are They

Two days later, Lt. Jack McNamara is sitting in his office when he hears a commotion going on in the detective's room. Jack gets up to check it out.

Lt. Mike Richards is standing in the entryway and all of the guys in the room are crowding around him. You can see the smile across Mike's face, happy to be alive and happy to be welcomed back by his peers.

The crowd of detectives wouldn't let go of Mike until they reached Jack. One of them states, "Lieutenant, we have a package for you."

Jack smiles and says, "Great to see you, Mike. When did you get out of the hospital?"

"Two days ago. They told me to get plenty of bed rest, but I'm going buggy home alone. I called the captain and he told me I could come in to do some desk work. When I feel tired, I should leave. I thought this was a great idea."

"Come on, have a seat in my office."

Jack pulls a chair up closer to his desk and guides Mike into the seat.

"I'm thrilled to see you up and around," says Jack.

"I was lucky, I caught one round in the chest but nothing vital was hit."

"Well, you nailed one of those suckers right between the eyes. He was dead before he hit the ground."

"Too bad I couldn't get a couple more of them. I hear three got away. Do you believe they are the same group that hit us over the Thanksgiving weekend?"

"Three are the figures the local Worcester police and the FBI are giving out. Because of what we had happen here, we are wondering where the others are. To answer your question completely, yes, I believe they are the same group."

"Do you think they are still in the area, Jack?"

"We doubt it; we think they went south to Connecticut or New York."

Mike shakes his head, "What do you want me to do in the office while I am here?"

"What would you like to do? You used to tell me you were a platoon leader in the military. Can you put those skills into something similar to coordinating our guys in the field? We are still active on the bombings issue. At least we will be for another twenty-five days is what I hear."

"Give me a desk and I'll put something together. I'll need you to make a presentation of what we want to accomplish. I don't feel I am up to that yet!"

"What's wrong with your office? It's still your office, you've not been replaced."

Mike smiles and says, "Thank you, it's good to hear."

At that moment Jack's phone rings. "Lieutenant, I have Alice Broadwell from the FBI on the phone."

"Thank you, put her through."

Jack's phone rings again as he held the receiver buttons down without putting the handset down.

"Alice, this is unexpected. We figured once the FBI left Natick we would never hear from you again."

"Jack, are you aware that the Charlton shooting of the state trooper and the killing in Sturbridge are all related to the same people?"

"I've heard of the two killings and suspected something like that, but had no evidence to confirm it."

"It's true, the commander of the state police just supplied us with a 9mm casing found alongside the body of his trooper and the cruiser camcorder got a good facial of the one who calls himself Ahmad. The video matches our composites."

"How about the Sturbridge killing, any proof who did that?"

"We are working that right now, especially since we believe this is now an interstate situation."

"I'd appreciate it if you kept me posted, Alice, because I would like to stay on top of this myself."

"That is why I called. I felt you had a need to know."

Sure, sure, Alice. Any way to keep me in your clutches, thinks Jack.

"I have to go, Alice. I have someone in my office."

"Oh, okay, we'll talk again sometime."

Jack merely hangs up.

Alice feels a little empty because Jack is not returning her overtures.

"Mike, do you want to come in tomorrow?"

Mike's head snaps as if his thoughts were far away. "Yes, can I come in for nine?"

"Oh, banker's hours, I'm only kidding, Mike, that will be fine. While I was talking to Alice, I thought you might want to put a strategic plan together of what we learned in this situation. It could be helpful in future situations. I'm sure that idea would be better than my first one."

"That's a great idea, Jack. I'll keep that in mind."

Mike gets up with a little difficulty but does okay.

Jack is proud to see his self-determination working, whether Mike realizes it or not.

*   *   *

At four o'clock that afternoon, a detective from the Connecticut state police and another from the Massachusetts state police meet with Peter Bent's sister in her home in Vernon, Connecticut.

Vernon, Connecticut, is a wealthy community and each of the detectives raises an eyebrow as they proceed to the front door.

Carolyn Bent Collins answers the door. Her eyes are swollen and red. They introduce themselves and show their identifications.

Carolyn steps aside so the men can enter. After closing the door, she leads them into a living room. Both men seem uncomfortable as where they should sit. Their homes have the lived-in look and this house looks like it belongs in *Better Housekeeping Magazine.*

"Have a seat anywhere. None of this is very special," says Carolyn.

The two had already decided who would lead the questioning and the other would be additional support for the investigation.

The Massachusetts state detective says, "Could you please give us a little briefing about your brother's trip here for the holidays."

"Sure, but I don't know where to start. My head feels like it wants to explode."

"Let me help. Does your brother make this trip often?"

"Peter," she has to pause with tears coming down her cheeks, "always comes for the Christmas get-together. He is my only sibling. My parents are deceased and Peter always enjoyed being with my husband's relatives. It gave him a sense of belonging.

"Peter would come down during the summer to spend time with our children and that gave my husband and me time to get away by ourselves. He is, or was, a marvelous uncle. Peter never married and he lived just outside of Boston."

"We have the address and vehicle information from the Motor Vehicle Department. Do you give us permission to go into his living quarters?"

"Yes, of course, anything that will help. Peter left me with a spare key and I only ask that you leave the condo as you found it and you return the key to me."

The Massachusetts detective says, "Not a problem, ma'am. We will send it out to you priority mail with a signature required."

"Do you feel that Peter's stopping at the place to eat was being in the wrong place at the wrong time?"

"Carolyn," the Connecticut detective says, "right now that is what it looks like. Unfortunately these things do happen."

"One more thing," the Massachusetts detective says, "do you have someone to stay with you through this? I mean, where are your husband and your children?"

"My husband is traveling in Europe right now on a project for work. I am waiting for him to return my call. My three children live far from here, but our daughter is grabbing the first flight here from Utah. She was very close to Peter."

The two men leave and sit in the Connecticut detective's car. "What do you think?"

"Right now I think you hit the nail on the head with the wrong place and time. Damn shame, isn't it," says the Massachusetts detective.

Chapter Forty-Six

Following Leads

The second-in-command of the FBI's Boston office contacts Alice later that afternoon. The cell phone number in Vermont belongs to a male in college in Brattleboro, VT. Since Brattleboro is not that far away, Alice plans to go there tomorrow with another agent. This is too important to pass up. The real reason that tweaks her interest is the Barre, Massachusetts, number is connected to Ahmad.

*   *   *

The commander of the Massachusetts state police sends a team to Boston to check out Peter Bent's living quarters. His detective receiving permission to do so makes it easier, even though he probably should have passed this over to the FBI. His reasoning is the bureau has enough on its plate with the Natick and Worcester incidents. He cannot logically come to the conclusion that Trooper Andrews' death would be given the time it deserves. The team is instructed to treat the residence with courtesy and he is to be given back the key.

*   *   *

FBI lab reports coming in from Washington are given to AD Doug Risner. The reports are telling him that the three terrorists killed in Worcester were green card holders based on their fingerprints. Each one of them is from a different portion of the country. The same goes for the two of the weapons found on the stairs of the church. These two are also green card holders and from very different parts of the country. The third's set of prints are unknown to the FBI database.

An attachment is sent with this email spelling out the names of the five terrorists, photo IDs, and where they listed their residence for their green cards.

Doug is not surprised about the green cards. Since 2011, anyone applying for a green card was photographed and fingerprinted. This is great information. What surprises him is each one of the five terrorist comes from a different part of the country. He needs to think this out.

Now that he has the prints and identification of two of the others who escaped from the Worcester bombings, he wants to publicize this on the media.

Nothing works better than the fear factor on criminals. Criminals hell, these people are animals and deserve to die.

Doug also realizes that the one set of prints they cannot get an identity on is the ringleader, who is heading this operation. He is the one who calls himself Ahmad. He is the one they must locate to put an end to this.

Chapter Forty-Seven

Consulting with Washington

Assistant Director Doug Risner places a call to his boss. When his boss, Brian O'Keefe, answers, Doug says, "Brian, I need some time with you. What do you have available this morning or this afternoon?"

"Well, this morning is tied up, but I am free, if you want to call it that, after 3:00. What's going on, Doug? You don't usually call me like this."

"I'll call you at 3:00. This is a very unusual situation. It is even going to get bigger than we thought."

Before answering, Brian looks up at the ceiling and lets out a breath of air.

"I'll be waiting for your call. Will Alice be on the call with us?"

"Not this one, just the two of us."

Brian felt that was a little strange not having the SAC on with the two of them. He wonders what the hell is going on.

* * *

Alice and a fellow agent named Tom arrive in Brattleboro, VT. Brattleboro is a sleepy little town in southeastern Vermont. It abuts the southwestern border of New Hampshire and sits in the middle of Route 9, which goes east and west.

They stop for coffee and then follow the GPS directions to the police station.

Entering the station, they are met by a pretty brunette dispatcher. "Can I help you?"

"Yes, I am SA Alice Broadwell. I called your chief a couple hours ago and he said he would see us when we got to town."

"He is in his office. Let me check with him." She makes the call and is directed by the chief to send them in.

Chief Murphy, at least six feet tall, trim, and well-muscled, opens his office door before they reach it, Alice introduces herself and Tom.

"Have a seat. What is this all about?"

Alice begins, "We're sure you are aware of the bombings in Massachusetts right after Thanksgiving and then again on Christmas Eve?"

"Yes, I think everyone in New England is aware of them. How does Vermont fit into this?"

"After the Thanksgiving bombings, we located where the bombers were staying and met the realtor who handled the transaction. She gave us a phone number that she had as a contact number. It turns out the number is from a disposable phone. With a warrant, we were able to identify other calls from and to the phone. We have the NSA monitoring the numbers.

"Yesterday, one of the other numbers located in Barre, MA, received a call from this area. The Vermont number is not a disposable phone. With the help of the cell service, we have the name William Foley listed as the owner of the phone. According to the cell records, he is a college student in the area here. We would like to talk with him."

"You want to interrogate him to find out what and who is in Barre?"

"Yes, I felt the proper way to handle this is to invite you to join us in going to the college."

"Let me make a call to the dean. I think it would be unfair if three of us merely walked in on him. I'll also ask him to arrange for us to meet with this Mr. Foley."

"Chief, is it possible if we could use your interrogation room to speak with him? I feel the security of the college might work against us getting to the bottom of this."

"It's important enough a matter, I will arrange with the dean to excuse Mr. Foley from whatever class he is in. After I make the call, you can follow me over there."

*   *   *

At the college, the dean agrees to have Mr. Foley present for their arrival. He goes out to his secretary and asks her to find which class Mr. Foley is in and have him come to the dean's office.

While she is in the process of locating William Foley, another student who works part-time in the office overhears the conversation. She excuses herself to go to the ladies' room. Inside a stall, she pulls out her cell phone and sends a text message to Bill.

"PD arriving shortly with FBI. What did you do?"

Foley looks at the message and says, "Shit, what has my uncle done?"

Bill's uncle chewed him out yesterday, saying he knew he was never to use that number unless it was an emergency. Bill realizes he cannot call his uncle by phone, but he will use a pay phone to call his pager to warn him. He leaves class and uses the first pay phone he sees. Just as he is finished with the call, he sees the messenger who is sent to retrieve him.

Sean, the messenger, sees Bill. In small colleges, everyone pretty well knows everyone on campus.

"Bill, I have instructions to bring you up to the dean's office."

"What's up, Sean?"

"I have no idea. I'm just following instructions."

The two young men walk to the dean's office. As they arrive, the chief of police's cruiser pulls up as well as the FBI vehicle. They enter the office and Sean goes back to class wondering what the hell is this all about.

The chief introduces the agents to the dean, while Bill Foley is standing near the receptionist's desk. She is the one who warned Bill. Their eyes are giving signals to each other that hint at not being aware of what is going on.

After being introduced, Agent Broadwell tells the dean she and the chief have agreed to speak with Mr. Foley at the station house.

Dean Southerland is not expecting this and asks, "Is Mr. Foley being charged with anything?"

Alice continues, "Right now we merely want to speak with him. He may be aware of certain situations that could aid in our solving two crimes."

Chief Murphy offers to have Bill ride in his cruiser to reduce the tensions that are building.

* * *

Inside of the station house, Chief Murphy escorts Bill and the two FBI agents into the small interrogation room in the rear of the station.

"Would anyone like some coffee or water?" asks the chief.

He receives three negatives so he closes the door and leaves them alone.

* * *

In Barre, MA, Jerry Walsh is cramming every piece of weapons and explosives he can into his van. He is thankful that Bill sent him a warning, but knows it will be only a short time when the FBI will be on his tail. Jerry has a friend who might be willing to put him up on short notice. He is going to trust his instincts.

Jerry hops behind the steering wheel and starts his van. About a hundred feet away he points a remote at his home, and hits the button he has it programed for. The house explodes with a tremendous force and a huge fire begins to destroy everything and anything in its space.

Jerry wonders how long the FBI will be delayed by this move.

As he drives off, he hears the fire engines from town coming toward his property.

The town of Barre utilizes a volunteer fire department. Their members come from different directions as well as the fire station.

Arriving at the scene, the chief says, "Jesus Christ, what the hell happened here? Did Jerry go up with the house? There's nothing we are going to save, so we need to stop the fire from spreading and destroying anything nearby. Water down the area good before you put water on the blaze. We will probably wind up letting this thing burn itself out."

One of the volunteer firemen heard the chief wonder if Jerry died in the blaze. "I don't think so, Chief. I thought I saw his vehicle heading into town right after I heard the blast. At least I think it was his."

* * *

Alice sits opposite of young Bill Foley.

"We have information that a call was made from your cell phone to another cell in Barre, MA, yesterday. Can you confirm if that is true?"

"Sure, I called my uncle."

Alice goes on, "Do you call your uncle often?"

Bill pauses so that he doesn't look as if he was scripting this interrogation. "No, I probably call him three or four times a year."

"And you just happen to call him yesterday."

"There isn't any law against me calling my uncle. Why is the FBI interested in when I call my uncle?"

Alice ignores the question. "Your uncle's phone number was listed on a cell phone that may indicate he is involved with terrorism."

Bill cracks a laugh, "My uncle involved with terrorism. No way, he is a meek and mild guy."

"You didn't talk long on the call. Is there a reason for that."

Now Bill realizes why his uncle was upset and feels he screwed up. "Yes, he said he was in the middle of things and he would get back to me in a day or two."

"Have you heard from your uncle, Bill?"

"No, as a matter of fact I haven't and it slipped my mind with my class schedule to call him again." At this point, as cool as Bill is trying to act, Alice notices a line of sweat breaking on his forehead.

"What is your uncle's name and address in Barre?"

"His name is Jerry Walsh. He lives just outside of town and right now I cannot think of the address. I don't get interviewed by the FBI every day. I know how to get there as it's a small town. We don't write to each other. You can ask anyone in town and they can tell you how to get to his place."

"Let me give you a word of advice, young man. Your uncle is not the man you think he is. Right now I have no grounds to hold you; however, I suggest you stick around the campus in case we need to speak again. If your uncle contacts you, I am going to give you my card for you to contact us."

"Are we through?"

"Yes, for now, I'll ask the chief to take you back to the college."

All three stand and leave the back room.

Bill Foley goes outside the station house and waits for the chief. He feels the cool breeze beginning to dry up the sweat running down his back.

Chief Murphy agrees to give him a ride, but wants to know what came out of the questioning.

"Right now nothing, but I think he knows more than he is telling us."

Alice and Tom leave to return to the Worcester area.

In the car, Alice tells Tom, "I want you to take two other agents and return here. I want this young man under surveillance. If need be, rent a car in case you need more than one."

"Yes, ma'am."

*   *   *

It is three in the afternoon and ADA Doug Risner calls the director. When Brian O'Keefe answers he says, "Boy, you are prompt!"

"I try to be."

"How come Alice isn't on the call with us?" asks Brian.

"She and another agent are up in Brattleboro, Vermont, interrogating an individual."

"What's going on, Doug?"

Doug goes on as to how the investigation is progressing. What his main concern is after the autopsies of the terrorist bodies he found and was able to identify each of them by their fingerprints because they had green cards and photographs. What he also found out by the same method is that a couple of the other weapons had identifiable prints by green cards. The others did not.

What really troubles Doug is each one of the three are from very different parts of the country. Indicating they were cherry-picked from different terrorist cells across the US.

"Does this really surprise you, Doug?"

"In a way, no, but I was hoping this would be more of a regional situation."

"Now you know it's not! Give us the details and that will be our problem. You solve the one in New England."

"Yes, I have the three bodies; I know who they are and the others I have no clue right now where they are. I am going to put a nationwide manhunt for the one plus expand the photos off the state police camcorder hoping someone will see these creeps before they do any more damage."

"I'm in agreement with your decisions on this. It appears someone came into the country and has put together a group of Iranians from cells across the country. The good news is now we know where the five came from and we can focus on finding those cells as well as what you are working on."

"This is the main reason for my call when I said it is bigger than we figured."

"Tell Alice I said hello when you see her and keep me up to date." Brian hangs up and so does Doug.

Doug feels a little relieved. Why he doesn't really know, but he does.

Chapter Forty-Eight

Media Works and Fire Damage

The next day, Ahmad and the nine remaining members of his group are watching television and the evening news starts with "Breaking news: the Massachusetts state police, along with the FBI, have issued a nationwide alert for the following three men. If you see them, do not try to detain them as they are armed and dangerous." Immediately the pictures of Ahmad, Kazem, and Marduh are posted on the screen.

Ahmad is not surprised to see his picture, but the other two men's jaws just dropped.

"How did they get our pictures?" asks Kazem. "This is serious. Anyone spotting us could turn us in."

Marduh says, "Ahmad, how are you going to handle this so we don't wind up captives of the Americans?"

"You saw my picture up there as well. Do you two have green cards?"

"Yes!" says Kazem. "All of us do, otherwise we cannot get employment."

"The FBI matched your prints from the weapons we left behind. I am not in their database, but they got my picture from that damn camera on the dashboard of the state police cruiser. Let me think about this. In the meantime, you two are also limited to staying inside until we are ready to launch our next project."

Both men are beginning to show signs of regrets of being involved with this cause.

*   *   *

SA Alice Broadwell along with two other agents arrive in Barre, MA. One of the two agents gets out of their vehicle and heads into the post office to inquire where Jerry Walsh resides.

The clerk at the counter says, "I can tell you where he lived, but he doesn't anymore!"

"What do you mean?"

"The house blew up and burned down two days ago!" replies the clerk.

"Did he die in the blast?"

"Don't know, you're going to have to ask the fire chief."

"Where can I find the chief?"

"He owns the hardware store down the street. We only have a volunteer fire department."

"Thank you!" the agent replies and heads back to the car.

After advising Alice, the same agent heads for the hardware store.

Inside of the hardware store, Agent Gene asks for the fire chief.

"He's out back; I'll get him for you. Call I ask who's calling?"

"Tell him a law enforcement officer is looking to speak with him."

The fire chief comes out front and says, "Can I see some identification?"

Gene shows his identification and asks, "Was a body found on the property that burned down two days ago?"

"No body that we found. What's going on here?"

"This is official FBI business and we will be declaring the area part of a crime scene. Please spread word around town for everyone to stay clear of the place, which we will have taped off."

The agent goes out to the car and advises SA Alice what he just did and what he was told.

"All right, let's go look for ourselves and tape off the area," says Alice.

* * *

After securing what was Jerry Walsh's home with crime scene tape, Alice calls AD Doug Risner. She gives him all of the details and requests that a crime scene tech squad is sent to verify if there was an explosion and what was used to cause it. If they could begin matching types of explosives to what was used in Natick and Worcester, then they have a lead to follow. She gives Doug the GPS coordinates of the site for the team to find the place. Alice and the other two agents will be heading back to Worcester. They cannot do any more here.

* * *

Barre's local reporter of their weekly gazette hears the word being spread around town about the FBI investigating the fire at Jerry Walsh's home.

To her this is the biggest news she's had since one of the local farmer's horses got loose and tore up Mrs. Grady's garden a week after she planted it.

Andrea decides to call her contact at the Worcester newspaper. "Look, Jamie, here is what is going down. The FBI is in town checking out a house that exploded and burned to a crisp. I've got a feeling this is connected to the tragedy at your church on Christmas Eve. Come out here and you will have first break on the news before anyone else. I just want some of the credit, okay."

"Oh my God, how did you find this out?"

"Thanks to my source is how I found it out."

"I'll be out within two hours with a crew."

"Meet me at the paper and I'll direct you there."

"Great, see you then!"

* * *

Meanwhile at the towing garage, the owner is frustrated that no one is trying to claim the vehicle they hauled out of the garage in Queens, NY. He decides that if no one claims it in one more week, it is going to the salvage yard for scrap.

* * *

Jerry Walsh is in Groton, Connecticut, with Jennifer, a lady friend he met years ago. He gave her the story that he was on his way to New York City and thought he would stop in to see her. Fortunately for him, she didn't have anyone at home to interfere with his coming.

Jerry knew she was a high-class hooker: she did it by appointment and not walking the streets or having a pimp. In other words, she was her own boss, you might say,

At first Jennifer was happy to see him, but she missed being out on her own and Jerry was beginning to interfere with her livelihood.

"Jerry, I thought you were headed to the city?"

"I am, but I missed you and we've had a couple of good days together."

"Yes, we have, only now I have to do it as a business and not for free."

"I thought you said I could always drop in any time."

"Drop in, yes, but now you're been here for a couple of days and I am not used to someone around all the time."

"Why don't we go out to dinner and I'll leave after dinner and head out to the city."

"Really? Sure, I would like that. Do you want one more for the road?"

"No, I think you've dried me out for a while."

"Let me go shower and change and get dressed to go out."

Jennifer steps out of the bathroom with a towel wrapped around her that she is holding up with one hand.

Jerry steps from behind the door where he was hiding and grabs her chin and head, twisting and snapping her neck in one quick motion. The towel drops as she fights to get away. Jerry hears her neck break. Jennifer drops to the floor.

He bends down to check to see if she is breathing. He hadn't used that move in a long time and he is glad it worked quickly. She was good in bed and he wouldn't want her to have suffered.

Ever since Jerry arrived, he began figuring a way to remain here at least for a while. Her house is secluded and there isn't a neighbor for a mile.

He pulls her body outside of the back door and drags it over to the garage. Jerry pulls her car out and removes the plates from his vehicle. Then he pulls his vehicle inside.

His next move is to transfer all of the materials he has in his van to her car. Once that is done, he places Jennifer into the trunk of his vehicle. It is cold enough so that she shouldn't decompose quickly and he will be long gone before anyone comes looking for her. Her clients always met her at a hotel. For some reason she had let him come here years ago.

He knows the FBI will be after him within days.

Chapter Forty-Nine

Situations Happening

It is two days before New Year's Eve. Tensions are building up in Manhattan with thoughts of the terrorists striking the New Year celebration at midnight on Times Square. Rules have already been set up and public notices are being made through all forms of media that no one will be allowed into the celebration area with a backpack.

The police are drawing up grids for each precinct to carefully monitor their areas. All leaves and vacations days are cancelled for the period of December 31 to January 2.

The governor arranged to have some portions of the New York National Guard located around all the perimeter of the Time Square festivities area.

*　　*　　*

SA Broadwell and AD Risner are reviewing the report from Washington, regarding the explosive residue found at Jerry Walsh's home in Barre, MA.

There is no question about what they found. Residue from Barre matches residue found at the Catholic church bombing and the bombing of the retail stores in Natick, MA.

"What do you think, Alice?"

"This clearly links Jerry Walsh with whoever did the bombings. I venture to say he has been their supplier. Now we need to find him and get some answers about who they are. Someone or some nation is financing this operation and we need that information."

Alice says, "We need to get his DMV information and his photo out to the media. I can feel we are getting somewhere in this investigation."

Doug replies, "Go ahead, run with it and let's see what happens."

*　　*　　*

Unbeknownst to Jerry, he is not the only man who knows where Jennifer lives. One of her former clients works at the local post office. Even though he is now happily married, he always had a special admiration for Jennifer. He notices her post office box is full and hasn't been emptied out for seven days. He wonders if she is ill or forgot to place a stop-mail order until she returns. If she's not in tomorrow, he will take a drive out to her place.

*　　*　　*

Ahmad gathers everyone together in the living room after the news is over. "We know the media is still broadcasting our faces, hoping someone will see us and turn us in. I've decided that those of you who they cannot identify will continue our surveillance of the subway system. You will do this on a casual basis because I have changed our plans slightly. We can see from the news they expect us to hit Times Square on New Year's Eve.

"That was my original idea. Then I changed it to the subway system when everyone is heading home and are not as keenly aware of their surroundings.

"Now, we will wait them out until they feel more comfortable and believe we left the area. My second thought was to hit them on Martin

Luther King Day. Then I realized it is too close to the first of the year. We will hit them on President's Day in February."

The men begin to smile as they realize their leader is very shrewd. They feel less threatened now.

Chapter Fifty

A Break

That evening on the six o'clock news all over New England and New York, Jerry Walsh's picture, plus his vehicle information, is posted along with a warning not to try and apprehend as he could be armed and dangerous.

*   *   *

When Ahmad sees the FBI report on how they found Jerry Walsh and that he escaped, he is beginning to get concerned more than he has been in the past. He could not allow his feelings to be known to the men around him.

Ahmad knows Jerry doesn't know his itinerary, but he doesn't know what Jerry knows that could trace back to him and Iran. He has a great deal to think about before his next project.

*   *   *

Donald, the postal clerk who knows Jennifer, sees that she hasn't picked up her mail yet. He cannot move it out of her postal box without authorization from her; however, he is concerned that maybe she is ill. He knows where she lives and plans to stop by on his way home to see if she is well.

A mile close to Jennifer's home, Donald has a vehicle pass him, which he swears is Jennifer's car. The puzzling thing is, there is a man driving it.

Donald parks his car before he nears the bend in the road near Jennifer's home. All kinds of thoughts are going through his head and he doesn't want to barge in on Jennifer if she has company.

Taking his binoculars from its case, he exits his car and walks to a slope where he knows he will get a view of Jennifer's house.

The same car is parked outside of the garage, which is strange because Jennifer's car is one of her prized possessions and he never knew her to leave it outside.

As he is looking through his binoculars, a man exits the house, heading to the car. The man lifts a bag out of the trunk, which Donald assumes is groceries.

When he sees the man's face, he thinks he's seen it somewhere before. Right at the moment, he cannot recall where.

Donald decides to leave and not get involved in Jennifer's life.

Placing his binoculars in its case, he starts his car and realizes where he's seen that face.

It was on last night's news posted by the FBI. "Oh shit, what is Jennifer involved in?"

Donald heads home and immediately places a call into the Connecticut office of the FBI.

*   *   *

Upon receiving the call and checking out that Donald is a responsible individual, the Connecticut field office goes into action.

Two SWAT teams are assembled and a senior field officer head for Jennifer's location. They expect to arrive in one hour.

Information on Jennifer's property is being relayed to the senior officer. He plans to locate his vehicles near the same spot that Donald parked in. It will provide concealment for his vehicles and he can arrange to position his men around the house.

One problem the agents will have is the fact that when they arrive, they will have very little daylight left and might have to use night-vision equipment.

*   *   *

SA Alice Broadwell receives a phone call from the Connecticut office. "Yes, this is Agent Broadwell!... When and where?"

When she finishes the call, Alice contacts AD Doug Risner. Alice relays the information that she received from Connecticut.

"When they have him in custody, you and I need to go to Connecticut," says Doug.

"I expected you would say that. I'm ready to go!" says Alice.

"I need to make one more call."

Alice calls the Natick Police Department, looking for Lt. McNamara.

She is told Lt. McNamara is out of the building and they would be glad to contact him and have him call her.

"Please do that. This is urgent."

*   *   *

Lt. Jack McNamara receives word from the station that Alice would like him to call her ASAP.

Jack looks at his Android for her phone number and places the call. "Alice, what's up?"

Alice fills him in. "Jack, we need a favor from you. Look, this character comes from Barre, MA, and being a small town, you understand how they might feel if we start asking questions. Could you contact the local police chief and see what you can learn about Jerry Walsh?"

"Sure, Alice, no problem and I fully understand what you mean. Nice work finding out where this guy is, and hopefully he will lead us to the others," says Jack.

"Let's hope so!" says Alice.

"I'm heading back to the station and will make the call to Barre within the hour."

"Call me if you have anything that you think will help us."

"You can count on it!" says Jack.

Chapter Fifty-One

Taking Jerry

The senior agent has four snipers and ten agents with the combined SWAT teams. He explains to the snipers how each of them will cover one side of the house. Eight of the agents will also be stationed around the house with two on each side. The snipers will be positioned between two agents per side.

The two additional agents will work their way around the garage and see what is inside they should be aware of.

The men are set in motion. When everyone is in position, the senior man dials the number of the house. He lets it ring eight times before hanging up.

Jerry doesn't want to answer Jennifer's phone. Whoever is calling will assume she is not at home.

When the phone stops ringing, Jerry hears a bullhorn call out his name from outside of the house.

"What the fuck is going on?" he yells out.

"Jerry Walsh, this is the FBI. The house is surrounded. You are to come out with your hands in the air."

Jerry steps over to the front window. Peering around the corner of the glass, he sees two agents clad in black from top to toe, wearing helmets and body armor, holding automatic rifles. *Damn, how did this happen? Who could have spotted me?*

Jerry knows it is impossible to escape. Yet, he doesn't want to give in easily. It is not his nature to do so. He could commit suicide and take some of these guys with him by blowing up the house, but he's a coward at heart and knows even though he will go to prison, at least he will be alive.

Let them wait, he thinks to himself. *It's pretty cold out there.*

The bullhorn sounds again and tells him he has five minutes to come out.

"Five minutes and then what are they going to do?" Jerry thinks out loud.

Jerry walks around each room, closing the shades and making sure no lights are on.

* * *

Each side of the house has agents reporting that shades are being closed and lights are out throughout their areas of vision. The senior man knows this guy isn't coming out too soon.

The FBI is pleased this is a one-story home and easier to deal with. The problem they have is they don't know if Jennifer is working with Jerry or if she is even inside.

Jennifer could be a hostage.

At the end of five minutes, one agent on each side of the house fires a weapon with tear gas canisters at windows. The containers break through the glass but don't travel far into the rooms as the shades are blocking their entrances. However, they are inside and should do the job.

Inside the house, the tear gas canisters are dispersing their powerful agents and Jerry is trying to evade them by crawling on the floors. He has a wet towel wrapped around his face and neck. The gas is filling each side of the house and making Jerry's vision almost impossible.

Desperately, Jerry opens the cellar door and shuts himself in the basement. Tear gas tends to rise and now that he is below the floor level, he feels he can breathe a little easier. His eyes are starting to burn.

Using a flashlight, he looks around the dark cellar hoping to find a way out. Once it gets dark, maybe he can exit the basement and get into the woods.

Then what am I going to do? I'm not wearing heavy clothes to be out in this weather.

Taking an assessment of what he is wearing, not having sufficient funds on him to get away, he decides to walk out. He realizes once Jennifer's body is found, he will be facing a murder charge.

Jerry waits a half hour for the gas to clear up from the main floor.

The commander is wondering what is taking the gas so long to have an effect on Jerry.

* * *

Suddenly, the sniper in the front of the house reports, "Inside door opening. One male is exiting the house. His hands are raised."

The senior agent directs the two agents who were inspecting the garage to meet with the man and take him into custody.

* * *

With his hands cuffed behind him, Jerry is read his Miranda rights and placed into one of the SWAT vehicles.

The commander then sends four agents to look through the house to see if they can locate Jennifer.

The agents indicate the house is empty. There is no sign of the woman.

The commander says, "Let's hope she is away and safe."

* * *

The commander calls in to his headquarters and reports they have Jerry Walsh in custody. There appears to be no one else on the premises. A team is going to have to come out and repair the windows they broke from firing the tear gas.

The communication is acknowledged and he is directed to bring Mr. Walsh to Hartford. Headquarters will handle informing the Groton police and turn everything over to them at this time.

The Groton police will be informed that any possessions they feel belong to Mr. Walsh must be taken into custody and turned over to the bureau.

*   *   *

As the SWAT team members head to Hartford, they are relieved this situation went as easily as it did. When they receive a call, they never know what they are walking into.

Chapter Fifty-Two

Daylight Hours of New Year's Eve

At eight in the morning, the Groton Police Department receives a call from the FBI. The chief takes the call. It is explained to him how the SWAT raid was done and there was no time to involve his department as darkness was almost upon them.

The chief could buy the alibi, but he is really incensed that his department doesn't know about it until the next day. "Fucking feds, they do what they damn well please" is his remark to his officers.

The chief sends over two teams of detectives. Their biggest concern is the whereabouts of Jennifer.

The detectives plan to meet with Donald from the postal department and go from there.

By the time the Groton forces arrive on scene, the FBI cleanup crew has replaced the damaged windows they shot out with tear gas. The detectives are amazed at how efficient they are to cover their tracks.

*   *   *

Anxiety in the New York area of Manhattan is growing by the hour. There are numerous fears and leads which are going nowhere. The police cannot make a mistake as people could die and careers will end.

* * *

Lt. McNamara reaches the chief of police in Barre, MA. He explains he is the lead investigator of what happened in Natick and a go-between with the FBI and local police forces.

Jack explains that the bureau has arrested Jerry Walsh and needs some feedback from him to completely interrogate him.

"What do you want me to say, he was a criminal? Look, Jack, he was a quiet reserved individual who paid his taxes and never gave my department any cause to look at him. Not even a speeding ticket or a drunken situation. I guess he played his role real well here. We really never knew he existed.

"Do you have any ideas of who he dealt with?"

"Like what terrorists, Jack?"

"Look, I have two full-time and three part-time officers besides myself. What do you want from me?"

"Chief, I understand and take this with all sincerity; I can understand what you are dealing with. Thank God for men like you!"

"Thank you, Jack, I wish I could give you more but I can't."

* * *

Jack calls Alice and gives her what little he has from the chief of police of Barre, MA.

While Alice was hoping for more, she knew it was a pipe dream. Her next call is to her agents in Brattleboro to take them off their surveillance assignment.

Alice and her boss Doug Risner are on their way to Hartford, Connecticut, to the FBI facility there.

* * *

At eleven o'clock that morning, Jerry Walsh is arraigned as a terrorist. The judge orders five million dollars' cash bail. The judge instructs Jerry to notify the court if he selects a lawyer within seven days. If not, a court-appointed defense lawyer will be arranged for him. The case will go to a grand jury in two weeks.

Jerry had not asked for a lawyer, nor has he offered any information. The FBI believes he will be a tough nut to crack.

*　　*　　*

The two detective teams from the Groton Police Department are scouring the house and searching for anything they can tie Jerry Walsh to Jennifer. If they can, they could get a crack at Jerry for a local crime.

One of the detectives goes into the garage and smells a rotten odor coming from the back of the vehicle. He raises the garage door to attempt to get some fresh air.

There are no keys in sight to open the vehicle. He walks inside to get another detective to work with him on popping the back door.

When the second detective comes into the garage, he says, "What the hell is that smell?"

"I'm not sure and I'm afraid to guess that what I am thinking is true," says the first detective.

With special tools that they use, it took five minutes to pop the back of the van.

Sure enough, Jennifer is lying inside completely naked and it appears her neck is broken. Time to get the MEs involved.

"Fuck," says the second detective. "She's been out here for a couple of days based on how the body looks. We got this sucker by the balls, not even counting the explosives the feds want to take."

"I'll call it into the chief," says the first detective.

*　　*　　*

"You found what?" the chief is shouting into his phone. "Get the whole place taped off and don't move the other car with the explosives in it. The feds will be picking that up later today. They said they had a towing trailer coming for it.

"Have two of you stay at the house until the MEs are through. I want a piece of this guy's ass before the feds can tuck him away. I am assuming we can get him on a murder one charge based on what you just found."

Chapter Fifty-Three

Times Square

Beginning with the noontime news, all of the media outlets are staging discussions on what might happen tonight in Times Square. Following the bombings in Natick, MA, on Black Friday, and in Worcester on Christmas Eve, a lot of media speculation is coming forth about possible terrorist attacks here in New York. The thoughts of the Boston Marathon bombings are on everyone's mind.

The talks range from Al-Qaeda attacks to lone wolf attacks from ISIS. The fear they are generating is worrisome to both the public and to the administrations.

The governor and the mayor had jointly decided that local police, state police, and National Guard troops would encircle Times Square to ensure the safety of the public. Police helicopters circle the area overhead and coast guard cutters patrol the shores of Manhattan. All of this is being broadcast live as news helicopters are taking in everything they can get about the situation below.

The politicians are not going to take a chance that bombings could occur in their territory.

Every conceivable entrance to Times Square is covered. No one is allowed to enter with anything looking like a backpack or fanny pack.

* * *

The media on the ground is moving around fairly easily as the size of the crowd at three o'clock in the afternoon is relatively small for a New Year's Eve celebration. Normally, couples with small children bring their kids out early to have some sort of participation in the festivities.

Cameramen and women reporters are approaching individuals, asking them how they are doing, whether they are enjoying the festivities, and anything else they can think of to keep the cameras rolling for newsbreaks.

Local vendors are feeling a bit frustrated. By this time in the past, they have sold almost half of their products.

The men and women of the police, state troopers, and National Guard have planned to work three-hour shifts to keep their people alert, and not be bored with the inactivity.

* * *

This year is different and people are looking over their shoulders, watching others and visibly looking uncomfortable. They watch the armed patrols and the police on horseback moving through the crowds. Yet, they have the courage to remain and uphold an American tradition. More than one child asks its parents why the police and soldiers are here. They don't recall seeing this many last year.

* * *

One reporter corners a man in the center of the square. Placing a microphone near his face, the reporter asks, "Seeing all of the security here, aren't you concerned that something disastrous might happen?"

"After watching television as to what happened in Massachusetts on Black Friday and Christmas Eve, I feel the city and the state are being safety conscious," replies the man.

The reporter continues to push, "Isn't this mood going to ruin the joy of the season?"

"Your station could report it as the government seeking safety for the public instead of your typical sensationalism."

Frustrated the guy didn't bite, the reporter and her cameraman move onto another attendee.

"Nice going. She wasn't too pleased with your response," says a man standing next to the person who was interviewed.

"They're just a pack of wolves looking for ratings; they don't really care about us."

*   *   *

Watching the six o'clock news, the ten remaining terrorists see how people are reacting to the tensions they have created.

"Yes, yes," Ahmad shouts, "we have won without a third round of attacks. They act like frightened children who cannot go out without the assurance of safety."

At that same moment none of his fellow terrorists feel the same enthusiasm. They are worried how they will safely get away from this madman. They are in a precarious position. If they run away, they will be hunted down by their cells and killed. If they stay, they might die for Ahmad's causes or for whoever he works for. Getting arrested may be the safest outlet for them.

*   *   *

At seven o'clock, the mayor and the governor appear in Times Square. It is very apparent they are there to demonstrate the safety precautions being used are sufficient for everyone's protection. One television station also notes on the air the number of bodyguards surrounding each man. Everyday citizens don't have that pleasure.

Both elected officials realize this event could make or break their political careers even if there is no bombing. "What do you think will come of this, Governor?" "I think you might have more to lose by being mayor than I do. Let's hope this works out well for both of us." They know the negative thoughts of the voters will fade away in time if nothing terrible happens. They feel they are doing what is best for the community. They pray it is enough.

*   *   *

As the evening goes on, there are fewer and fewer people showing up for the celebration. It is obvious the nature of the protective means and the fear of a bombing are keeping many families away from the event.

*   *   *

Lt. McNamara and his bride-to-be are snuggled up on the couch with a drink, waiting for the ball to drop. They began watching television after seven o'clock, following the negative reports on the evening news about the attendance.

"Do you think there will be a blast when the ball drops, Jack?"

"No, I have inside information that from the beginning of the installation of the ball and up to the current time, this ball has more security that the tomb of the Unknown Soldier has in Washington."

"You mean they were that worried?"

"Wouldn't you be in their shoes?"

Hesitating a minute, Jennifer says, "I guess I would be too."

"Look, it will drop in about three minutes. Let's just enjoy the New Year and hope it is a good one."

"It will be next summer when we get married," says Jennifer. "We have that to look forward to. As a matter of fact, we have a lot of work to do to put together for our wedding."

"I promise I will start on it tomorrow with you," says Jack.

Then they hear, "Ten, nine, eight, seven, six, five, four, three, two, one. Happy New Year!"

Jack and Jennifer give each other a warm kiss and look lovingly into each other's eyes.

There is no explosion!

Chapter Fifty-Four

The Day After New Year's

Lt. McNamara enters the department's detective quarters and is stopped by the captain. "Jack, the chief wants you and I to meet with him in his office at 9:00."

Jack looks at the captain and says, "What gives?"

"I know as much as I just told you."

Shrugging Jack says, "This is unusual, I'll be there."

* * *

At precisely nine, the lieutenant follows Captain Green into the chief's office. The chief is on the phone and he points to the two chairs located in front of his desk.

When he hangs up his phone, the chief looks at the two men and says, "I hope both of you enjoyed the holiday. I know the city of New York enjoyed not being bombed, but the costs of that event are staggering. However, I am not planning to talk about what didn't happen.

"Early this morning I received a call from SA Alice Broadwell. She and her boss are planning to interrogate this fellow Jerry Walsh from Barre, Massachusetts. The FBI caught him in Groton, Connecticut, and have him in custody in Hartford.

"Jack, do you have a thing going on with this lady? She just invited us to come down to Hartford and talk to this guy this afternoon after she and her boss are through. She specifically asked that you represent the department."

Jack looks up at the ceiling and rolls his eyes. "No, Chief, I do not have a thing going on with this lady. You know I'm engaged to be married in the middle of this year."

"Well, can someone explain to me what the hell is going on?"

Captain Green speaks, "Chief, let's say that Jack has an admiration groupie by the name of Alice. You know the FBI has offered him a position. I feel she is trying to prime him to make that move."

The chief looks at Jack, "What's your opinion?"

"I think the captain hit the nail on the head. I also think this could be a plus for us."

"How!" says the chief.

"From what I've learned just before New Year's, the FBI has connected this Jerry Walsh with explosives in his van and those explosives have residues that match the bombings we suffered, and also occurred in Worcester. I know for a fact that the Groton Police Department has filed a charge of murder against this character since they found the body of the homeowner in the back of his vehicle, in her garage.

"I would like to talk to this guy and see if I can penetrate his armor to give us the names of the actual bombers. My God, we lost hundreds of people on Black Friday. I'm hoping to convince him he is guilty of conspiracy charges involving terrorism and murder. I believe a judge could give us priority over Groton's charges. I know Groton will go for murder one, which they can prove, and that is a death sentence. Our charge would give him life without parole when he is convicted."

"Okay, I want you in Hartford by one thirty. Alice says they should be through by then and the prisoner can get a lunch break."

"Does the prisoner know I will be coming?"

"I doubt it," says the chief. "If you run a long time, get some accommodations in Hartford. Don't try driving back in the dark. Those highways down there are nuts."

Smiling, Jack says, "Thanks, Chief."

Captain Green says, "Are we through, Chief?"

"When Jack gets back, I want the three of us to sit down and study what the hell is happening."

When the captain and Jack leave the chief's office, Captain Green turns and says, "He must be getting a lot of pressure from the mayor and the governor."

"I'm sure he is," says Jack.

"Look, Captain, I need to call Jennifer and tell her our plans for this evening have to change."

"Good luck with that!"

"Thanks!"

*   *   *

After Jack hung up with Jennifer, Lt. Mike Richards is standing in his doorway. "Do you have a minute for me, Jack?"

Jack looks at his watch realizing he needs to be in Hartford by 1:30. He will also need to eat lunch somewhere before he arrives at the FBI facility.

"Yes, just a minute though, Mike. I have orders to be in Hartford by 1:30."

"Okay, I'll make it quick! The captain spoke with me this morning and advised me that I need to see the department's shrink because of my gunshot wound. He said I could not go back on full duty until he had a report from the doctor. Is this standard procedure?"

"Thankfully, I have never been shot before. Shot at but never been hit. I know this is standard policy by the department. Look, take it as a positive thing. Once the doc clears you, you'll be back full time."

"The captain told me to take my time making my decision. I just wanted to check with you."

"Mike, if it was me, I would do it."

"I'll tell him to set me up with an appointment after lunch. Thanks, Jack, have a safe trip."

*   *   *

Lt. McNamara advises the detective's receptionist he will probably be away for two days on department issues. He heads home to pack an overnight bag in case he needs it.

Chapter Fifty-Five

Same Morning

Early morning on the day after New Year's, the owner of the yard that stores towed vehicles tells one of his mechanics to get the vehicle they picked up in the Queens parking garage and take it to the salvage yard. He is tired of it sitting around. No one seems to want to pick up the tab for its space.

Andy heads out to the spot where the van is located. He removes some of the snow that has collected on it and is happy there isn't too much of it. Andy knows the process: you remove the license plates then the VIN number in front of the driver's seat located very close to the bottom of the windshield.

When he removes the front license plate, something pops into his memory, but he shrugs it off. As he is removing the rear plate he hollers, "Holy shit!"

Andy gets off his knees and walks toward the office. Entering, he hears the boss say, "You ready to get it moving so quick?"

"Boss, are you sure you want to get rid of that van?"

"Why wouldn't I want to get rid of it?"

"The FBI has been posting that plate around for almost two weeks now. You could go to jail for obstructing justice."

"What are you talking about?"

"Look, I work for you, but I'm not about to be involved with the feds. Call them and have them check the van out before you get in more trouble."

Andy's boss looks like he swallowed a lemon. "You're serious, right, you're not shitting me."

"Call them and see what happens. If it's nothing, nothing will happen. If it's what they are looking for, they'll be crawling all over this place like stink on shit."

"Go back to something else; I need to think about this."

Ten minutes later with a great deal of hesitation, Andy's boss calls the New York office of the FBI. He is first placed on hold, then a young lady's voice asks how they could be of help.

He tells her what is in his storage yard and for how long without his realizing it.

"Wait one minute, sir! I will have someone else speak with you."

An agent gets on the phone and asks enough questions to realize this is the van belonging to the man killed in Sturbridge, MA.

"We will have a team of agents at your office within the hour."

"I'll be waiting," he says and his imagination starts working overtime as to what is going to happen to him and his business. "Oh fuck!"

* * *

It took Lt. McNamara two and a half hours to get to Hartford because of the traffic. Normally he would expect to be there in two hours. He's glad he grabbed a quick lunch at a fast-food place on the way down. He arrives at the FBI location and enters the lobby.

A pretty young redhead asks, "Can I help you, sir?"

Jack shows her his credentials and says, "I have been invited by SA Alice Broadwell to do an interrogation this afternoon. Is she available?"

"SA Broadwell, along with the assistant director and the station chief agent, have gone to lunch. Is there anything I can get you while you wait?"

"Do you know when they will be returning?"

"Agent Broadwell said they should be back around two. She said someone would be coming that she was expecting. I assume that you are the one."

"Can you call her on her cell phone and advise her that I have arrived?"

"Yes, I would be more than happy to make the call."

The receptionist makes the call. As she speaks to SA Broadwell, she says, "Hold on, Agent Broadwell, I will transfer your call to the lobby phone for Lt. McNamara to speak with you."

Jack picks up the lobby phone, "Alice, when can I meet with Jerry Walsh?"

"I have it scheduled for 2:00. He will be brought down to the interrogation room and then you will be invited in."

"Is there anything special I should know?"

"Play this by ear, Jack. Doug and I would like you to join us for dinner tonight so we can compare notes. There is something else I want to discuss with you, but not over the phone. I assume you were planning to spend the night here."

"Yes, the chief directed me to stay the night."

"Good, then we won't have to rush dinner. I will be back to the offices after we finish lunch and chat with you when you are through. Have our receptionist make a reservation for you at the Holiday Inn we normally use here in Hartford."

"I'll do that, thanks, it saves me the trouble."

When Jack finishes speaking with Alice, he asks the receptionist to make him a reservation per Alice's instructions.

"I'll be more than happy to," she says, giving Jack a big smile.

Five minutes later, the receptionist hands Jack his reservation number with the address and phone number and directions to the Holiday Inn downtown.

*   *   *

Precisely at 2:00, an agent enters the lobby and asks, "Lt. McNamara?"

Jack stands and replies, "In the flesh."

The receptionist thinks his reply is funny and she smiles.

On the other hand, the agent escorting him acts like a robot.

The agent opens the interrogation room door and allows Jack to enter. "When you are finished, use the phone on the wall and I will come to escort you to the lobby."

Jack nods his understanding; he didn't want to waste any breath on Mr. Nice Guy!

Jerry Walsh is clothed in what appears to be typical prison garb. Only instead of the usual color orange, these are blue. Jerry is handcuffed to a chain that extends down to the floor and connected to a ring in the floor. His hair is messy and he could use a shave.

Jack pulls a chair out from the opposite end of the table. He sits and stares at Jerry without saying a word for five minutes.

When he speaks, Jack asks, "Were you told I would be coming in to talk with you?"

"The FBI said someone from Massachusetts would be coming. I didn't get a name."

Before he continues, Jack takes out a pocket-size tape recorder. He turns it on.

Jack speaks into the tape recorder. He gives his name, rank, and position on the Natick Police Department. It also gives the time of day and the date. He says before him is a Mr. Gerald Walsh from Barre, MA. Mr. Walsh is currently in custody of the FBI in Hartford, Connecticut. Mr. Walsh may be the provider of explosives to terrorists operating in New England.

"I was told you have been given your Miranda Rights and you understand them."

Jerry nods.

"The recorder is the latest technology, but cannot identify nods yet. Is that a yes or no?"

Very angry, Jerry shouts, "Yes, okay, this is all bullshit. I've spent most of the morning with a honcho FBI guy from Washington and some dizzy-ass broad out of Boston. What the fuck are you here for?"

"Did you have a lawyer present this morning?"

"No, I didn't, and I don't need one now!"

"Fine, then let's continue. What are the names of the bombers who created the explosions on Black Friday?"

"I don't know what you are talking about!"

"The explosives found in the car in Groton are being compared to those used in the bombings."

Jerry smiles and doesn't reply.

"Your former home in Barre blew up and the FBI said residue from that explosion is linked to the bombings on Black Friday and Christmas Eve."

Jerry continues to smile and remains mute.

Jack sits back in his chair and just observes. Jerry is relatively calm and doesn't seem to be phased by the questioning.

Jack uses a new tactic, "You know the Groton police found a body in the van that is listed in your name. Why did you kill her? The FBI plans to turn you back over to the Groton police to face a murder one charge, which could bring the death penalty."

That remark seems to have stirred something inside of Mr. Walsh.

"Why would they turn me over to Groton? They're accusing me of terrorism and homeland security violations. Seeing one dumb broad dead shouldn't be as big a deal as the picture they are painting."

"Maybe they think their evidence is circumstantial and her death will get a sure verdict. Either way, you're going to fry or take the lethal injection. Your only saving grace is going to help them and me get the bombers. You are petty cash to us, unless you become useful.

"Now what are the names of the bombers who created the terror on Black Friday and Christmas Eve?"

Jerry sits very still; however, Jack can sense he is boiling inside with anger.

Jack continues, "The FBI has located all of your financial assets, even the accounts in the Grand Cayman Island and the one in Switzerland."

This did the trick. "How the hell did they do that?"

"I'm not privy to their sources, but SA Broadwell told me this before I came down."

Of course Jack is baiting him and wants to see how he reacts to being vulnerable.

"I only know one name," Jerry says.

"What is the full name?"

"The only name I know is for the leader of the group. It is Ahmad."

"Sorry, that doesn't cut the mustard. We already know his name."

"That is all I can tell you."

Jack takes a moment to rethink his next statement. "Who pays for the explosives you provided and where do you obtain what you provided?"

Jerry doesn't say anything for a couple of minutes. "Now I want a lawyer."

Jack knows the interrogation is officially over until a lawyer is present. Jack turns off the recorder and calls Mr. Nice Guy telling him he is through.

Chapter Fifty-Six

A Sit-Down with Alice

Lt. McNamara is waiting in the lobby while the receptionist spends time trying to locate Alice in the building. When she finds which office Alice is in, she connects the lobby phone to that room.

"How did the interrogation go? I hope you got more out of him then we did," she says.

"Can we talk somewhere in private?" said Jack.

"Give me fifteen minutes to wind up what I am doing, and I will be down to pick you up."

* * *

"I spent an hour and a half with him. At first it was like talking to a wall. Then I tried a few different tactics."

"Like what?"

"I told him the FBI was going to turn him over to the Groton police because their case against him was unbeatable whereas yours is circumstantial." Jack continues, "I let him know unless he was useful to us, he was going to get a death sentence."

"And?"

"It shook him a little, but not as much as he shook when I said you've tied up all of his financial assets."

"We haven't made all those connections yet?"

"I figured that he doesn't know I was bluffing!"

"What else?"

"He says he only knew Ahmad's name, I'm sure he's telling the truth. What happened next is the important issue."

"Yes, you're teasing me bit by bit."

"I told him we already knew Ahmad's whole name. Or at least the one he used on the credit card. Then I told him we wanted to know who paid him and where he got the explosives."

"What happened after that?"

"He demanded a lawyer!"

"Doug and I spent two hours with him this morning and he never hinted he wanted a lawyer."

"I think he is more afraid of us knowing his sources than he really is of us," said Jack.

"That is his Achilles' heel," remarks Alice. "It's nice to know you found it. Good work, Jack. Why don't you take some time to check into the Holiday Inn. Doug and I will pick you up for dinner."

Chapter Fifty-Seven

Dinner with the FBI

After checking in, Jack makes a couple of phone calls. The first one to Captain Green. When the captain comes on the line, Jack informs him the FBI is planning on taking him out to dinner. He would be staying over and he gives the captain the location of the Holiday Inn as well as its phone number and room number if he needs to speak with him.

Captain Green, being in a playful mood, says, "Going to dinner with your lady friend, Jack?"

"Captain, you and the chief are becoming a pair of ball busters."

Green laughs for a moment before continuing. "How did the interrogation go?"

"Fair, ask the chief to plan a meeting for the three of us at one tomorrow. By the way, Alice's boss will be along for dinner."

"I'm not worried about Alice, Jack. Watch out for old smooth tongue Risner. He is my worry. Risner may try to promise you the moon to get you to switch."

"I'm not changing. Remember, I want your job when you retire in two years."

The captain laughs, having forgotten he told Jack about his retiring.

*   *   *

The second call is to Jennifer. She answers her phone when it is transferred to her, but she is very busy and he makes it quick.

"I'll be back in the station tomorrow at noon. Let's plan dinner tomorrow night."

Quickly she says, "I'll cook at your place. I have something special in mind."

"Great, love you!"

"I love you, too!"

*   *   *

As the FBI are working to solve the bombing problems created by Ahmad and his men, Ahmad goes about changing his strategy in his surveillance methods on the New York subway systems. His men will only make trial runs at night when they will actually be planting their explosives and they will rotate every week so all of them will be familiar with each and every run. Martin Luther King Day is close and after that they will have five more weeks to prepare.

*   *   *

The phone rings in Jack's room. "Hello."

"Jack, Doug and I will arrive at the Holiday Inn at 6:30. Meet us in the lobby with an overcoat. We are going to have dinner elsewhere."

Jack looks at his watch. He has another hour before they arrive. "Fine." He hangs up his receiver.

*   *   *

At 6:25 Jack is standing in the lobby with his overcoat over his arm. He browses the pamphlets left in the lobby for local tourist attractions.

As he is reading one in particular, Alice walks up to him. "Doug is waiting outside in the car. Are you ready to go?"

"Ready and hungry. It's been a long and tiring day."

When they get to the car, Doug asks, "Do you like seafood?"

"Are you kidding? Being raised in New England, I love it."

"Good, we have a great chowder house not far from here and the booths will give us plenty of privacy."

"You're the driver," says Jack.

In front of the chowder house, Doug drops off Alice and Jack. The two of them walk inside as he proceeds to park the car.

Inside Alice walks up to the podium near the door for the hostess on duty. "We have a reservation for three. The third member is parking the car."

"Name please!"

"Alice Broadwell"

"Checking the list, yes, I have you right here. Please follow me."

She smiles and begins to select three dinner menus for them. A moment later, Doug walks through the front door and sees Alice and Jack following the hostess. He joins the procession.

As they get seated, Doug and Alice on one side and Jack across from them. The hostess hands out the menus and advises them that Grace will be their waitress.

Jack nods while Alice and Doug have already buried their faces into their menus.

Doug says, "Their clam chowder is absolutely out of this world. If you like chowder, you should try it."

"Thank you, I'll keep that in mind."

Grace appears before them and asks if they would like to order cocktails. The three of them order their own personal choices. "I will be back with water momentarily."

While they are deciding what to order, Grace appears with water and their drinks. "I will give you some time to make up your minds." She leaves to attend another table.

The three decide they've made up their minds, Doug flags Grace and she comes to the table to take their orders.

Alice orders a cup of chowder and the baked trout, Doug orders a bowl of the chowder and the same entrée that Alice ordered. Jack orders a cup of chowder; Jack likes to watch his calories. His entrée will be shrimp stir-fry.

After Grace departs, Doug said, "Alice gave me a heads-up on your interrogation of Jerry Walsh. It appears that you struck some nerves with him. Do you think those will be door openers for us?"

"Look, Doug, I appreciate the invite to interrogate Jerry and the dinner this evening. What I really want is for the bureau to let Natick have him as an accessory to Black Friday and Christmas Eve."

"You don't think the FBI can satisfy the homeland security issues we are dealing with on Mr. Walsh."

"Since you put it that way, I think Groton has a better case than the bureau does. They have a murder one warrant out for his ass. Right now they are fighting in the courts to get custody of him."

Doug replies, "Well, if you feel Groton has a better case, why do you feel Natick deserves him?"

"Because in Massachusetts he will not get the death penalty for what he has done. He'll get life without parole. I really don't give a shit about him. However, I do feel if I can get my hands on him, I'll find our real killers."

While the two men are going at it, Alice signals Grace to get everyone a second round.

Grace delivers the drinks to the table saying "Your chowder will be out momentarily."

Eating their chowder slows down the conversation. Doug is developing a greater desire to have Jack within the FBI.

Just as they finish their chowders, Doug says, "Jack, I like your style. I am asking you to join the bureau. With your current credentials and experience, you would not be starting at the bottom. Yes, you would have to go through the academy, but that is only procedure. What do you think?"

Just then their entrees arrive and Jack has a minute or two reprieve.

"Doug, to be honest with you, my captain is retiring in two years. Our chief and he want me to fill that position. At some point the chief is going to retire and I expect to fill that role."

Doug and Alice don't know what to say. "We didn't know you had those aspirations," says Alice.

"You call them aspirations, that is exactly what you are offering me. I feel I can be more effective as a leader than a number. I plan to stay in Natick."

The remainder of dinner was a little cool but pleasant. Jack knows that Alice should realize she cannot get her claws into him.

When the three completed their meals, Doug says, "Anyone for dessert?"

All three declined.

While the table was being cleared and coffee was served. Jack says, "I hope you can understand where I and my department are coming from. We are out to get these guys come hell or high water."

Doug smiles and says, "Jack, it is written all over your face and your performance in the interrogation room. That is why I want you on my team."

Now Jack drops the bomb on Alice, "I realize my potential, but my career is only part of my life. I have a fiancée and we are going to be married later this year. I want more than work out of life."

Doug and Alice look at each other, realizing they have totally misjudged Jack.

Jack continues, "When will I know what the bureau decides about Walsh?"

Alice, feeling left out of all of this, says, "We'll let you know."

Jack sees the resentment in her eyes that he is in love with another woman.

Doug says, "I'll call you in a week. Is that okay? I have to talk to the director first."

"Fine with me, I understand the chain of command," said Jack.

Doug puts the tab on his American Express credit card and the three of them walk out to the parking lot.

Arriving at the Holiday Inn, each says a polite good night to each other.

Jack hopes that Alice's dashed dreams of a romantic relationship with him are over. He also hopes she will not be vindictive. She doesn't realize he now has an in with Doug who is her boss. Score an A+ for him.

Chapter Fifty-Eight

Meeting with the Chief
and the Captain

Lt. McNamara leaves the parking lot of the Holiday Inn in Hartford, Connecticut, at 9:30. He waits until most of the morning commuters are at their work locations. His breakfast was on the light side. His reasoning is he wants to have an early lunch at Rein's Deli in Vernon, Connecticut. He's had their sandwiches years ago, and the memory of how good they are is hard to forget.

*   *   *

At 10:30, Jack pulls into the parking lot of Rein's Deli. Most of the breakfast crowd wouldn't be there and it is early for a lunch crowd. Most of those eating at this hour are travelers heading north or south on Route 84.

Inside he sees there are only three people waiting in line to be seated. He could have selected a stool at the counter, but with the long drive ahead of him, he prefers the comfort of a table and chair.

Within minutes he is seated at a table alongside the far wall in the restaurant. A dish of two kosher-style pickles is placed in front of him along with a menu.

Jack reviews the menu and it appears that nothing has changed on it since he was last here. When the waitress appears, he orders a hot pastrami sandwich on rye with mustard and a side order of their delicious potato salad.

"Would you like some coffee with your meal or something else to drink?" she asks.

"Regular coffee would be fine."

As Jack is waiting for his food, he runs over everything from this trip in his mind. He also notices how many people glance over to take note of who he is. Their thoughts are that he is probably another traveling salesman just passing through. Well, in a way he is. Jack takes his first bite of one of the pickles. "God, these are good!" he quietly states.

The waitress arrives with his meal and he smiles, seeing the sandwich is as large as he remembers from the past. *Hmmm, this is going to be good.*

When the waitress brings his coffee she asks, "Will there be anything else?"

"Please bring me the bill so I can pay at the counter. Your tip will be on my credit card."

She smiles and walks off.

In half an hour, Jack is back on the road heading for Natick.

* * *

Just before 12:30, Jack pulls into the station's parking lot. He knows he will have messages waiting for him. At least he will have time to prioritize them before his meeting at 1:00.

* * *

Five minutes to one, Jack heads toward the chief's office. He meets Captain Green, heading in the same direction.

Captain Green asks, "How did dinner go last night?"

"Hold off a minute because I want you and the chief to hear how dinner went besides the interrogation."

"Now you're busting my balls, Lieutenant?"

"Oh, I wouldn't do that, would I?"

Green smiles and pats Jack on the back, "Touché."

* * *

The chief is on the phone as they enter and take seats without making any disturbance so he is not interrupted in his conversation.

When the chief gets off the phone he says, "Well, how was your night in Connecticut on the taxpayers' expense?"

"The taxpayer only has to pay for one night in a Holiday Inn. The FBI picked up my dinner last night and I paid for my breakfast and lunch today."

"I am tempted to ask you if your girlfriend at the FBI paid for dinner, but I think I've teased you enough about that."

"After last night, she and her boss know where I am coming from. I'm not saying he won't try again, but I know she won't."

Captain Green says, "Jack, now you're being a ball buster, and are leaving us hanging in mid-air?"

Jack smiles. He loves it!

"The assistant director made me a very nice offer to switch to the FBI. I made it quite clear I was planning on staying in the Natick PD. As far as my girlfriend is concerned, I announced I am getting married later this year. I saw fire in her eyes. However, Risner likes me and she won't be a problem. If she becomes one, I will tell him."

The chief says, "You think he likes you that much?"

"I think he likes the way I operate and inside or outside of the FBI. I could be an asset that will pay off for him somewhere down the road."

Chief replies, "Now, you talking like a politician."

"No, I really hate politics, but I know what must be said and done to get things accomplished."

Both Captain Green and Chief Winters smile as they know he has a future in the department.

"Now tell us about the interrogation, that is why you really went down there," says Captain Green.

* * *

Jack creates the scene where he and Jerry Walsh sparred together. Jack said, "The interrogation was a fair episode, but information in a couple of ways." He made a big point that Walsh acts like you're talking to the wall. He likes to play the tough role.

"Walsh acts like he thinks the feds will protect him from a murder rap in Connecticut. I let him think he may be on shaky ground there. The feds right now have a circumstantial case against him. Groton has a solid murder one case."

The chief asks, "Do we think we can get him up here?"

"Chief, that was exactly my idea. I told him we will ask the courts to have him booked as an accessory to the Black Friday bombings and the Christmas Eve bombing and shootings. This way he would get life the most in Massachusetts."

Jack continues, "I also told him the FBI had seized access to all of his financial assets. I saw him get nervous there."

"Do they really?" asks the captain.

"No, I learned at dinner they haven't connected all of his dots yet, however, Doug says they will continue the charade."

"The big thing that really shook him was I told them we and the FBI want to know his sources and how he obtains explosives and weapons. He didn't like that at all. I don't know, maybe it's some kind of code they operate with that you never divulge that information."

Captain Green replies, "Or that makes you a marked man in or out of jail."

"Might be," says Jack. "He sure was uncomfortable when I brought that up."

"What happened next?" says the chief.

"He lawyered up and I shut off my recorder."

"Nice work. Jack, Captain, notify the FBI in Hartford we are proceeding to take custody of Jerry Walsh as an accessory to our holiday traumas. Then contact our department attorney so they can work with the attorney general's office."

"Nice work, Jack."

The captain and lieutenant leave.

Chapter Fifty-Nine

Sturbridge Vehicle

A pair of FBI agents left the towing garage yesterday giving explicit instructions to the owner that nothing was to happen to the vehicle picked up in Queens. They told him a flat-top will arrive tomorrow to remove the vehicle. They left around four in the afternoon.

*   *   *

The following morning while Lt. McNamara is driving back to Natick, the FBI tow vehicle arrives to remove the van. Along with the flat-top is another pair of agents. They begin to question the owner regarding all of the pertinent information about where in Queens was the vehicle picked up, what time of day, what level of the garage it was on, and other details.

When they are through, they insist he come with them to verify the information he provided when they visit the site.

"Don't you think it would be a better choice if the driver of my tow rig went instead of me," he asks. "I'm not refusing to go, but I have no clue of what to verify other than what I have on my pickup ticket."

The older man looks at his partner and says, "I guess you're right, that would be better. Where is your man?"

The owner calls out to his secretary, "Tammy, get Sam on the horn and find out when he can be back here ASAP."

While Tammy is trying to locate and communicate with Sam, the agents wander around the small lobby.

Tammy gets up to give the owner Sam's reply.

"Gentlemen, my driver said without a snarl in traffic he could be here in forty-five minutes. He just loaded a car on his rig and will head right in. There's a good coffee shop up the street if you guys want a break."

The two agents nod and say they will return.

*   *   *

Lt. McNamara is sitting at his desk, sorting out his messages, after meeting with the chief and the captain. There is a knock on his door post. Looking up he sees Lt. Mike Richards.

"Mike, how is it going?"

"I'm meeting with the department's therapist once a week. So far I'm comfortable with it. I have a feeling that she wants to discuss my military experience as well as the Christmas Eve shooting." Mike sits down.

"Do you have a problem with that, Mike?"

"I'm not sure yet."

"Look, take it slow with her. She and the department want you back on your feet."

"Yeah, I guess so! Look, if I need to talk to someone besides the therapist, can we talk?"

"Mike, we can always talk. Let me know when you want to get together."

Mike rises and says, "Thanks, Jack!"

*   *   *

Forty-five minutes on the dot, the two FBI agents who took a coffee break re-enter the towing garage.

"Is your man back yet?" says the senior agent.

"He called in five minutes ago, said he is stuck on the Cross Bronx Parkway in traffic up to his ears. He figures another half an hour."

The younger agent says, "We'll wait!"

It's too damn cold to wait outside so they sit in the uncomfortable chairs along the window and thumb through magazines.

True to his word, Sam pulls his truck into the yard a half hour later.

"He's here now," says the owner. "Do you want me to introduce you two?"

"No, we'll handle it," said the younger agent.

"Picky, picky, picky," remarks the owner as they walk out the door.

Tammy his secretary replies, "I guess if your job was boring like theirs seems to be, you probably would be in the same mood. Look at us, we don't have to wait around. We always have something to do."

As Sam is backing the truck, with the towed vehicle on it, into a space on the lot, the two agents walk over to him.

"Sam, we need some of your time and your boss has okayed it. Feel free to double-check with him," remarks the senior agent.

Once Sam drops the vehicle he brought into the yard, he heads for the office.

Inside, "Did you sic those two feds on me?"

"Sure did, I didn't want to deal with those stuffed shirts."

"What do you want me to tell them?"

"Answer all of the questions they throw at you about the vehicle you brought in from the Queens parking garage."

When Sam goes outside, the agents suggest the three of them ride in the bureau car to the parking garage.

* * *

After spending an hour with Sam, they realize that they are no further ahead than they were before. The agents drop Sam off at the garage and head toward their office.

Chapter Sixty

Home with Jennifer

Around four in the afternoon, Lt. McNamara calls Jennifer at work. "Honey, I have a lot of messages I need to go through and phone calls to return. I don't expect to be home before seven."

"Jack, that works out fine, I cannot leave before five and it will take me at least a half hour to get to your place. I'll need time to prepare what I want to plan for dinner so take your time. If you are later than fifteen minutes after seven, give me a call so I can keep everything warm."

"Thanks for understanding; I have a lot to share with you tonight."

"Oh, this sounds interesting, you run off to Connecticut, then you want to share things with me."

"Jenn, you will like what I have to say. Oh, by the way we should do a couple of things tonight."

"Like what?"

"Like pick a definite wedding date and to get away for the President's Weekend to New York. Nothing happened on New Year's Eve like everyone expected, and if Martin Luther King Day goes by without a hitch, maybe the bombers have left New England."

Jennifer hangs up her phone. *Setting a wedding date tonight would be fun and scary too after working here and seeing so many marriages fall apart.*

* * *

At six fifteen Jack closes his office door and heads down to the parking lot. He has a department vehicle and he had it serviced while he went to Connecticut. Walking toward the garage, he calls out to the lead mechanic on the afternoon shift,

"Wally, has my vehicle been serviced?"

"We did what you asked for, Lieutenant; however, there are some other items you need to have addressed very soon."

"Okay, make a list for me and leave it at the desk. I'll pick it up in the morning."

"You got it, Jack."

Jack smiles. He and Wally have teased each other for all of the years he has been on the force. Wally is a good man besides being a good mechanic.

Jack pulls his vehicle out of the lot and heads for home.

Thinking to himself, Jack figures he will arrive there at seven.

* * *

Pulling up in front of his condo, Jack parks his car and walks toward the front door. Taking his keys from his pocket as he usually does, he prepares to open the door.

Before he can get it open, Jennifer is standing there in a beautifully decorated Mexican senorita's outfit and a rose in her mouth.

"I guess we're having Mexican tonight!"

Jennifer takes the rose out of her mouth and says, "You could have at least offered to kiss me when you saw me in this outfit!"

Jack grabs her, lifts her off her feet, and gives her a very passionate kiss.

"Keep that up and dinner is going to burn."

They both start laughing!

"So are we going to have Mexican food tonight?"

"Not just Mexican, but homemade Mexican. We are going to have albondigas, rice with turmeric, refried beans, and guacamole. I made the albondigas, added turmeric to the rice so it doesn't look anemic. I did refry the beans and I purchased the guacamole."

"I'm with you on everything except the albondigas. What the heck is that?"

"Albondigas are Mexican-style meat balls. I haven't made them for years and I wanted something special for tonight.

"Let me tend to finishing up with everything on the stove and in the oven. There is a glass of SKYY in the freezer for you. I don't want a drink until after dinner and we talk. I want my head to be clear for what you requested today."

Jack headed for the refrigerator and wondered what he said today that she doesn't want a drink until after dinner.

*　*　*

Fifteen minutes later, the two of them are seated and having dinner.

"My God, these meatballs are fantastic."

"I made them with hamburger since you are a meat eater. I've also made them with ground turkey for when my family visits as I try to watch how many calories my dad eats."

"Has he noticed any difference or did you tell him what you did."

"Nope, it's my secret. I did tell my mother. So what happened on your trip?"

Jack starts off by telling her the FBI asked that he make the trip. He inserts Captain Green's warning about the assistant director, who has already made an offer to Jack to come on board with the FBI.

"Let me take things in the order they happened." Jack notices she is anxious!

He explains what developed with the interrogation. "Chief Winters told me I did a good job this afternoon when we met."

Then he tells her about the dinner with Doug and Alice.

Jack and Alice had met before they went out to dinner and she knew what he learned in the interrogation. What he sensed from Jerry Walsh made the AD realize how good he is at his job. They made him a unique offer to join the FBI. This was exactly what Captain Green warned him about.

"Are you going to change jobs?"

"No, I set the record straight. I am staying with the Natick PD. I expect to receive Captain Green's position in two years and who knows, maybe I'll become chief. Then I, added, I am getting married later this year and I want more out of life than a job."

"How did that go over?"

"Like a fart in church."

Jennifer, on pins and needles, busts out laughing.

"Jennifer, what is wrong? You appear very anxious tonight."

"I am feeling that way. You asked to set a wedding date tonight and I'm seeing all of these clients coming in looking to get divorced, it makes me nervous."

"Look, you cooked and I'll clean up. Why don't you relax and sit in the living room. We can always talk about setting a wedding date another time. I didn't mean to make you anxious.

"I would like to plan a weekend getaway to New York if you are up to it."

"When?"

"I'd like to do it President's Weekend if you can get off."

"Done, I would like that too! The office will be closed that Monday and we can have a three-day weekend."

"Would you like your drink now?"

"Yes, and bring me the rose again. I want to make sure I didn't purchase a dud."

Chapter Sixty-One

FBI Report

At 6:00 in the morning, Lt. McNamara gets a call from his captain. "Be in the station at 7:30. The chief has a report from the FBI on the vehicle they took from the Queen's towing garage. We have a lot to talk about."

Jack left his condo at 7:00. Without too much traffic, he should be at the station at 7:25.

Entering the police station, Jack remembers to pick up Wally's to-do list for his department vehicle. He glances at it and says, "Holy shit."

Jack is glad he doesn't have to pick up the tab for all of these repairs. He'll schedule something with Wally.

Dropping his briefcase into his office, he heads for the chief's office and arrives exactly at 7:30.

"Boy, you timed that right," says the chief. Captain Green is sitting across from the chief with a smile on his face.

"What is all of the urgency?"

"The van the FBI picked up in New York is definitely the one that was stolen in Sturbridge and the owner found dead nearby. Prints of the owner and the same prints from three terrorists were found in the vehicle dumped in Sturbridge.

"Right now the bureau doesn't have a clue what to do next. They are uncomfortable with this situation. They are looking for help."

Captain Green picks up the conversation, "What are they looking for from us?"

"They're fishing and hoping we will come up with something."

"Like what?" remarks Jack.

"Look, they have a vehicle that was parked in Queens right after Christmas. We all know there were a dozen shooters here on Black Friday. Anyone with half a brain in the bureau should put two and two together, and see they are meeting up with the second half of their group," Jack continued.

"They've got that figured out, but where do they spend their resources?"

The captain joins the conversation. "It would be an impossible task to canvass Queens looking for these guys. If we were the terrorists, where would we be planning on doing our next bombing?"

The chief says, "I believe with all of the publicity for New Year's Eve, they decided that wasn't a good choice. They might try to do something on Martin Luther King Day, or they may just split town and head somewhere else."

"Or they may hit on President's Day," replies Jack.

The two men look at him. "Are you serious, where would they hit?"

"If you ask me, I'd say they want everyone's guard to be down. If I was planning this I would hit the subways around dinnertime when people are traveling back and forth."

"Do you have a crystal ball or something, Jack?"

"No, you asked if I were doing this, what would I do."

"I see, I guess you also have a criminal mind."

"It helps in this business!"

*   *   *

After a few minutes of quiet contemplation, the chief goes on, "What should we tell the FBI?"

Captain Green says, "Tell them about the President's Day scenario if nothing happens on Martin Luther King Day."

The chief continues, "I know the mayor and the governor are planning more security around Manhattan, but not to the extent they did New Year's Eve."

"That is a typical conclusion," remarks Jack.

"Are you saying they are wrong, Jack?" asks the chief.

"Look we all look at things differently. We are also all human. Shit can happen with the best of plans."

The chief smiles! "Okay, I will call the AD and tell him what we think."

"Captain, have you approached the department lawyer to contact the AG regarding Jerry Walsh?"

"That was accomplished yesterday after our meeting."

"Good."

"Anything else from you, Jack?"

*   *   *

"Yes, something happened in my personal life that I need you to be aware of."

"What, is Jennifer okay?" asks the chief.

"Yes, she is okay. When I got home last night she had a beautiful dinner cooked and we had an enjoyable evening. I told her I was hoping we could set a wedding date for later this year. She seemed anxious and wouldn't have a drink until after we talked. It seems working in a law firm that deals with divorce cases has caused her to be concerned about the longevity of marriages today."

Captain Green speaks out, "She wouldn't think that you might step out on her, would she?"

"She never brought that up!"

"I need to know if the comments of Alice Broadwell being my girlfriend go beyond the three of us."

The chief and the captain look at each other. "No, this was just in fun, Jack. You know male humor," remarks the chief.

"That is what I missed, that it was privy to us three. My concern is that when we have department functions inviting wives and girlfriends, with a few drinks under your belts, you two may forget yourselves."

Both men assured Jack that would never happen.

"I'm okay with that so long is it doesn't happen. If for some reason should it ever happen, you will receive my resignation the next day."

Jack rises and shakes both men's hand to relieve some of the tension he just brought up. "Thank you for listening."

After Jack leaves, the chief says, "He really loves her, doesn't he?"

"Yes," replies the captain. "They are good for each other."

Chapter Sixty-Two

Preparing for MLK Day

The mayor of New York City and the governor of the State of New York have just concluded their third meeting regarding security for Martin Luther King Day in Manhattan.

The press has put them through a wringer because of all of the stringent security they had on New Year's Eve. They spent all of that money, and nothing happened, which proved their intelligence is the luck of the draw. Both men will suffer in the next elections.

The two men agreed to have the full force of the local police departments and the state would provide a large contingent of state troopers. There would be no National Guard units, although some units would be on an alert status. Both men are also hoping and praying that nothing will happen, because the media will not remember their complaints about too much money. They will only talk about the blood and guts that might get spilled.

Today, is Thursday, Martin Luther King Day is Monday.

*　*　*

Local media is announcing that there will be security but not as tight as New Year's Eve so that the citizens can feel more comfortable.

Hearing this, the mayor and the governor wonder how they received this information so quickly, and wish who ever offered it would learn to keep their mouths shut.

*   *   *

On the other hand the FBI is taking a different approach. They are announcing to the public they found the van parked in a garage in Queens, it was stolen from a man in Sturbridge, Massachusetts, after he was murdered. They are suggesting to people to be on the lookout for anything suspicious. Photographs of the three terrorists are being broadcast daily with a great deal of frequency.

*   *   *

Ahmad knows the city and its citizens are running in fear. He makes changes to his plans. There are five more weeks to go to President's Day. He wants each of his men to wear their fanny packs on a daily basis. They can be empty or merely loaded with trinkets. He wants the local metro police to be lulled into accepting the fanny packs as an everyday thing.

Chapter Sixty-Three

Martin Luther King Day

The sun is shining and the temperature is lingering around the high thirties at noontime. The parade is due to begin at 2:00 and the local police and state troopers are beginning to take assigned positions along the parade route to ensure the safety of the public.

*   *   *

At Battery Park, organizations and bands planning to march in the parade are starting to assemble at 1:30. As they do, citizens are amassing along the parade route to commemorate the achievements Martin Luther King accomplished in his short lifetime. The parade will enter Broadway from the Battery and march along Broadway up to Fortieth Street. From there they will turn onto the Avenue of the Americas, where they will head up to Central Park. At Fifty-seventh Street, they will enter the southern entrance of Central Park where the dignitaries will make their speeches.

At the front of the parade are large numbers of members from five black Christian congregations in the New York area. They will be marching across the streets arm in arm as Martin Luther King and his followers did so many times years ago.

Following the marchers are seven high school and college bands coming from the New York area. Behind the bands are the dignitaries riding in limousines, waving at those who come out to see the parade.

The parade begins at 2:00 p.m. and everyone should arrive at Central Park for the presentations by 4:00.

*   *   *

Ahmad and his men are watching everything on television. They notice the lower amount of security put forth for this event.

Ahmad says, "Either they believe we left the area or they feel we will not attack for some reason."

After watching the parade for the full two hours, Ahmad knows how he will handle the attacks on President's Day. He feels exhilarated that they will have one more opportunity to strike at the Great Satan.

Meanwhile his men are beginning to feel bored at being cooped up for so long and tired of the propaganda that Ahmad dishes out every dinnertime. Each member will be happy to go back to his own sleeper cell when this is over.

Tomorrow Ahmad has to text his superiors and explain to them why he is delaying the third strike for another five weeks. By the message he received, he knows they are not happy with his change of plans.

Chapter Sixty-Four

Day After MLK Day

The next day Lt. McNamara is seated in front of his captain. "Did you watch the Martin Luther King parade yesterday in New York?" asks Jack.

"No, Jack, I had more pressing things to do. What did you learn from it?"

"Captain, it is just my gut feeling. I think New York is being lulled into a false sense of security."

"Why, what grounds do you have to make that conclusion?"

"That's the problem. I have none, but something is going to go down."

"Look, Jack, we can't police the whole world. We are only responsible for Natick."

"Yeah, I know. This is not over. Mark my words."

Jack rises from his chair and leaves the captain's office.

* * *

Arriving back at his office, Lt. McNamara sees Lt. Mike Richards waiting for him.

"Hi, Mike, come in and take a load off."

"Thanks, Jack, I was wondering if you could spend some time with me today?"

"How much time?"

"I guess an hour should be enough."

Looking at his schedule, Jack says, "Do you want to meet in the station or somewhere else?"

Mike thinks about that a moment and decides, "Your office will be fine for me."

"Mike, let's do 3:30 to 4:30. If we run a little over, that's okay."

Lt. Richards rises and extends his hand to shake with Jack. "Thanks, right now, you're the only friend I feel I have."

Mike departs and Jack says to himself, *Shit, this is going to get complicated.*

*   *   *

A half hour later, Captain Green knocks on Lt. McNamara's open door case.

Jack looks up. "What's up, Captain?"

"The chief just spoke with me and it seems that Connecticut is willing to concede on us bringing Jerry Walsh to trial and agrees we should have first priority."

"Wow, they didn't offer much resistance, did they?"

"No, I think the Connecticut state house got involved somehow and there are members of their government who had relatives die on Black Friday."

"Connecticut does want to have the option on Mr. Walsh in case we don't receive a good verdict."

"That's fair! Now what do you want me to do?"

"I want you to put together a two-man team to pick up Walsh as soon as you can. I don't want anyone changing their minds."

"I'll work on it as soon as you walk out of here. Oh, there's one thing you need to know."

"What's that?"

"Lt. Richards has asked me to be a confidant along with his therapy sessions. We will be meeting at 3:30 here in my office."

"Jack, I don't want a word-for-word report on Mike. Just if you feel he might not be able to perform his duties, let me know so I can get a report from the therapist."

"Fair enough!"

The captain leaves and Jack picks up his phone. He dials Detective Sergeant Alan Singer's phone.

"Singer, what can I do for you?"

"Alan, where are you right now?"

"I'm about a half hour from the station."

"Can you break away or are you working on something hot?"

"It can wait, Lieutenant. I'll be there as soon as I can."

"See you then," says Jack.

* * *

In forty minutes Detective Singer is knocking on the open-door case of Lt. McNamara's office.

"Have a seat, Sergeant!"

Alan looks across the desk at Jack and wonders what the hell is going on now.

"The department has filed to have the explosives man, who is sitting in a cell at the FBI office in Hartford, to be brought back to Natick to stand trial. We are going to take possession of him. I want you and someone else of your choosing to go and pick him up tomorrow."

"Who is going to file all of the necessary paperwork to transfer him up here? I hate that part."

"I will take care of that this afternoon. Who would you like to travel with you? It is only a couple hours down and a couple back. No stopping on the way. I don't want to create a scene."

"I hear you. You mean, like the last time we transported a prisoner?"

"Let's not go into that, all right."

"I want Henry Kostovich to go with me."

"Fine. Contact Henry and tell him that he is being assigned to work with you for one day. Have him meet you here around eight in the morning. The two of you should be back here by three in the afternoon. I want you to take a department vehicle with a screen between the seats, got it?"

"Where will the paperwork be for us to pick him up, including the address that we need?"

"The desk sergeant will have everything for you. I will call once you are on your way so they know to expect you."

"Sounds fair to me. Where are we going to dump him?"

"I need to go over that with the captain later today, and I will tell you when you check in leaving Hartford."

Chapter Sixty-Five

Three-Thirty the Same Day

At three-thirty, Lt. Richards has not shown up. Jack continues to work on paperwork.

At three-forty, Lt. Richards walks through the door. "Sorry, I'm late, I got tied up."

Mike sits in a chair across from Jack.

"Mike, why don't you close the door before we begin."

"Oh yeah, good idea!" Mike gets up and closes the door.

When Mike is seated, he merely looks at Jack without saying a word.

Jack allows a minute to pass by then goes on, "Mike, you wanted time to talk together. Something must be on your mind that is bothering you. I cannot help you if you don't open up to me."

"Maybe this isn't a good idea!" the lieutenant begins to get out of his chair.

Jack takes the bull by the horns and says, "Is this what you do to your therapist?"

"What has she told you?"

"Mike, I don't even know who she is, but you are not helping yourself handling things this way."

Mike sits back down. "It's hard, Jack. It hurts!"

"Whatever you are going through must hurt like hell, Mike. Not dealing with it is only going to allow it to fester more."

Tears begin to streak down Mike's face. "Iraq, my divorce, and seeing those people killed at the church, when will it all end, Jack?"

"What have you been able to discuss with your therapist?"

"We talk about my divorce and the church bombings. She gives me the impression those are my troubling circumstances."

"Is she right, Mike?"

"Only partly. What happened in Iraq is still tearing me apart inside."

"Are you willing to tell her that she only sees part of the picture?"

"I think so!"

"Look, Mike, you have a fine record with the department. What is affecting you is not fair to you and to the department. You and your therapist can work this out."

"I don't want anyone to say I have PTSD."

"Why, because too many people have labeled it a mental illness? Do you realize that everyone walking the street has some level of PTSD in their lives? You don't have to go into combat to get that. Combat may bring it on more severely. Besides, it is not a mental illness. The government is using that term for their own political agenda."

"What do you think I should do, Jack?"

"I believe we have already covered that area and now it is time for you to make a decision."

"What decision, Jack?"

"Think about it and let's talk again before your next therapy session."

"You really want to talk with me again?"

"Why not, you've been a friend of mine for six years. Let's start using that friendship time to work together to help you heal."

Mike looks at the clock, "It's almost four-thirty. I've stayed my time."

"Call me, Mike, and let me know well in advance of your session so we can meet again."

"Okay, Jack, I promise."

$$* \quad * \quad *$$

For the first time in weeks, Ahmad announces he will be going out for a short while. He has a phone call to make and wants a breath of fresh air before he begins.

He no sooner walks out the door when the rumors start amongst the men about who he is going to call and what they should expect.

Ahmad walks down to the parking garage where he dropped off the vehicle they had picked up in Massachusetts. He heads up to the top level and opens his cell. Dialing a special number that will send a signal to Switzerland and bounce another to Iran, he waits for someone to answer. The phone rings six times before someone answers.

The imam answering says, "Why are you calling?"

"I think I have misunderstood the email I received earlier today. It sounds to me that you are dissatisfied with our mission."

The imam hesitates because he knows Ahmad has correctly acknowledged the intent of the message.

"Let us say, we were expecting quicker results from you!"

"We have law enforcement chasing us from three states and there is a nationwide alert for us with three of our pictures on the nightly news. I have one more mission to accomplish in five weeks and then we will be done."

"Let us hope that Allah makes the last one successful."

"Our first two missions were successful, were they not?"

There is a delay before the imam answers and no matter what the response is, Ahmad knows he is in trouble.

"Of course, of course," says the imam.

The phone line goes dead in Iran and Ahmad stands against the outside wall overlooking the area of Queens lit up by the household lights.

He shuts off his phone. Ten minutes later, he leaves the parking garage and walks back to the house.

*   *   *

When the phone call ends in Iran, the imam Ahmad spoke with places a call to the senior mullah of the mosque.

Chapter Sixty-Six

Inside Iran

The senior mullah returns the phone call from the imam. He advises him to meet him in his office in an hour. "We need to discuss how we are going to close this out," says the mullah. The imam is wondering what the mullah means by closing this out.

*   *   *

Ahmad walks back to the house wondering why the religious leaders cannot comprehend the real world. His group is a small group trying to survive among those who seek to kill them or place them in prison.

He is tired of trying to carry this load alone. He will talk with Renza when he returns.

In ten minutes, he is at the front door and rings the bell. One of the men checks him out before opening.

Stepping inside he asks, "Where is Renza?"

"He went upstairs, let me get him!" replies the one who opened the door.

A moment later, Renza is walking down the stairs.

"You want me, Ahmad?"

"Yes, put on your coat. I would like you to walk with me."

The two men walk out the door. Both of them have their collars turned up as it is breezy as well as cold.

"What is going on, Ahmad? The way you left caused the men to become anxious about what is happening. Most of them have never been to a large city before and are uncomfortable being here. Never mind seeing their leader act out in a way that looks like he is becoming unglued."

"I received a text message this morning from Tehran. I was told, in no uncertain terms, they are unhappy that we have not completed our mission."

"I thought you had the authority to make those decisions."

"When I left Iran, that was the way it was to be."

"What changed? We have been successful so far. Yes, we lost a couple of men, but that is to be understood."

"They wouldn't say. However, I believe the capture of the munitions man has them rattled. They were the ones who set that up from the beginning. I think they are worried they will be traced from whatever he tells them."

"You told me he never knew of our plans."

"He was never told any of our plans. They are refusing to believe he doesn't know."

"We are going to proceed with our plans and then we will split up right afterward. Tomorrow, when you send out the men, I want you to stay back so you and I can agree on everything."

"I will do as you ask. Will you be all right when you return to Iran?"

"We will discuss that and all of our plans tomorrow."

*   *   *

The senior mullah and the imam who spoke with Ahmad are seated in the mullah's office. "Imam, we need to close this operation down. Somehow we need to connect with Ahmad and make him quit or terminate him. We must also work out a plan to eliminate the munitions man whom the police have captured."

"The munitions man I understand. Why Ahmad? Sure, they are running late on this project, but you gave him total liberty in doing it!"

The mullah is not pleased to be reminded of what he did. Those below his stature should not be criticizing him. "I have spoken with him today by messages, and I see he is running scared and that is dangerous."

"To him maybe, not to us!"

"Don't you understand, you fool, that if they are captured, it will cause a major international incident."

The imam realizes at this point he's said too much. He shuts his mouth and merely waits to be told what to do next.

*   *   *

Alan Singer and Henry Kostovich are on their way to Hartford to pick up a prisoner. They make a stop at Rein's Deli just off Exit 65 on Route 84. Both men enter, are given seats quickly, and it only take minutes to decide what they will have for lunch. With Jack issuing orders of not stopping for lunch with a prisoner, they at least want to have something in their stomachs before noontime.

Their meals are served quickly and both men are having hot pastrami sandwiches on rye with pickles and coleslaw. They are also drinking plenty of coffee.

Less than half hour later, they finish lunch, pay their bills, and leave for Hartford.

Henry says, "I hope Jack appreciates how fast we chowed down our lunches to accommodate his wishes."

"Let's say we threw down lunch so we wouldn't be starving going back. I doubt if the prisoner is going to get a take-out lunch bag."

"Yeah, you're right, Alan."

In another half an hour, they are in front of the FBI building.

*   *   *

Inside of the FBI building, each detective shows his credentials and Alan passes over the papers to transfer Jerry Walsh to the Natick police station. Alan hands over the transfer hardware that they want Jerry wearing. "Please make sure he hits the men's room before you turn him over," says Alan.

The two are invited to sit in an interrogation room while the bureau processes the necessary paperwork for them to have possession of Mr. Walsh.

A half hour later, the two detectives walk Jerry out to their vehicle. His wrists and ankles are shackled, which causes him to take short steps instead of a normal stride.

Once Jerry is seated reasonably comfortably, Alan and Henry enter the two front seats.

Henry is driving the first hour of their return trip. Alan is dialing Lt. McNamara's phone to find out where they are dropping off Jerry Walsh.

*   *   *

Lt. McNamara grabs his phone on the third ring. "Lt. McNamara, can I help you?"

"Lieutenant, we are leaving Hartford with Mr. Walsh in tow. Where do you want us to deliver him?"

"The powers to be want him placed in MCI Walpole."

Alan continues, "Isn't that for sentenced prisoners?"

"Normally, yes, it seems our chief has called in some markers to make it happen!"

"Do you have contact information so we can get entry when we get there?"

"Call me back when you hit Worcester. I will have everything you need by then."

"Thanks, Lieutenant, one of us will call you back."

*   *   *

Henry calls the lieutenant for the contact information after he and Alan switched drivers.

With the information in hand, they need to head out to Route 495 south to get near the Walpole prison.

It takes them another hour and a quarter after leaving Worcester. The first gate they drive up to, an armed guard approaches their vehicle and Alan gives him his ID and asks for the admissions secretary so they can drop off the prisoner.

The guard heads back to his booth and places a call.

Returning back to the car, the guard says, "Just pull over to the right and park your vehicle. They are sending a vehicle out so you can follow it to the area you will be turning him over."

"Thanks, we'll sit and wait for them," says Alan.

The whole process of bringing Jerry Walsh took another hour and the detectives were glad to have been relieved of his presence. Now they need to head north and pick up the Massachusetts Turnpike westbound to get back to their station house.

*   *   *

After turning in the cruiser, they walk into the front door leading to the detective's squad room. The sergeant at the front desk says, "Lt. McNamara wants to see you two as soon as you arrive."

Alan and Henry look at each other and shake their heads.

Knocking on the doorpost of the lieutenant's doorway, they enter his office.

"How did everything go?"

Henry begins, "It took more time than we expected at Walpole, but other than that, everything went as expected."

Alan continues, "Walsh never said boo the whole trip."

Jack says, "That doesn't surprise me. I know it's been a long day. Take off."

Chapter Sixty-Seven

Tehran Nervous

Right after noontime prayers, Imam Azim is headed over to the main office of the revolutionary guards. On instructions from his mullah, he will meet with the head of foreign activities.

The imam enters the front entrance way. He is greeted by a guard and another one pats him down for weapons. Once it is determined he has no weapons, he is allowed to enter the inner office.

The woman behind the desk asks who he is here to see. He gives her the name supplied by the mullah. "I will call his office and leave word with his secretary that you are here for your appointment. Take a seat while you are waiting."

Azim moves over to the waiting area. It is small with only six cushioned chairs. As he sits down, he realizes the chair is more comfortable than anything they have at the mosque.

The receptionist advises him, "You will have to wait at least fifteen minutes."

The imam nods his head as a sign of acceptance. He has no choice in the matter.

Twenty minutes later, an escort comes out to the reception area and takes the imam back to the office.

Inside the office is a small man who looks to be around fifty with a bald head. He wears wire rim glasses and seems to have a scowl on his face. He doesn't stand to greet him.

He doesn't even offer the imam a chair so the imam takes one on his own.

"Your mullah called yesterday and wants me to work out some operations with you. Why didn't he come here himself?"

"I cannot speak for his thoughts, sir. I only wish to ask your cooperation on this situation so that an international incident does not occur."

"What are the circumstances of this event as you call it?"

The imam goes on to tell him about how everything developed and where it is supposedly at for the moment.

When he is finished, the director says, "You religious, overzealous leaders keep doing this shit over and over again. When the hell are you going to learn that these types of operations take trained individuals. Individuals we could have supplied."

Director Adel shouts, "Go back to your mullah and tell him I will give it some thought. When I make my decision, I will get back to him. Or do I get back to you?"

"Either one of us will be adequate, sir."

"You can leave now. There is nothing else for us to discuss until I decide what I want to do."

*   *   *

Inside of the mosque, the imam advises the mullah about the meeting.

"When is he going to get back to us? It must be acted on immediately."

"He did not say. I suspect he needs to think how he will approach a solution so his operatives do not get caught."

Chapter Sixty-Eight

Ahmad and Renza Plan

After the last of the group leave to continue to do their surveillance work of the subway system, Ahmad says, "Let's pour some coffee and talk about what we are going to do." They sit at the kitchen table and begin.

"Are we still going to attack on President's Day?"

"Yes, but we need to make some changes."

"What kind of changes?" asks Renza.

"I have noticed you are keeping the men to a rotating weekly schedule. I want you to change that so it is not noticeable by anyone."

"Why?"

"Change always interferes with observation. I don't know if it will really affect anything, but I want you to work out a program for the men," says Ahmad.

"I am seeing the men getting restless with all of this waiting. I want you to break them up into pairs or small groups and get them out of the apartment for at least two hours a day, after their surveillance work. They are getting lax and sloppy."

"Is there someone or more than one that you are noticing this with?"

"Yes, Kazem and Marduh—the two that survived the church bombing with me. I cannot place a finger on what I feel, but they are making me feel uncomfortable. I want you to observe them as well. We will discuss our findings a week before the bombings to see if we need to address any issues," said Ahmad.

"Now, I want to know if anyone sensed the fact they were continuing to wear fanny packs on the trains and if it drew attention to them?"

"Ahmad, I have been sitting down with each of the men weekly. No one seems to find anything unusual in their surveillances."

"Okay, I am being extra cautious!"

"I understand, now what do you wish me to do with the rest of my day?"

"Take the day off and get rid of some of your own tensions. Be back here by three. I plan to get some rest while all of you are out."

"I will go into Manhattan and see some sights for myself," says Renza.

"Enjoy yourself. We have a stressful two weeks coming up."

*   *   *

At the Natick police's detective division, Lt. McNamara receives a call from Captain Green.

"Jack, I would like to talk with you about a couple of things. Do you have fifteen minutes to break away?"

"Yes, Captain, I'll be right down to your office."

Knocking on the doorpost of the captain's office, Jack enters.

"What's up, Captain?"

"First, I've met with the chief this morning. Both of us agree that you should be the person who interrogates Walsh. We want you to do three one-day visits with him in Walpole."

"Do either you or the chief have an agenda you want me to follow?"

"No, we feel your report of seeing him in Hartford meant you have touched on some issues that you might be able to break through."

"When do you plan on having me start this program?"

"Why don't you contact Walpole and find out their visiting hours and number of times you would be able to visit Walsh. Compare that to whatever else you have on your plate and set up your own schedule. Keep me posted when you will be going."

"That's fine with me. What else do you want to discuss with me?"

"The chief told me the FBI is holding a one-week counter-terrorism program at Quantico in May. He thought I should go, since I am retiring in two years. I convinced him you are the one who should go. What do you think?"

"I would be glad to go. Is the department going to be too short-handed, especially with Mike on leave?"

"We'll survive; I think this is very important, especially with what we have experienced last year and a great opportunity for you and the department."

"I'll be glad to go!"

"Good, I'll book you for the event and get all of the details to you."

"Anything else, Captain? I have a pile of paperwork to finish."

"No, we're all set for now anyway."

*   *   *

Entering his office, Lt. McNamara is a little surprised to see Lt. Mike Richards there. "What can I do for you, Mike?"

"The last time we spoke, you said you would speak with me before I had my next therapy session. I have one on Friday afternoon. Can you make time for me before then?"

"Sure, let me look at my schedule here." Jack brings up his schedule on his database and says, "How about Thursday at four?"

"Good, I'll be here. Thanks, Jack."

After Mike leaves, he is going to have to spend some time to create notes for himself based on what Mike said their last session.

*   *   *

Realizing it is almost lunchtime, Jack decides to call Jennifer before he gets tied up with Walpole. He dials her phone and she answers: "Jennifer Stone, may I help you?"

"Hi, beautiful, can you break away for dinner tonight and no cooking? I want to take you out."

"I'd love to go! My schedule has been booked solid and now I realize why they hired a third person. This is a very busy law practice. Where do you want to meet?"

"Can you meet me at my place at five thirty, and then we can go together to the Moroccan restaurant in Worcester. We haven't been there for a long time."

"I'd love it. I'll meet you at your place. I love you."

"I love you too."

Chapter Sixty-Nine

Alone with Jennifer

Lt. McNamara pulls into his parking space in front of his condo at 5:20 p.m. He sees Jennifer's car in the visitor's section and he knows she is waiting for him inside. He heads for the door. Opening the door as he nears the entrance, she gives him a quick kiss as he passes by.

"Let me wash up and I'll be ready to roll."

"Good, I'm starved, that is why I got here earlier to wash up before you arrived."

"Give me five minutes!"

They left in Jennifer's car because it is smaller in size and easier to park in crowded parking lots. Besides, Jennifer drives a sports car.

Traffic was a little heavy but not too bad. It did take forty minutes to get there.

Shrewsbury Street in Worcester was the worst of the traffic.

Entering the restaurant, they were escorted to a table in the back of the room, giving them a good deal of privacy.

"We haven't been here in a long time. What is the occasion?" Jennifer asks.

"A number of things. I have been assigned to be the interrogator of the man we recently transferred to Walpole from Connecticut. The captain is enrolling me in a counter-terrorism weeklong program at the FBI's facility in Virginia."

"When will you be going?"

"Sometime in May. He hasn't given me the details. He and the chief want me to go."

Before they can continue to talk, a waiter arrives at the table with menus and looking to take drink orders.

Jack orders a Wild Turkey 101 on the rocks and Jennifer orders a Black Russian on the rocks.

They decide to look at the menu so they can place their orders when the drinks arrive.

When the drinks arrive, both of them order the roasted lamb special. They've had it before and it is amazing.

As the waiter walks away, Jack lifts his glass and says, "To us." Jennifer seconds the salute and they sip their drinks.

"Do you still want to do New York on President's Day weekend?" asks Jack.

"I thought we had previously agreed on it and you were going to set it up. I've applied to have off half a day on Friday and the firm is closed on Monday. Will you be able to get the time off?"

"I will take the whole day off on Friday. I don't want to get dragged into something I cannot get away from."

"I'll make the calls tomorrow. Let's take your car. It is better on gas. What would you enjoy doing over the weekend?"

"I've never been to New York City."

"Really, you are in for a treat. I hope the weather isn't bad so we can get around. One thing I know is that there are plenty of indoor activities we can visit with. I want to use a cab getting around the city, plus there is always the subway. Parking your car and using a cab all weekend is the best idea. You think Boston drivers are bad. Wait until you see New York drivers."

Dinner arrives with the traditional Moroccan salad and home-baked bread to start.

They eat about a quarter of their meals before conversations continue.

"Tomorrow I will email you various activities that are being held on President's Weekend. You can review the choices and let me know where you would like me to purchase tickets to."

"Where will we be staying?"

"I haven't decided yet. It will be a whole new experience for you from any place we have stayed before. As a matter of fact, I will make it a surprise to build up your imagination about the hotel."

"Now, you're going to make my brain work overtime."

"Not really, but I know you will begin to do some dreaming."

Jack orders another round of drinks for them.

They do some small talk about preliminary preparations for their wedding even though they haven't set a firm date.

Jack feels that Jennifer is starting to loosen up about getting married after dealing with all of the divorce cases she is handling.

"Look, why don't you stay at my place tonight rather than drive home. I see you are very tired and I am tired too!"

"No pretty negligee tonight?"

"Tonight, we can take a rain check. It's easier for you to get to Boston from my place than yours."

"I'm glad I have some clothes at your place. I don't have to wear the same things tomorrow that I'm wearing."

Jack smiles. He sees Jennifer is relaxing.

They finish dinner, have some coffee, and skip dessert. They leave the restaurant around 8:30 and head for his condo in Natick.

* * *

Jack's alarm goes off at 5:30. He needs to remove his arm from around Jennifer to shut off the alarm. She is still sound asleep. He gets up and heads to his bathroom to take his shower. He loves to watch her sleeping and looking peaceful and resting.

He dresses quickly and heads down to the kitchen to start the coffee.

When he is finished making the coffee, he heads back up the stairs and bends over Jennifer to kiss her cheek. "Hey, beautiful, the alarm will go off in two minutes and I've started coffee."

"How can you say I'm beautiful the first thing in the morning?"

"Because you are, with or without your makeup."

"You're real good for a lady's ego, you know." She throws the covers off her and he admires those gorgeous legs of hers. "What are you having for breakfast?"

"I'm having a quick bowl of cereal with some fruit and I will be on my way."

"I'm in the mood for eggs. Do you have any?"

"You know where they are, so help yourself. I have a full day ahead of me."

"Kiss me goodbye now, so I don't have to rush my shower."

Jack grabs her and lifts her off her feet while kissing.

"Whoa, save some of this for another time, big boy!"

Chapter Seventy

Full Day of Scheduling

Lt. McNamara has been at his desk since 7:30. He has created a to-do list on his desk calendar that needs to be completed today without any excuses. When the clock reaches eight o'clock, he calls a travel agent he has used in the past and tells her what he is looking to book for President's Day weekend. She promises to call him back after lunch with the arrangements.

After his travel agent call, he looks up the number for the Walpole State Prison. He dials the main number and asks for the visitors department. After identifying himself, he learns that officers of the law have more flexibility than regular visitors. Looking at his schedule on his computer, he makes an appointment to meet with Jerry Walsh Friday at 2:00 p.m. The attendant informs him that Mr. Walsh will be advised of the appointment. Jack is told that Mr. Walsh has the right to refuse the visit.

That statement takes Jack back a little bit. "This is going to be an interrogation, not a social call." He ensures the attendant understands the situation.

"Oh, I didn't realize this was the case."

"Well, now you know," says Jack.

Hanging up his phone, Jack shakes his head in disbelief. He wonders what kind of intelligence level guards working in the state prison have.

*   *   *

The next item on Jack's list is to compile a half dozen items he wants to discuss with Mike when they meet before his next therapy session. Jack doesn't want to wing it as this is important and he wants Mike to know he has a friend who is willing to work with him.

This part of his agenda takes him a half hour of writing down questions, reviewing them, exchanging some of them for better questions until he is satisfied with the list.

*   *   *

Nearly 11:30, Captain Green knocks on the doorpost of his office. "Can I interrupt your train of thought for a moment? Something has come up that I would like to include you in the decision process."

"Sure, come in, Captain. Close the door if you feel it is necessary."

Captain Green closes the door. Detectives still in the squad room look around and make faces indicating, *What the heck is this about?*

"The chief just received a call from the commander of the state police. He's learned we transferred Jerry Walsh back to Massachusetts. Jerry isn't who he is after, but he wants in if we get this Ahmad fellow."

"What does 'he wants in' mean?" asks Jack.

"The chief said he was very vague?"

"Look, Captain, if, by the grace of God, we can get this Ahmad fellow, we deserve first crack at him. I know, I know, the commander lost a trooper shot in the back. We've had hundreds, mostly women, killed, many of them blown to bits. To tell you the truth, this lowly detective wants time alone with him in a room where only one of us would walk out."

"Please, don't say that in front of the press. I feel the same way. The chief asked me to talk to you because you have really been the one

257

leading this investigation. The chief merely wants your okay to stall this commander and see where the chips fall."

"Tell the chief to say, 'We will do the best to accommodate you',' says Jack. "This way we can soft-pedal the damn thing and see what happens. I know the chief wants good relations with the state police and so do I. What I can promise the chief is, we will use the best case against this Ahmad to get a conviction."

Captain Green looks at his watch, "Let's have lunch, Jack, I'm sure you have something to discuss with me that makes it legit."

"As a matter of fact I do!"

Jack grabs his sport jacket and the captain and he walk down to the captain's office for him to pick up his jacket.

When the two of them walk out of the department, the desk sergeant says, "Damn, this is a first if I've ever seen one. The captain and a lieutenant going to lunch together."

* * *

They dined on Mexican food where Jack had taken Alice Broadwell to lunch.

"What do you have to tell me to address our business together?"

Jack laughs as he knows what the captain is hinting. The captain will put this lunch on his business expenses and needs an excuse to declare it as such.

After Jack tells him of his appointment at Walpole, the captain asks, "Do you want me to come along?"

"I might at some point in the process, but right now let me go it alone."

"It's your call."

"One more thing before the food arrives, how is Mike coming along?"

"He has another therapy session on Friday and we will be meeting on Thursday to go over some things."

"Are you comfortable with this, Jack?"

"Yes and no. Yes, because I believe Mike deserves the help. No, because I know my responsibility to the department and I feel I'm torn in two different directions."

"Look, if it becomes a problem for you, let me know and I will have someone else work with Mike."

"Yes, I realize that, but you still want me to assess him. Either way I am in a catch-22 situation. I'll handle it."

Their lunches and iced tea arrive. As they eat, they both begin talking about personal issues that neither one has ever shared with the other.

Both men realize their relationship has risen to a higher plane. It feels good to know each other as people, not merely co-workers.

* * *

Meanwhile in Tehran, the revolutionary guard director in charge of foreign assignments calls the mullah at the mosque.

The phone rings six times and goes into voice mail. He leaves a message for the mullah to return his call.

* * *

Shortly after Lt. McNamara returns from lunch, the travel agent returns his call. "How did you make out, Jan?"

"I got you booked at the Wyndham near Times Square. They are four-star rated and I got you a rate of $124 per night for three nights. It is located in the heart of Manhattan and you will love it. I suggest you leave your vehicle there and use cabs, the subway, or walk, depending on the weather."

"What else did you find?"

"In tomorrow's mail you will find brochures for various shows, fine dining, and areas of interest around the island. You still have the same address correct?"

"Yes, that is great. Thank you!"

Jack hangs us and calls Jennifer. When she answers he says, "We have three nights booked at a four-star rated hotel near Times Square. Over the weekend we need to review some shows and points of interest you would like to see."

"Wow, I am so excited!"

"Enjoy your day; I still have plenty to do."

"I can't wait to get away now," says Jennifer.

* * *

An hour after Jack heard from his travel agent, the mullah at the mosque returns the revolutionary guard director's call.

When the director picks up his phone, he is all business. "I want you in my office first thing in the morning. We have important matters to discuss."

"I will send the imam you met before as I take care of morning services."

"You didn't hear what I just said," repeated the director. "You are to be here tomorrow first thing. Let the imam do the service."

The mullah doesn't enjoy being bossed by this man. He is a military person and probably has no spiritual life. Yet, he feels he has no choice, except to go.

"I will be there!" he said with a great deal of distaste.

When the mullah hangs up, the director smiles, he speaks to no one, just to hear his own thoughts. "Now I've got him where I want him and he doesn't like it."

Chapter Seventy-One

Inside of Tehran

At 8:00 a.m. in Iran, the revolutionary guard director is talking to the receptionist at her desk. "I am expecting a mullah from one of the mosques this morning. I told him to be here first thing. I want you to note how late after eight he arrives. When he comes in call me, but this will be a dummy call. I will answer and hang up. I want you to continue talking as if I was on the line. After you hang up, I want you to tell him I will available by the number of minutes he is late arriving. Do you understand me?"

"Yes sir!"

Pleased with himself the director walks back to his office.

Twenty minutes later the mullah arrives. He tells her he has an appointment with the director.

She calls the director's office and as instructed play-acts speaking with someone.

She tells the mullah the director is on the phone and expects to be late for fifteen or twenty minutes.

The mullah takes a seat but his scowl tells the whole story.

* * *

Twenty minutes later, the receptionist phone rings. "You can send the mullah in now."

"Sir, the director will see you now. He is the last door on the right side of the hallway."

The mullah grumbles something she cannot hear; she assumes it is not a pleasant statement. He heads down to the director's office, knocks on the door, and is asked to enter.

Entering the director's office, the mullah is not greeted with a smile. "I asked you to be here first thing."

Stunned by someone else being as blunt to him as he is usually the one who is in control, the mullah says, "I got a late start this morning."

"Look, you approached me because you and your little band have fucked up once more. I don't want to hear excuses. I am going to ask you some questions and I want straight answers, no crap."

The mullah shrinks back in his chair, "What do you want to know?"

"Let's start at the beginning, when did this operation start?"

"Nine months ago, we sent an operative over to the Boston area to create a hit team of bombers. He was given a large cash reserve in an encoded account located in Switzerland. His assignment was to secure one individual from each of twelve cells we have in the United States for this project."

"He was able to achieve this without any difficulty?"

"Yes, the twelve cells we gave him were more than willing to send him someone."

"You now know that if he is captured and interrogated, he could expose twelve cells that have been concealing themselves for years for projects greater than your petty bombings. Your project is small potatoes compared to what other agendas these cells might be working on."

The mullah stops to think. That idea had never struck him before.

"The first bombings were held on what the Americans call Black Friday. It was successful and our people got away free and clear."

"So you think or maybe it's because the investigation has not caught up with your people. What happens next?"

"Ahmad the leader created a second bombing, which affected a church on one of their holy nights. It was successful but he lost three volunteers."

"You are now concerned that this Ahmad and his little band are more vulnerable to be arrested and then you and your religious zealots will be exposed."

"Yes, he admits and adds that their munitions supplier has been arrested as well."

The director shakes his head, "Have you tried to contact this Ahmad?"

"Yes, he was told that the project is taking too long and he needs to abort the remainder of it and return to Iran."

"What is his reply?"

"He says the third project is near completion and then he will release the remainder of his group and head back to Iran after it is completed."

"Where is this third project to take place?"

"He was given full rein of selecting the targets and not disclosing any information that could jeopardize his mission. We only know it is somewhere in New York City."

"Where was this munitions person arrested?"

"On the news we saw that he was arrested by the FBI in Connecticut. For some reason they have transferred him to a prison in Massachusetts. That is the only thing we know."

The director's rage is building up inside of him as to the stupidity of this operation. They sent a man halfway around the world and had no way to control the circumstances.

"When will you be speaking with this Ahmad again?"

"He has cut off communication with us."

"What, cut off his funding so he is forced to come back somehow."

"We have learned that he has transferred all of the funds that were in Switzerland into another bank somewhere."

"So now he's got you by the balls, doesn't he?"

"In a manner of speaking, yes."

"Well, you have given me quite a task. Now I must send two separate teams into the United States. One team will eliminate your munitions person, and one to take care of this Ahmad."

The mullah shakes his head, knowing full well he and his people are now indebted to the revolutionary guard who despises them.

"I will get back to you when I have permission from the Supreme Leader to handle this fuck-up. He will not be pleased with you."

The mullah rises and leaves the director's office with his emotional tail between his legs.

Chapter Seventy-Two

Following Friday

Lt. McNamara is working through the weekly reports from the detectives under his responsibility. Most of them are routine, and there is hardly any mention of another clue from the Black Friday bombings. This in itself is frustrating as Jack wants to see more results about the bombings.

At 10:15 a.m., Jack's phone rings and he notices it is a call directly to him from Lt. Richards. "Hello, Mike, how did the therapy session go this morning?"

"I thought it went well and that is why I called. I followed your suggestions this morning with the therapist and she has agreed to work on the possibility that what I am dealing with began in the military."

"That's good news, how did it feel to you?"

"I guess it's okay, but I'm pretty nervous about it. That isn't why I called; I want to ask you to lunch if you will go with me."

"I'll be glad to go, only I need to have an early lunch as I have an appointment at the Walpole prison this afternoon."

"I can be at the office by 11:15. We can go for lunch before the crowds are out and I will bring you back," says Mike.

* * *

Mike Richards is true to his word and he knocks on the door of Jack's office at 11:15.

"Shall we head out?" says Mike.

"Give me a minute and I'll be right with you."

Jack and Mike walk past the duty sergeant's desk and leave for lunch. Captain Green sees them leave and he smiles.

"Where do you want to go?" said Mike.

"There is a D'Angelo's sandwich shop two blocks down. Are you up for that?" asks Jack. "They make a wicked good steak sandwich."

"Sounds good to me."

The two enter D'Angelo's and place their order for the number nine steak special, medium sized, with lettuce and tomato added along with American cheese. They each select a bottle of water from the cooler and Mike pays for lunch.

Since they are early, their order comes off the grill quickly. They select a booth down at the end where no one else is sitting.

Jack asks, "So tell me why I am seeing a nice glow on you this morning."

"The therapist and I spoke back and forth about what has transpired since our last session. Halfway through, I mentioned that in speaking with a friend, my friend recommended our discussing my military time in the Middle East."

"What was her reaction to that?" asks Jack.

"I felt at first she resisted, but then thought it over before she gave me an answer. After a few minutes she said, 'It might be beneficial to you and I see no reason why we should not, especially if it is important to you.'

"She asked me to bring her a couple of instances we could work on."

"Are you comfortable with her on that?"

"I think so, we'll see how next session goes."

"I'm glad my ideas opened some doors for you with her. Keep up the good work, I hear that the inside staff really like having you around. It has taken some of the load off them."

"Yes, I heard from some too. Only I want to be back on the streets as soon as I can."

"Take it slow, Mike, sorting things out in your mind and emotions doesn't happen overnight."

"I know and that is the frustrating part of all of this."

"Look, let's finish our sandwiches and get back. I need to be in Walpole soon."

*　　*　　*

Lt. McNamara parks his vehicle in the visitors' lot in the Walpole Prison parking area. He walks over to the security guards and shows his ID and tells them he has a two o'clock appointment.

One of the guards escorts him to the visitors' reception area. Without a word, the guard leaves to return to his post.

Stepping inside, Jack walks over to the officer at the reception desk. He explains he is from the Natick Police Department and has a two o'clock appointment with a prisoner named Jerry Walsh.

The officer checks his log and notes that the appointment is on the list. "Do you require a separate room that we use for law enforcement and lawyers?'

"You know, that would be great. This is my first experience doing an interrogation at a prison so I can use all of the help you can give me."

"Give me five minutes and I'll see what I can arrange."

"Thanks again."

Ten minutes later the guard says that he has a room arranged for him and Jerry Walsh to meet.

Jack nods in appreciation.

Jack is still ten minutes early so he needs to learn to cool his heels while the wheels of the prison system work.

Exactly at two o'clock, an officer enters the reception area and asks for ID from Lt. McNamara. When he is satisfied, he escorts Jack to the room where Jerry is handcuffed to the table and is sitting in a chair with a leg iron attached to his left ankle.

Jack moves to the end of the four-foot-tall table and pulls out a chair.

The officer says, "Use the phone on the wall when you are through and one of us will escort to back to the reception area."

Jack begins, "Jerry, you were moved here to Massachusetts because you will be indicted in Worcester County as an accomplice in the Black Friday bombings and the Christmas Eve bombings. If for some reason you are not sentenced with those charges, you will then be sent back to Connecticut to face a murder one charge. Do you understand what I am telling you?"

"When is the indictment procedure supposed to happen?"

"I understand it is on the court's docket for next Wednesday."

"I asked for a lawyer in Connecticut, do I get the same lawyer?"

"No, the Massachusetts court system will appoint a lawyer for you when you are indicted."

"So why are you here?" ask Jerry.

"I thought we could talk and hopefully you could shed some light on what really happened and how you are involved in all of this."

"You're a cop. Anything I say could be held against me. No fucking way, pal!"

"If you could give us some details on this Ahmad character, maybe something could be worked out to lower your jail time. Look, Jerry, right now a lawyer can work with you for your trial, but I can work with the attorney general's office and they're the ones who can make your life a little easier or more miserable. Take your pick, give us something and if it is any good, they will work with you. Ahmad is the guy we really want."

"Why don't you give me time to think about it?"

"I'll be back next Thursday. You need to think long and hard about what you could say to save your own ass."

Jack rises and walks to the phone on the wall. He calls the guard room and lets them know he is through.

When Jack gets to the reception room, he asks the guard who he needs to speak with about setting up another appointment next Thursday.

"I can schedule that for you, Lieutenant. What time on Thursday?"

"Let's do two o'clock again. I have a feeling that session will be longer that today's."

"I hope you're not wasting your time, sir!" remarks the guard.

"Thanks, now I need you to get me my escort to take me back out front."

"Sure thing," and he calls out to the entry gate area.

*   *   *

In Tehran, the director of the revolutionary guards calls the mullah at the mosque. "The Supreme Leader has approved my request to send two teams to save your ass. He told me to tell you this better be the last time this occurs."

The mullah is pleased and also a little nervous about what the Supreme Leader will require of him as payback.

Chapter Seventy-Three

Week Before President's Day

Sitting in his office at 7:30 a.m. Lt. McNamara ponders what he has been thinking over the weekend. He feels he must make his commitment to Captain Green regarding Lt. Richards, but he doesn't want to destroy the friendship Mike and he have developed. He lifts the receiver off his phone and hits the quick dial button for the captain's phone.

Captain Green answers by stating his name.

"Captain, it's Lt. McNamara. Could I have a few moments with you?"

"Sure, Jack, come right over." The captain feels leery about the sound of Jack's tone of voice.

Within two minutes, Jack knocks on the doorpost of the captain's office.

"Come in and why don't you close the door. I have the feeling you want this conversation to be private."

"You're right," Jack enters and closes the door.

"Is everything all right with Jennifer?"

"Jennifer is fine and we're going to New York for the long President's Weekend. I posted that I am taking Friday off as well as taking the holiday on Monday."

"Good, glad to hear you're taking some time off. What is the problem you want to discuss?"

Jack hesitates for a few minutes and then says, "It's Mike Richards, I'm beginning to feel torn about the issues involved.

"I want you to know that he feels I am his friend and he is using my suggestions with his therapist. I don't want anything to break that bond. Mike needs a close friend he can trust.

"I promised you I would report anything I felt you needed to know about Mike to help you evaluate him. I am going to tell you what he and I spoke about and how his therapist has accepted the idea."

"Okay, Jack, lay it on me!"

"Mike and I spoke before his latest therapist visit. I suggested that he tell his therapist he wanted to discuss his military background looking for PTSD."

"Did she accept this?"

"Mike says she hesitated at first then allowed that it might be a good idea. My idea is for you to speak with his therapist periodically saying you need to access his progress for departmental needs."

"So you want me to go directly to her."

"That's the idea, Captain, and then I feel I can honestly work with Mike as his friend."

Captain Green sits back in his chair and smiles. "Jack, Mike will never know how much of a friend you are. He is a lucky man!"

"Thanks, Captain, that is all I have to say."

"Consider it done, Jack. I will deal with his therapist directly."

Jack returns to his office, feeling a great burden has been lifted from his shoulders.

*   *   *

This same Monday morning Ahmad is rehearsing their subway assignments with his men, and how he wants them to begin taking two trips each day on their particular routes. They should take one run in the morning and then return to where they got on board. They should do another one around mid-afternoon in the same manner. Friday will be their last run and they will strike on Monday, the holiday, after he decides what will be the best time.

These men are not impressed with Ahmad's leadership and want to be rid of him. After he asked if anyone had questions, no one responded.

The men are anxious to get this part of the plan over with. They are bored with hanging around and need to be active. Even with all the different sights and sounds of New York City, all of them cannot wait for next Monday to arrive.

Ahmad plans to discuss with Renza on Sunday night the final times he wants the attacks to take place.

*   *   *

Meanwhile at JFK airport in New York, five businessmen unload from a flight that originated in the UK and are headed for customs and then their luggage. The next portion of their travel will take them up to Yonkers, New York.

Two hours after the five arrive in New York, five more businessmen arrive in Boston from a flight that originated in France. They too are headed for customs and their luggage, then to take a taxi to an address in Somerville, Massachusetts.

Neither team is aware of the other; their missions are totally different.

Chapter Seventy-Four

Tuesday the Next Day

The five Iranians dressed as businessmen who are heading to Yonkers, New York, arrive at their destination at 2:30 in the afternoon. They are warmly greeted by the owner of the home and invited in to rest and relax before their evening meeting.

Those five who headed to Somerville, Massachusetts, arrive around the same time as those who went to Yonkers since travel time to Somerville is short. In similar fashion, they are invited inside to rest and relax before their evening meeting.

* * *

At the Yonkers location where the men are meeting, they are sitting in the living room with two of the cell's leaders.

The leader of the five says, "We understand the people we are looking for are somewhere in New York and that is really the only information we have that is definite. What can you tell us?"

The tall slender man who portrays himself as the cell's leader says, "There were hints that they might be in the Queens portion of the city. The rental car that was dropped off in a parking garage seems to make sense they were there. If it is true or not that they are still in Queens, no one knows."

"We have time restraints placed on us by Tehran. We need to find them quickly. Where do you suppose they might attack next time? We need to stop them as soon as possible!"

"There are dozens of places they could be contemplating to attack next. Do you have any idea of the identities Ahmad hired from other cells around the country?" says the cell leader.

The man shakes his head and says, "No, and this is a major screw-up. However, we must try our best to locate them and get them to call the rest of their mission off."

"Why is that so important?" the cell leader asks.

"That is not up for us to decide. Our mission is to find them before they do..."

"Where are you staying? We will give you a call if we learn something."

"Thank you for feeding us. We must leave now and get busy organizing a plan. Please call a service that can carry five. If dispatch asks where we are going, just say into the city. Here is my cell number if you have anything."

When the car and driver arrive, they depart.

The cell leader turns around to his second-in-command, "What do you think?"

"I wouldn't want to be in their shoes when they report they couldn't find anyone and the third attack goes off. I really am curious why they want to cut off an attack!"

* * *

The team working in Massachusetts is getting the opposite of what the New York team received.

They are being fully appraised about Jerry Walsh from the time the FBI began their investigation of him to his flight and arrest in Connecticut, then his being moved to Walpole prison in Massachusetts.

Somehow the team became aware of the Natick Police's keen interest in Jerry Walsh, and that a lieutenant has interviewed Walsh one time to date. Walsh is expected to be before the grand jury tomorrow.

Tehran's group leader asks, "What happens when the grand jury makes their decision for Walsh to stand trial?"

The cell's leader replies, "Depending on caseloads, a court appearance will be held for Walsh to go to trial."

"How long with this process take?" ask Tehran's leader.

"It could take weeks or, depending on the prosecutor, it could take months."

"Will this information be made public?" asks one other member of the Tehran team.

"Yes, this is a case getting top publicity in the media. I think they want to smoke out your Ahmad!"

"I doubt that will happen!" says a third man from the team.

With nothing more to learn, the team moves out to the hotel arrangements they have for the night. They have bookings at the Holiday Inn in Sullivan Square.

Chapter Seventy-Five

Wednesday

As Lt. McNamara walks into the detective squad room, the receptionist hands him a note from Captain Green. "Hi to you too, Mary, no hello this morning?"

"Lieutenant, this morning has already started off the wrong way. I am dying to get away from this desk for a long weekend, and the chief wants umpteen items on his desk by Friday."

"Any way I can help?"

"Not really, Lieutenant, but thanks for offering."

"Well, the next best thing for me to do is connect with the captain. Keep smiling, Mary, the weekend is almost here and I have it off too, and cannot wait for the week to end."

Walking into his office, he places his jacket on the coat rack in the corner behind his desk, then sits down to dial the captain.

"Green, can I help you?"

"It's Jack. Captain, when do you want to see me?"

The captain looks at his watch and it is 7:35. "Give me until 8:30 and come to my office."

"Will do!"

* * *

At 8:30, Lt. McNamara is knocking on the doorpost of Captain Green's office.

"Come in, Jack! You don't need to close the door on this one. Have a seat anywhere you wish."

"The chief got on my case last night about the grand jury situation with Walsh. I told him it was scheduled for today. Do you know if it is morning or afternoon?"

"No, I don't, my focus has been building an itinerary to interrogate him with it tomorrow. I planned my next visit right after the grand jury is held so he should begin to realize his ass is on the line and we mean business. Captain, may I suggest you have your secretary call the attorney general's office and find out the information you are looking for. I believe Eileen is very qualified to handle the situation for you."

Captain Green looks dumbfounded for a minute. "You know, Jack, I should have thought of that, I felt sure you would know."

"I'll fall back on my old saying, Captain. Good I am, God I'm not."

"After Eileen advises me, I'll have her call you."

"Thanks, Captain, I would appreciate knowing too! Is there anything else you want to discuss?"

"One more item, give me a quick brief about your interrogation with Walsh tomorrow. Just in case the chief asks me on Friday and you're not around."

"I'll be glad to do that for you, sir."

Jack turns and leaves the captain's office.

* * *

The five men from Iran who are now located in Massachusetts are formulating plans in which they will assassinate Jerry Walsh. They are touring the areas around the Walpole prison and are waiting to find out where his court appearance location will be.

The two members who are topnotch snipers are viewing the areas from their approach and the three bombers are viewing the same areas.

When they have a plan A and a plan B, they will decide which team will lead the group to take Jerry out.

Now it is a matter of time and precision planning to complete their task.

The group leader sends an encrypted message to Iran indicating they are making progress on their mission.

* * *

At 1:30, Eileen, Captain Green's secretary calls Jack. "Lieutenant, the grand jury will be convening at 2:00 this afternoon regarding Jerry Walsh. The captain asked me to call you."

"Thanks, Eileen, I will be meeting with Mr. Walsh tomorrow afternoon."

"Good luck, Lieutenant!"

* * *

By 3:00, Lt. McNamara has decided his list of questions for Jerry Walsh is complete. He knows mentally he will be reviewing this list in his head to fine-tune it up until he meets with Jerry again.

He hopes going before the grand jury will shake up Jerry's idea that this case is going to be a cake walk.

Chapter Seventy-Six

Second Interrogation

The five-man hit team in New York is trying to determine where Ahmad's group will attempt their next bombing. There are so many targets that could be considered it seems to be an impossible task to stop them before they attack. Not only are there so many targets, they only know of Ahmad's identity and appearance. They could walk by the rest of his group and never know it.

This challenge is very frustrating to say the least. As the team struggles to research areas that will give them a chance at being successful, they are about to be rewarded with some information.

*   *   *

Two hours later, the leader of the cell they met with yesterday calls the cell phone number he was given. "I have some information for you that one of our people picked up this morning."

"Go ahead, I am listening."

"Within two weeks there will be an incident on the subway system somewhere between Seventh and Eighth Avenues. That is all I have and we hope this makes your mission easier."

"How large of an area does that cover?"

"It is huge and underground in downtown Manhattan. At least you have something more than you had before I called."

"How confident are you that this is not disinformation."

"I'm confident enough to give it to you, because if you don't stop them, we might be in a great deal of jeopardy."

"Thank you, this should help us. We will put this to good use. Tehran will know of your assistance."

Closing his cell phone, he tells his people. "Tomorrow we eat very early and begin staking out the subway system in downtown Manhattan. Tonight we must look on the Internet for everything that will assist us."

At the moment he feels better than he did two hours ago. They will face whatever they must.

"Let's order some food in and begin working on the Internet for the schematics of the area."

*   *   *

It is 1:30, Thursday afternoon before President's Day weekend. Lt. McNamara pulls into the identical parking spot he used a week ago when he visited Walpole prison. He sits in his car for a few minutes, running everything through his mind. Will Jerry Walsh feel the pressure of the grand jury decision yesterday and be willing to cooperate with the department? He gets out of his car and similar to last week, he approaches the first guard shack.

Jack is led to the visitors building. When he enters, he sees the same officer on duty that was at the desk last week.

The officer says, "I've already arranged for an interrogation room for you, Lieutenant. Hope you get more time with the prisoner this week."

"I hope I do too, Jeff. Thanks for the heads-up on the room."

"Someone will be out for you momentarily; they are bringing him up for you."

As Jack says, "Thanks again!" his escort arrives to take him in to see Walsh.

*   *   *

Jerry Walsh is sitting very erect at the end of the table, chained once more like he was last week.

Jack takes a seat at the opposite end of the table. He sits and doesn't say anything for about five minutes. His focus is on Walsh to make him sweat.

Before Jack says a word, Walsh goes on a tear, "Fuck you, Lieutenant, and the horse you rode in on."

"Just for your info, Jerry, the Natick PD stopped using horses decades ago."

"Well you know what I mean!"

"Sounds like you're pretty upset. Grand jury decision didn't go your way. Have they assigned a new public defender to you yet?"

"No, they told me that would take at least a week. You must have known that when you scheduled this visit."

Jack replies, "Yeah, I expected as much. You still have the right not to talk to me or you could make it easier on yourself."

"Copper, you are full of shit. At the grand jury I learned part of what they are going to hit me with at the trial. It's not a pretty picture."

"Can't say I blame the district attorney. She is only doing her job."

"Doing her job, that bitch had half the grand jury in tears with what she presented. There is no way you are going to make my life easier."

"Well, now that you've got the anger out of your system, are you ready to talk?"

"I might as well tell you about Ahmad and what materials he bought to do the attacks he did. Did he complete his New York mission yet?"

The hairs on the back of Jack's neck stood up. He tried his best not to look that he was a little rattled. "So far he's done Route Nine and a church in Worcester. Do you know what he was going after in New York?"

"He always thought he was so smart: Keep him in a conversation and he would tell you things he never realized he did. He was planning to hit Times Square on New Year's Eve. I wonder why he didn't or why you haven't heard anymore about him. Hopefully, he's crawled in some hole somewhere and died. Yet, I don't think so!"

"Fine I would like to tape this conversation about what your transactions with Ahmad were. Jerry, I find it hard to believe he is your only client. I would like to know the rest."

Walsh looks him straight in the eye and says, "After you come back with what you can do with the Ahmad situation, maybe we can talk some more."

Jack took a tape recorder from his briefcase and for the next 45 minutes, Jerry talked all about his dealings with Ahmad.

When Jack felt the interrogation could go no further today, he stood and called the officer from the wall phone. Before he leaves the room, he says to Jerry, "I'll be back in a couple of weeks. I need to spend time with the district attorney's office with the information you just gave me."

Walsh doesn't reply.

*   *   *

It is 3:30 and Jack realizes with traffic, he will have a hard time making it back to his office by 5:00. The only real pressing item he has is to honor his commitment to Captain Green about how the interrogation went down.

He calls the captain in his office.

After telling Captain Green what went on, the captain says, "Good work, Jack! It also feels like you might get more out of him. Have a great weekend in New York with Jennifer."

"Thanks, we will enjoy ourselves."

Chapter Seventy-Seven

Manhattan Bound

Jennifer and Jack wake up at 7:30 a.m. when the alarm begins playing music. They tease each other about who is going to shower first. Jennifer stayed overnight at Jack's condo to make it easier to get started on their long weekend vacation. Jennifer gives in. She heads into the shower first.

Jack walks out into the kitchen and puts on some coffee. He takes out his frying pan, butter, eggs, and bread he wants to toast. Breaking four eggs into a bowl and adding some milk, he gets the idea of chopping up some onions then adding them, plus some cheese, to the scrambled eggs he is preparing.

As Jennifer walks into the kitchen, she announces, "Whoa, a man who can make more than cereal for breakfast. This smells so good, who taught you this?"

"A cookbook, if you really need to know. Please get the juice out of the refrigerator these eggs and toast will be ready in about two minutes. I've already set the table."

As they eat and smile at each other, both of them feel relieved that the stresses of work are out of their lives for four days. They can be themselves and plan some fun times together.

"I can't wait to see this Wyndham hotel you booked us at."

"I'll be honest with you, I've never stayed there; however, I trust my travel agent. We should love it."

As they finish their meal, Jennifer says, "I'll clean up. Go take your shower. We want to get an early start, remember."

"Yes dear!"

"Would you say that again. I love it!"

"Yes, dear," and both of them bust out laughing.

Fifteen minutes later, Jack is back dressed very casual as is Jennifer. They don't want to travel for four to five hours feeling like mummies.

Jack does a last-minute check on his place and remembers to put his Sig Sauer.40 cal. pistol in his belt holster, as well as carrying his two spare magazines.

"Do you have to carry a pistol on vacation?" asks Jennifer.

"It's part of me and part of my job. Don't worry, I will always have enough covering it so no one will notice I have it on. Just think of me as your private security firm."

"I think of you more than that!"

"Oh, this is going to be one hot weekend," say Jack.

"Yep," Jennifer replies.

Jack closes up his condo and they place their luggage in Jennifer's car. Jack doesn't want to take a department vehicle on vacation. He wouldn't feel right doing it.

Jack takes the first turn driving. They head for the Massachusetts Turnpike.

* * *

Since Jack talked about Rein's Deli in Vernon, Connecticut, so much after his trip to the FBI office in Hartford, he promised Jennifer they would have lunch there.

An hour and a half into their ride, they are nearing Vernon and Jack says, "Are you ready for lunch?"

"I'll have a small lunch since I expect we will be eating a large dinner this evening."

"Why don't you look at the menu first before you make that decision? We can always eat dinner later. I would like to take you to Rockefeller Plaza before dinner. Since it is wintertime it will be dark early. We can watch the skaters under the lights of the plaza. I have fond memories of doing that when I was young. They sell hot chocolate there."

"That sounds good. You keep building Reins up. I'm anxious to see this place."

"You'll love it, I am sure you are going to want to stop there on the way home."

Ten minutes later, they are at Reins and the waiting line to be seated is short. Jennifer is amazed at the take-out deli business they do. The assortment of foods and baked goods smells terrific.

Within five minutes, they are seated. A small dish of pickles is delivered to the table along with menus. The waitress asks what they would like for a beverage.

Jack responds, "An unsweetened iced tea for me."

Jennifer says, "I'll have the same and make mine with lemon."

She leaves them to make their choices from the menu.

"I see what you mean, Jack. This is one hell of a selection and the atmosphere make one think they are sitting somewhere in downtown Manhattan."

"After we place our orders, take a moment to read your table mat. It gives the reader a history of their beginning and up to the current times."

When the waitress returns with their iced tea, they place their orders. Jennifer asks for a corned beef with mustard on a bulkie roll and Jack orders hot pastrami with mustard on rye. Both ask for coleslaw instead of French fries.

Jennifer takes her first bite. Once she swallows what is in her mouth, she looks at Jack and says, "This is utterly delicious."

"See, I told you!"

*   *   *

Back in Jennifer's car, she says, "I don't know if I can eat anything else today. How do people put away those French fries that come with those sandwiches?"

"I have no idea, I wouldn't try it."

Jennifer starts the car; she will drive until they get closer to the New York border.

*   *   *

Jennifer and Jack switch drivers once they get off Route 287 West and head for the Saw Mill Parkway South.

A half an hour later, Jack switches onto the Henry Hudson Parkway, which is Route NineA. This road will take them into downtown Manhattan and they need to look for 345W Thirty-fifth Street. Here is where both of their sets of eyes are important.

It is difficult trying to find a location in New York when you have plenty of traffic to contend with and you aren't familiar with the area. Jennifer keeps her eyes on the street signs.

"Take the next left and a second left. We are right around the corner." Jack follows her instructions and sure enough, they are almost in front of the Wyndham.

Jack pulls up in front of the hotel and a valet asks if they are checking in.

"Yes, we will be here for a couple of days!"

The valet gives him a stub and moves their vehicle after their luggage is removed from the trunk.

Jennifer grabs his arm, "Jack, this place looks gorgeous."

"Let's go check in so we can unwind from the trip."

*   *   *

Under the city streets, the New York hit team hoping to find Ahmad and his men are beginning to realize the magnitude of their problem even though they have somewhat of an idea when and where Ahmad will strike.

Their leader curses internally, knowing how futile this project is.

They will need a great deal of luck to achieve any success here.

*   *   *

Jack and Jennifer's room is on the sixth floor. Jennifer cannot get over the luxury they are in the midst of. "I've never been in a hotel room this exquisite before," she says.

"We members of the working class have a right to celebrate once in a while," says Jack. "I'm going to fix myself a drink from the liquor bar. Will you have one with me?"

"Sure, tell me what they have."

Jack opens the cabinet door and whistles, "Wow, they have the largest stocked bar I've ever seen in a hotel. Come over here and pick something out."

Jack grabs two bottles of Maker's Mark and Jennifer grabs an apricot brandy.

They pour their liquor into glasses with a little ice and walk over to the window to look down upon the city. It is beginning to become dusk and the city's lights should go on shortly.

Chapter Seventy-Eight

Saturday Before President's Day

Jennifer and Jack are eating breakfast at the Wyndham. Over veggie omelets, fresh fruit, and coffee, they talk about last evening's viewing of Rockefeller Plaza.

"I loved watching the skaters enjoy themselves in the middle of this huge city. I also enjoyed watching you reminisce. Your thoughts were being displayed by your smiles."

"The Plaza has always been a favorite of mine since my grandparents took me there numerous times when I was a child."

"Do you still want to stick with the plan we had for today, or do you want to do something else?" asks Jack.

"Let's do the Empire State Building this morning and take the afternoon ferry from the Battery to visit the Statue of Liberty. You were so fortunate to have your grandparents. They left you with many positive memories."

"I am fortunate and I hope to do the same for my children when they get to the age they can appreciate most of New York."

Jennifer places a hand across the table, holding Jack's, then says, "We'll work on that idea together."

Jack smiles.

*   *   *

Ahmad is seated on one of the chairs in the living room. Everyone else is crowded into the room onto chairs or on the floor.

"Yesterday, you completed the last of your surveillance. If the authorities are anticipating an attack this weekend, I would say they might expect it to happen on Monday the holiday. We will attack tomorrow on Sunday. I will give you an exact time tomorrow. I will be giving you American dollars. Once you plant your explosives and dial into your cell phones, you are to head back to wherever you live. Do not come back here. Are there any questions?"

He receives no questions and thinks this is sort of odd.

"Renza, you and I need to take a walk."

Renza rises and gets his overcoat and meets Ahmad at the front door.

Outside in the cold air, Ahmad says, "I sense an air of indifference than from when we did the first two attacks. Do you feel it?"

"Yes, I do; however, I believe it is because they have been cooped up so long they just wish this to be over."

"I hope that doesn't make them careless tomorrow!"

"I don't expect it will. Do you still want to shadow Kazem and Marduh tomorrow?"

"Yes, for some reason those two trouble me."

"I will place them on a train out of Penn Station. It will be easy for you to follow them in there."

"Good, let's plan to be successful one last time."

*   *   *

Jennifer and Jack are eating in a restaurant a few blocks from the Battery piers. She loved the Empire State Building and insisted on going to the top even though it was the middle of February and very cold out.

Jack is pleased she is enjoying herself. For him this is sort of old hat, but still remains enjoyable for him.

They finish their soup and salad and head out to the ferry to purchase tickets to the Great Lady in the Harbor. At least this is what his grandfather always called her.

At the Battery, they find there is no line for tickets. Jack can only attribute this to the cold. He purchases two and he and Jennifer only have ten minutes to wait before the next boat leaves.

Arriving at the Statue of Liberty, Jennifer steps off the ferry and looks upward. The statue is huge and she feels a sort of a chill down her spine. Not because of the cold; it's because of the impact the history of the statue is having on her.

Jack begins to smile then says, "Let's see if the crown is open for visitors. If it is, you'll need to be ready to do some climbing."

The crown is open for visitors and he explains what it will be like to walk up to the top. Do you want to do that?"

"Oh, yes, I wouldn't miss this for the world. Please, let's go!"

They join a line of visitors who will begin to ascend the stairway that winds around and around all the way up to the crown.

At the top Jennifer is awed by the sights she can see and to realize she is standing at the top of the Statue of Liberty. She turns around and gives Jack a big kiss. "This is wonderful. Thank you for bringing me here."

Some of the other visitors smile as they see her so involved with her emotions.

They spend a half hour at the top and then proceed to come down.

*   *   *

The five-man Iranian hit team is going nuts trying to figure out how they are going to cover all of these train rails with only five men.

Their leader makes a decision and hopes for the best. They will return on Monday the holiday when they expect the attack will be, if there is one.

*   *   *

"Have you had enough for the day?" asks Jack as they return to the Battery.

"Yes, it's four o'clock and I think a drink at the bar or maybe two and some play time might be in order. What do you say?"

"Your wish is my command!"

Jennifer punches him in the shoulder and laughs, "You're funny, like I really have to twist your arm."

They head back to the Wyndham and look forward to sitting inside of the bar.

Chapter Seventy-Nine

Sunday

Jack orders a continental breakfast for two sent to the room. Both he and Jennifer wish to relax, have the noontime brunch, and then head out to the museum of National History for the afternoon.

Last night Jennifer suggested they slow their pace down on Sunday and Monday by only seeing one visitor's site each day. They should plan to check out early on Monday, visit the Metropolitan Museum of Fine Arts and after a quick lunch begin their journey home. At this pace they wouldn't be dragging their behinds on Tuesday. Hopefully if they leave early, the traffic will not be too terrible. After all this is a vacation, not a marathon. They can always come back another time.

After taking a shower, Jennifer walks out of the bathroom dressed in a Wyndham's bathrobe. At that same moment, room service delivers their breakfast.

"I guess I timed this right!" she says.

"I'll eat before I take my shower. My stomach is beginning to growl," remarks Jack.

"Good, by the time we eat and you shower, my hair should be fairly dry."

*   *   *

Ahmad is lecturing his men, something they really do not enjoy. "Enjoy a large lunch, we are leaving at 4:00 p.m. and you are going to your positions. I want you to walk in pairs and take your time to relax. Enter the subway systems at 5:00 and get on the trains as soon as they arrive. You know the rest of the plan. Good luck and praise Allah for this blessing in your lives.

"At 3:00 p.m., I will give each of you an envelope containing one thousand American dollars. Make sure you are not carrying any identification and anything that can leave a trace back to this apartment."

*   *   *

The New York Iranian hit team has been dissecting the subway system, hoping to get a clue where this team of Ahmad's may stage another attack. They have been working on this project for a week and find they are no further than when they started.

The leader suggests they refresh themselves by resting on Sunday. It makes sense that if the attack is to happen, it would be done on President's Day to make the most horrific effect on the local population.

They hope they are right, but trying to find them has been almost impossible.

*   *   *

At 12:30 p.m. Jack and Jennifer enter the Museum of Natural History and decide to sign up for a guided tour that will take four hours. Jack has been to the museum three times prior to this visit. He loves to come here. His first visit was a ninth-grade class trip, Jack is as excited today as he was then. For Jennifer this is all new and she is totally engrossed in what she is seeing.

*   *   *

At four 4:00 p.m. the first pair leaves the terrorist apartment, and each of the following pairs will leave ten minutes apart. There are four pairs with Renza following up alone. Ahmad will tail Kazem and Marduh to Penn Station.

They walk with a mission on their minds and the opportunity to be free of this long and screwed-up assignment. Each man plans to tell his cell leaders how bad the leadership was over the past six months.

As they near their subway entrances, each pair makes note of the time, so they are synchronized to arrive into the subway at the same time.

At 5:00 they all enter their designated rail lines.

* * *

Leaving the museum Jack says, "Let's take the subway to Chinatown. You should never go to Manhattan without having a meal in Chinatown. Are you up to it?"

"Lead the way, my faithful security guard."

Little does Jennifer realize how true her statement will become.

"We should head over to Penn Station and catch the rail there. Then we can come back to Penn Station and walk to our hotel to work off dinner."

"This sounds romantic, let's do it."

They enter and pay the fare for two to head into Chinatown. Once inside of the turntable, they look for the platform for their ride.

For some reason Jack feels the hair on the back of his neck standing up.

He has always paid attention to his intuition; it has saved his life a couple of times.

Suddenly, Jack is hearing a man yelling in Farsi. He wonders what is going on. Then he sees two men are the reason the man is yelling. However, they aren't paying attention, as they seem to be dropping something in trash bins. The man yelling is beginning to run toward them.

"Jennifer, please listen to me. Get up to the main street and seek out the first police officer you find and tell him to get the subway system shut down now."

"I'm going, but they're going to think I am nuts."

"Go and stay on the street level. Do not under any circumstances come back down."

Jennifer looks at Jack and she realizes he is dead serious. She takes off running to the exit.

Jack follows the man who is still yelling and when he gets close enough he shouts, "Ahmad, stop right there."

Instinctively, Ahmad reacts to his name; he looks to see who is calling him. No one is supposed to know he is here.

When Jack sees Ahmad look, he pulls his weapon. People around him begin screaming and scattering in all directions.

Ahmad realizes he cannot control the two traitors any longer; he heads for the exit stairs himself.

Jack follows. He doesn't want Ahmad to get away.

*   *   *

On the street level, Jennifer sees two police officers near the subway entrance. She runs to them and almost out of breath she gives Jack's message.

"Lady, are you nuts?" says the short fat guy.

"That is exactly what I told my fiancé you would say. Now, I'm going to give it to you straight: a terrorist is running around the subway system with who knows how many accomplices. My fiancé is a Massachusetts detective working on this very case. If you don't do something quick, I will make sure both of your futures will not be with the police department. You'll be lucky if you are collecting trash after this. Here is my card."

The taller man takes her card and sees she is a lawyer. "Don't fuck around, Jimmy, call it in."

*   *   *

While Ahmad is heading for an exit, two metro police officers overhear what is going on. "Johnny, call the bomb squad to see what those two dropped off in the trash and I am going after them."

Johnny calls the bomb squad and begins clearing the area around the container where the materials were dropped into.

Dispatch receives the call and the dispatcher calls for a supervisor to make a decision. Minutes are ticking by and Johnny is wondering if he will be blown into bits any time now.

The decision from high up arrives quicker than anticipated. "Execute plan to evacuate the subway system. On the subway's cars system the riders hear 'All cars will halt at their next stop and everyone is to depart from their respected trains. This is an emergency.'" When the cars stop, riders are rushing and shoving to get to the exits and the upper street level.

While Kazem and Marduh are struggling to get through the crowd formed at the exit, Jack has a clear view of Ahmad. "Stop or I'll shoot."

Ahmad laughs to himself knowing no police officer is going to take the chance to hit an innocent bystander. He keeps moving.

The next time Jack has a clear view of him, he blows out Ahmad's right knee cap.

"Allah, why do you forsake me?" Stumbling, Ahmad keeps trying to escape and Jack shoots out his second knee cap. Ahmad collapses on the stairs.

At this same time New York police are coming down the subway stairs and sees Ahmad get shot. Seeing Jack holding a gun the officer shouts, "Drop the gun now, drop the gun now."

Jack bends down, puts his weapon down and places his hands in the air. In his left hand is his badge and ID.

When the officer approaches him he says, "You are under arrest."

Right now Jack has had enough, "I put my gun down raised my hands so you police officers now know you are safe, the least you can do is look at my ID and my badge. When I can put my hands down, I am going to walk over to that body and arrest that son of a bitch."

The officer looks at his partners and they all look as if they don't know what the hell to do.

Jack looks over to Emmons, the officer closest to him. "Emmons, I want to arrest that man and I am going to walk away from my gun. If it is touched by anyone, I will hold you and your department responsible. Do you hear me?"

Emmons says, "Yeah, go ahead, but it still has to be confiscated to go to the crime lab."

"No shit, Shakespeare, what do you think I do as a detective?"

Jack walks over to Ahmad as EMTs are caring for him; he gives him his Miranda rights. He asks what hospital they will be taking him to.

Then Jack walks back to Emmons saying, "Now I need to speak with your brass. Before I do that, I want to make sure my fiancé is safe. I sent her upstairs with a message. We were on our way to Chinatown to have dinner. I guess this episode blows the day for us tomorrow."

The officer laughs and says, "You could have let him escape and saved yourself some headaches."

Jack whirls around, "Look, asshole, do you know what the Black Friday bombings were? That's the prick who engineered the job, and the Christmas Eve massacre too. Get out of my sight, will you. If you've got enough brains, get me one of your partners to escort me to the street level."

The officer turns beet red and says, "Jacobs, take this hotshot fucking lieutenant up to the street. I'll call in for a command car."

Jack turns to Emmons and smiles, pissing Emmons off some more.

Chapter Eighty

Aftermath of the Shooting

As Officer Jacobs walks Jack up to the street level, he tries to apologize for Emmons's bad behavior.

Jack says, "No need to apologize for him, Jacobs. He thinks he's a badass, he just met his match. When your brass gets through with him, he's in for big trouble. He should have arrested the man I shot; now the prisoner belongs to the state of Massachusetts and every glory hound in New York is going to be pissed.

"Before you leave me, call what happened into your precinct and have them contact the FBI. Now help me find my fiancé."

Jack and the officer walk two blocks and they see Jennifer surrounded by four officers.

Jack walks up them and says, "Sorry guys, this lady is already taken."

"Jack, are you all right?"

He nods his head yes.

One of the officers says, "We have orders to remain with this lady until the brass arrives."

"Well, I guess I'll have to join your company. Thank you, Officer Jacobs, remember the phone call I told you about. It will make you some points. I'll tell the brass it was your idea."

"Thanks, Lieutenant!"

Jack stands behind Jennifer and makes a call on his cell phone.

"May I ask how you got this number?"

"Captain, it's Jack, look I'm in a situation here in New York where Ahmad and his merry men were trying to take down the subways system. Please listen carefully. Ahmad is on his way to the hospital. I shot him twice. Call the chief and tell him to contact the local FBI because I arrested Ahmad before anyone else got the opportunity. When he is well enough to travel, I want his ass up in Massachusetts. I'm sure you will see everything on television very shortly."

"Jack, are you and Jennifer okay?"

"Yes, we are and she helped too. I'll tell you another time."

*   *   *

Captain Green hangs up and immediately calls Chief Winters. When the Chief answers his phone, the captain goes on to tell him what Jack said.

"Holy shit," says the chief. "Is Jack and his lady friend okay?"

"Yes, however, he wants us to contact the Boston office of the FBI immediately."

"Make the call, Captain, you say Jack arrested this Ahmad?"

"Yes, but he's not going to be up and around for a while."

*   *   *

On the street level of the subway station, media crews are arriving. Reporters with their camera crews are circulating like sharks around a victim. They heard the news on police broadcasts. Right now no one knows what is really happening. Somehow a story is being put together of a hero detective.

*   *   *

The NYPD command car arrives. The captain of the local precinct gets out of the car. "I hope that someone has some answers for us shutting down the subway system in this area. Otherwise the media is going to kill us."

Right at that very moment, four explosions are heard from below ground within the subway system.

"I believe you just got your answer, Captain."

"Who are you?"

"My name is Lt. Jack McNamara of the Natick, MA police department. This is my fiancée Jennifer and we were spending the weekend in the city. Right now except for the explosions we just heard, everything else is under control. I know I will have to go back and give you a report on what happened. I just hope you will arrange for Jennifer to go back to our hotel. She doesn't need to go through this."

The captain looks at Jennifer and agrees, "Wilson, get a squad car over here to take the lady to her hotel. Jennifer, we will return the lieutenant after we understand everything that went on."

"Thank you," Jennifer says.

"Now back to the explosions we just heard. Who are these people?"

*   *   *

The bomb squad arrives just as the explosions happen. The officer standing guard around the trash receptacle is more than certain the container will explode next so he tries to give himself more cover.

As the bomb squad comes down to the platform level, the officer known as Johnny directs them to what he and his partner suspect to be bombs.

The bomb squad relieves him of his post and sends him to safety.

They begin to dissect the trash container of its contents, very carefully looking for explosives. Near the top they find two fanny packs packed with semtex. The semtex is inert since they are not connected to something to charge them to explode. This is a first for the squad, a bomb that is not a bomb. Either the bombers had screwed up or had a change of heart.

Next on the squad's agenda is tending to the bombs that did explode to collect evidence.

*   *   *

Officer Johnny heads up to the street level and finds his partner. His partner has both Kazem and Marduh in custody, along with two other officers. It seems that the other officers were coming down the stairs to the subway and they saw the pair running upstairs. They ran right into the two officers, quickly followed by Officer Davis. They are being held as possible terrorists right now.

*   *   *

Four subway cars were damaged in the explosions. The city is prepared for a situation like this, allowing passengers from cars to get off before the explosions detonated. While there is considerable damage to cars and terminals, there is no loss of life.

*   *   *

Lt. Jack McNamara knows the drill. Now he will be interrogated as if he was a criminal. There will be some professionalism, but the facts and details must come out. His pistol will go to the crime lab and will be returned to him when all of the facts agree with what he says.

He has been told that one of the NYPD officers arrested two men who were escaping. The officer believes they are part of the terrorist group, although it is not known why they were bolting from the scene. There are also questions about the two bombs that were retrieved that were duds. It is hoped the two men will place some light on that matter.

Jack is informed that Chief Winters has already called and advises the NYPD that Jack is of the highest caliber as a police officer. He has been working this case since Black Friday last year. The chief also told the department the Boston office of the FBI has been informed that Jack arrested the leader of the terrorist group.

*   *   *

At the Wyndham, Jennifer is a bundle of nerves worrying about what Jack is going through. One thing she realizes is, he is safe and out of harm's way and she thanks God for that.

*   *   *

On the 6:00 p.m. news, the headlines hit the air waves and the Iranian hit team in New York is in an uproar. Not only did the attack happen, but Ahmad has been taken prisoner.

The group leader advises Tehran of the circumstances and they have now been told to execute plan two.

*   *   *

The hero story plus pictures of the detective are now live on television and will be in tomorrow's paper. No one knows much about him except he is not from New York.

Chapter Eighty-One

Jack Returns

At 8:30 p.m. Jack returns to their hotel room. "Oh Jack, I was so worried, how come this took so long?"

"In police interrogation the same questions are asked time after time in different ways to see if you can be tripped up. In other words they never believe your first version of the story."

"Is this what you went through?"

"A milder version of it, but it was a constant searching for the answers to see if they come out differently. I did learn that one of their officers has arrested two of what they believe are members of Ahmad's group. I guess the fact that I arrested Ahmad first doesn't hurt as much now that they have two sitting in jail."

"Can we go home tomorrow? Or do you have to stay around here?"

"I told them we were leaving tomorrow and they know how to reach me. There is nothing more that I can tell them about what happened. I find it hard to believe it happened the way it did."

"Jennifer, I need to eat something and would like to go downstairs to the dining room. Are you hungry?"

"I snacked wondering how you were. I can eat something although I don't know if my stomach will accept it."

They head down to the dining room and ask for a table in a quiet corner. The hostess realizes that she has seen Jack's pictures on television being the hero of the subway incident.

The hostess seats them and advises them their waiter will only be a moment. She goes back to her podium and calls the manager.

The waiter shows up promptly and takes their drink orders. Jack orders a double of Makers Mark on the rocks; Jennifer has a martini straight up.

They quickly choose an entrée and when their drinks arrive, they place their orders.

Jennifer asks, "Do you still want to go to the Metropolitan Museum of Fine Arts tomorrow or just head home?"

"To be honest with you, I would rather go straight home. Too much has happened today. It is a lot to digest."

"Those are my exact thoughts, we can come back another time," remarks Jennifer.

"We were having such a wonderful time. Jennifer, are you okay with what happened today?"

"Yes and no. Today I truly realize how dangerous your job is."

"What does that mean? You might not be able to handle it?"

"That is not what I said; it's just that I realize every time you leave home, something could happen to you."

"It will be okay, Jennifer, I'm still here and the bad guy is in the hospital not me."

"Thank God!"

* * *

Just before their entrees arrive, the manager of the hotel comes to the table.

"Excuse me, you are detective Lt. Jack McNamara, am I correct?"

"Yes, did we cause you a problem somehow?"

"The Wyndham South would like to thank you for your brave deeds this afternoon. When you check out tomorrow, your bill will be paid in full by the hotel. We want you to know New York thanks you." He shakes Jack's hand and leaves.

Jack doesn't know what to say, except "thank you" in return.

"Wow, that was powerful. It also made me realize that I asked you to go get the bad guys when they did the Christmas Eve massacre. You've done exactly that. I love you, my hero!"

It is a good thing their food arrives as people are coming to their table to congratulate Jack, and he needs an excuse not to get into long conversations.

* * *

As they are packing to check out and head back home, the phone in the room rings.

"Mr. McNamara, we know you are checking out this morning, we request a favor from you."

"Sure, what would you like me to do?"

"Since 6:00 this morning there are numerous media vans and crews hanging around the front of the hotel. The police can only do so much. When you are ready to check out, we can have a valet driver bring your car to the rear of the hotel so that you will avoid the media. Once you have left the property, we will announce you have left and they should disperse."

"Give us ten minutes and we will be down. We will leave our room keys on the dresser so we are not seen at the front desk."

"This will be greatly appreciated and the driver will be there."

"You can send a bell boy up to take our bags downstairs. He can direct us to the exit you want us to use."

"He is on his way!"

* * *

Jack tips the bell boy before they head downstairs. Within minutes they are exiting the rear of the hotel and loading Jennifer's car. Jack tips the valet driver and says, "I need directions to the Henry Hudson Parkway."

The valet driver gives him the shortest route and Jack pulls away from the Wyndham.

"My God, this whole event seems so strange with all of this attention," says Jennifer.

"I'm glad the hotel asked us to leave the way they did," remarks Jack.

"Let's hope this doesn't happen at Rein's when we stop for lunch," replies Jennifer.

Chapter Eighty-Two

At Rein's

Jennifer pulls the car into the parking lot for Rein's Deli. She shuts the motor off and looks at Jack. "Do you think we can eat in peace this time or should we go somewhere else?"

"Hell, if it is going to happen, it can happen anywhere, let's go inside."

Jack and Jennifer enter Rein's and stand in the line to get seated. When it is their turn, Jack asks the hostess, "Can we have a table behind the glass partition on the other side of your stand. We would like some privacy."

"Sure, let me see what is available."

Coming back, she says, "Another couple is nearly done. When we clean the table it is yours."

Jack replies, "Thank you."

Other couples in line are moved around them and seated elsewhere in the dining area. Their wait is only five minutes.

When they are seated, Jennifer says, "I'm glad you asked for this."

"I ate behind the partition once and it enabled me to have some quiet. I figured we were less visible here than out in the open seating."

"Good call, Jack!"

Both of them ate a large lunch since they knew once they got home to Jack's place, they would be too tired to cook. They planned to send out for a pizza.

*　　*　　*

Jack takes over the driving after leaving Rein's Deli. He continues driving north on Route 84 toward the Massachusetts line.

Almost an hour later, they cross the border and are heading for the Massachusetts Turnpike, when Jack notices a state police cruiser parked perpendicular to the road watching traffic. He has Jennifer's car on cruise control so he is not concerned.

Two minutes past the cruiser, Jack notices the cruiser come out of its space and pull onto the highway.

What happens next he doesn't expect. The cruiser pulls up behind Jennifer's car, its lights begin to flash, and the officer inside says, "Pull over," on his PA system.

Jennifer looks confused at Jack as he pulls over according to the instructions.

Jack shuts off the car and he and Jennifer sit there wondering what is up.

The officer comes out of the cruiser and walks toward the car.

"Are you Jack McNamara, Lt. Jack McNamara?"

"Yes, Officer, can you tell me what this is all about?"

"I'd like you and the lady to step out of the car then stand over on the grass with me."

Jack looks over at Jennifer they both nod to each other. They begin to get out of the car.

Jack sees the officer is a sergeant and the three of them are facing each other.

"Lt. McNamara and Jennifer Stone, as a representative of the Massachusetts State Police, I would like to congratulate you on the outstanding police performance you did in New York City." He shakes both of their hands.

"That character you shot killed one of our own last December not far from here. We are very pleased you've arrested him. We have word that Jennifer also played a part in this.

"I have orders from our commanding officer to escort you to your home in Natick. I would like you to follow me onto the turnpike."

Jack is curious, "How did you know to look for Jennifer's car?"

"We thank Captain Green for that information. Are you ready to get back on the road?"

"Sergeant, lead the way!"

Jack and Jennifer get back in her car. "I don't believe this is happening!" she said.

"I don't either and I have a feeling this is not going to be the end of it either."

The cruiser pulls into the lead and with flashing lights escorts Jack and Jennifer back home.

*   *   *

As they pull up to Jack's condo, he and Jennifer see three media vans parked in the condo area's parking lot.

"Oh, no!" he says.

The sergeant says, "Thank you again, Lieutenant. I'll leave you to the wolves now."

"Thanks, I don't believe all of this."

As Jack parks the car he says, "Let's put our bags in the house. I'll come back out to speak with them."

They make their way to the door with reporters and cameramen trying every which way to get a word in edgewise.

Inside, Jennifer sits down on the couch once their bags are in the bedroom.

Jack goes out, "Look, I know everyone is hot for what happened. Tomorrow I must make my report to my chief. I suggest you contact Chief Winters as to what time all of you can attend a press conference at the Natick station.

"Other than what I just said, I don't plan to make any further statements." Jack goes inside and slams the door.

"I need a drink!"

"Me too!"

*   *   *

Jack's cell phone rings. "Hello, yes sir, we were escorted home from Sturbridge to Natick. Look, Captain, there were three media vans sitting here when we arrived. I told them to call the station tomorrow and find out when there will be a press conference."

"You're funny, Jack now you're running the station. I'll call the chief at home and let him know what to expect. I'm glad the two of you are back safe and sound."

Chapter Eighty-Three

Returning to Work

At 7:30 the next morning, Lt. McNamara walks into the Natick Police Station. All of a sudden people are getting up from their desks and applauding him.

"Thank you, thank you, please sit down and just let me feel like myself again."

Hearing the commotion, Captain Green enters the squad room. "Jack, the chief wants the two of us in his office. He wants a verbal report so he can answer any questions people throw at him. This way, you only have to tell your story once before you write out your report."

"Let's go and get it over with!"

As they enter the chief's room, the chief stands, "How is our hero?"

"I need a long weekend after this past weekend."

"Why don't we sit down and get started," says the chief.

*   *   *

For two hours, Jack reviews the events of how he and Jennifer were preparing to take the subway into Chinatown for dinner. Then he goes on to describe how he heard someone yelling in Farsi and sees two men not paying attention to whomever was hollering. He explains how he was able to identify Ahmad, and to stop him from escaping by taking out both of his kneecaps. Jack even includes the police officer who was a jerk, plus the second one who was helpful. He makes note that the NYPD crime lab has his weapon so he needs a replacement until his is returned. Jack includes how Jennifer ran up to the street level and was able to get the subway system shut down. Jack gives a full explanation of how the police brass treated him, how they were polite to Jennifer and how his interrogation went.

He tells the chief how the Wyndham hotel picked up his bill for the whole weekend as a way of saying thanks. Jack learned there were four explosions in the subway system and two bombs that were recovered. He didn't know the bomb details. Also the NYPD did arrest two of Ahmad's group. He said that he would be guessing they felt better after he had placed Ahmad under arrest before they did.

The chief and the captain have a number of questions. When Jack answered their questions, the chief said, "I have scheduled a press conference downstairs in the large conference room at 3:00. Will you handle the questions they ask?"

"I promise you I will handle it so long as it is only surface questions, nothing that the public needs to know."

"Good, we're all proud of you, Jack, I am putting you in for a accommodation."

"Thank you, sir! I'm glad I got the bastard. I request that I be the officer in charge of what transpires?"

"It's yours, Jack, you deserve it!"

Chapter Eighty-Four

Jennifer Returns to Work

When Jennifer enters the law firm where she works, the receptionist says, "What a weekend you must have experienced."

"Pam, that is an understatement."

"We weren't sure if you would be in today."

"Jack and I are working today, his day is going to be much harder than mine, believe me."

Pam's phone rings, she answers it. "Let me check to see if she is available?" Pam places the caller on hold.

"Jennifer, the *Boston Globe* is on the line and wants to set up an interview with you."

"Pam, advise any media who calls that they need to contact the Natick Police Department. I am not giving interviews."

"Good for you, I'll will be glad to pass your wishes on."

Pam connects with the caller and gives them Jennifer's message. The caller tries another tactic. She merely hangs up.

Harry and Ben, the owners of the law firm, enter the office at the same time Harry says, "Our heroine has arrived. When you go to New York, you do it in a big way."

Ben hands Jennifer a dozen of yellow roses to help her get through the day.

"These are beautiful, thank you. I don't know what to say."

"Don't say anything, there are a lot of people in New York thanking you and Jack."

Ben says, "We are going to close the office at lunchtime and bring in food for everyone. We are dying to hear what happened. I'm sure you are willing to share with us."

"After getting these roses, how could I say no?"

*   *   *

At 2:50 in the afternoon, the chief, the captain, Jack, and a dozen media are sitting in the large conference room while the camera men get everything set for a 3:00 broadcast nationwide.

Exactly 3:00 the camera begins rolling. Chief Winters speaks a little about this particular group they have been investigating since Black Friday. "They created a massacre in Worcester on Christmas Eve and then fell of the map. Fortunately, they turned up in New York, just as our senior detective was having a getaway weekend with his fiancée. I know you don't want to hear anymore from me so I will turn the microphone over to Lt. Jack McNamara. I might add that Jack is not the senior detective due to age. He has more time with the department."

That gets a laugh from the media.

Jack stands in front of the microphone and says, "Ladies and gentlemen, you make me feel more uncomfortable than I felt chasing Ahmad the Iranian killer."

That draws another laugh from the media.

"I am going to paraphrase what transpired. First of all, I want you to know there were others who made this event successful. My fiancée rushed to street level to contact the police. She did it knowing they would think she was nuts. That is exactly what one officer told her. Her next statement was, I was below and chasing an unknown number of terrorists alone. She advised this officer and his partner that if they didn't call her warning in, she would do everything in her power to make sure they weren't on the police force any longer. She handed the other officer her card and when he realized she is an attorney, they made the call. That was one situation.

"Anticipating a terrorist attack since New Year's Day, the city of New York devised a plan to protect the subway's passengers and the system. Thank God it worked. There were four bombs that did explode. Sorry, I don't have the details on those. I do know they caught two others of Ahmad's group.

"I was too busy chasing the leader. By sheer coincidence, I hear him yelling at two of his group in Farsi. Since I recognize the language, I tested him.

"I called Ahmad by his name. Instinctively he looked at me as you or I would do if someone shouted our names.

"I knew I had the right man. I was not about to let him escape.

"Yes, I did shoot inside the subway system; however, I trusted my own skills and his belief that I would never shoot with innocent bystanders around. That was his downfall.

"While EMTs worked on removing him to a hospital, I arrested him and gave him his Miranda rights.

"Now he belongs to the state of Massachusetts and the town of Natick.

"That is all I have to say."

Everyone sitting in front of Jack stands and applauds him for nearly five minutes.

* * *

Captain Green moves in front of the microphone, "We have arranged for any questions to be answered by Jack to be done in the smaller conference room. Thank you for coming."

* * *

The chief and the captain both pat Jack on the back and tell him what a great job he did. The chief told him to go home and get some rest after he answers questions from the media. He could see Jack was emotionally exhausted.

*   *   *

Likewise, Jennifer's bosses did the same for her. They could see she is fighting to keep her concentration. Jennifer was headed for Jack's condo; she needed to be close to him after going through this episode.

Chapter Eighty-Five

Media Blitz

Jerry Walsh is eating dinner with one hundred and fifty other prisoners at the Walpole, MA prison. Dinner is the usual prison food, small quantities, without taste and lousy selections. Sometimes Jerry wonders how someone who is in charge of these meals doesn't know anything about dietary standards. He finishes his meal and decides he would go to the recreation room before returning to his cell.

As he enters the room, he sees the wide screen television display a full screen message saying, "Breaking News." Jerry wonders what is going on in the outside world today. He decides to take a seat and pay attention.

Jerry nearly shits his pants. The press release given by the Natick police clearly discusses the capture in New York of the Black Friday and Christmas Eve Massacre bomb leader. Jerry starts to sweat. So long as Ahmad is a free man, Jerry felt the charges against him wouldn't hold water. Now with Ahmad in custody, Ahmad could sell Jerry down the river to make a deal for himself.

Jerry's mind is racing a mile a minute. Should he contact Lt. McNamara to have another interrogation sooner that what is scheduled?

Or should Jerry wait for the lieutenant to show up and not seem too anxious.

A court appearance is scheduled in two weeks; Jerry decides to wait for the lieutenant to make a move after the court date.

* * *

The Iranian hit team in Massachusetts has learned of the court date and its location, where Jerry will be officially charged in order to set the trial date.

They have decided to use explosives to destroy the vehicle carrying Jerry to court. The team will take a week to select where they will place their explosives to ensure Jerry is terminated.

The team planning where and how they will accomplish this feat now goes about figuring everything out. They will only get one chance at this.

* * *

Chief Winters and Captain Green along with Lt. McNamara are in the chief's office. "Lieutenant, I want you to step back from your regular duties and devote your total time on the court proceedings of this fellow Ahmad and also Jerry Walsh. I have been discussing with the captain, who could fill in for your position doing on-the-job training. We believe Alan Singer would be a good choice. Do you agree?"

Jack knew the court happenings would fall into his lap. He was surprised that he would be spending his total time on the process.

"Yes, I do agree. I do have some questions for you about how this could affect Mike Richards."

"I figured you would. The captain has advised me he received word from Mike's therapist that Mike is improving; however, his emotional recovery may take some time. What I am saying is, I am trying to get someone else trained as a lieutenant for when our captain retires, and you step up. We will still have two lieutenants in the detective division.

"Captain Green will sit down with Mike and explain to him what we are doing, so he doesn't think he is being phased out. If we and Alan are satisfied, he will get promoted to lieutenant at the same time you are promoted to captain."

"I think that is an excellent idea. I wouldn't want Mike to feel his position with the department is in jeopardy. It should come from the captain."

"When will all of this come about, Chief?"

"Captain Green needs to sit down with Alan and ask if he is willing to accept this responsibility. It will be announced shortly afterward."

"I don't expect Alan to turn this down, sir. He will do a good job."

"Now back to your responsibilities. I want reports about what is going down every Monday, Wednesday, and Friday by 4:00 p.m. I know the state police commander will be climbing all over you. If he gets annoying, let me know. I want you to have good communications with the attorney general's office and let me know if you think they are missing the boat.

"What I am saying is: I want both of these guys' asses."

"Understood, sir, I believe we all do!"

"That's all I have, let us know if you need anything. Captain Green will make it happen."

Captain Green hasn't been speaking; he nods his head in the affirmative and gives Jack a big smile and handshake.

Jack heads back to his office.

*   *   *

Back in his office, Lt. McNamara sits behind his desk to contemplate the huge responsibility that has been handed him.

This is new waters for him. He has never heard of any other detective in history having this type of assignment.

He knows he will do his best and the rest is up to others to do their part.

The first assignment he gives himself is to make two phone calls. Jack picks up his phone and dials the hospital where Ahmad is recovering in New York.

Jack leaves a message with the nurses on Ahmad's floor to please have the attending doctor contact him. He leaves his cell number.

Next on his list, Jack calls the attorney general's office and asks to speak with the prosecutors who are handing Jerry's case. Similar to the first call, he leaves his cell number.

*   *   *

Waiting for the returned calls, Jack calls Jennifer.

"Jennifer Stone, can I help you?

"Hello, honey, how about dinner out tonight?"

"Sure, where would you like to go?"

"Meet me at my place after work and we can try the new steak house that opened."

"That's a great idea, see you around six."

Chapter Eighty-Six

Next Moves

Before he leaves for dinner, he calls the secretary for the detective squad. "I have placed a call to the hospital taking care of the man I shot and arrested in New York. It is almost five and I doubt if the attending doctor will return my call before I leave for the day. Tomorrow, I would like you to contact the hospital again for me and try to have him return my call."

"Lieutenant, email the name of the hospital, the doctor, and the phone number along with any other information that will assist me in getting to the correct floor."

"Janice, I will. Also, I need you to contact our local attorney general's office and get the prosecutor's name who is handling the case for Jerry Walsh. I left a message there this afternoon. You know how these things work. Janice, the chief has given me a special assignment and I am going to be needing your help so I don't have to duplicate my efforts. Can you handle this extra workload?"

"Lieutenant, the word is already spreading around the department that this is your big project. You will be my first priority, believe me. We will nab these bastards, excuse me, sir."

"I couldn't have said it better, Janice."

*   *   *

Jack realizes this will be the first email he has ever sent to the chief. The chief is going to need to get used to it. *I cannot keep running back and forth in between his other responsibilities.* Jack realizes he should always copy the captain on every email.

To Chief Winters: It is my recommendation that when it is possible to move Ahmad from the NY hospital, we put him up in another prison. I don't want Ahmad and Jerry Walsh under the same roof. Email me your opinion. There is the Souza-Baranowski Corrections facility in Lancaster. It is acclaimed to be the most modern maximum security prison anywhere. I will handle all arrangements when needed. Lt. McNamara.

*   *   *

The Iranian hit team in New York is discussing how they would handle their attempt on Ahmad's life. They are looking at the number of options they have and come to the conclusion their best bet is to follow Ahmad up to Massachusetts and see where they place him in prison.

Once they have an idea of where he will consistently be located, they can come up with a site plan to eliminate him.

At least they won't have to go hunting for him in a subway network again.

Chapter Eighty-Seven

Dinner with Jennifer

Jack and Jennifer leave his condo at exactly 6:00. This is a date night to catch up on what they missed, when the two of them experienced the subway episode in New York. They agreed to go to the new Longhorn Steak House in Marlborough, Massachusetts. Both of them love steak.

The steak house is only twenty minutes away without heavy traffic. Both of them are hungry and have a great deal to share about their lives.

Seating is done promptly and they are given a seat with a window view. It appears that Jack's reputation is preceding him and he is being given special treatment.

When the menus arrive and the drink order is placed, both take their time to inspect the choices.

"I'm in the mood for a starter; would you share one with me?"

"What are you thinking of getting?"

"They list grilled cheddar stuffed mushrooms. Are you up for that?"

"Yes, that should go nicely with my martini!"

"What kind of steak are you selecting?"

"When we left for dinner, I had in mind to get a sirloin, but they have a grilled citrus salmon that has caught my eye."

"Salmon sounds good to me; I am choosing the smoky garlic outlaw ribeye. I know you don't mind my having garlic."

Their drinks arrive along with the appetizer. They order their entrees.

"Now tell me what you seemed so excited about over the phone," says Jack.

"My bosses called me into their conference room yesterday. They are a bit concerned that the media is tying up our phone lines trying to get me to do an interview."

"So where is this going?" asks Jack.

"They have a couple of ideas. I told them I wouldn't do anything until I spoke with you. When you called to have dinner tonight, they were excited we would be together with a chance to talk."

"What, are you comfortable doing with the suggestions they gave you?"

"Their first suggestion was having the media into our conference room. The second was to rent another location so they could get as many people there at one time."

"I can see where this is headed," says Jack. "They want the publicity of your interview to attract business. It's not something I object to; however, you don't represent the town nor are you employed by the town."

"I figured you would say this, I'm really not sure if I want to do it anyway."

"Although, if you were to give one station an exclusive for an interview, you can do it on site and also promote your firm on their screen."

"You really think that will work?" asks Jennifer.

"It could and I believe we can create a script of questions they are limited to ask you and kill two birds with one interview."

"Oh, Jack, am I good enough to go on television for something like this?"

"Yes, you are a beautiful lady and what you experienced is something you've had no training for. We will need some time to create the questions so you tell them enough, but not get into the criminal investigation details. My suggestion is for you to contact Fox News to arrange for someone to interview you. You should tell your bosses how you want to handle this and let them work out the details of advertising the firm. See mission accomplished."

"You will help me compile the questions for the interview?"

"Of course, I want you to look good and I don't want the town hall down on our backs at the department."

"This can get complicated, can't it?"

"You don't know the half of it. This will be good and when you have a set date I will have the department watching it."

"Oh great, just what I need is more pressure."

"Jennifer, you can handle it and we will rehearse it together until you are comfortable."

"Thank you, I guess this is one of the reasons I love you so much. You worry about me as well as take care of yourself."

"Why shouldn't I?"

Their entrees arrive and Jack begins to realize he has not told her of his new responsibilities yet. *That can wait until after dessert.*

*   *   *

Jack and Jennifer finish their meals and are thoroughly impressed by the good service and the quality of the food.

Jack says, "Would you care for a dessert or maybe split one? How about another drink?"

"You devil you, you know I am trying to watch my weight and you want to have dessert. Okay, we can share one. However, since I am not driving and planning to stay the night I will also have another martini."

"Be my guest, my lady! You pick the dessert and I will have coffee while you have a martini. I am driving tonight. I look forward to your spending the night and possibly we can talk about more long-term living together at some near time. I'll have another drink when we get to my condo and you change into that lovely peach colored lingerie you have."

"That's a deal, I wouldn't have it any other way," says Jennifer.

$*$ $*$ $*$

While Jack has his vodka and Jennifer has some brandy, Jack tells her what his new responsibilities are regarding the trial of the terrorist.

Jennifer says, "That is a heavy load on you. I have never heard of this being done before."

"I haven't either," says Jack.

"This is new ground for me and I will need your legal input into how to handle it."

"You are more than welcome to it, sir, besides having my body."

Chapter Eighty-Eight

Next Day

When Jack arrives at the office, his receptionist says: "Lieutenant, the hospital in New York says the doctor will return your call around noontime. He is sorry he hasn't returned your call sooner. The second message is from the attorney general's office wanting to know why you are getting involved in this case as it is not normal procedure."

"Janice, thank you, fine job. I'm sure the AG's office is put out. I will let the chief handle this as he assigned me."

"Please call the chief's office and have them ask him to call me in my office."

Wow, a lieutenant asking a chief to call him back, this guy is something else.

* * *

"Lieutenant, what the hell is this AG's office complaining about you working with them?"

"Chief, you assigned me to this project and I am not going to be caught between us and the bullshit with the department of the AG's office. I think you should make it clear what our goal is."

Hearing Jack's statement, he realizes he has more than the typical officer on his staff. He will do what Jack insists, but he expects results from Jack.

"Fine, I will call them. Once you have the go-ahead, you need to proceed."

"Chief, I want a contact name inside of the AG's office who is handling Walsh's case. I also want one from their case officer when we set Ahmad up in Lancaster."

"You know, Lieutenant, you are more demanding than your captain."

"Well, sir, if you want me to get the job done, this needs to happen. If you want a yes man on your staff, you are looking at the wrong boy when the captain retires."

The chief is lost for words because the lieutenant just said if he wasn't what the chief wanted for a captain, he shouldn't be upgraded to captain. The chief has never had anyone talk this way with him before.

* * *

At, 12:15, Jack receives a call from the doctor caring for Ahmad in New York.

"Lieutenant, I understand you want to move him. Will he have adequate care where he is being incarcerated?

"Yes, the facility he will be in is of the latest technology and medical facilities."

"All right, I will agree to release him a week from today. Does that work for you?"

"Yes, it gives me time to arrange transportation and protection for him."

"Protection, Lieutenant, is he in danger?"

"Doctor, I hate to tell you we live in the real world, not one protected by your medical cocoon. Yes, I will arrange protection for him."

The doctor cringes, "Let us arrange for him to be released at 11:00 a.m."

"That will be a good time for us. See you then!"

Chapter Eighty-Nine

Chief Follows Through

Jack is reading an email the chief's secretary sent him. It explains how he is to work with the attorney general's office and who his contact person is to be. Rachel Goodwin will be informed to be expecting a call from the lieutenant in a day or two.

The memo goes on to state the lieutenant is authorized to contact the maximum security prison in Lancaster, Massachusetts, where the department will deliver Ahmad when he is moved from New York.

Jack reads the email a second time as he wants to make sure his eyes aren't playing tricks on him. The chief followed through with what he requested even though he seemed a bit put out by the requests.

He creates two files on his computer, one named Walsh and a second named Ahmad. He files the chief's email under the Ahmad file.

*　　*　　*

In the law firm where Jennifer works, she is involved in a meeting with the two partners regarding the suggestions Jack made, how to handle an interview that would satisfy the media, and promote the law firm as well.

Both partners listen and admit the idea has merit. They will talk it over and get back to her.

When Jennifer leaves Ben's office, she doesn't quite feel convinced they are sincere about going ahead with this type of interview.

The positive thing is that she discussed it with Jack, and now the ball is in their court.

*   *   *

Detective Alan Singer places a call to Jack's office.

Recognizing Alan's cell phone number, Jack says, "Lt. McNamara, how can I help you?"

"Lieutenant, this is Alan Singer, I called to say thank you. I heard you recommended me to cover your duties while you are working on your special project."

"Alan, you've earned the opportunity to get some advancement. There will be days you are going to swear at me. I expect you will do fine and come through it okay. Look, I am also going to need your assistance at times and we can discuss this tomorrow. I want you to arrange for the transfer for our terrorist in New York. Meet me in my office tomorrow after lunch. We have a great deal to work out."

"I'll be there, thanks again."

*   *   *

Captain Green is standing in the doorway of Jack's office. "Can I interrupt you a moment?"

"Sure, Captain, come in and have a seat."

"I'm going to close your door."

"Uh-oh, what gives now?" asks Jack.

"I was meeting with the chief an hour ago and he filled me in on what you are looking for and he seems to think, you were giving him orders."

"Ha ha ha," laughs Jack. "I'm glad you closed the door. I merely told him that since he assigned me this special project, I expect him to work with me when I need him to use his influence. I told him what I want; surprisingly he got me my answers without it sitting on his desk for a week."

Captain Green smiles, "You know he has a tendency to do that."

"Oh yeah, I've been that route before with him. At least you've given me two years to train him the way I want him before you leave."

"Just a word to the wise, Jack, learn when to push and when to back off; don't forget he's still the chief. Look, I wanted to let you know what he told me and just keep it between the two of us."

"Thanks, Captain."

*   *   *

Jack looks at his watch and wants to place one more call before he calls it quits for the day.

On the third ring he hears, "Souza-Baranowski Maximum Security Prison, please listen carefully. Our menu has changed, etc. etc."

Jack allows the phone system to run through the directory until he hits the warden's number. He pushes that speed dial and waits for someone to answer.

"Warden's office, this is Jo-Ann, how may I help you?"

Jo-Ann takes his name and phone number, along with a message that he requests to meet with the warden as quickly as possible.

Jo-Ann hangs up before he is finished speaking with her.

"Oh well, we'll see what happens on my next call."

Chapter Ninety

Numerous Meetings

Shortly after 8:00 a.m., Lt. McNamara calls the Lancaster Prison once more to try and get a face-to-face appointment with the warden. Frustrated with their telephone menu, he remembers a little trick he learned years ago. When the menu keeps spouting out orders, keep pounding the zero button until something happens. After ten tries it works, he is about to have a conversation with a real human being.

He impresses upon the woman he is speaking with about the highest priority of the prisoner he wants to deliver to their facility next week. Not only is the Natick Police Department involved in this, also the commander of the state police, and the Federal Bureau of Investigation.

The lady gets the message from his tone of voice as well as his words. She promises to contact the warden directly and will personally have a reply for him by the end of the day.

Jack hangs up the phone. He wonders why with all the technology; we still have people who cause it to be stupid.

* * *

The detective's group secretary walks into his office as he is finishing his call with the prison.

"Sorry, you're finding this very frustrating, Lieutenant. Welcome to the club. By the way, here is the direct line number to a Rachel Goodwin who says she is with the AGs office. Let me warn you, she doesn't seem pleased to be calling you."

"Thank you, I'll call her in a minute after I compose myself."

She laughs and turns around to exit his office. "Don't give up, Lieutenant, all of us are counting on you."

*   *   *

The phone is ringing, "Rachel Goodwin, attorney general's office, how can I help you?"

"Rachel, this is Lt. McNamara of the Natick Police. Thank you for returning my call."

"What can I do for you, Lieutenant?"

"I have been assigned a special project of working with the AGs office on the Jerry Walsh proposed trial and the upcoming grand jury decision for the terrorist who was arrested in New York."

"First of all, Lieutenant, this is a highly unusual procedure. We don't normally have police working with our staff. Second, why would we be interested in a prisoner who is in New York?"

"Well, Rachel, I can understand your resistance to this. However, we both work for others higher on the food chain than we are. Do I make myself clear? I would like to make these situations easy and less difficult than what I am hearing from you. Besides, the New York prisoner will be in the state of Massachusetts in one week."

"I never received word on that."

"I guess we have a good reason to begin communicating, don't we?"

"I suppose you want a face-to-face meeting to review what we are doing with Jerry Walsh."

"That would be a good start!"

"I'll call you back, Lieutenant, as I have a number of cases and I am very busy."

"Rachel, I don't think I am getting across to you. These two cases are of the highest priority in the state right now. If someone were to drag their feet on them, there could be political repercussions."

"Are you threatening me, Lieutenant?"

"No, and since I know this call to your office is recorded, let me make myself clear. I have been given this assignment to provide the AGs office with every bit of evidence we have to allow you to get a positive decision in court. My other responsibility is to make sure this case doesn't go on the back burner or slip between the cracks."

"I'll call you on Monday as to when we can get together and where that will be."

"That will be fine, thank you, Rachel."

Jack hears her slam her phone down. He smiles.

Rachel is livid. She is so pissed off she needs to take a break to calm down.

"Who the hell does he think he is," she says to no one.

* * *

After his phone call with Rachel, Jack decides to take a break. While he is out getting coffee, he bumps into the captain who is walking around the department.

"How are things going, Jack?"

"Just as I expected captain!"

Captain Green laughs knowing Jack in now confronted with dealing with a lot of others who interfere with his progress. *Welcome to the real world,* he thinks.

* * *

The phone in his office is ringing as Jack enters his office. He picks it up before he sits down. Jack responds, "Lt. McNamara."

"Lieutenant, Jennifer would like you to call her at work. She couldn't hold on while you were out of the office."

Jack needs some good news although this morning was not all bad.

When Jennifer's phone rings, "Jennifer Stone, how can I help you?"

"Sorry, I missed you, honey. It's been a crazy morning here. What's up?"

"The partners like your idea and they have me calling Fox News to set up an interview. How much time do we need to put this together?"

"Give us a two-week window so we can create questions and do some rehearsal."

"Great, I like that! Are you going to be home tonight?"

"Yes, why?"

"I'm going to come over and give you some stress reduction."

He can't help it. Jack laughs and says, "This is the best thing I've heard all day after your firm agreeing to do the interview. I won't be home until at least 6:30."

"I'll be waiting. I'll pick up something on the way over, and I really don't have time to cook either."

* * *

Jack has a steak sandwich delivered from the local D'Angelo's in the area. He needs the time to make a list of items he will be discussing with Detective Alan Singer.

* * *

At 1:15 Detective Alan Singer knocks on the door of Lt. McNamara's office. "Can I come in?"

"Yes, that chair has your name on it."

"Uh-oh, am I in trouble?"

"No, it's just been one of those days and the day isn't over yet. Here is what is going to happen. A week from today, we are going to remove the terrorist I arrested in New York and bring him to the prison in Lancaster, Massachusetts."

"Lancaster, not Walpole?"

"Yes, the chief and I agreed that we do not want both of them under the same roof. Lancaster is even more modern and with newer technology than anything else in Massachusetts.

"The doctor whose care he is under agreed to release him next week. Now, here are your responsibilities: You need to connect with the NYPD and work out the paperwork for us to remove him from New York City and New York State. When you are an hour away from Lancaster, you need to call me. I will meet you at the prison so we do this together."

"None of this sounds difficult, what's the big fuss"

"Alan, this guy is a major liability to some nation and I don't know what that party will do to stop him from being transported or to arrive safely in Massachusetts.'

"You're shitting me, right?"

"No, Alan I am not. I want you to draft a proposal, which will include an ambulance and protection for us to review together. When we are satisfied, we will jointly present it to the chief and the captain."

"You're serious about this, Lieutenant, aren't you?"

"Yes, very serious, I believe somewhere in transit or going to trial, someone or some party is going to try and eliminate him."

"Why, what's the gain?"

"Just think about what you just said, Alan, and we can discuss it further when we review your draft."

"When do you want this draft by?"

"I expect you after lunch on Monday."

"Aw, Jack, we have a barbecue to go to this coming weekend."

"Remember what I said, there will be days you will hate me for recommending you."

Alan said, "I guess this is the first one, right"

"You keep score, I don't have time. While you are learning to do the duties of a lieutenant, you have the golden opportunity to say no someday if you're not happy with the responsibilities."

Alan rises and says, "I'm going to work on this at home."

"I have no problem with your working at home. Just make sure your regular reports are in on a weekly basis."

"You are a ball buster, aren't you?"

"It comes with the job!"

*   *   *

Just as Jack checks the time on his watch, his phone rings. "Lt. McNamara!"

"Lieutenant, there is a lady named Roselynn Gibbs who says she works at the prison in Lancaster and she desires to speak with you."

"Thank you, transfer her."

"Roselynn, thank you for keeping your word of getting back to me."

"I made a promise and would call you back even I didn't have the information you are looking for."

"I hope that is a positive statement," says Jack.

"Yes and no! You didn't hear this from me. You do have an appointment with the warden next Tuesday at 2:00 p.m. Just be aware he tends to be a real politician and I think he is afraid that this is too hot a potato for him to be involved."

"I understand, Roselynn. As far as anyone knows you only told me the appointment information."

"Thank you, sir, and good luck with it."

After speaking with Roselynn, Jack focuses on a point on the wall opposite his desk. He is trying some mindful thinking so he can keep all of the balls in the air on this project. Ten minutes later, he shakes his head and leaves for the day.

Chapter Ninety-One

Monday Morning

At 7:30 a.m., Lt. McNamara's phone rings on his desk. Seeing it is an inside call, Jack says, "Hello."

"Jack, the chief read your first report Friday evening. He wants us in his office at 8:00."

Jack walks up to the chief's office just as the chief's secretary tells the captain to go inside. She says, "You might as well follow him, Lieutenant. I know you're expected too."

Jack smiles. Here is a lady with a sense of humor, especially this early in the morning.

Watching both the captain and the lieutenant enter at the same time, the chief says, "Take a seat."

For a moment the chief doesn't say a word, then he begins. "Jack, I'm impressed that you've accomplished so much in two and a half days. However, I believe you are really stirring the pot."

"Stirring the pot, sir?"

"Yes, creating problems or, let me say, difficulties. I spoke with the warden from the Lancaster Prison at five on Friday. Yes, I know you have an appointment with him on Tuesday. He's not too happy about what you want to do."

"Chief, we have two maximum security prisons in the state. Where do you suggest I put Ahmad if not Lancaster?"

The chief gives Jack a frown and replies, "I think the warden knows that and probably agrees with your choice. He just needs to let off some steam.

"Next the attorney general calls me and says he has one pissed-off lady on his staff named Rachel Goodwin. Do you want to explain this one?"

"Sure, I tried to be nice with her. She played the control game with me. She is supposed to call me back today to let me know when she and I will meet on the Walsh trial. I promised to tell her about Ahmad's transfer when we meet. I kept that out of the conversation as leverage. She slammed the phone down at the end of our conversation. You can tell the attorney general for me, she is not very professional."

"I will give you credit, you have things moving, Jack."

"I've been given an assignment and I have no idea what my time parameters are. I cannot sit around while other people pussyfoot around. That is the problem today. No one prioritizes."

The chief looks at Captain Green and the captain doesn't comment.

Chief Winters continues, "Your report says Detective Singer is working up a draft for transferring the prisoner from New York."

"That is correct, sir. Alan's assignment was to work over the weekend so we can meet after lunch today. Sir, if you want to give this assignment to someone else you won't hurt my feelings."

"Jack, for some reason your having this assignment has improved the morale of this department since Black Friday. Everyone sees you fighting to get results. Your style is not my style, but I will say it is doing wonders for our people. Keep up the good work and try not to get too bloodied in the process."

"I'll do my best, sir!"

Captain Green and the lieutenant leave the chief's office.

Halfway down the hall, the captain stops Jack. "I'm sure you felt pretty uncomfortable in there. What I want you to know is that he is covering his bases by the questions he asked you. When he has to deal with those who want your neck, he needs the ammunition to shoot back. You received one hell of a compliment in there about the morale of the department. Be proud of yourself. We all think you are doing a good job. Believe me, I know what it's like when people want to shove you under the rug to get rid of you." The captain shook Jack's hand and they left each other's company.

"Thank you, Captain," Jack said as the captain is leaving.

* * *

Jack looks at his appointment calendar and remembers he has another interrogation with Jerry Walsh on Thursday at 2:00. He needs to prepare for this and it is a good time to put his mind to it.

He will develop his interrogation questions for Jerry and afterward will build a presentation for the warden in Lancaster. It's nice to know his meeting will be a hostile one before he gets there so he is prepared.

* * *

By 10:30, Jack has a list of the interrogation questions he is satisfied with for his meeting with Jerry Walsh on Thursday. He looks at his watch and decides to get a cup of coffee before starting to put together his ideas in meeting with the warden in Lancaster.

* * *

Iran's hit team assigned to New York learns Ahmad will be moved to Massachusetts sometime near the end of the week. What they realize is they will have a better success rate of killing him in Massachusetts than if they were to try a hit-and-run during the transfer. This will take some surveillance work on their part to see where he will be dropped off. Their plan is to rent two vehicles so that they can follow whatever vehicle is used to move Ahmad. While this is more work and time consuming, it has a greater chance of success.

The team leader sends out one of his men to purchase two-way radios they can use while on the road. The key is to purchase a set that has a good maximum range.

*   *   *

Jack returns from stretching his legs and having some coffee. He brought a second cup back to his desk. He glances at his watch and it is 10:45. He begins creating a list of why the Natick Police Department wants Ahmad in Lancaster.

At 11:45 he feels he has a list he is satisfied with. Knowing Allen Singer is due at 1:00, he relies on his old standby for lunch. He calls the local D'Angelo's gives his name and his rewards card number then asks them to deliver a medium No. 9 steak special sandwich.

"You know, what I always order, so make it the same way. Nothing to drink. We have water here in the department. Oh yeah, add a small bag of baked potato chips. Thanks."

Chapter Ninety-Two

Rest of Monday's Schedule

Jack receives a call from the desk sergeant that his lunch has arrived. Could he come down to pay the delivery lady and collect his food?

Jack pays the young lady and gives her a tip. "Thank you," he says.

The young lady turns and leaves without saying a word.

"So much for communication," remarks Jack.

He glances at his watch and sees it is only 12:15. He has plenty of time to eat his lunch without getting indigestion from eating too fast. He hates when that happens. Jack walks back to his desk so he can also have some privacy.

After finishing his sandwich and the small bag of baked potato chips with a bottle of water, Jack clears the papers the lunch was wrapped in off his desk, and wonders what Detective Alan Singer is going to propose.

* * *

At 12:55, Alan Singer knocks on the door of Lt. McNamara's office.

"Come on in, Alan, I've been waiting for you."

"Is that a good sign or a bad sign?"

"It is definitely a good sign and after my meeting with the chief and the captain this morning, I think we are on the right track. Now what do you have?"

Alan looks at Jack and says, "I thought about this all day Saturday. It hit me late Saturday night to give you this proposal."

"Okay, let's hear it."

"You are very concerned that someone or some country would want to remove this guy from the scene, before he can open his mouth in court."

"You've got that right, so go on!"

"If what you feel is correct, and I don't doubt your suspicions, whenever we move him, there will be surveillance watching us to take him out or to follow us to our destination."

"I agree and I'm with you, so what have you got?"

"Since their surveillance team will somehow learn who I am and will be watching me closely, I want to do the following: One, I along with another detective will be in the lead car leaving the hospital; two, there will be an ambulance behind us carrying a body along with an EMT; three, we will have a follow-up car with two more detectives behind."

"This sounds reasonable; however, I have a feeling this is not your real solution."

"If I were looking to do surveillance work on this event, I would have one vehicle set to follow the procession. Another vehicle would continue to stay near the hospital looking to see if another procession leaves, causing anyone to wonder which one is the dummy ambulance."

"I like your thinking, Alan, continue."

"If we wait an hour or an hour and a half, we could arrange for a helicopter to land on the roof of the hospital and fly the real patient to Fitchburg Municipal Airport. That is the closest small airport to Lancaster. No one would be expecting the arrival.

"This way the second car figures there is only one procession and they haul ass to get close to the first procession."

"Sounds reasonable, have you figured out how to get the prisoner to Lancaster yet? I did expect you would want to be involved meeting the helo and taking him to Lancaster."

"Lieutenant, I haven't figured any costs out yet. I wanted to see what you thought of the plan."

"I like it and I believe I can sell the idea to the chief if it's not astronomical."

"Right now I would like to brainstorm with you about all of the ifs and buts we could encounter before I present this. I knew you would come up with something unique.

"If we can sell the idea to the chief, I want the first procession to arrive at Walpole and take whatever or whoever you use for that body for deployment there."

"I like that idea," says Alan.

"Alan, you put together a great proposal. Find out what the approximate costs will be vehicle wise, including a helicopter and manpower wise, so I can give the chief a budget figure."

"When do you want these figures?"

"Let's say Wednesday at noontime."

"I'll have them for you, Lieutenant."

*   *   *

It is after 4:00, when Alan and Jack separate from their meeting. Jack looks at his watch and wonders if Rachel Goodwin will call by 5:00.

He sits down to prepare a Monday report for the chief and the captain per the chief's instructions. His final remark in his report asks the chief and the captain to hold 2:00 this Wednesday, open for a briefing on how they plan to move Ahmad on Friday.

When he has finished, it is 4:55 p.m. Jack calls the receptionist and tells her he will be in his office until 5:30. He is expecting a call from the attorney general's office.

*   *   *

Jack isn't the only one watching the clock. Rachel knew she owed him a phone call. She planned to call at 5:15 expecting he would be gone for the day.

At 5:15 Rachel calls and tells the receptionist that she is sorry to be calling so late, but she promised to return a call to Lt. McNamara today.

"Oh, the lieutenant told me he has been waiting for your call. Let me ring his extension."

"DAMN, DAMN, DAMN," Rachel repeats to herself.

"Hello, Rachel, thank you for calling me."

"Sorry, I'm late. It's been hectic here all day."

"I can imagine!"

Rachel says, "I have time to meet you Friday. Is that okay with you?"

"Monday would be better. I have a full day Friday. Would you like to go to lunch?"

Rachel is a little taken back as no one has ever offered to take her to lunch before unless they were dating.

"Monday lunch will be fine. Would you care to eat here in Worcester or somewhere else?" she says.

"I'll meet you at your offices and you decide where we should go. See you then."

After Rachel hangs up, Jack realizes he threw her a curve by offering lunch. Her status with the AGs office normally wouldn't allow that. However, this could be an exception. If she cancels lunch, I know someone told her not to go.

With this completing his day, Jack shuts his computer down and heads for home.

Chapter Ninety-Three

Tuesday

It is 8:00 and Jack's phone rings. The chief's secretary says, "Lieutenant, the chief wants to see you in his office in ten minutes."

"I'll be there," replies Jack. *He wonders what brought this on.*

Jack knocks on the chief's door and enters.

"Have a seat, Jack."

The chief hangs up his phone from the call he is on. "Jack, you've called a meeting without much notice. What the hell is going on?"

"Let me explain before you hit the roof, Chief. Alan Singer has come up with an excellent plan to transfer Ahmad from New York. I need to present it to you and the captain because I want to move him this Friday."

"Why this Friday?" asks the chief.

"That is what I worked out with his doctor last week."

"All right, tell me about the plan so I can think about it for twenty-four hours and decide what to do when we meet. Jesus, Jack, you sure do make things happen."

Jack gives the chief the highlights of the plan and says, "I think it is an excellent plan. I am sure you will agree."

The chief looks up at Jack and smiles, "Lieutenant, you are becoming one hell of a pain in the ass. However, I have to say I wouldn't want you any other way."

"I guess I'll take that as a compliment, Chief."

Jack leaves the chief's office and heads for a cup of coffee. Right now he needs one.

*　　*　　*

Jack plans to have lunch at 11:30 so he can arrive at the prison in Lancaster at 2:00. While Lancaster is not normally a one-and-a-half-hour drive, he is preparing for any circumstance that would cause him to be late with the warden. In other words, Jack doesn't want to give the warden an excuse to cancel their meeting and refuse to accept the prisoner.

The time at this moment is 9:30. He knows the captain is overloaded with detective reports with Mike Richards being on desk duty. He decides to ask the captain if he could use him for two hours.

"Jack, thanks for asking, yes, come down and pick up a couple of these reports so I can make sense out of them."

"I'll be right down."

*　　*　　*

The paging system in the department starts asking for Detective Lt. McNamara to call the main desk.

As soon as Jack returns to his desk, he responds to the page. "Lt. McNamara!"

"Lieutenant, you have two messages: the warden in Lancaster has changed your meeting time to 3:00. He wants you to confirm. Second the doctor in New York wants to know if you can pick up the prisoner after lunch on Friday."

"Thank you, I will take care of both situations."

Jack calls the receptionist for the detectives, "Janice, I need you to make two phone calls for me. Please call the prison in Lancaster and tell the warden or whoever, I am confirming the change of appointment to 3:00. Next, I need you to call the doctor in the hospital in New York where we have our prisoner. Tell him, yes, we will pick him up after lunch, we want a time. Then tell him on Friday morning he will be called by a Detective Alan Singer with some other details for picking up the prisoner."

"I will, Lieutenant, and I will get back to you when I have satisfied your instructions."

* * *

At 11:30, Lt. McNamara leaves for lunch. He needs to be away from his desk so he can clear his head and be set for the meeting with the warden. He decides to have lunch at a local sushi bar that is a favorite of his.

Waiting for his sushi to arrive, Jack's cellphone rings. Looking at the number on his screen he sees it is Jennifer. "Tracking me down are you?"

Jennifer laughs, "Yes, they told me you were going for an early lunch because you have to leave this afternoon. I only want to tell you the interview with Fox News is set for three weeks from today. Can we work on the statements over the weekend?"

"Sure can and bring your bathing suit. We will use the indoor pool at the condo in between sessions," says Jack.

"How about if I come over Friday night and cook dinner for you?"

"I'd love it. Plan to stay the weekend. My lunch has arrived. Here is a quick kiss for you until Friday."

Smiling Jennifer hangs up and feels how lucky she is to have Jack.

* * *

At 1:30; Lt. McNamara leaves Natick and heads for Lancaster. He arrives at the prison at 2:45. He parks in the visitor's lot and heads for the main entrance. At the main entrance, he is asked to wait for an escort to the warden's office. His escort arrives and takes him in the administration building, where he is asked to be seated and wait to be called to meet with Warden Edwin Cooper.

At 3:00, no one is giving him any hint when he will meet the warden. Finally, at 3:20, the warden's male secretary comes over and asks Jack to follow him.

Entering the warden's office, Jack sees a man somewhere in his late fifties, white hair and metal rimmed glasses. The warden doesn't offer to stand.

"Have a seat, Lieutenant!"

Jack reminds himself to keep his cool!

"I understand you have a prisoner you want us to house."

"Yes, sir. I assume you know the background about this man."

"I do, and if it wasn't such a high-priority case with a lot of agencies involved, I doubt I would accept him. When are you delivering him?"

"I will be delivering him Friday late afternoon."

"You will be delivering him?"

"Yes, Warden. Lieutenants do work!" Jack couldn't resist the response. He knows there is no way Cooper is going to reject this prisoner. He has already said so himself.

"Is he going to need medical treatment?"

"Some depending on how his knees are healing."

"His knees. What the hell did you do to him?"

"It will be a matter of court records. I shot him in both knees while he was trying to escape."

"His doctor is willing for him to be moved?"

"Yes, his doctor wants me to move him on Friday from New York."

"This is highly unusual, Lieutenant."

"This situation is highly unusual. If you have no further questions from me, I will leave."

"You don't have any more questions for me?"

"Warden, I believe you know your job. I will suggest this prisoner is carefully monitored and treated in a manner so his physical appearance doesn't show any injuries."

"Are you accusing our people of brutality, Lieutenant?"

"Warden Cooper, I never used those words. You did."

Jack rises from his seat and leaves the warden's office. He asks the warden's secretary to get him an escort to the main gate.

* * *

While Jack is being escorted to the main entrance, the warden's secretary advises him of his next appointment.

"I want you to cancel it. I need time to think some more about this lieutenant that just left. He is a bit arrogant."

"Yes sir!"

Chapter Ninety-Four

Wednesday

Sitting in his office at 7:30; Jack is running yesterday's meeting with the warden through his mind. He knows he isn't going to get anywhere with the warden, the god of the rock pile. Still he is happy they have a separate place to house Ahmad away from Walsh. He doesn't want them to communicate and there is no way the word will spread that Ahmad is in Lancaster at least until next week.

* * *

A knock sounds from Lt. McNamara's door. He looks up to see an attractive blonde standing in the doorway.

"Got a minute, Lieutenant?"

"May, I ask who you are, and how you can come into the detectives section without notifying anyone."

"Doris Metro, *Worcester Telegram*. Let's say I have some friends. Can I come in?"

"Take a seat! What are you looking for?"

"In all honesty, an exclusive on the prisoner you are planning to move from New York."

"Who might that prisoner be, Doris?"

"Lieutenant, I would like to work with you and create a great story for the Natick police and portraying you as a hero in the whole affair. The people need to know they are safe from the dangers of mad bombers when they are out shopping or even going to church."

Jack smiles. This lady in not only good looking, she is very shrewd and knows how to play the game.

"I'll tell you what, Ms. Metro. When we are ready to have a press release for items we are working on, I will make sure you are on the do-call list."

"Lieutenant, the press has ways of making your position more glamorous or more difficult. Work with me and I'll show you it will be worth your while."

"Right now, I have work to do and should you decide to come again, call for an appointment."

Doris stands and looks at him as if he were a thing to be toyed with. "I'm sorry you see it this way. We could have had a good relationship together."

"See you, Doris!"

She stomps off and you can hear her high heels clicking down the aisle to the outer doors.

Henry gets up and stops at the lieutenant's doorway. "Sounds like you pissed her off, Lou."

"Yep, sure did. I want you to find out who is the leak we have in the department. Make that a priority, Henry. We will be having serious confidential meetings soon and I don't want to see her face here again."

"Okay, let me see what I can do."

Jack dials the captain's number. "Captain, we need to talk. Your office or mine it doesn't matter."

"What's going on, Jack, you sound upset?"

"Nothing more than the usual. I would like a few minutes of your time."

"I'll be down in five minutes."

When Captain Green arrives at Jack's office, he doesn't even bother to knock. He steps inside. Taking a seat across from Jack he asks, "What's going on?"

"Do you know a reporter, Doris Metro, from the *Worcester Telegram?*"

"Not really. I hear she is not a regular, gets paid as a freelance reporter, why?"

"She just left my office after coming here unannounced. Doris tried to connive me into giving her an exclusive on moving Ahmad."

"How did she know he is being moved and when?"

"My suspicions are it is probably all over the New York papers. How much is being said, I really don't know and don't have the time to follow it. I remembered you came and talked with me one time because you felt we had a leak in the department. Now I am suspicious and have assigned Henry to find out who the hell it is."

"I don't blame you for being upset, Jack. Let's see what Henry finds and we'll take it from there. Do you want me to advise the chief about this?"

"I think it's a good idea. Thanks for coming down. I've got to put my head together to what Alan and I are going to discuss."

"I know the chief and I are anxious to listen to your proposal at 2:00."

* * *

"Lieutenant, I know, it's earlier than we planned to meet. What I have will take more than one or two hours. How about I come in at 11:15 and we order some pizza or something?"

Jack starts laughing to himself because Alan is now starting to take his lieutenant-in-training mode seriously. "I think it will be a great idea. Order a pizza and we can eat it in the small conference room where we can spread out."

"What do you like on your pizza, Lieutenant?"

"Onions and anchovies?"

"Got it. See you in twenty-minutes."

* * *

Detective Alan Singer arrives with a large pizza loaded with onions and anchovies. He is the envy of everyone he walks by. He cannot help but smile and think, *Too bad, suckers.*

Jack is already in the small conference room with his share of the paperwork to finalize what they plan to do Friday.

"Let's at least have one slice or two before we get involved with this mess, Lieutenant."

"I'm with you. Would you like some water?"

"Yeah, that would be great."

Jack heads out to the machine that dispenses bottled water for the department at no charge.

As they begin to eat, Jack says, "How do the figures work?"

"Not bad really, Lieutenant. The manpower costs are no different than what they would normally cause the department. The vehicles have some extra mileage; however, that is not a major hurdle. We can obtain an ambulance from the Natick Fire Department and that is going to be a freebie if you understand what I mean."

"Sure, everyone is willing to do anything to get this guy's ass."

"You've got that right!" says Alan.

"What about the helo—what are the costs involved?"

"You really don't want to know, Lieutenant. The sky is the limit with these people."

"Fine, I think the plan is a great plan. I'll let the chief worry about that one."

"Alan, the doctor who is releasing Ahmad wants us to pick him up after lunch. I will arrange a 12:30 or 1:00 pick-up time. I want you to call the doctor and arrange a dummy pickup for 11:00. He is aware that you will call him. Use your influence and don't let him crap out on this."

"Lieutenant, I won't. Tell me who is going to meet you in Fitchburg?"

"After the chief okays this, I will arrange an ETA in Fitchburg. I want you to arrange for the ambulance."

"No problem, just give me the word."

"After I meet with the chief and the captain at 2:00, I'll call you with the results."

"We need to celebrate by finishing this pizza. Two more slices for you, Lieutenant, and two more for me."

Jack realizes he better cut back on his carbs for dinner.

*   *   *

Jack begins his presentation in front of the chief and the captain. As he continues, he is surprised at all of the facial expressions. They seemed to be positive and not questioning his and Alan's position.

That is until he hits the costs of the helicopters.

"Are they serious, they want that much money?" says the chief.

"Alan went out for three quotations. Not much we can get away with here."

The chief sat back and began smiling. All of a sudden Jack was wondering what is coming next.

"Jack, I knew these helo people would be ridiculous so I threw a bone to the commander of the state police."

"What kind of bone, sir?"

"I told him he wants in to see Ahmad get the death penalty so he needs to get his hands dirty."

"Well, what did he say?"

"We have full use of his department's helo to go to New York and fly to Fitchburg."

"Really, wow, how did you pull that off, Chief?"

"Don't ask, you'll learn how later in your career."

Jack notices Captain Green smiling. He realizes the captain knew this all along before the meeting began.

The meeting ends and everyone is pleased.

* * *

Jack puts in a call to Detective Singer. He leaves him a voice message.

"Everything is a go! Helo is taken care of by the chief. Once I get an ETA I will arrange with whoever you select for me to work with in Fitchburg. Nice job, Alan, I am impressed. See me tomorrow morning to finalize everything."

Chapter Ninety-Five

Thursday

Lt. McNamara works at putting some final thoughts together to his interrogation with Jerry Walsh this afternoon.

At 8:00 a.m., his phone rings. He sees the number is from Detective Alan Singer.

"Alan, we need to get together this morning to finalize your project plans. I will be in Walpole this afternoon."

"Is it okay with you if I come in at 10:00 as I need to meet with one of the detectives about his part in the plans?"

"I need to be out of here by 12:30 and be in Walpole at 2:00."

"We should have enough time and you can even squeeze in lunch."

"See you later, Alan." Jack hangs up smiling.

*   *   *

Captain Green calls Jack. "Lieutenant, we may be having some fed problems with Ahmad."

"What kind of problems, Captain?"

"The chief is hearing they want to claim him as a national security risk."

"National security risk. He is going to be locked up in a maximum prison."

"The chief asked me to speak with you to see if you have any ideas why the fed shouldn't gain possession of him."

"Well, to begin with, the only assistance the feds gave us was to confirm everything we generated. Ahmad was in New York for at least six weeks right under their noses and they never knew it. Ask the chief to call the governor and some members of the Massachusetts Supreme Court for a recommendation. Besides they bailed out of Natick and Worcester without so much as a clue."

"I'll pass this on to the chief."

"You know, Captain, they don't surprise me one bit. They are glory seekers!"

* * *

It is almost 10:00 when Alan Singer is due in. Jack decides to get some coffee and try to get rid of this latest frustration about the feds.

Jack no sooner returns to his office when he finds Detective Alan Singer standing in the doorway.

"When I saw you were out, I figured you were going to use the john or get some coffee. Is there any left downstairs?"

"Go grab yourself a cup. It's pretty good today. Then we can get started."

Alan returns and sits down in front of Jack. "I'm ready."

"Lay it all out for me so I know the details," says Jack.

"I plan to call the New York doctor on our way down around 9:00. I will give him a heads-up about how we are going to do a distraction run leaving the hospital at 11:00. I will tell you are arriving by helo at 1:00 for the actual move.

"Steve Donavon will be riding with me in the lead car. The Natick Fire Department ambulance will be in the center with a real live EMT inside. The follow-up car will have Peter Chang and Mark Rosen in it.

"We will make like we are actually moving a body out of the hospital and head for Walpole, like you suggested."

"How are you going to go into the hospital with an empty transporter and come back with the transporter carrying a body?"

"Easy, Lieutenant. The fire department is loaning us a blow-up dummy, which will be deflated going in and inflated coming out."

Jack smiles, "I like it. See if you can spot a tail following your procession."

"Oh yeah, we are looking forward to finding one. Now Lieutenant, you say the helicopter will arrive at 1:00. What time will you get to Fitchburg?"

"Our ETA should be around 2:30. I have it worked out with a Lancaster ambulance service to meet us there and take us to the prison."

"How are you getting back to Natick?"

"Captain Green is meeting me at the prison. He wants to get a look at Ahmad."

"Everything should work like clockwork and Ahmad should be all settled in by dinnertime."

Alan says, "Let's hope so!"

Jack looks at his watch and says, "I need to be out of here in twenty-five minutes, which means I get to eat something out of our vending machine instead of real food."

"Sorry, Lieutenant, duty calls," Alan says smiling.

*　　*　　*

This is Lt. McNamara's third visit to the Walpole Prison. He is very familiar with the routine he must go through to visit with Jerry Walsh.

Entering the visiting area, he is happy to see the same officer on duty that was here his first two visits.

"Lieutenant, I hope you're making headway with this prisoner. Word around the lockup is that he is a real loner."

"I'm hoping to make use of that fact. What is happening outside of these walls may be making him very nervous. Hopefully that will work in our favor. Thanks for the comment. I can only do my best."

"As soon as I saw you come through the door, I called down below and they are arranging to bring him up."

"Thanks, I'll wait to be called in."

Jack waits nearly ten minutes before being called into the interrogation room he had used twice before.

Jerry Walsh is seated at the table chained to the seat and to the floor.

Lt. McNamara takes his usual seat opposite the prisoner.

Jack goes for the juggler vein right at the beginning. "I'm sure you know we have arrested Ahmad."

Walsh doesn't say a word.

"Tomorrow he will be transferred from New York."

Walsh seems startled by this.

"Why, I thought he was arrested in New York?"

"Yes, he was, by me. I happened to be at the right place at the right time."

"So what does that mean?"

"It means I get to interrogate him and see if I can play the two of you off against each other."

"Ahmad would never fall for that and besides, I've already given you information about our dealings. What did the legal eagles say about a deal for what I told you?"

"Their exact words were 'it's not enough.' You may never get the death penalty, but you will never see life outside of four walls again. Unless..."

"Unless what?"

"You tell us about all of your clients and the appropriate contacts in each situation."

"If I do, you know I'm as good as dead, and I'm safer here than outside."

"This is our last meet unless you begin to open up. I've had enough of your games and I've got more important situations to deal with. Either you open up, or when you walk out that door I will spread the rumor throughout the prison you told me everything you know."

"That's a lie and you know it. Don't you have any ethics?" hollers Jerry.

"Jerry, I am learning how to play by your rules—cheat and deceive. How does it feel to be on the receiving end?"

Walsh stares at Jack for a good five minutes. "Put your fucking recorder on and don't say a fucking word until I finish. You can take that back to the AG's office. Maybe I can do one good deed before I am removed from this earth."

Jack would love to smile, but the time is not right. He takes his recorder from his jacket pocket and turns it on facing Walsh.

Jerry begins and his statement goes on for eighteen minutes. When he is finished, he lets Jack know to shut off the recorder.

"One more thing, Lieutenant, you wouldn't really spread a rumor about me, would you?"

"Let's put it this way. Maybe spreading that rumor might take away some of the nightmares I still have because of what you and your friend Ahmad did. I might just have tried it to see if I felt better."

"Fuck you!"

With that statement from Jerry, Jack gets up and calls the guard to remove the prisoner.

*   *   *

Back in his car, Jack begins to wonder if he would really have followed through on his threat. He begins to realize what he has witnessed has begun to change a part of him.

Chapter Ninety-Six

Moving Ahmad

Lt. McNamara is on the phone making last-minute confirmations to the Lancaster Prison, the state police, for the helicopter which will transport him and Ahmad back to Massachusetts, and finally the Lancaster ambulance that will meet him at the Fitchburg airport.

With his phone calls completed, he calls Detective Singer's cell phone. "How are we looking, Alan?"

"I'm getting ready to contact the doctor in about ten minutes. Our little convoy is doing fine, Lieutenant."

"Call me if there are any changes. Remember to tell the doctor the helicopter will be on the roof at 1:00 p.m."

"I haven't forgotten. Funny, all of us feel very excited about this run. It's totally different from what we normally do."

"You never know what comes next in our business, Alan."

Jack signs off with Alan knowing this operation is in good hands.

As he ends the phone conversation with Alan Singer, the captain knocks on the door of his office. "I need a few minutes of your time."

"Come in, Captain, do we need to close the door?"

"No, I don't think so. Let's do the easy item first. Henry reported to me who leaked the word of Ahmad being moved today.

"It seems one of our office ladies told her husband over dinner and Doris Metro is his cousin. I don't feel it was done maliciously, I believe she has learned a lesson. I feel our leak is plugged. She will never tell her husband anything anymore that he doesn't need to know."

"That is fast on Henry's part. I didn't expect such a quick result," says Jack.

"What is the harder item you seem reluctant to discuss?"

"The Boston office of the FBI is pissed about what was shared with the governor and some judges regarding their professionalism. The governor has issued an executive order that Ahmad must remain under the jurisdiction of Massachusetts. The chief and I know all of us have just made some enemies; however, we feel it is only appropriate that Ahmad is handled this way."

"Do I need to speak with the chief about this?"

"Right now I would leave it alone. You sure know how to get right to the heart of things in a situation, Jack. I personally feel the chief used your wording and now maybe he wished he would have whitewashed it."

"I only spoke the truth, Captain."

"I know, and it got results."

"How is your transfer going this morning?"

"I just got off the phone with Alan and they are halfway to New York. He is about to contact the doctor about the whole mission, which is new information for the doctor."

"Do you think the doctor will play along?"

"I think so! He shouldn't have any problem with it at all."

"All right, if I don't see you before you leave for the helicopter, I'll meet you at the Fitchburg airport."

"Thanks for the heads-up, Captain."

*　　*　　*

The Iranian hit squad located in New York City has rented two vehicles. Two of their members will follow whatever transfer means the

Massachusetts police use to remove Ahmad. They have been following the newscasts and newspapers regarding when this is going to happen. The second set of two members will remain in the hospital parking lot to see if there is a second transfer. Since they would not know which one might be the real event, both vehicles would have to follow their targets to wherever their destinations end up. The two pairs will keep in contact by phones.

* * *

Close to 10:45 a.m. the detail from the Natick Police Department pulls into the parking lot at the emergency room entrance. The doctor gave Alan instructions on how they were to enter the building and there will be a designated room for them to use and inflate the dummy they have with them.

The doctor thinks it is funny that he has a part in this covert plan.

The ambulance pulls up to the entrance way and orderlies from inside come out to assist the EMT with the move. They guide the ambulance's stretcher into the designated room and the orderlies assist the EMT with inflating the dummy.

When the dummy is fully inflated, they reverse their procedure by adding some accessories to make the dummy humanlike. A sheet is placed over the dummy's body and they aide the EMT in wheeling the stretcher back outside to the ambulance.

Alan Singer is overseeing all of this and signs a blank form for anyone watching to make this look authentic. The procession lines up again and they are on their way by 11:15.

Alan contacts Lt. McNamara and advises him they are beginning their return trip.

"Everything went okay," asks Jack.

"Yes, and the medical staff got quite a kick out of what we just pulled off."

* * *

As the three vehicles leave the parking area, Team One starts their vehicle and begins to follow at a distance of three vehicles long, so as not to be noticed.

Detective Peter Chang says, "Did you catch the silver sedan pulling out from the emergency area parking lot, Mark."

"Yeah, he's three vehicles behind us and I'll keep an eye out to see if he stays on our tail."

Mark calls Alan, "We think we have our tail, a silver Honda sedan four-door. Don't know how many are inside of it."

"Play it casual like you don't know he's there. Let's see what happens," replies Alan.

Alan calls Jack, "We think we have a tail, that is all I can tell you right now."

Jack replies, "We expected this!"

Close to Hartford, Connecticut, Mark calls Alan once more. "Our friend in the back is still there. Are we going to do anything about them?"

"Where we are headed is exactly what Lt. McNamara wants them to think. We will play this out all the way to Walpole."

*   *   *

After waiting another hour and a half, the second car with the terrorist leaves the emergency room parking lot. They have relayed their thoughts to the team leader. "We don't feel there is another transfer going to happen. It looks like you have Ahmad in front of you. We will try to catch up somehow."

*   *   *

Captain Green has a driver deliver Lt. McNamara to the Worcester airport. There he will meet the state police helicopter and they will fly to New York City.

Jack arrives at the airport at 11:45. He finds the helicopter has already landed. He asks security to take him to meet the flight crew.

After introductions are done, the flight crew states, "Let's get this show on the road. Have you ever ridden in a helicopter before, Lieutenant?"

"First time for everything," says Jack.

As they enter the helo, the co-pilot makes sure Jack is strapped in and he gives him some instructions.

The helo rises and begins a smooth assent to their flight attitude.

Jack is wearing a helmet with a microphone inside in case he needs to speak to the flight crew.

At 1:00 p.m., they are descending onto the roof of the hospital in New York City.

The pilot has called ahead and Jack can see four individuals standing on the roof waiting for their descent. Three of them are dressed in medical outfits.

When they land, the shortest man comes over and introduces himself as Ahmad's doctor. "I would like to inspect your helicopter to ensure it is satisfactory to transport the patient."

Lt. McNamara steps out of the way as this is not his equipment.

The pilot takes the doctor into the helo and shows him how well equipped this helo is to transport medical emergencies. The doctor is pleased and he escorts Jack along with his two staff members to load Ahmad onto the helo.

As Ahmad is being loaded onto a stretcher, the doctor turns to Jack and says, "That was quite a ruse you pulled off this morning. Was it really necessary?"

"I received a call from the convoy after they left here this morning. Yes, it was necessary. They told me they have a tail that followed them out from your parking lot."

"Really, what is going to happen?"

"I don't know, Doctor. All we can do is try and be one step ahead of them."

The pilot announces, "We are loaded and ready to return."

Jack shakes the doctor's hand and boards the helicopter. He turns to look at Ahmad and can see the hate in Ahmad's eyes for him.

*   *   *

Shortly after 2:30 the helo descends onto a platform at the Fitchburg Municipal Airport. This is a small private airport mostly used by local companies and those executives wealthy enough to afford expensive toys.

Jack is pleased to see the ambulance from Lancaster is waiting for them.

Lt. McNamara gets out of the helo and stands back, allowing others to do their job.

When Ahmad is loaded into the ambulance, Jack tells them where they are to meet him at the Lancaster Prison. As he says this, he sees Captain Green coming across from the main building to give him a ride.

"How did it go, Jack?"

"Like clockwork, Captain. Alan had a good plan. Also, as we suspected would happen, they have a tail following them back to Massachusetts."

"Is that good?"

"In a way, yes, it is. Alan and his merry men are on their way to Walpole."

Captain Green looks stunned. "Wow, this operation has been well thought out."

"Yes, Alan and I work well together. Whoever is following them is going to be pissed when they find out they have been suckered."

"Look, let's get to Lancaster so we don't have to pay more for this ambulance than we need to," says the captain.

*   *   *

Around 3:30 Ahmad is fully checked into the maximum security prison in Lancaster. Captain Green takes Jack back to Natick and when they arrive, they report to the chief.

Inside the chief's office, Chief Winters says, "Is he tucked away in Lancaster?"

"Yes, sir, mission accomplished," says Jack.

"One more thing: before you leave for the weekend, Jack, what do you believe those who are tailing our people to Walpole will do?"

"Chief, right now I don't have the foggiest idea!"

* * *

On the way home Jack pulls over to the side of the road and pulls out his cell phone. "Alan, it's Lt. McNamara, I realize you must almost be in Walpole. You and your men should finish the day after your phony delivery is made. Good work. I want you and your people in the small conference room at 8:00 Monday morning. This is important!"

Chapter Ninety-Seven

Planning Ahead

Jack pulls up in front of his condo at 6:30 p.m. He sees Jennifer's car and knows dinner and a drink will be ready for him. This has been an exhausting physical and emotional day getting Ahmad to Lancaster, and trying to throw the terrorists off the track of where Ahmad was placed.

Alan Singer reported to Lt. McNamara that his convoy played their role to the hilt suggesting that Ahmad was delivered to Walpole. Alan and his group are heading for home. Alan also stated, "I received your voice mail about Monday morning. All of us will be there."

Jack gets out of his car and heads to the door.

"Welcome home, sir, I cannot wait to hear how today went for you." Jennifer hands him a double SKYY vodka on the rocks with a lemon twist and gives him a quick kiss. Dinner will be ready in about fifteen minutes."

Jack takes the glass and heads toward his bedroom to get rid of his jacket, pistol, and his tie.

*   *   *

Jack is finished for the day and looking forward to the weekend. Those terrorists who were following his men to Walpole have made contact with the two behind them. They saw the ambulance delivery to the Walpole prison and now must rethink their plans. The four men are driving to Dedham to register at the Holiday Inn on Route 1. It has been a long day for them as well, and now they need to rest and recoup.

* * *

Jennifer's fish dinner was fantastic. She put a great deal of work into making this a very special meal for her very special man.

The two of them clean up the kitchen and make another drink to sit in front of the television to watch the evening news.

When the national news comes on, Jack sits up straight. He sees the convoy that Alan led to Walpole on television. He wonders how the media found out about this trip. Damn he is pissed, but in a way he is pleased. This will further confuse the terrorists looking for Ahmad.

Both Jack and Jennifer head to bed early tonight.

* * *

After an early-morning swim at the indoor pool, Jack and Jennifer sit down to have a breakfast of bacon and eggs along with some toast, juice, and coffee. Jennifer made the coffee in Jack's largest pot knowing they would want to have some coffee while they work on the interview questions.

Jack pulls out a lined yellow pad he uses when he brainstorms ideas. They sit across from each other at the dining room table along with fresh cups of coffee.

Jack begins: "What do you expect them to ask you?"

"I've been thinking about that. They could start a number of ways such as why I was in New York, etc."

"You're right, they could and probably will. I say they really want to get into the meat of how you got involved in this whole affair."

"What am I not allowed to say, let's start there. This way if I am asked questions I don't want to answer, I need to know how to address them so I don't look ridiculous."

"They shouldn't ask you any questions relating to how the police handled the situation. You can always tell them to check with the authorities because you don't feel you should get involved with such matters."

For the next three hours Jack and Jennifer create a role play that he and Jennifer will practice, so she feels comfortable being addressed with these issues.

When they are finished, both of them shower. Jack drives Jennifer's car to the Berkshire Mountains in western Massachusetts for a weekend getaway. It is the beginning of March and the temperatures are ranging in the fifties. They can feel spring in the air and its new beginning is refreshing.

*　*　*

At 8:00 on Monday morning, the four detectives of Friday's trip to New York are sitting in the small conference room when Lt. McNamara walks through the door.

"I'm glad to see everyone is bright and shiny this morning," says Jack.

Alan replies, "Who are you looking at, Lieutenant, not this crew."

The other three guys give Alan dirty looks.

"I want to commend all of you and the EMT as well on the remarkable way you handled everything. Did you realize you made national television on the evening news Friday?"

Alan and Peter acknowledge a yes by shaking their heads. Mark and Steve don't say a word. They look mystified.

"How did things go when you went inside the prison?"

Alan leads, "Actually they were very nice to us. We were led to a visitors section, which was empty. It was great to get out of the vehicles for a while and stretch. The EMT handled bleeding the air out of the dummy. That took about ten minutes. I suspect the ten minutes added to our cover story about delivering Ahmad."

"Do you have any idea how the media got wind of your procession?"

None of the men could figure out how that happened.

"Now I have a couple more things I want to address. I need you to check with the news rooms and see if there is a shot of your tail anywhere in their pictures. If there is, I want you to get a blow-up of the vehicle and the plate. Hopefully we can run the data down and see who was following you. Second, I want each of you to keep this next statement in mind. Whoever was following has something in mind, what could it be? When you think you may have an answer, contact me. This could be very important.

"Let's break for the day. Thanks again for a great job!"

Jack heads upstairs. He wants to speak with the captain.

Seated in front of Captain Green, he fills him in on what was discussed at this morning's meeting in the conference room.

When he is through, the captain says, "Do you think they have a chance of learning who followed them?"

"I say it's a million to one shot but one worth taking. Asking them what they believe could happen next just adds four more minds to the process. Hopefully we can come up with an answer. They were being followed for a good reason. Someone or some nation wants to shut up Ahmad before he says something. Now the question is how are they going to try?"

"Keep me up to date with whatever they come up with, Jack."

"I'm leaving in another hour to have lunch with a member of the AG's office in Worcester. I should be back no later than 3:00."

"Who's buying?"

"We are. I asked her, hopefully it will calm the waters."

Captain Green starts laughing.

Chapter Ninety-Eight

AG's Meeting

At 10:00 on Monday morning, Rachel's boss sees how nice she is dressed. "Is this a special day, Rachel?"

"Not a special day. One I want to make a good impression on with my luncheon appointment."

"Oh, I see a gentleman caller."

"Well, not exactly. This is AG office business, so I want to look presentable."

"Enjoy your lunch, Rachel."

"Thank you."

*   *   *

At 11:30 Lt. McNamara parks his car in the visitor's lot and walks to the main doors of the attorney general's office building. He already knows that he needs to take the elevator to the fourth floor and look for Room 422.

Entering the designated office, he walks over to the receptionist and asks for Rachel Goodwin.

"Who may I say is calling?"

"Lt. McNamara of the Natick Police Department."

"One moment please!"

Rachel answers her phone and explains to the receptionist she will be out in five minutes.

"Rachel will be out in five minutes, Lieutenant."

"Thank you!"

When Rachel turns the corner to come out to the lobby, Jack is impressed with her outfit. *He figures the AG's office must pay pretty well.*

Rachel is carrying her briefcase. She looks to be all business.

When she walks over to Jack, she extends her hand to shake his.

Jack asks, "Where would you like to eat?"

"I don't live in the city so I'm really not familiar with a place to go. I usually eat at my desk or in the cafeteria."

"So, since I have you at my mercy, do you like Moroccan food?"

"Never had it, but I'm willing to try."

The two of them head out to the elevator and take it down to the main floor. They cross the lobby and walk outside to the parking lot.

Jack is driving his department Ford. He opens the passenger door for Rachel and closes it after she swings her legs inside.

"My fiancée and I like this restaurant so I am sure you will enjoy it."

She smiles at him, one, for the fact she feels he's not going to hit on her and two, because he is very polite.

The restaurant is only fifteen minutes away even with the traffic. They enter and walk over to the podium to meet the hostess.

A small table for two is provided and a waiter appears quickly as the luncheon crowd has not arrived yet.

They both order unsweetened iced tea with lemon and are handed menus to select their order.

They order the same item, which is the roasted lamb special with potato and vegetable. Rolls and butter are delivered to the table and now they have time to talk before the food arrives.

"I believe the two of us got off on the wrong foot last week, I would like to apologize for my behavior," says Rachel.

"I accept, we all have our bad days and I believe we are even on that score. I've had tremendous pressure on me with moving the ring leader of a terrorist group from a New York hospital here to Massachusetts. Now that is accomplished and I can breathe a little."

"Is he involved with Jerry Walsh in any way?"

"You're going to hear it in court so I will be up front with you, yes he is."

"So why are we going to work together on this? Our jobs are so different."

"This is an idea that our chief came up with. Since I am the lieutenant in charge of this operation you are stuck with me."

Rachel smiles, "Stuck with you doesn't seem so bad."

Jack returns the smile. "Look, I really wanted to have lunch with you so we could get off on a new beginning. I feel we've just overcome our first hurdle and can go forward."

"I agree, what confuses me is no one in our facility has ever worked with the police before other than have them testifying in court."

"I understand, I'm not trying to make this difficult for you. What I see is I can offer some suggestions where I feel the AG's office is not addressing an issue. Then you can have your PIs check them out. My chief just wants to make sure you have an iron-clad case. Between Natick and Worcester, there have been over a thousand deaths caused by Mr. Walsh's explosives."

"You know this is going to take hours and hours of time together. For me to show you what we are planning to do in court is a major undertaking."

"Look, neither one of us can really do what we are setting out to do over this luncheon. Why don't we enjoy our meals and get back to each other for us to have convenient meetings. We could split the driving so that you come to Natick some of the time and likewise I can come to Worcester."

"I like that idea. I'm just not used to be out on assignments. It will be good practice for me."

"Good, we agree and by the way, lunch is on my department."

"Thank you!"

Their meals arrive and they each have a small house salad with their entrée. The waiter says, "If you need anything, just signal for me."

As soon as Rachel takes her first bite she says, "Oh, this is good, now I won't have to cook tonight."

"Funny, you should say that, I was thinking the same thing. I won't have to cook tonight either."

The two of them did some small talk about their careers and their lives. This may be the first experience this AG's office ever had with working this way, but Jack feels it will have positive results.

They finish lunch at 1:30.

"Oh, my god, I didn't know it was so late. The time just flashed by."

"If anyone asks, you had a working lunch and I will verify it for you."

"Thanks, why don't you drop me off at the main entrance. That will be fine for me."

Jack knew this luncheon was new experience for her. He hopes she's not in trouble.

When Rachel exits his car, she says, "I will call you by Friday and before 5:00. We can create a working schedule."

* * *

Jack arrives back at the station house at 2:45. As soon as he enters, he receives a note from the duty sergeant to see the captain.

He knocks on the door of the captain's office and receives a come-in motion from the captain's hands since he is on the phone.

Jack seats himself and as soon as the captain hangs up he says, "How did it go?"

"Well, we had a lovely luncheon at the Moroccan restaurant and I believe everything will work out very well. We have tentatively agreed to meet in both locations to cut costs and get this assignment done. She is a nice young lady who I believe has very little social experience. I think this assignment will be good for her in more ways than one."

"Great to hear, the chief wants to know, so I'll pass that on."

"Captain, unless you have something else, I have other things to finish up."

"No, we are done here."

*   *   *

Arriving at his desk, Jack notices the red light flashing on his phone. He calls the detective's receptionist.

"Lieutenant, a Lieutenant Sullivan from New York City called to speak with you. He would like you to call him back."

Jack thanks her and begins dialing the number she gave him.

The number Jack dialed is a direct line to Lieutenant Alexander Sullivan. It sends him to voice mail and he leaves a message that he returned the phone call.

A half hour later, Lt. Sullivan calls him a second time.

"Lieutenant, let's dispense with the titles and the full names. My name is Alex and I assume you are Jack."

"You are correct, Alex, and I like your style. What can we do for you?"

"I assume the transfer for the ring leader went well last Friday. I hear the feds are bullshit at your department."

"Right on both counts, but I know that's not what you really called for."

"Very perceptive, Jack. The two terrorists we arrested in the subway have a unique story to tell. Of course they didn't come right out with it; however, when they learned what prison life was really going to be like for twenty or thirty years, they decided to talk."

"I assume you are going to tell me why you called, Alex."

"Yes, because this is going to knock your socks off, my friend. I am going to place both of their interrogations in priority mail to you. Expect them by Wednesday or Thursday the latest. There is too much to say over the phone. Besides, I feel you will want a hard copy of these issues before you begin to act again."

"What do you mean act again?"

"You'll see, Jack, believe me!"

* * *

Jack no sooner hangs up with Alex than he receives another call from the captain. "Make sure you are available all morning tomorrow and early afternoon. The chief is having another press conference with the media.

"What about this time, Captain?"

"His legal eagles tell him to, that's why!"

"Oh shit!"

Chapter Ninety-Nine

Tuesday

Lt. McNamara is writing a report for the chief based on what transpired with the AG's office representative and the strange phone call he received from a New York City detective yesterday. As he continues Detective Henry Kostovich raps on his door post.

Looking up, he sees Henry and says, "Come on in, Henry, you have something of interest for me."

"I think so. Wait until you hear the following: My source on Iranian information tells me he hears the following. The mullahs in Tehran have been getting nervous since the first of the year that this fellow Ahmad is not executing his orders. He supposedly told them he is waiting for a more opportune time. He was told to cease from the next assault and come back to Tehran after sending his group to their respective cells here in the United States."

"Then why did he go ahead with the subway bombing?"

"Your guess is as good as mine, Lieutenant. I have no idea. What I am hearing is he is afraid to go back and has gone rogue."

"Why would he do that?"

"There is word around the mullahs have issued a fatwa on his head. They are embarrassed he didn't complete his missions clean and now they want to eliminate the connection between him and Iran."

Jack sits back and whistles while Henry shakes his head.

"Henry, how accurate do you feel this information is?"

"My source has always been right on, sir. I say it is as true as I am sitting in front of you."

"Thank you, I am going to have to take this up with the captain and the chief."

*   *   *

The original hit team sent to Massachusetts to eliminate Jerry Walsh has been desperately trying to find out when and where his trial will be held. Each of the five members are working independently to see what they can come up with. Once they have an idea of where and when, they can plan to set their trap.

*   *   *

"Notice to all media sources, at 11:00 this morning in the Natick Police department's large conference room the second press conference dealing with the bombers of Natick and Worcester will be discussed." The news media is going nuts; they only received a two and a half hours' notice to this press conference.

*   *   *

Chief Winters is standing behind the podium with Captain Green off to his right and Detective McNamara off to his left.

Precisely at 11:00 he begins. "Ladies and gentlemen of the media, this press conference was called without much notice due to a number of factors. I am going to do our best to give you a picture of what we are dealing with regarding the capture of those involved with the bombings in Natick and Worcester.

"Let me explain. Due to the heavy losses of life we experienced over the Thanksgiving weekend and the Christmas holiday, the Connecticut police and the FBI saw fit for a Mr. Jerry Walsh to be returned to Massachusetts as an accessory to the fact and the supplier of explosives used in those bombings."

Those media who have recorders are desperately trying to get each word and those who are taking notes are going spastic with the chief's delivery.

"Over the President's Day holiday, our Lt. McNamara along with his fiancée, Jennifer Stone, were visiting New York City. They were using the subway system on Sunday night. By sheer coincidence Lt. McNamara was able to identify the ring leader of the terrorists, who were in the midst of setting off explosives in the subway system. His fiancée aided by notifying the metro police to shut down and evacuate the subway system. To make a long story short, the lieutenant arrested the terrorist and he is now within our prison system and will be standing trial.

"I want to point out one error in the media; the ringleader is listed as being housed at the Walpole prison. That is not correct, he is currently being held at another facility. He will appear before a grand jury shortly, and stand trial for mass murder. We are going to push for a death penalty.

"There will be no questions taken and you can proceed to your respective employers to announce what we just made public."

*   *   *

Noontime television stations and radio announcers are all breaking the news given by the police department.

Reporters are listing many questions they were not given the time to ask.

One question on their minds is: Why are the two prisoners in separate facilities?

Second: When can the media and the public see what the justice system is doing in taking them to trial? Why is everything so secretive?

Chapter One Hundred

Thursday

Captain Green and Lt. McNamara are with the chief in his office discussing the information Detective Kostovich gave to the lieutenant. Suddenly the chief's phone rings and it is his secretary. The chief places the call on speaker phone.

"Chief, the attorney general's office is calling for the lieutenant on line five. Does he want to take the call now or should I get a name for him to return the call?"

Jack responds, "Take a name and I'll return the call, thank you."

"Well, that call sounds promising," says the captain.

"Rachel promised to call back by the weekend and I assume this is what she wants to discuss. Other than that, I have no idea why the AG's office would be calling me."

"Let's get back to the topic at hand," says the chief. "What do you gentlemen suggest we do with this information?"

Captain Green responds, "Right now I don't think there is much we can do except watch out for the safety of the prisoner. The surveillance team that followed us getting him to Massachusetts is now beginning to make sense. They want him out of the picture."

*   *   *

Seated back in his office, Jack dials the attorney general's office and asks for Rachel Goodwin. He is told Rachel is in a meeting and will be given the message he called.

"Well I guess today will be telephone tag day," Jack says to himself.

*   *   *

The New York hit team is furious they were outwitted and have lost sight of their target. Now the major problem will be to find out where he is currently in prison and how can they get to him to make their score.

The team is also wondering why they didn't receive orders to take out the explosives supplier.

*   *   *

The chief calls Jack and tells him he wants to review the tape he took on his last visit with Jerry Walsh, "Come down to my office around 3:00."

*   *   *

At 1:30, Jack's phone rings and the receptionist tells him the attorney general's office is calling and the lady is Rachel Goodwin.

"Thank you, please put the call through."

"Hello, Lieutenant, I promised to call you back before the weekend. I met with my boss after our lunch and he is interested in seeing how our project could work. Do you have a better day we can meet next week? I am willing to drive to Natick."

"Let me look at my schedule, Rachel. By the way, if we are going to work together, please call me Jack. My Wednesday and Thursday next week are pretty open. Which day is better for you?"

"Thursday would be a better day for me. Would 10:00 be fine?"

"Yes, and as of right now you are in my calendar. Do you have the address and need directions?"

"I have already used Google Maps and I use a GPS so I won't have any problems. I will see you at 10:00."

"Thank you, Rachel, and I look forward to your visit."

*   *   *

Two minutes before 3:00, Lt. McNamara knocks on the chief's door. He hears the instruction to come in.

As he expected, Captain Green will also be involved with this meeting. That is a positive sign as it shows the chief is looking for a consensus.

"Grab a seat, Lieutenant, I only have an hour before I have to leave," says the chief.

Chief Winters continues, "Both the captain and I have listened to the tape and I am sure you have as well."

"Yes, I listened three times to make sure I understood everything on it."

"What do you make of it, Lieutenant?"

"Chief, before Walsh offered to make the tape, he wanted to know what kind of deal the AG's office is going to give him based on what he told me on Ahmad."

"And...?"

"I told him they didn't feel there was enough information to give him a deal."

"He acted like he was going to do one last good deed in his life, but I think he is hoping everything on that tape will win him some favor."

"So you think the information is authentic?" says the captain.

"Authentic as far as he gave it firsthand, good information to take what we know

to the next level, I'm not sure. I do feel this is above our level of investigation and the feds should be called in."

"The captain and I agree with you on that measure. However, before we do that, I want to pass the tape over to the AG's office and have them make a duplicate so they can use it in court."

"When are you meeting with the representative of the AG's office?" asks the captain.

"Rachel will be here on Thursday next week at 10:00. I think she will be surprised when we give it to her. It might be a feather in her cap with her boss as well."

"Lieutenant, I want you to make it clear to this Rachel that we want the original returned ASAP, so we can pass it on to the FBI. Maybe this will take some of the sting out of their hard feelings about getting Ahmad here instead of to them."

The chief looks at the clock on his wall and says, "I've got ten minutes before I leave. Do we need to continue this discussion?"

Both the captain and Jack nod their heads saying no.

Chapter One Hundred One

Hectic Day

Monday morning has Jennifer Stone sitting in the Boston office of Fox News. She is scheduled to tape an interview in ten minutes. She is nervous about the outcome of the interview and how it will be judged by viewers.

Ten minutes go by and Jennifer is still sitting in the waiting room.

Five minutes later, an attractive blonde addresses her, introduces herself, and asks Jennifer to follow her into the studio where they will tape the interview.

The host explains this will only be a fifteen-minute interview with information provided by her firm to be displayed at the beginning and at the end of the event. She is seated in a high-back chair and fitted with a mike attached to the lapel on her jacket.

The lady recognizes the first-time nerves that Jennifer is experiencing. "Try and relax. Once you start and focus on what you say, the nerves will disappear. Believe me, many of us have been there before. If I ask you questions that you are uncomfortable with, merely say you are not at liberty to discuss that information."

That statement began Jennifer's moment of relaxation. She didn't want to place the Natick Police in any bad light to the public.

The cameraman adjusts the lighting on the two ladies and tells them he will give a countdown of five before they need to begin.

Five-four-three-two-one. "Hello, I am Carol Snyder and this morning I am interviewing Jennifer Stone. Jennifer is an attorney for the firm sponsoring this program. Jennifer is also somewhat of a hero.

"Good morning, Jennifer."

With a big smile, Jennifer says, "Good morning and thank you for having me on your program, Carol."

Carol smiles. She sees Jennifer relaxing.

"I understand you and your fiancée were visiting New York City during the President's Day weekend."

"Yes, I had never been to New York before, and we wanted to get away from the stresses of work."

"Who is your fiancé?"

"My fiancé is Lieutenant Jack McNamara on the Natick Police force."

"Please tell us what happened, how you and he were involved in saving lives on the subway system and capturing the head of the terrorist group that was also involved in the Black Friday and Christmas Eve bombings."

Jennifer proceeds to tell Carol what occurred in the subway tunnel, how Jack sent her up to the street level with a message for the police to have them shut the subway system down.

"The police actually believed you?"

"Well, not at first, but I convinced them to change their minds."

"How did you do that?"

"I became very assertive and told them something that caused them to rethink what they were saying."

"You threatened them?"

Jennifer laughs, "Right, a woman in high heels is going to threaten police officers. No, I made them a promise!"

"A promise, that is why they changed their minds?"

"I handled them my business card to my law firm and I promised them if they didn't call in my message, I would work very hard to make sure they became unemployed police officers."

"Really, and they called it in."

"Yes, fortunately they did, and to give the city credit, they had already designed a way to safeguard the subway and its passengers."

"What did you do then?"

"I really wanted to go back down to Jack, but he had given me strict instructions to go to the street level and stay there no matter what happens.

"The city's streets became alive with squad cars, and SWAT teams all over the place. The security plan worked to the extent there was no loss of human life. Six bombs did explode on trains that were shut down."

"How did Jack get out to safety?"

"Carol, I cannot give you all of the details of how he exited. Those are matters for police departments. I will tell you he was smart enough to arrest the terrorist he shot before someone else arrested him."

"He shot the terrorist?"

"Carol, this is all I will say about the incident."

"You cannot or will not tell us more?"

"Both!"

Right then the cameraman went into the post-program advertising of Jennifer's law firm.

When the cameras were down, Carol, says, "This is an amazing story!"

Jennifer leaves the studio and heads to work in Boston.

* * *

At the same time Jennifer is being interviewed, one of the terrorist hit team members assigned to take out Jerry Walsh is reading the *Boston Globe* and says, "Look at this, Walsh's trial date and location is posted in yesterday's paper."

The team leader says, "Let me see that."

Reading the notice in the paper, the leader continues, "We now have something to work with so let's begin laying out our plans. We must also have an exit plan to leave the country immediately. Tehran doesn't want us involved with the Ahmad fellow. I believe they have another team here to take care of him."

* * *

When Jennifer arrives at her office, everyone is excited to hear how the interview went. "It will be on the noontime Fox News, and this evening at 6:00." Jennifer enters her office and dials the Natick police to leave Jack the same message.

* * *

At 12:45, Jennifer's phone rings. "Jennifer Stone, how can I help you?"

"Hey, beautiful, you were great."

"You saw it?"

"The chief put the television on in his office at 11:55. He had the captain and myself in with him. All of us thought you did a great job and you didn't let the host weasel anything out of you that shouldn't be on the air."

"Oh, I'm so glad. Ben, one of the owners, did the same thing with his television and had the whole staff in his office. Everyone here felt it was good! Besides it got the law firm a chance to run two ads alongside a hot topic."

"I'm taking you to dinner tonight. Pick the place and email me. I will be tied up all afternoon," says Jack.

"Okay, I'll do that. See you tonight!"

* * *

The duty officer calls Lt. McNamara and tells him he has a priority envelope waiting for him. It just arrived.

Jack remembers the detective in New York saying he was sending him a priority package. He heads downstairs to pick it up.

Back in his office he opens it and sees it contains five pages of a report. He begins to read and cannot believe his eyes. He read through the report twice before he calls Captain Green.

"Captain, can you squeeze some time in for me this afternoon?"

"Sure, will 4:00 be fine with you?"

"I'll be in your office at 4:00."

Jack reads the report a third time and sits back thinking about how he is going to discuss this with the captain.

*   *   *

Jack knocks and steps into the captain's office. "Sir, I think we should close the door."

"Go ahead, Jack, if you feel the conversation warrants it."

After closing the door, Jack hands the priority envelope over to the captain. "There are five pages, take time to read them and then we should talk."

Jack sits watching the expressions on the captain's face as he reads the report. He figures the exact or similar expressions must have been on his face when he read the report.

"You say this came from a detective in New York?"

"He called me last week and told me he would be mailing me something to review. He said he figured I would be interested to know what is in it."

"Let me call the chief."

Chief Winters answers, knowing it comes from the captain's phone. "Yes, Captain."

"Sir, I would like to drop something off to you that was just mailed to us. After you read it, you, Jack, and I need to talk with you sometime tomorrow."

Chapter One Hundred Two

Events Begin to Unfold

Jack and Jennifer are having dinner in their favorite Italian restaurant in the North End of Boston. The north end has a large population of Italians and most of their restaurants have some sort of Italian-style meal selection. This particular restaurant makes everything to order and it is made to perfection.

While enjoying glasses of Chianti wine, Jennifer explains everything to Jack about how the interview was held. She is pleased it went over so well.

As they talk, their salads are delivered to the table and homemade breads are placed alongside the candles burning in the center of the table. It is a lovely romantic setting for the two lovebirds.

Jennifer says, "Ben, one of the owners, told me there were five phone calls to the front desk asking how the callers could schedule time to meet with me regarding their legal matters. Ben is thrilled and realizes how well the ads did for the firm. He figures the five are just the beginning."

*   *   *

Rachel Goodwin normally watches the standard local media channels but for some reason she clicks on Fox News this evening.

As Jack and Jennifer share dinner, Rachel views the interview Jennifer made for Fox News.

He really is engaged and wasn't giving me a line, she thinks to herself. Jennifer's story impresses her and she wonders if she can obtain more details from Jack when they meet on Thursday.

* * *

The next day, Captain Green calls Jack as soon as he arrives at the department. "Jack, the chief wants us in his office at 10:30."

Precisely at 10:30, both the captain and the lieutenant enter the chief's office after Captain Green knocks.

Both men take chairs in front of the chief as he finishes a phone conversation. They are both used to the drill.

When the chief gets off the phone he asks, "I want to know your comments starting with the captain."

Captain Green is surprised as he is used to having the lieutenant answer before him. He wonders what is going on here. He explains how the FBI has taken over the two terrorists arrested in the subway incident and they have been given immunity.

The chief says, "Lieutenant."

The lieutenant is also caught a little off-guard but recovers quickly. "Detective Sullivan mailed me this packet after phoning me last week. I read it a couple of times and then took it over to the captain. Based on what I read in the report, the two terrorists that were arrested by the New York police were turned over to the FBI after a few weeks of arm twisting. It appears that the FBI gave these two immunity and offered to place them in the witness protection program in return for the information on the cell locations of those who were not captured."

"Captain, do you agree?"

"Yes, I agree!"

"Did either of you wonder why we received this packet? I mean it is a bit unusual for one agency to send information to another especially when it is unsolicited."

Jack speaks, "My personal opinion is this detective is fed up with how terrorists are being treated in the legal system. Sure, maybe the FBI can dig up information on the others. However, I think that is a real shot in the dark."

"Why?" asks the chief.

"Based on past performances there are numerous cases where witnesses are turned over to the witness protection program and their information sucks."

"What do you suggest we do with this report then?"

Jack responds, "Now we know that two of the team Ahmad was working with come from Massachusetts. We should take advantage of that information and see where it leads."

"You know those locations of North Adams and Hyannis are out of our jurisdiction," says the chief.

"Yes, I do; however, you are sending me to counter-terrorism school at Quantico. I feel this would be the perfect time to put what I learn into practice."

The chief looks at the captain, "Do you agree with Jack?"

"We would have to create a new position and be able to budget the costs. Can we do that?"

"I will need to review everything before I give my blessings on this idea."

Both the captain and the lieutenant stand to leave the chief's office, wondering where this will lead.

"There is one more thing we need to discuss, Chief."

"What do you have in mind, Lieutenant?"

"When I transferred Ahmad to Lancaster from the helicopter, I could see the hatred in his eyes he has for me. I understand you have placed me in charge of this project, but I recommend that someone else interrogate him. It will be difficult for me to get an honest answer from Ahmad."

"Who do you have in mind?"

"Either Captain Green or Detective Singer would be good choices."

"What do you think, Captain?"

"Ahmad saw me at Lancaster; I think the lieutenant should select Detective Singer."

"There's your answer, Lieutenant."

Chapter One Hundred Three

Meeting with Rachel

Early Thursday morning Lt. McNamara holds a conversation by phone with Detective Singer regarding a new assignment for him. Alan is to be the department interrogator for the terrorist Ahmad who is located in the Lancaster Prison.

Alan is pleased to be able to have this assignment and he tells the lieutenant he will send him regular reports. He plans on making his first scheduled appointment next week.

*   *   *

At 9:55 the duty sergeant calls Jack and tells him he has a visitor from the attorney general's office waiting for him.

Jack says, "Tell her I will be down in a couple of minutes."

Reaching the bottom of the stairs, Jack sees Rachel sitting on a chair in the waiting area. He walks over to her and asks, "We can use the small conference room if you wish to spread anything out or we can use my office. Which do you prefer?"

Rachel smiles and replies, "Let's use the conference room."

Jack leads the way down one of the passages to the rear of the building.

Entering the room, he hits the light switch and Rachel sees a brown rectangular table with six chairs neatly set around it.

"I think this will work out fine as both of us can sit on one side and not have to raise our voices to each other to be heard," Rachel remarks.

Jack pulls out two chairs from the side of the table they are standing at. They sit and get comfortable. Or to be comfortable as you can be on these chairs.

"Before we start, I want to tell you I saw your fiancée's interview on the evening news the other night. She did an excellent job."

"Yes, Jennifer did a great job on the interview. Yes, she is very photogenic and can handle most conversations with ease."

Rachel says, "Where would you like to start, Jack?"

"Why don't you begin to lay out the evidence your office is going to present in court. I'll see if I can add to it or make some suggestions to ensure your success."

Rachel begins by listing the witnesses they will be using.

1. Members of the FBI
2. Members of the Natick police
3. Members of the Worcester Police
4. Forensic materials based on bombs residue in Natick
5. Forensic materials based on bombs in the Worcester Church
6. Forensic materials from Walsh's home in Barre, Massachusetts
7. Bomb-making materials found in vehicle in Connecticut before Walsh's arrest

* * *

"This is a fine list. Let's look at how each of these will stand up in court," says Jack. They talk for three hours before breaking for lunch.

Following lunch, Lt. McNamara has been saving the best for last. Seated in the conference room, Jack says, "I have a surprise for you and your boss."

"A surprise, what could that be?"

"My last interrogation visit with Walsh enabled me to record all of his contacts and operations he has been working with for ten years."

"Is this for real, Jack?"

"Yes, I am going to give you the original. However, our chief wants your office to make a duplicate and to return the original to us within 72 hours. Everything we discussed before lunch can be shot down by a shrewd lawyer who knows how to cast a shadow of a doubt. This will crucify Walsh in a way that there is no other choice than to judge him guilty. Walsh actually gave this willingly in order to avoid the death penalty."

Holding the tape in her hand, she says, "This is wonderful. You just made my day."

Rachel heads back to Worcester with a large smile on her face.

*　*　*

The Walsh hit team has been studying the area where the courthouse is located and the street layouts for them to utilize a bomb to eliminate Walsh.

Today, they have come up with a workable plan and their idea is to locate bombs under sewer covers in the street. There are two near the courthouse and the prison vehicle will be traveling slowly when they cross over these locations. The idea is to use the first cover to explode under the vehicle with Walsh and the second one to destroy any vehicles following so they immobilize any police activity.

Now they must work out a plan to install the bombs without being detected.

*　*　*

After Rachel leaves, Jack sends the chief an email along with a copy to the captain. The message reads: "We have made one attorney general's office very happy this afternoon. I will keep you posted, Jack."

*   *   *

Meanwhile the Ahmad hit team is beginning to generate plans on how to accomplish their hit when Ahmad is transferred to the grand jury.

Chapter One Hundred Four

Walsh's Death Squad

They've selected the sewer cover locations. Next they have to install the bombs. The bombs must be strong enough to shoot upward and large enough to drive the sewer covers as well as the charge through the underbelly of a vehicle. What will happen is the cover will act as shrapnel. They've used them before in the Middle East and this is not a problem. The difficulty they face is installing them and not being seen or detected, which could cause operations failure or being arrested and maybe both. The local streets are not like the desert where no one usually travels at night.

Each member of the team is sent out with a message to secure enough information in order to bring this plan into reality. They split up five ways.

*　　*　　*

After two days of seeking possibilities to have a successful mission, they decide on one they feel will achieve their goal. It is somewhat daring yet very innovative. They will attempt it on Friday night. Walsh is going to trial on Monday.

After dark on Friday night, two of the team head over to the town's parking area and find they can easily open the lock on the sliding gate, which the vehicles pass through. They enter the area and close the gate behind them without attaching the lock. Coming upon the office entryway, they find the door lock is even easier than the gate lock to open. Now the question is, would there be a security system inside they can deactivate? The senior man of the two looks at the sensor pad and realizes it is a simple system that doesn't even appear to be able to signal the local police. He cuts the wires and deactivates the alarm on the exterior of the building just in case he's made a mistake. No alarms sounds. They look for the storage of the truck keys. It takes them five minutes to find a set. Going outside, they quickly learn which truck the keys belong to. Fortunately, the accessories they need are spotted easily and they load them onto the truck.

The senior member gets into the driver's seat and starts the vehicle. Without using headlights, he moves the truck through the gate that his partner has moved aside. Once the truck clears the gate, his partner closes the gate and attaches the lock without snapping it shut. Jumping into the passenger side of the truck, the two men move out into the street before putting on the headlights. Each man looks at the other and both release a breath they have been holding. The decal on the truck says Water and Sewer Department.

It is a fifteen-minute ride for them to meet their other three team members. They pull up to the first cover they want to detonate. Three of the men dress in utility uniforms and wear hard hats. This is merely cover if anyone questions why they are there.

The two who met the truck have the explosives near the first cover. The men set up four sides of a guard rail around the hole after they remove the cover. They rig lights so they have sufficient lighting and it helps to play the role of them being legitimate. Those same two men who met the truck climb inside the sewer and begin the necessary implementation to build their first bomb.

It takes a half hour before sufficient bomb-making materials are loaded into the sewer and attached to the underside of the cover before it is replaced. All four men wipe perspiration from their foreheads and begin loading the accessories to move to the second sewer cover.

When they begin setting up around the second cover, a local police cruiser comes by.

"You guys are working awful late," the officer says.

The senior man with the good English accent replies, "We have an emergency situation and we should be done no later than two hours."

"Good luck, you guys must be happy making all this overtime."

"Yeah, we are!"

The cruiser pulls away.

"Dumbass," says the leader. "He merely took our word for it."

At the second cover, they go through the same process they did at the first one. A half hour later, they are finished and begin taking down the accessories so the truck can be returned and hopefully no one will be the wiser.

*   *   *

Monday morning at the Water and Sewer Department, the first indications something happened is the alarm system was tampered with. A search begins to see what is missing or damaged. An hour later nothing is found out of the ordinary. All of the trucks are accounted for and their keys are where they should be.

The department head makes a note to speak with the police; however, right now he has other pressing matters on his mind.

*   *   *

The police officer who drove the cruiser made a note in his report that he came upon a water and sewer group working late at night under lights. The person he spoke with said they had an emergency, which should only take about two hours.

His supervisor who read the report Monday never paid any attention to this occurrence.

*   *   *

At 10:00 am Jerry Walsh is being driven to the court room. His trial is set to begin at 10:30. He wonders about his future.

The Walsh assassination team is set back from the street about one hundred yards. As the vehicle carrying Jerry crosses the first sewer cover, a call is made on a cell phone. An enormous eruption is made beneath the vehicle, which causes it to lift a dozen feet in the area and burst into flames.

As the vehicle bursts into flames, the car carrying prison guards crosses the second sewer cover and the explosion is identical to the first one.

There are no survivors in either vehicle.

Chapter One Hundred Five

After the Fact

The media is going wild with the breaking news of two vehicles demolished by explosions that seems to have come from below the street. Are these natural gas explosions?

* * *

Lieutenant Jack McNamara is seated at his desk when the phone rings. The receptionist tells him he has a call from the attorney general's office on line two.

"Lt. McNamara, can I help you?'

"Jack, it's Rachel. Have you heard what happened?"

"You mean about the possible gas explosions, only what I heard on the radio this morning coming in."

"Jack, someone or some people killed Walsh. I don't believe those were gas explosions."

"What, they killed Walsh? Why would they do that?" Then Jack begins to remember his intuition has been bugging him and he didn't realize what it is.

"Look, I am leaving the courthouse now. Can I come to your office so we can talk?"

"Sure, I'll be here."

* * *

While Rachel and Jack are wondering what is going on other than they lost a prisoner, the five Walsh team members split into single units and are leaving the country in different ways. Yes, they will ultimately return to Iran; however, they were successful and have the luxury of taking their time.

* * *

Rachel enters the Natick Police Department at 10:45. She tells the duty sergeant Lt. McNamara is expecting her.

* * *

Ahmad is watching the newscasts in the recreation room at the Lancaster Prison. He hears the news and understands everything that is happening. He knows Iran has taken out Walsh and he is next.

Ahmad has a detective coming to interrogate him in two days. He wonders if he can work a deal. Otherwise he will never see the end of the winter.

* * *

Jack has refrained from calling the chief or the captain. He wants to speak with Rachel before he does.

Jack receives the call that Rachel has arrived and he heads downstairs to bring her up to his office.

Rachel begins speaking very rapidly even before they arrive at Jack's office.

"Hold on a minute, Rachel. Let's go inside and I need you to calm down. I understand the anxiety you are feeling. I need to have you reflect on everything you learned."

Rachel smiles then seems to relax a little as she sits in Jack's office. "My God, this is America. How is it happening?"

"You're right, this is America and shit happens. You are just beginning to get a taste of what happens in the world around us. Now let's start from the beginning, you were at the courthouse."

Rachel begins and she goes on and on about how she learned about the explosions killing all of the men in two vehicles on their way to the courthouse. Rachel is so intense she repeats herself at times. Jack doesn't interrupt her.

When she is finished, Rachel says, "I don't know who is investigating this incident."

Jack replies, "Mostly likely detectives from Framingham will head the investigation and maybe the FBI. I know you are upset and understandably so. Would you like to take a lunch break before you go back to Worcester?

"Let me call my office and tell them I am meeting with you to discuss this. I'd like the chance to relax and have lunch. It will do me some good just to talk."

"You can use my phone or your cell, whatever you choose."

"I'll use my phone. Will we go to lunch soon?"

"Let me call the chief and the captain and see when I can meet with them regarding this. Based on what they say, will schedule our lunch."

Jack picks up the phone and calls the captain. Captain Green's secretary advises him the captain is out until 2:00 p.m. Jack asks her to schedule a meeting this afternoon with the captain and the chief regarding the explosions.

"It is nearly 11:30. Let's get an early lunch and the two of us can get back to what needs to be addressed."

"Thank you, Jack."

*   *   *

HEADLINES IN THE LOCAL MEDIA STATE MYSTERIOUS EXPLOSIONS CAUSE THE DEATH OF PRISONER AND PRISON GUARDS ON THE WAY TO COURTHOUSE.

* * *

The other assassination team, whose target is Ahmad, smiles realizing the other team has been successful in eliminating Jerry Walsh. They need to rehearse their plans sufficiently to ensure they have the same success when they assassinate Ahmad.

* * *

The commander of the state police places a call into the chief's office at the Natick Police Department. He is advised the chief will be returning later this afternoon and he should expect a return call.

* * *

Inside of Tehran, the head of the revolutionary guards is made aware that one subject has been assassinated and he will be advised when the other team is successful. He knows it will take his team some time to safely return to Iran. He doesn't worry about them.

Chapter One Hundred Six

What's Next?

The commander of the Massachusetts State Police has learned the explosions which killed Walsh and the prison guards were not gas explosions. He is positive Walsh was targeted by someone or some group. He plans to share this with the Natick police. The commander is also positive that Ahmad is the next target and he desires to eliminate their success of that situation. He will work with local police departments to ensure Ahmad goes to trial and receives a death sentence.

* * *

The chief's secretary calls Jack and advises him he has a meeting with the chief and the captain at 4:00 p.m.

* * *

Lt. McNamara knocks on the chief's door and enters his office. The captain is already sitting.

The chief points to a chair indicating Jack should sit there and then holds up his hand in a halting sign so he doesn't speak.

When the chief hangs up his phone, he says, "That was the commander of the state police. He has word the bombings this morning taking out Walsh and the prison guards were a deliberate assassination. While Walsh hasn't been someone on his radar, now he wants to be involved because he figures the next target is Ahmad.

"Jack, the floor is yours!"

"The first time I became aware of this happening was this morning after receiving a call from the attorney general's lawyer I started working with. She seemed pretty convinced the bombings were against Walsh."

The captain says, "Let's look at the facts. Walsh is dead and so are prison guards. That means we have a hit team looking to do assassinations. It is quite clear someone wants Ahmad next. We cannot keep worrying about Walsh since it will not be our investigation. What we do need to do is focus on keeping Ahmad alive."

"How do you anticipate doing that?" asks the chief.

"Jack and I will work together to make sure he stays alive. Will the state police assist us?"

"We have the word from the state police if we ask for help, we will get whatever we need," says the chief.

"Jack, you seem to be daydreaming. What's on your mind?" asks the chief.

"Alan is scheduled to interrogate Ahmad tomorrow. I'm sure Ahmad is already aware of the bombings. I will talk to Alan and get him to pressure Ahmad or else we can threaten to give him up without any resistance on our part. After all we really want him dead."

The chief and the captain look at Jack, then the chief says, "Talk to Alan, have him scare the shit out of Ahmad."

Chapter One Hundred Seven

Meetings

Lt. McNamara's first meeting this morning is with Detective Alan Singer. He and Alan are going over what he should address with Ahmad. Jack tells Alan how the chief wants him to scare the shit out of him. The Iranians want to kill him and let's use this as a tool.

Alan explains he understands and will get back to Jack when he completes the interrogation this afternoon.

* * *

The lieutenant's next meeting is with the state police commander-in-chief in the commander's office. Jack needs to be there at 10:00 so he must leave the station now.

Jack arrives at the state police office at 9:50. Entering he is met by a lovely lady who looks and handles herself very professionally. She offers the lieutenant a seat and calls into the commander's office.

"Lieutenant, the commander will only be five minutes before he sees you."

"Thank you!" replies Jack.

Jack has never seen the commander in person before and he is surprised when he arrives to invite him into his office. While most state troopers are tall, the commander appears to be less than six feet.

"Have a seat, Lieutenant, and if you would like to remove your jacket, feel free to hang it behind you on the rack."

"Thank you, I will."

The commander says, "Let's begin: Do you mind if I call you, Jack? We have a great deal of thinking to do and I would like to give you an idea of what I would like to see happen."

"Feel free to call me Jack, sir."

"Since Ahmad's trial is to be held in Worcester, that is a plus for us. We can use state police, Worcester police and some from Natick as well. Rather than have three command units I am comfortable, if everyone agrees, with heading the task force. In order for us not to suffer the same situation that happened with Walsh, I plan to cordon off an area five square blocks around the courthouse. After midnight, we will have K-9 dog patrols smelling for explosives on sewer covers and anything else we deem appropriate. Once the area is cleared, I want the Worcester police to set up a sleep cot in one of the rooms in the courthouse and we will have Ahmad delivered there at 4:00 a.m.

"Are you with me on this?"

"Yes, and I am beginning to like what I am hearing. How are we going to evade the media?"

"We are going to do our best so that the media is not aware of the 4:00 move and we will be having a dummy run from the prison beginning at 9:00."

"All right, we have Ahmad in the courthouse now, how do we handle keeping him alive? The hearing will not end in one session."

"You're correct; it is my feeling the hit team will make an attempt on his life before he ever steps through the doors of the courthouse. That is what they did to Walsh. We have to be sharp to anticipate what they might do. Do you have any ideas?"

"I've been doing a lot of thinking about the site around the courthouse. If they don't plan on using explosives a second time and I doubt they will, I think they will use a sniper."

"If you were that sniper, where would you position yourself?" asks the commander.

"I expect the prison van would let Ahmad out right in front of the courthouse instead of using the alleyway they normally do. For two reasons, the guards are less restricted in the open and second, there is lots of publicity on this trial and they want to feed the public. If I were the sniper, I would position myself on the roof of the hotel right across from the courthouse, which gives a good view of the whole area. It would only be a 100-yard shot. For a good sniper, that is no sweat."

"Interesting that you say that. I've asked three of my SWAT snipers where they would position themselves if they were doing the shooting. All three of them said what you stated. I feel you have the right conclusion and now we need to come up with a plan to ensure our success no matter what they pull off."

"Sir, if you could use one of your helos and oversee the area, maybe we can get a jump on them."

"I like that, Jack. I can handle it. Now how much support from Natick can I expect?"

"I want to be personally involved at some level. I go back with this thing since last November. The numbers you want will have to be decided by our chief."

"Fair enough and yes, I'd planned on asking you to be involved. You deserve it."

"Thank you, sir, if we are finished here, I need to attend to other things."

"I understand. We can always sort out other matters by phone."

Jack rises, shakes the commander's hand, and leaves the office.

* * *

On the way back to the office, Jack stops off at D'Angelo's to get one of his favorite steak sandwiches to take back with him.

* * *

Before he starts his sandwich, Jack emails the chief and the captain saying he is back from the state police and he would like to report to them on what transpired.

* * *

Jack sees a note on his desk that Jennifer called and asks if he would return her call. He decides to eat his sandwich while it is still warm. He knows his call with Jennifer will not be brief.

Finishing his sandwich along with a bottle of water, Jack places a call to Jennifer only to find out she is with a client and will call him back.

* * *

Shortly after 1:30, Alan Singer calls Jack and gives him the feedback on what happened with the interrogation.

"Lieutenant, as soon as I started, he got obnoxious, started shouting and swearing and really carrying on. I sat there until I told him to knock the act off. 'You are pissed at your own countrymen who now want to assassinate you. They already got Walsh and you're next unless you work with us.' He tells me to fuck off and I stood up and said 'good luck asshole' and began walking out.

"'Where are you going?' he shouted. 'I'm leaving. If you really know what I think, for what you did to my people in my town, I want you dead. So stick one finger up your ass and the other one in your mouth and learn to play switch.'"

"What did he say after you told him that?"

"He asked what he needed to do and I told him he needed to play ball with us and give us a lot of information."

"What kind of information?"

"I said, 'Ahmad you are not fucking stupid. You either have a choice of working with us or we are going to release you.'"

"'Release me, you can't do that.'"

"'Oh no, you're dreaming, guy. We Natick guys are taking bets on how far you will get once we let you go. We have a lottery going.'"

"You didn't say that did you, Alan."

"Sure did and since I know our conversation was not recorded, I could say anything I wanted to."

"All conversations are recorded."

"Not when you have a friend who needed to work on the equipment just when I interviewed Ahmad."

Jack sits back in his chair and smiles. "This conversation will go no further than me, okay."

"Yeah, okay, I guess up-and-coming lieutenants shouldn't use that kind of language."

"Well, I would say shouldn't but since nothing happened, it is only among friends."

"Thanks, Lieutenant, I was pissed."

"You're only human, Alan, and stay that way. Just so long as you always remember some items stated to the higher-ups are held against you. I will give your report to the captain and the chief. When can we start working with him?"

"I would suggest the captain handles this one. He doesn't really know him so Ahmad will be on unknown ground with Captain Green."

"I'll pass that on."

*　　*　　*

Five minutes after talking with Alan, Jennifer calls. "Sorry, I was with a client," she says.

"That's to be expected, I'm not always available when you call."

"Honey, I am just hoping we can get together this weekend. I need my batteries recharged."

"Oh, I can take that a number of ways."

"You can try all of the ways you know how. I just want to be together and away from the rat race."

"Sounds good. Let's go out to the Berkshires again."

"That's a plan. Do we do dinner on Friday?"

"So long as something unexpected doesn't come up."

* * *

An hour later the chief's secretary calls and advises the that lieutenant the chief and the captain are meeting in the chief's office and would like to have him there.

Jack thanks her and laughs at the way the two officers are requiring him to come to meetings. What sissy games humans play.

Sitting before the chief and the captain, Jack tells them everything that transpired in conversation with the state police commander. "I agree with his plan. He wants to include our force in the program."

"Chief, I think you should call the commander and work out how many men you will send to aid his force. He wants me in the program doing what, I don't know yet. I want to be there."

"You should be there," says the chief. "I'll call him this afternoon and we can work something out. Do you think this will work?'

"It will if they attempt to take out Ahmad before he ever gets to the courthouse."

"This operation will be one for the books," says the captain. "When will this begin if it goes as planned?"

"Midnight a week from Sunday is D-hour."

Chapter One Hundred Eight

Falling into Place

Lt. McNamara receives an email from the commander of the state police. "I want you to be my second-in-command on this special operation. Is this fine with you? I want to plan a meeting with you, the Worcester officer in charge and my helicopter people next Monday. It will be scheduled for noontime in my office conference room."

Jack responds to the message: "Thank you for the compliment. I accept. I'll see you next Monday before noon."

The lieutenant knows Natick is going to send twenty patrol officers for his assignment. Worcester is supplying thirty and the state police are supplying thirty.

Jack removes any unimportant tasks from his calendar scheduled for next week. As second-in-command, he is going to be busy with this special operation.

* * *

Jack sends an email report to the chief and a copy to the captain of what will be happening with the operation. He is pleased to announce he has been assigned second-in-command.

Two hours later both the chief and the captain send him an email congratulating him on his position. They both want him to keep them up to date on how to work in the twenty patrol officers Natick will send.

*   *   *

The Iranian hit team is spending numerous hours scouting the area of the court room. They have come up with a tentative plan which is on the ground, two of their men will position themselves in a diagonal parking spot fifty yards from the entrance of the courthouse in an SUV. The team leader and his spotter will get up onto the roof of the hotel across from the hotel. There they will position themselves to kill Ahmad when he exits the prison wagon. Their fifth man will man the roof as a guard.

*   *   *

Jack calls Jennifer. She answers her phone. "Hi, I didn't expect to get through directly to you. I am straight out. Can you book the Berkshire hotel we stayed at before for Friday and Saturday night. I am going to need to be fully relaxed for next week."

"Yes, I can do that and I will make sure you reach your goal by Sunday noontime."

Jack busts out laughing and says, "I'm sure you will."

"Consider it done, sweetheart, I'll take care of it right now."

"Thank you, I love you!"

*   *   *

Jack and Jennifer's getaway weekend is exactly what they needed. The pressures each of their jobs imposes on them, not counting the pressures they impose on themselves, are enormous. The weather was great for them to spend time outdoors and spring is starting to show signs of coming around.

Jack's best surprise was when Jennifer said, "I'd like to plan a fall wedding in September. Are you up to that?"

Jack lifted her off her feet and kissed her deeply. "Yes, I am up to that. You just made my day."

Jennifer knew he would be and she is thrilled.

* * *

Back at the station house Monday morning, Jack is tying up loose ends so he can attend the meeting scheduled for noontime with the department heads for the special operation.

The receptionist calls with a question. She has someone on hold that needs to speak to a detective. Do you want to handle it?"

"Normally, I would. This week I have a special project that will consume most of my time. Give it to Alan Singer."

The receptionist says, "I will flag your schedule not to take routine calls this week. Good luck, Lieutenant, with whatever you're working on."

"Thanks."

* * *

The state police commander greets Jack as soon as he enters the front office. "Go ahead to the conference room. It is the door to the left of my office. The lieutenant from Worcester will be here momentarily. Our helo landed and the crew should be here shortly."

Within minutes, Lieutenant Daniel Foley enters the office and the receptionist directs him to the conference room. She also says, "There is coffee on the table along with bottles of water if you would like something to drink."

Dan replies with "Thank you."

Entering the conference room, the commander and Jack rise and each man shakes hand with the other two. The three men helo crew is right behind the Worcester officer.

"Shall we get started?" says the commander.

Two hours later they close with the reminder the state is renting a local hotel to host all eighty patrol officers and their commanders for a preview of their operation, which begins at midnight on Sunday.

All three leaders leave the conference room with the intent to speak with their own groups before Friday.

Chapter One Hundred Nine

Sunday at Midnight

At 11:45 Jack, with Detective Alan Singer riding with him, four K-9 patrols in marked cruisers, and four unmarked cruisers with four patrolmen each, arrive at their staging area on the northeastern quadrant of the square created by the commander of the state police. They will park their cars in the city parking garage on the inside walls so that they cannot be noticed from the streets.

Beginning midnight, all four quadrants of the square will contain officers assigned to certain tasks that will seek out explosives laid out to incinerate Ahmad and his transportation from the prison.

Worcester police and the state police have each brought six K-9 teams into the area. The state police commander uses a radio check with all groups, and then they begin their tedious search.

By 3:00 there is no indication the streets have been set up with any kind of explosive materials. The noses of the dogs are what the officers trust and there is no sign of any charges.

At 3:00 Jack notifies the commander he is leaving for the Lancaster Prison. He expects to be back by 4:00.

As Jack leaves, a group of Worcester officers begin setting up a cot inside one of the rooms used by attorneys when court is in session.

Ahmad will be secured to the bed and Detective Singer will begin his interrogation. What the attorney general will offer him will depend on how the information from Ahmad is received.

The remainder of the force is free to relax and stand down, but to remain out of sight. The key to their success is to keep the media away from the area before they are normally expected.

* * *

Lt. McNamara arrives at the prison at 3:25. He is escorted to the warden's office, something he didn't expect.

Inside the warden goes on and on how this is against policy and he plans to report this to the governor.

"Warden, you are free to report this to whoever you choose so long as it is not the media. If you pull the plug on this operation, there will be hell to pay. You have a nice cushy job up here. Why don't you keep it that way?"

"Are you threatening me, Lieutenant?"

"No, sir, just promising you that you will not be happy with the results if you don't play along with this charade."

"I am sending three guards because we have never been involved in anything like this in the past."

"It's fine by me, I am sure the state police commander will not mind either."

The warden suddenly realizes how big this operation is and immediately keeps his mouth shut.

Jack leaves the warden's office and heads down toward the prison gate where the van is located.

"My car is in your visitor's lot. You can follow me to the courthouse. There is almost no traffic on the road."

The senior guard acknowledges the instructions and they head out in a column of two.

* * *

Jack's vehicle and the prison van pull up in front of the courthouse. Ahmad is almost carried inside. No one wants to spend too much time in the open. The van is moved around to the rear of the building and secured. Jack moves his car.

Ahmad is loaded onto the cot and one of the prison guards will always remain with him even when Detective Singer interrogates him. His left hand is cuffed to the frame of the cot.

"Why are you doing this?" asks Ahmad.

"We are trying to keep your sorry ass alive is why!" replies Singer.

Detective Singer begins his questioning.

It is decided by all parties involved that Ahmad will appear in prison garb, not civilian clothes, which can make him look innocent.

*   *   *

By cell phone Jack contacts the commander and says he plans to take a look at the hotel roof they talked about.

The commander gives his go-ahead. So far everything is working to plan. Hopefully, the terrorists will make an attempt today.

*   *   *

The State Police SWAT team member who is keeping the area around the courthouse under surveillance reports to the commander that someone exited the hotel roof top door.

"That's a good eye, Johnson. It's okay though it is Lt. McNamara. After he leaves, I want to know if that door opens for any reason at all."

"Yes, sir!"

*   *   *

At 5:15 the hit team drives around the area looking for a reason to postpone the operation. Finding none, they drop the team leader and his shooter, plus their fifth man off at the rear entrance to the hotel. The team was able to pick up a stolen guest pass and the outside door opens and allows them to enter undetected.

The two remaining men head for a local diner to have something to eat and to kill some time. They are the men who will be diagonally parked around fifty yards from the courthouse steps. Their job is to spray the area with AK-47 rounds if their leader misses his shot.

* * *

The commander hears his earphone key, "What is it, Johnson?"

"The rooftop door opened and we have three individuals entering the roof and heading toward the wall facing the courthouse."

"Keep an eye on them and let me know their every move."

"Yes, sir!"

* * *

The commander calls Jack on his cell. "We have three on the hotel roof since you looked around. I'll keep you informed."

"Thanks!" Jack says.

* * *

The sniper and his shooter peer over the edge of the roof looking at the courthouse. The fifth man stands guard next to the roof door. Everything appears normal and they are satisfied they will accomplish their mission. The sniper begins to set up his rifle and the tripod he uses to give him a way of steadying his aim. The spotter begins to set up his optical lens that will enhance the images below them on the street level.

* * *

Johnson keys the commander's mike. "Sir, we have a shooter setting up his rifle and tripod. He has a spotter along with him. There is a third man with a weapon by the roof entrance door."

"Let me know if anything changes, Johnson."

"Yes, sir!"

The commander pushes his mike button to speak. "SWAT Team One, come in."

"SWAT Team here, loud and clear."

"We have a shooter and a spotter on the hotel roof. There is an armed man standing by the roof entrance door. I want six of your men up behind the door to the roof by 8:00. When I give the word, they are to enter the roof and take the three men there."

"What are my rules of engagement?"

"Use whatever force you need for capture or self-defense."

"Team One out!"

* * *

The two men, who went to the local diner, finish their meals and pay the bill. It is time for them to get into position. They move their vehicle toward the courthouse and park very close to the entrance to the courthouse. The time is: 8:15. The men remain in the car.

* * *

Johnson reports in again. "Sir, we have a maroon SUV parked diagonally near the front entrance of the courthouse. I was able to notice there are two men inside as they drove up. They have shut off the engine and are remaining stationary in the vehicle."

"Thanks, Johnson. SWAT Team Two, over."

"SWAT Two go ahead."

The commander repeats the information of the SUV and its location.

"Get your men in position around the vehicle; I believe it is part of this operation."

"What are your instructions, sir?"

"Use whatever force to stop those two men that are inside. Keep them alive if you can."

"SWAT Two over and out!"

*   *   *

The time is 8:30; the prison van without Ahmad is heading toward the courthouse and will be there within ten minutes.

Everyone taking part in this operation is tense and realizes the waiting is the most difficult part of what they are doing.

The spotter sees the prison van two blocks away from the courthouse. "Prison van approaching; everyone get ready."

The sniper sees the van pull close to the curb and the driver opens a sliding side door. A wheelchair is lowered and the sniper expects Ahmad will come out and sit in the chair. He is pleased as this exercise will give him extra seconds to take the shot.

Suddenly, the driver walks away with the empty wheelchair.

The sniper screams, "Abort, abort this is a setup. Get away."

At the same moment, the commander yells to Team One, "Now."

The SUV below on the street starts its engine and begins backing out to leave. All four tires are shot out from underneath the car. Team Two cautiously surrounds the vehicle and demands its inhabitants raise their hands and get out of the car

The two men oblige.

On the roof as Team One enters the roof and takes out the sentry. The sniper and the spotter are shocked. The sniper screams in Farsi and dives over the side of the building falling toward the pavement. He doesn't quite make it as he lands on the metal cover over the entrance of the hotel with a loud thud and blood running off the cover.

The spotter surrenders and is taken below. He is more shaken up over his teammate committing suicide than being arrested.

*   *   *

The media that have been congregating around the courthouse don't know what to make of what just happened. One of the cameramen heard a scream when the Iranian jumped to his death, then a couple of shots; however, no one recorded the fall.

Some media people run toward the SUV with the shot-out tires and others run toward the hotel where a body is lying just over the entrance canopy.

The state police commander is sorry to have lost one terrorist by his suicide mission, but he is pleased with how the operation went. The death of the armed sentry didn't bother him.

Jack meets with Detective Singer to see if he was able to obtain more information.

Alan says, "Once Ahmad heard the shooting and the scream in Farsi, he knew that he must work with the authorities in order to live. He didn't stop talking until they took him into the courtroom."

Both Jack and Alan along with their patrolmen are pleased and happy to be heading back to Natick.

* * *

Understanding the politics of the situation, the state police commander holds a quick interview about how the operation went down and how successful it was. He has high hopes of obtaining information about those who ordered out this team to kill Ahmad, hoping it will lead back to the people who sent out Ahmad. He praises the work of the men and women of the Worcester Police Department and the Natick Police Department, along with his own people.

"Ladies and gentlemen, it has been a long night. I am going to give you a quick rundown on what happened. We learned of an assassination attempt to take place tonight on the person going to court who is the alleged bomber leader. We dealt with a hit team of five and lost two of them, one when he jumped to his death. At this time that is all I can say, thank you."

Some of the media are happy and some are miffed realizing the police put one over on them.

* * *

Inside of Iran, the head of the Revolutionary Guard is screaming and throwing things off the wall, He is bullshit. He has just lost one of his best teams and its leader died jumping off a building.

The imams who caused this shit are going to pay.

Chapter One Hundred Ten

Wrapping Up

The time is 11:00 a.m. The patrol officers and the K-9 units return to the department. Lt. McNamara and Detective Singer arrive ten minutes later. The men have been on the Worcester operation since 10:00 last night. All of them are exhausted from the stress of the events.

Lt. McNamara along with Detective Singer report to the captain, upon arriving at the station.

Captain Green immediately calls the chief for a meeting.

The captain tells the lieutenant the chief will see himself and Jack in half an hour.

* * *

Twenty-five minutes later the captain and the lieutenant enter the chief's office.

Jack appears to be exhausted. The lack of sleep and the emotional strain of the operation are taking a physical toll on him.

"Lieutenant, I saw the press conference the state police commander made to the media. It looks as if everything went well. Is there anything you want to add to it?"

"I can go over everything that happened if that is what you want. Or you can read my full report after I have it completed, sir."

"I don't need a blow-by-blow account from you, Lieutenant. Are you satisfied with what went down?"

"Not trying to be confrontational, Chief, what do you mean by satisfied?"

"Do you feel the operation was handled well?"

"No one could have handled this operation better than the commander did. I enjoyed working with him. He assigns responsibility and allows people to function without micromanaging."

"Look, I understand you are fatigued by all of this, yet I have the feeling you have some unresolved issues about what happened."

"Chief, Ahmad spilled his guts out to Detective Singer when he heard all of the shooting and yelling outside the courthouse. He was scared shitless. Ahmad knows he is a marked man by his own countrymen. From the bits and pieces I picked up, Ahmad is going to be sent somewhere outside of Massachusetts by the feds. That is the deal the AG's office gave him in return for the information they learned. A sweet deal if you ask me."

"You disagree with that, Lieutenant?"

"Right now, I'm very tired and all I can see in my mind are the bodies of women and children in Natick and in the Worcester church."

"Are you hoping we get revenge, Lieutenant?"

"Revenge, no, that's not the answer; however, there must be better ways for our society to get these pricks before all of these deaths occur."

"The captain and I would like you to consider seeing our therapist if you feel it's necessary. You leave in two weeks for the counter-terrorism training. Maybe you can pick up some ideas when you are in Quantico for the future."

"I feel the results of this affair will lead me to something better than playing cops and killers."

The chief places an inquisitive look at the captain with Jack's remark.

Captain Green speaks, "Jack, go home for the rest of the day. Write your report tomorrow; you have done more than most men are asked to do."

Jack stands, "If neither of you desire more information right now, I will take that as a good suggestion." Jack leaves the chief's office.

When Jack leaves the office, the chief says, "What do you think, Captain?"

"I think he needs some time to sort everything out, which I believe he will. Don't worry about his abilities, Chief. I trust that man with my life."

The chief stares at the captain for at least three minutes before saying, "I hope you're right. We don't need another lieutenant dealing with emotional issues."

"Chief, if I were you, I would worry if he had not expressed his feelings."

"I guess you're right. Do you have any idea of what is happening to those captured on the scene?"

"No, Chief, when I find out, I will let you know. I'll let you know about the two that NYPD arrested in the subway system too."

The chief nods and the captain leaves his office feeling very frustrated by the way the chief handled the meeting.

*   *   *

Jack leaves the station house in the next fifteen minutes. He is too tired to call Jennifer; he needs to get some rest.

On the way home he realizes he has vacation time on the books. Tomorrow he will discuss this with the captain when he turns in his report. He needs some time to clear his head before heading to the counter-terrorism workshop.

Arriving at his condo, Jack parks and exits his car. Opening his front door, he is surprised to see Jennifer there. He didn't notice her car in the parking lot because of his fatigue.

"Wow, honey, I'm so tired, I can't think straight."

"I know, Captain Green called and asked me to stay with you. He's worried about how exhausted you are and maybe you need someone to talk with."

Jack tosses his sports jacket onto the couch and sits down. "Come here, hold me, I need some reassurance there are good people in this world."

"First, let me remove your weapon and holster; otherwise it could get in my way."

Jack laughs, "Yeah, I don't want to hurt your boobs."

"Nasty, nasty man, I wasn't even thinking about my boobs. After some rest, I can see there is really nothing wrong with you. Let me get you a drink. Take off your shoes and put your feet up on the couch."

Jack smiles and complies.

After the drink, Jack rests his head back on the arm of the couch and he is out like a light. Jennifer smiles at the wonderful man who will be her husband in a couple of months.

* * *

The following day, Jack hands the captain his written report of the Worcester incident in which the Natick department participated along with the Worcester police and the state police.

The captain says, "You look much better today. I think some tender loving care did wonders for you."

"Yeah, thanks to you. I felt too tired to call her myself, and I didn't want her worrying about me."

"I'll read your report later; your message said you had something else on your mind."

"Yes, I have fourteen days of vacation on the books. I want to take five of them, two before next weekend, and three, right after the weekend. Do you see a problem with that?"

"No, I assume you are saving the rest for your honeymoon."

"You've got that right. The one we're going to take in September."

"I'll arrange the schedule and have Alan Singer cover while you're on vacation and also down at Quantico."

"Thanks, Captain, I really appreciate your calling Jennifer and I know she thinks the world of you for doing it. One more thing, it's in my report. Alan Singer did a hell of a job on this last project. He deserves to be the next lieutenant."

"I'll keep that in mind considering the source," the captain says as he winks.

*   *   *

Jennifer didn't have to do a selling job to her bosses when she asked for the time off to be with Jack. They had heard all of the media reports of who was involved in the Worcester incident. They knew being with Jack means an awful lot to Jennifer. They like her and respect her future husband.

Jennifer calls and tells Jack she has the same free time off that he worked out with the captain.

"Great, let's plan on going somewhere that gives us a chance to rest and have fun before I go away to Virginia for a week."

"We'll plan it tonight over dinner, my favorite detective."

CPSIA information can be obtained at www.ICGtesting.com
Printed in the USA
BVOW08s1228170516

448421BV00001B/1/P

9 781514 487815